9/08

FINDING MAGIC

Other Books by Tanya Huff

NOVELS

Child of the Grove, 1988
The Last Wizard, 1989
Gate of Darkness, Circle of Light, 1989
The Fire's Stone, 1990
Blood Price, 1991
Blood Trail, 1992
Blood Lines, 1993
Blood Pact, 1993
Sing the Four Quarters, 1994
Fifth Quarter, 1995
Scholar of Decay, 1995
No Quarter, 1996
Blood Debt, 1997
Summon the Keeper, 1998
The Quartered Sea, 1999
Valor's Choice, 2000
The Second Summoning, 2001
The Better Part of Valor, 2002
Long Hot Summoning, 2003
Smoke and Shadows, 2004
Smoke and Mirrors, 2005
Smoke and Ashes, 2006
The Heart of Valor, 2007

COLLECTIONS

What Ho, Magic!, 1999
Stealing Magic, 1999
Relative Magic, 2003

FINDING MAGIC

by
Tanya Huff

ISFiC PRESS
Deerfield, 2007

Published by ISFiC Press
707 Sapling Lane
Deerfield, Illinois 60015
www.isficpress.com

Series Editor: Steven H Silver

ISFiC Press Logo Design: Todd Cameron Hamilton

Book Design by Robert T. Garcia / Garcia Publishing Services
919 Tappan Street, Woodstock, Illinois 60098
www.gpsdesign.net

First Edition

10   9   8   7   6   5   4   3   2   1

ISBN: 978-0-9759156-5-3

PRINTED IN THE UNITED STATES OF AMERICA
by Thomson-Shore, 7300 West Joy Road, Dexter, Michigan 48130-9701
www.tshore.com

CONTENTS

Finding Magic
by Julie E. Czerneda

FINDING MAGIC. THAT'S THE EASY part, for a writer with as rich an imagination as Tanya Huff. The hard part? Delivering a great story that grabs a reader by the appropriate gonads. And that, my friend, is all about finding reality.

Consider, if you will, the art that graces a book cover or videogame. Many artists can—and do—create striking and imaginative dragons or starships or worldscapes. Far fewer can produce an image we believe could be a real, breathing person. It's because we're experts. We know how people look. We can spot the most subtle flaw in proportion or expression. Even if we can't put our finger on it, something's wrong and the image doesn't work for us.

We're experts in how people sound, too. Many writers can—and do—write meaningful conversations between their characters. But do they sound real? Sometimes. Not always. Unless you're Tanya Huff.

Tanya and I have the same editor/publisher at DAW Books, Sheila Gilbert. I remember Sheila telling me one day that Tanya's always right about dialogue, that she nails it, no matter what her characters are feeling or who they are. The words, the phrasing, how they're expressed—a reader is convinced by what Tanya puts in a character's mouth, because that character sounds absolutely real, even to experts like us.

Believe me, that's not easy, though Tanya makes it look that way. Skill is its own best disguise.

Of course, reality is more than looks-like-a-person, sounds-like-a-person, probably could-be-one-up-close. In story terms, reality encompasses every and any thing that could knock a reader out of the plot. Get it right, and those credible threads wind tighter and tighter around your heart and mind until you willingly believe it all.

Including the magic. Research and care for detail is part of it, as is worldbuilding, but arguably the larger part is creating scenarios where certain actions produce inevitable-feeling reactions. The trumpets blow. Your pulse hammers. You live with the story as much as read it. The ending is as true as fine steel.

How does she do it? I've mentioned Tanya's skill as a writer, which goes without question, but she brings another key attribute to the reality of her work, something gained only by a habit of grabbing life by the throat and staring it in the eye. (From a variety of angles and without pity or squirming.) Tanya experiences, she observes, and, oh yes, she remembers. Tanya knows what lurks in the hearts and minds . . . need I say more? Unlike The Shadow, however, she uses her knowledge to imbue her stories with reality, not to change anyone else.

If you are reading these stories for the first time, I'm envious. There are few writers I trust as I trust Tanya; few I read with such open abandon. While I do reread—as her occasional editor, some-times often—the first ride through a new Huff is always special. I put everything else aside. I open the file or page. And I willingly follow where she leads me.

Finding magic. You could ask for no better, surer guide than Tanya Huff. Enjoy this collection. Find more of her work. Cherish it. I know I will.

Julie E. Czerneda

FINDING MAGIC

I Knew a Guy Once

I'm not one of those writers who hates her stuff the moment she finishes it (and don't actually understand the writers who do). I quite like everything I've ever written. There is, in fact, stuff I wrote in high school I still enjoy reading—not that I'd ever let anyone else read it, mind. That said, while I like everything I've done, there's only about half a dozen stories that I'm actually proud of. Stories where I tried to say something and feel like I succeeded. Three of them are in this collection. This is one of them. It may be my favorite of everything I've ever written. It's also one of my rare SF stories and has a kickass song by Brenda Sutton to go with it.

ALTHOUGH THERE WERE ONLY TWO people in the passenger compartment of the supply shuttle, the cramped quarters had them practically in each other's laps. The company had no intention of wasting shipping space on privacy; nearly every square millimeter of the four by eight meter compartment they weren't actually occupying had been filled with labeled containers.

As the shuttle left Io, they were a study in contrasts.

The young man, his environmental suit still so new it crinkled softly when he moved, gripped his helmet tightly in both gloved hands. He wore his dark hair at the company's regulation length but it looked to have been styled rather than cut. His face was tanned with high spots of color on both cheeks and he was trying too hard to appear unafraid.

The older woman's short gray hair seemed to have been hacked off during a power shortage, when lights, as unessential, were the first thing to be shut down. Her skin had the almost translucent paleness of someone who'd spent her entire life protecting it from high UV and her environmental suit was so old it had digital readouts in the cuff. As soon as the main engines cut off, she closed her eyes and went to sleep.

Tried to go to sleep.

"They say that this last bit from Io to the station isn't as dangerous as it used to be."

She opened her eyes and turned her head enough to see him smiling at her, his teeth very white, his lips pulled back just a little too far. "They're right," she said at last.

His smile relaxed a little although the rest of him remained visibly tense. "I'm Simon Porter. Dr. Simon Porter. I'm the new station psychologist."

"What happened to the old one?"

"What? Oh. Well, actually, there wasn't one. The Company only brings a psychologist out to the mining stations when there's a problem they can't solve through the usual channels."

"Wouldn't it make more sense to keep you on staff?"

"Too expensive." He seemed proud of it.

"So, what's the problem?"

"I'm afraid that's privileged information." He seemed proud of that too. "But I can tell you that things seem very shaky on the station right now. Stress levels rising. You know . . ."

"Yeah." And something in that single syllable suggested she did. Probably better than he did.

"I specialize in isolation psychosis. This is sort of a dream job for me."

The following pause lengthened into expectation.

"Able Harris. I'm the new bartender for downside."

"So we're in the same line of work. You listen, I listen."

"You pour drinks?"

"No, but . . ."

"Well, there's your difference. I'm a bartender."

"Okay." His tone touched patronizing. "I've never been in a downside bar."

Able turned just enough to look him full in the face.

"I've never actually been *downside*," he admitted. "Or on a mining station at all." He cleared his throat, as though confused by his confession. "So, what happened to the old bartender?"

"He died."

Dr. Porter nodded sympathetically. Everyone knew death and downside were intimately acquainted. "Of what?"

"Well, they said it was the sucking chest wound but I suspect it was actually the wrench to the back of the head."

"He was *killed*?"

Able shrugged philosophically. "Might've been an accident."

"He was accidentally hit on the back of the head with a wrench?"

"It happens."

He studied her face, dark brows knit together so tightly they met over the bridge of his nose. After a long moment, he nodded and relaxed. "I may be fresh out of the gravity well but I'm not totally gullible. You're making fun of the new guy. I'm onto you, Able . . . May I call you Able?"

"Everybody does," she told him, unaffected by his accusation.

"It's an unusual name. I assume it's not the one you were born with?"

"Why?"

"Well, it's just . . . unusual."

She stretched as far as the straps allowed. "I knew a guy once named Strawberry Cho."

"He had a birthmark?"

"No, he had a mother who was so homesick she didn't consider the consequences."

"Consequences?"

"You name your boy Strawberry and there's going to *be* consequences."

Dr. Potter opened his mouth, closed it, and shook his head. "You're doing it again, aren't you, Able? You're pulling my . . ."

The klaxon's sudden bellow clamped his hands to the arms of his seat, his helmet floating out to the end of its tether.

Able glanced down at her cuff then reached out, hooked a gloved finger around the cable, and tugged it back. "They're warning us they're about to hit the brakes, start decelerating."

His ears scarlet, Dr. Porter clutched the helmet so tightly his gloves squeaked against the plastic.

"Pilot knows it's your first time out. Knows people have been feeding you bullshit stories since you blew off Earth. Probably hit the klaxon trying to get you to piss yourself."

Embarrassment rose off the psychologist in nearly visible waves.

"Don't worry, the suit'll take of it. I knew a guy once, had the shits all the way from L5 Alpha all the way to Darkside. Suit took care of it." Able closed her eyes and didn't open them again until the shuttle kissed its assigned nipple on the docking ring and the all clear sounded.

By the time Dr. Porter had fumbled free of his straps, the hatch was open and the dockers were barely controlling their anger as they waited to start unloading. Able snagged her carryall from behind her seat and followed him to the bottom of the ramp, arriving just in time to keep him from being flattened by a wagon piled high with containers from the aft compartment.

"They're on tracks," she yelled, leaning closer to make herself heard over the noise. "You get in front of them, they'll squash you flat. I knew a guy once, lost a foot under one. Crushed too bad to be reattached."

The doctor's cheeks paled, his embarrassment forgotten. "What happened to him?"

"Got himself a whole bunch of prosthetics. Got one with a full entertainment until in it."

"In his foot?"

Able shrugged. "Takes all kinds."

She slipped between two wagons and headed for a set of metal stairs against the starboard wall. The doctor trailed behind.

"There should be someone here to meet me," he shouted as they climbed.

"There is, back behind that glass."

At the top of the stairs was a wire enclosed catwalk. At the end of the catwalk, a platform. In the wall overlooking the platform, two hatches. Between the hatches was a mirrored window.

"There's no way you can know who's back there, Able." Safely above the wagons, he regained his professional voice.

"Presence of suits kept the dockers from hauling your ass out of the shuttle. Only place the suits could be is behind that glass. They're not going to be out here in the nipple risking a seal rupture. I knew a guy once, got sucked through a seal rupture and ended up in a low Mars orbit." When no question prodded her to continue, she grinned. "Bounce satellite signals off him now. This is your exit." She nodded toward the right as they clanged out onto the platform.

Dr. Porter stared at the hatches. Aside from the varying wear and tear, they were identical. "How can you tell?"

"Company policy; suits are always right. We're what's left."

He stared at her for a long moment, he glanced toward the mirrored glass, then he held out his hand. "I appreciate you making the effort to distract me, Able. Perhaps we'll meet again."

"Could happen. It's a small station in a big universe."

His grip was a little too emphatic. A young man with something to prove.

Don't need to prove it to me. Her grip matched his exactly.

EVS in a temporary locker, Able took a moment to watch the Company news on the small vid in lock. Possible layoffs. Cut backs. Accidents. Price freezes. One hundred percent bad. She sighed, scanned her chip into the station's database, stepped through the inner hatch, and went looking for the Quartermaster's office. QMO was never far from the docks so she expected to have no trouble finding it. And the yelling was pretty much a dead giveaway.

"I don't freakin' care what the invoice says, my people unloaded sixteen crates off seven dash seven three two *not* seventeen." Hands planted firmly on the desk, the quartermaster leaned closer to the pickup and went for volume. "You short-shipped us, you bastard! For the second god-damned time!" Then she straightened, flipped pale blonde hair back from her face and smiled across the room at Able. "Jesus, Able, what'd you do? Hijack a military transport?"

Able stepped over the threshold and shrugged. "Just made all the right connections."

"Just? You broke the freakin' Phoebus to GaMO speed record. And who told you lot to god-damned stop working?" she snapped, as the four clerks along one side of the room turned to look. "I can't say I'm not glad see you though, situation's been going to freakin' hell in a handcart since Rich Webster died. Asshole. I close the place down, the riggers riot. I open the place up, the riggers get drunk and riot. The fitters are talking freakin' union again and that's got the suits on my ass. Whole god-damned place is falling a . . ." The desk receiver chimed. "Hang on a nano, Able. I need to get this."

"I'm sorry Quartermaster Nasjonal but our packing orders clearly show that all seventeen crates were loaded. I suggest that you take the matter up with the transfer supervisor on Io."

"PJ's got more freakin' brains than to screw with me! Now get your thumb out of your ass, get Yuen on this thing, and stop wasting my god-damned time!" Shaking her head, she dropped down into the desk chair. "Freakin' distance delays make it impossible to hold a conversation. You've got standard quarters behind the bar. You got six servers, burn-outs for the most part—I think Webster was paying at least one of them in booze."

"I won't."

"I know. I'm the one who asked you to drag your ass out the armpit of the universe, remember? Usual drill. Company expects you to turn a profit and keep the workers happy. You should be fully stocked, I've kept supplies coming in during this whole freakin' mess. And . . . Jonathon!"

One of the clerks jerked and peered over the top of his monitor.

"Where's my freakin' ass-Quart?"

"He's at 07, Quartermaster. Supervising the loading . . ."

"Right. Okay, you take Able to the Hole."

"But . . ."

"Quartermaster Nasjonal, Supervisor Yuen is not currently available. Would you be able to call back after 1700 hours?"

"Tell Yuen, I'm about to start talking about what happened last December. And if that doesn't haul his skinny ass to a pickup, nothing will," she added, sitting back in the chair. "I'll be down to see you as soon as I get this freakin' short ship straightened out. Jonathon!"

He jerked again, the movement propelling him out from behind his terminal.

"Go!"

Able paused on the threshold, allowing Jonathon to proceed her into the corridor. "Always a pleasure talking to you, Quartermaster Nasjonal."

The quartermaster grinned. "Suck up."

Jonathon was waiting an arm's length away, nervously clutching his hands together in front of his belt.

"Do you know where the Hole is?" Able's tone made it clear she very much doubted it.

He flushed. "Yes, theoretically, but I've never . . . I mean . . ."

"It's downside. You drink amid." She slung her carryall over one shoulder, and started to walk.

"Not that I . . ." His protest trailed off as he hurried to catch-up. "It's just, it's . . ."

"Downside?" When he nodded, Able snorted. "Tell you what, take me to lower amid and the nearest shaft, give me decent directions, and I'll cover downside myself. We won't mention it to the quartermaster."

"She'll find out."

"Then tell her I didn't have the time to waste escorting you back and there was no way I was letting you walk through downside alone. She'll let it go if you tell her it was my idea."

"You've known her for a long time?"

"Pretty much since she was born."

Jonathon flattened against the bulkhead as Able and the approaching docker merely shifted their shoulders sideways and slid past each other. "She's actually really good to work for," he declared scrambling back to Able's side. "Her bark is worse than her bite."

"Most days." Able paused at the hatch that would take them from dockside into the station proper. "I knew a guy once that she bit."

Sucking chest wound or wrench to the back of the head, after a cursory inspection of the only bar in downside, Able was sure of one thing, Richard Webster had gotten what he deserved. The place was everything people like Jonathon expected a downside bar to be. Dark and filthy and stinking of despair and rage about equally mixed–as well as a distinct miasma of odors less metaphorical.

She ripped a yellowing list of rules off the outside of the hatch–splash marks making the vector for the yellowing plain–and stepped over the threshold. The panel just inside the door responded to her chip and once she'd pried the cover off, she hit the overhead lights. The amount of grime that had sealed the cover shut suggested it had been a while since the overheads had been turned on.

A pile of rags in the far corner coughed, cursed, and turned into a skinny person of indeterminate gender.

"I didn't do nothing," it whined, squinting across the room.

"That's obvious." Able pushed a dented chair out of the way and moved close enough to see that the rags had covered a balding man who could have been anywhere from forty to seventy, his mottled scalp a clear indication that hair loss had been caused by other than genetic factors. Toxic spills were endemic to downside. "Who are you?"

"Bob."

She'd be willing to bet that Bob was the guy Webster had been paying in booze. One way or another, and there were a number of ways, he'd gotten so far in debt to the Company that they'd written him off. He'd lost his access to the ship's database, his quarters, and his food allotment leaving him with two choices, the kindness of strangers–only people who'd burned off their friends fell quite so far–or the tubes. Clearing the tubes of blockages was usually a mecho's job but the little robots were expensive and they didn't last long. People like Bob didn't last long in the tubes either but they were cheap.

Arms curled around his chest, he rubbed his hands up and down filthy sleeves. "I need a drink."

"I don't doubt it."

"'s cheaper than paying me. Keeps your profits up."

"Who told you that?"

"Webster. Lets me sleep here too."

"Webster's dead."

"I didn't do it."

"I don't care."

If Bob was sleeping in the bar during the eight in twenty-four it was closed, he was using the bathroom sinks to keep clean. And not very often.

"I knew guy once who smelled like you. Somebody kicked his skinny ass out an airlock and nobody missed him."

Without waiting for a response, she ducked behind the bar. The door on the right lead to the storeroom, to the left, her quarters. Both smelled strongly of disinfectant. The QMO. If they'd been attempting to run the Hole, the only thing they'd care about was the stock. Wiping Webster out of her quarters had probably been a personal courtesy from Nasjonal. Able'd thank her later.

"I *need* a drink."

The whine came from directly behind her left shoulder. Up close the smell was nearly overpowering.

Fortunately, disinfectant was cheap.

Grabbing the back of Bob's overalls, she frog-marched him through her quarters, ignoring his struggles and incoherent protests, carefully touching him to as few surfaces as possible. The showers on downside all had the same two settings. Hard clean. Soft clean. Hard clean for when the riggers and the fitters came off shift. Soft clean for the rest of the time. The company saved money by keeping the pressure and temperature consistent.

Bob went in, as was, on Hard.

When the cycle finished, Able checked to see he hadn't drowned, efficiently stripped him of overalls and ragged cloth slippers, and hit the button again. By the time the second cycle finished, his clothes were dry, the industrial solvents in the Hard clean having taken care of most of the grime.

She dressed him, ran a depilatory pad over his head, and marched him back to the bar.

The whole thing had taken just under twenty minutes.

"I assume you sold your shoes?"

Bob stared at her, wide-eyed and trembling.

"Then the slippers will do for now. Here's the deal . . . you work for me, I pay you like everybody else. You can decide what you do with it. You can start paying down your debt to the Company, or you can drink it away—after you pay me what you owe me for the two showers. Until you're clear and can get quarters again, you can keep sleeping in the bar but not on that crap. I'll pull a couple of shipping pads out of stores. You don't do your job—well, a smart man will keep in mind that I'm the only thing between him and the tubes. Oh, and you will shower every two days. You can use a communal clean-up off the hives."

He was panting now. "I *need* a drink."

"You *need* to haul the big steam cleaner out of the storeroom. Or you need to let the company know they've got a new tube man. I knew a guy once, survived four trips down the tubes. His record still stands."

By the time Bob had dragged the cleaner out into the bar, the five other servers were standing, blinking in the light. None of them looked too pleased about being summoned.

"I didn't even know this place had overheads," one muttered.

"Then how did you see to get it clean?" Able asked coming out from behind the bar, wiping her hands on a dark green apron

"Fuck that, how clean do you need to get a place like this?" one of the others snorted. "Nobody who drinks here gives a crap."

"What difference does that make? My name's Able Harris and I'm the new bartender. You're Helen, Tasha, Toby, Nick . . ." With each name, she nodded toward an incredulous server. ". . . and Spike." She studied the last woman curiously. "Spike?"

Spike folded heavy arms over an ample chest. "Able?"

"Good point. So . . ." Her attention switched back to the group. "Is that what you wear to work?"

The four women and two men looked down at their overalls and exchanged amused glances.

Able waited.

Toby finally shrugged and muttered, "Yeah."

"It'll do for now but when the first shift's back for opening, I want the overalls to be clean. There's a dozen or so aprons like this one in stores. You're in them while you're working." When the protests died down, Able nodded. "Okay. You don't have to wear them if you don't want to. You don't have to do anything you don't want to do. If you work for me, you wear the aprons but you don't have to work for me."

"And if we could get other jobs on this fucking station, we'd be fucking working at them."

Toby moved up behind Spike's shoulder. "Webster didn't care what we wore."

"Webster's dead."

Bob jerked up from behind the steam cleaner. "I didn't do it."

After the snickering died down, Spike growled, "He wasn't killed because he wasn't wearing a fucking apron, was he?"

Able shrugged. "I knew a guy once, got killed by an apron. He lost his job and got so hungry he tried to eat it. Managed fine until he got to the ties and then he got one wrapped around that dangly thing at the back of his mouth and choked to death."

"Was that a threat?" Toby wondered as their new boss walked over to Bob and hauled a length of hose off him then hauled Bob back to his feet.

"I have no fucking idea," Spike admitted.

Even with the pressurized steam, it took the seven of them three hours to get the bar clean.

"Who the fuck washes the bottom of tables?"

"I'd guess nobody in living memory." Tasha swiped on more solvent and grimaced at the dissolving grime. "This is disgusting."

Helen nodded and sat back on her heels. "Well at least we won't have to do it again . . ."

"We'll do it after every shift."

The two women glanced over at Able, working the steam against the upper wall.

"Why?" Helen demanded. "Hell, with only the drinking lights on, nobody can even see the dirt."

"Doesn't mean it's not there."

"Are you fucking obsessive or something?"

"Keeping the bar clean's part of the job."

"But nobody cares!"

"That doesn't change the definition of clean. I knew a guy once, tried to change the definition of Tuesday. Ended up with a fish up his nose."

"That makes no fucking sense . . ."

"And that's what I said to him at the time. How long has the big vid not worked?"

Discussion narrowed it down to a couple of months.

"Bar's not making enough of a profit for the Company to send maintenance in."

Everyone turned to stare at Bob, who dropped his sponge, hugged himself, and announced that he needed a drink.

"Downside maintenance never drinks here?" Able asked after a moment.

"Well, yeah," Toby snorted. "But they can't shit without a Company work order."

"Okay, bar opens in half an hour. First shift go home, get cleaned up. Second shift, your time's your own." Standing by the light panel, Able looked around and nodded. "Good work people."

Spike poked Toby hard in the side. "Why the fuck are you looking so pleased?"

He shook his head. "I dunno. It just sounded like she meant it."

"Meant what?"

"When she said, good work. When was the last time you heard somebody say that, and mean it? Webster never said it."

"And when was the last time you did good work for Webster," Tasha snorted as they left.

With only the drinking lights on Able went back behind the bar put a new sponge in a shallow bowl, filled the bowl with beer, and kept filling it until the sponge was soaked through. She looked up to see Bob leaning on the end of the bar, his eyes wide.

Able pried the cover off the main air vent, set the bowl inside, and put the cover back on. "No one wants to drink in a bar that smells like disinfectant. It's annoying. They start out annoyed, they end up as nasty drunks. On the flip side, no one wants to drink in a bar that smells like old piss and stale sweat. They start out disgusted, they end up as nasty drunks. You don't want nasty drunks, you start your drinkers out in a good mood."

Bob opened his mouth and closed it again.

Carrying a box of textured protein patties in from the storeroom, she dropped a stack out on the counter and began cutting them into strips. "I knew a guy once lived on these things for twelve years. What he didn't know about making them edible you could write on the ass end of a flea. Lots of chili, a little oil, bake 'em until they're crisp and they're almost food. Works with garlic and onion too."

"They won't pay for it," Bob muttered, staring longingly at the taps.

"I'm not expecting them to."

"Company won't like it."

"Company expects me to turn a profit. You give the drinkers something to eat, they can drink more and it effects them less." She slid the first tray into the tiny oven on the back wall. The bar had a kitchen unit so her quarters didn't. "You make this stuff right and it's got a bite. The more they drink, the less they feel it, the more they can eat. Since the patties are enriched the serious drinkers are getting fed. Which makes them less shaky which means fewer accidents on the pipes. Fewer accidents puts everyone in a better mood. With everyone in a better mood, fewer nasty drunks. Fewer nasty drunks, fewer fights, fewer things get broken and need to be replaced, less drinking gets interrupted, the bar turns a profit. The Company's happy." The oven chimed and she slid the tray out, juggling a strip from hand to hand, finally passing it to Bob.

He took a cautious bite and sneezed. "It's good."

"I know what I'm doing." She drew a 500 of beer and handed it to him.

After emptying it, he blinked at her a few times, his eyes the clearest they'd been. "Who the fuck *are* you?"

"I'm the new bartender."

When she opened the hatch, half a dozen riggers and fitters stood in the corridor; weight shifting back and forth from foot to foot, hands curled into fists, a fight waiting to happen. They knew who she was. The only thing that got processed faster than the gas pumped up off Jupiter was gossip.

"What happened to Webster's rules?" one of them growled.

"You guys do the most dangerous work on the station, you don't need someone to tell you how to act like adults."

"So there ain't no rules?"

Able stepped back out of the way. "I didn't say that."

The big rigger leaned across the bar, grabbed a bottle in one scarred hand, and grinned at Able as he settled back on his stool. "Webster let us serve ourselves."

"Webster's dead. Put it back."

He cracked the seal and took a long messy swallow. "Make me, old woman."

A heartbeat later, he was lying on the floor and everyone in the immediate vicinity stood open mouthed, blinking away the after images of an electrical discharge.

"I knew a guy once took a second hit from one of these things." Able bounced the rod against the palm of her other hand. "He's still striking sparks when he takes a shit. I'm charging the bottle against your chip. Oh, and by the way," she raised her voice so that it filled all the listening spaces in the Hole, "it's coded to my DNA. Anyone else touches it, and . . ." A nod toward the rigger blinking stupidly up at her from the floor. "I knew a guy once who designed weapons systems for the military."

"Fuck," someone sneered, "you knew a lot of guys."

Able grinned. "Would you believe I used to be a raven-haired beauty?"

"Not without a few more drinks!"

"You're lucky his friends didn't rush you," Nick muttered under the laughter.

"First guy who tries something never has friends." Able drew a beer and set it on his tray. "That's why he's trying something. Second guy who tries something's always a little trickier."

She drew some beer, poured some shots, and scanned the crowd for maintenance overalls. They weren't hard to spot. Two women sitting alone in a booth; one of them had a bandage wrapped around her right hand, both of them were drinking boilermakers. Two beer, two shots, basket of chili strips on a tray and Able slid out from behind the bar.

They watched her approach and when she paused at their booth, the uninjured woman snarled, "We didn't order those."

"On the house." Able set the drinks down and picked up the empties. "My big vid's busted."

"So?"

"I'd like one of you to fix it."

"No." The injured woman downed the whiskey and took a long pull on the beer. "Crew boss'd stuff us naked out an airlock if we did shit without a work order. And the Company won't approve a work order until this place turns a profit."

"Your crew boss says anything to you, you tell him I knew a guy once, used to work maintenance on L5 Beta. He knew a seal was fucked but waited for a Company work order before he'd fix it. Six people died."

"You knew a guy?"

Able shrugged. "Haven't you heard, I know a lot of guys."

"Yeah, but . . ."

The uninjured woman raised her hand. "What's in it for us?"

"Repairs go on your tab. You drink free until it's cleared."

"You do know that the Company expects you to make a profit here, right?"

"Vid's fixed, people are happy and stay longer, they drink more, the bar profits. Excuse me." She slid the empties back on the table, took a long step to the right, pivoted on one heel and slammed the edge of the tray down on a fitter's wrist. He howled and dropped back into his seat.

"I was way over there and I distinctly heard her tell you to keep your hands to yourself. You want to grope my servers you make damned sure they're into it first or you find someplace else to drink."

"There is no place else to fuckin' drink!"

"So if you're going to keep drinking here, what are you going to do?" She met his glare with a steady gaze and waited.

And kept waiting.

Slowly, the room fell silent.

Able kept waiting.

He rubbed his wrist and sighed. "I'm gonna keep my hands to myself."

"Unless?"

"Unless the person I'm gropin's okay with it?"

Able smiled. "Spike, give him his drink."

The large vid was showing zero gee lacrosse from one of the L5's, the small vid behind the bar ran the station's news channel.

"Why the fuck is that on?" The rigger slid forward on his bar stool and squinted at the screen. "News is all bad."

"Eighty per cent bad."

"Bad enough."

"I like to know when it's getting better."

"Yeah? Well, what I'd like to know is where you get off tellin' us how to fuckin' behave."

Able wiped up a spill and pushed the basket of garlic seasoned protein strips down the bar, closer to the rigger's reaching hand. "I don't. I tell you what I won't put up with. You chose how to behave."

"No choices on a Company station, you should know that."

"There's choices in here."

He chewed, swallowed, and finished his beer. "What, you not gonna tell me that you knew a guy once who had no choices?"

"I knew lots of guys like that."

"Yeah." He tapped for a refill. "What happened to them?"

"That depended on the choices they made."

"Who the fuck *are* you?"

She threw her rag in the sink and held out a hand. "Able Harris. I'm the bartender."

"Took you three freakin' weeks to make a profit, Able."

"Took you three weeks to fix that short ship, Quartermaster?"

"I got busy. Freakin' sue me." She slid onto a bar stool. "Jesus, you got coffee running. Let me have a mug. Too damned early for booze. You know, I don't think Webster even knew what that pot was for."

"Webster's dead."

The quartermaster started as half a dozen voices chorused, "Bob didn't do it!"

"What the hell was that?" she demanded as Able snickered.

"Private joke." The mug hit the bar along with two packets of creamer and three of sugar. "So, I make the news at about sixty-forty."

"Yeah, things are looking up. What happened over there?"

Over there was a stack of chairs waiting repair and table that had moved significantly past *broken* and into *scrap*.

"Oh, one of the riggers told the two fitters in a suction pipe joke."

"Shit. What did you do?"

"Cleaned up afterwards. I like to make stupidity it's own reward."

"Able, you better get out here."

She rubbed a hand through her hair so that it stuck straight up in pale gray spikes. "Shift just started, what's wrong."

"There's a table of supervisors out there."

"I knew a guy once, insisted on hanging out with the guys he supervised."

"What happened to him?"

Able finished entering the top shelf and handed Toby her data pad. "Let's just say *hanging out* became the definitive phrase."

There were five of them at one of the big round tables; two women, three men. The tables around them were empty. In the booths and at the bar, the regulars sat scowling over their drinks.

Able walked over, drying her hands on her apron. "Evening. Don't you lot usual drink in lower amid?"

"We've been hearing good things about this place." He folded his arms and managed to simultaneously look up at her and stare down his nose. "Thought we'd check it out."

One of the women smiled, showing recently repaired teeth. "Downside drudge like you ought to be happy we're here. Might get the Company to put you someplace a little . . . better."

"Better?"

"Than this . . . hole."

Able reached out and touched her chip to the table's scanner then transferred the screen to the big vid. "I'm an independent contractor. I'm here because I want to be. You want to be here, that's fine. You're trying to make a point—make it somewhere else."

"The Company . . ."

"Doesn't care how I do it as long as this bar makes a profit. Now, what can I get you?"

"How about a little respect." His lip curled.

"I knew a guy once, wanted respect he hadn't earned."

The regulars sat up a little straighter.

"What happened to him, Able?" a senior fitter called.

Able's eyes narrowed. "I didn't know him long."

They didn't stay long.

Beckoning Bob forward to clean off the table, she started back for the stock room.

He caught at her arm as she passed. "Able?"

When she turned, every eye in the house on was on her.

"You chose to be here?"

"I did."

"Are you out of your fuckin' mind?"

"Hole's a downside bar, isn't it?"

"Yeah but . . ."

"I'm a bartender." She swept an exasperated gaze around the room. "Not a hard concept people. Bar. Bartender. Sorge, I just got that god-damned pool table. Get your beer off the felt or it'll be the last beer you have Bob hasn't pissed in."

* * *

"More good news than bad these days."

"You want bad news. I'll give you bad news." The rigger downed his shot, and slapped the bar for another one. "Fuckin' storms on Jupiter's flinging the lines around. We lock it down, we risk losing the gas pocket. We let it run, we got no control and we risk losing the whole fuckin' line."

"Does sound bad."

"Yeah. I don't suppose you knew a guy once who solved the problem?"

"Nope." Able polished another length of the bar, cloth moving in long, smooth sweeps. "But I expect to."

"You expect . . . Oh." Frowning thoughtfully he tossed back his shot. He was still looking thoughtful nearly half an hour later as he headed out the hatch.

Able polished her way down the bar—not so much because it needed it but because it was one of the things a good bartender did—and when she came back she smiled at the man sitting in the rigger's place. "Dr. Porter."

"It's a small station in a big universe, Able. How've you been?"

"Good. What can I get you."

"Coffee's fine."

She set the mug down, studied him for a moment, then slid over two sugars. No creamer.

"Nice trick." He stirred them in, his spoon chiming against the heavy porcelain sides of the mug. "You know that problem the Company brought me on board for? Seems to be solved."

"Congratulations."

"I didn't say I solved it, Able. Company thinks I did though. Upside, they're saying things started to change the moment I came on board. Except I wasn't the only one who came on board that day." He took a long drink and looked around. "So this is the Hole. It's not so bad; why the Hole?"

"Because this is downside, Dr. Porter. And they call this the asshole of the station."

"Do they, Able?"

"They do, Dr. Porter. I knew a guy once, his asshole seized up on him. Eventually, his head exploded." A sudden loud burst of music cut off the psychologist's reply. "Strawberry! Tell Logan to turn his damned foot down!"

The music dimmed.

Dr. Porter smiled into his coffee. "You knew a guy once?"

"I knew a lot of guys, Doc."

"And you say you're just a bartender."

"No, I don't."

"But . . ."

Able drew a beer and set it on Spike's tray. "I don't believe I ever used the word *just*."

Choice of Ending

Now, when you're invited into an anthology about the Maiden, Matron (I'm not sure why Matron rather than Mother) and Crone and you've already got a perfectly functional Triple Goddess setup in your fourth book, Gate of Darkness, Circle of Light, *it only makes sense to use that. Well, technically since I'd used Mercedes Lackey's* Wind's Four Quarters *as a way to evoke the Goddess I had a Quatro Goddess set-up but I fudged past that in the book.*

I'd always thought Mrs. Ruth was a wonderful secondary character and it was great to give her this chance to go out in style.

WHEN THE PHONE BEGAN TO ring several people within the morning rush heading for the Spadina subway station literally jumped. The incessant 27/7 warble of cell phones from pockets and purses hadn't prepared them for the strident and insistent ring of old technology. A couple of the older commuters actually moved to pick up–their responses set in a childhood before call answer when such a ring demanded immediate attention. One after another, they changed their minds upon actually reaching the booth. Perhaps it was the prevalent scent of urine or a perfectly valid fear of catching something virulent from the grimy receiver or the sudden certain knowledge that the call couldn't possibly be for them.

And the phone rang on.

"All right, all right, I'm coming. Don't get your damned panties in a twist!" An elderly woman dressed in several layers of grimy clothing pushed a heavily loaded shopping cart along the crowed sidewalk, scattering pedestrians like pigeons. Although collisions seemed unavoidable, no collisions occurred. A heavily perfumed young woman did snap one heel off a pair of expensive shoes after making an observation about street people and personal hygiene and asylums but that was probably a coincidence.

Possibly a coincidence.

Actually, not likely to be coincidence at all.

The shopping cart finally parked by the booth, a gnarled hand, gnawed fingernails surprisingly clean, picked up the receiver.

The ringing stopped.

The sudden silence turned heads.

"What?"

And the city dweller's innate ability to ignore the poor, the crazy, and most rules of common courtesy turned heads away again.

The voice on the other end of the phone was pleasantly modulated, genderless, and just a little smug. "Mrs. Ruth, this is your third and final warning. The power is about to pass. Please see that your affairs are in order."

Mrs. Ruth, the eldest avatar of the triple Goddess, She who was age and wisdom and kept council during the dark of the moon, slammed the receiver back down onto the phone, coughed for a while, spat a large gob of greenish-yellow phlegm onto the stained concrete and snarled, "Bite me."

She'd known her time was ending for months now. It was, after all, what she did. What she was. She knew things. She knew the name of every pigeon who'd lost its home when the university tore down Varsity Stadium. She knew the hidden places and the small lives that lived in them. She knew the pattern of the larger lives that filled the city with joy and laughter and fear and pain. She knew that something was going to happen only she could prevent and she bloody well wasn't going anywhere until it did and she had.

"They can come and get me if they want me to go that badly!" she told a passing driver as she crossed Bloor Street against the lights deftly moving her cart through the places the cars weren't. The driver *may* have questioned how he could hear her, given that his windows were up, his air conditioning was turned on, and he was singing along with a Justin Timberlake CD his daughter had left in the car, but she didn't stop to find out if he had. Another day she would have; questions were her stock in trade. Today, she didn't have time.

The trouble with knowing things was that not everything known was pleasant. There had always been dark places in the pattern, she acknowledged them, kept an eye on them, and if asked for her help, assisted in removing them.

Asked for her help. That was the sticking point.

"I can't just go fixing things willy nilly," she pointed out to a young man jogging past.

Without really knowing why he slowed and asked, "Why not?"

"Well, what will you learn from that?" Mrs. Ruth responded. "That I can fix things?" She blew a moist raspberry. "You have to learn to fix things yourself. I'm just a tool in the great toolbox of life."

"But what if you can't fix that . . . thing on your own? What if you've tried and it stays unfixed?"

"Ah, then you have to learn just who to ask for help. Your parents have been married for what, twenty-nine years?"

"Yeah but . . ."

"You think that maybe they know a thing or two about staying together?"

"My parents have always said they won't interfere in my life."

"Uh huh."

"So I should ask them . . ."

"Ask them what they had to do to make their relationship work." Which was, quite possibly, the most direct answer she'd given in thirty years.

"But . . ."

Not that it seemed to matter. "Just ask them, bubba."

He frowned at her then and reached into his belt pouch. "Power bar?"

"Sure."

And off he jogged, feeling good about himself because of a little effortless charity. He'd already forgotten the conversation but that didn't matter, the things he'd needed to know that he already knew were now lying along the surface of his thoughts where they'd do him some good.

Mrs. Ruth snorted as she watched him jog away. Time was she could have spun her answers out for blocks, switching between allegory and insult at will. No one appreciated words of wisdom that seemed to arrive too easily. Trouble with common sense was, folks had stopped appreciating anything considered *common.* Granted, they'd stopped some time between coming out of the trees and walking erect but it still pissed her off.

Time was . . .

Time wasn't. That was the problem.

The wheel of life turned. Sometimes, it ran over a few hearts on the way. As a rule, her job was to remind folk that there wasn't a damned thing they could do about it.

"Why did this happen to me?"

"Because."

"It's not fair!"

"No, it isn't."

"How can I stop this!"

"You can't."

But she could. It was within her power to change the pattern—if she could just hang onto that power long enough. She was *not* having her end and this particular bit of darkness coincide.

"I'm not denying that it's time," she muttered at her reflection, keeping pace in the windows of parked cars. "There are days I feel more tired than wise."

Her reflection snorted. "Then let go."

"No. I can't let it happen again."

"You can't stop it from happening again, you old fool."

Mrs. Ruth sighed and raised a hand to rub at watering eyes. That was true enough where *it* referred to the general rather than the specific. But she could stop this particular *it* from happening and she was going to.

With only one hand guiding it, the shopping cart twisted sideways and slammed into the side of a royal blue sedan. The car alarm screamed out a protest.

"Oh shut-up!"

The alarm emitted one final, somewhat sulky, *bleep* then fell silent.

Shaking her head, Mrs. Ruth dug into the deeps of the cart, shoving aside old newspapers, her entire wardrobe except for the blue socks which she'd left hanging on the bushes by the church, and eighteen faded grocery bags filled with empty Girl Guide cookie boxes and Tabasco sauce. Down near the top half of the 1989 yellow pages, she found a coupon for complimentary body work at Del's Garage on Davenport Rd at Ossington. Del had played high school football with the owner of the car and was about to be in desperate need of a good lawyer. The owner of the car had married a very good lawyer.

"There." She shoved it under the windshield wipers. "Two for one. Don't say I never did nothing for you. And stop staring at me!"

Her reflection suddenly became very interested in getting a bit of secret sauce off the sleeve of her shapeless black sweater.

Frowning slightly, Mrs. Ruth laid her palm against the warm curve of glass and wondered when her joints had grown so prominent, her fingers so thin. She remembered her hands fat and dimpled. "You look old," she said softly.

Under the crown of her messy grey braid, the lines on her reflection's face rearranged themselves into a sad smile. "So do you."

"You look older!"

"Do not!"

"Do too!"

"Excuse me, are you all right?"

Mr. Ruth turned toward the young woman standing more than a careful arm's length away—compassion's distance in the city. "When he asks you how you did it, tell him it's a secret. Trust me; things'll go a lot better if he never knows."

Or had that already happened? Past and future threads had become twisted together.

And why was she speaking Korean when the girl was clearly Vietnamese?

"No! Not now!" Her hands closed around the bar of her shopping cart and she closed her eyes to better see the fraying threads of her power and draw them back to her. Through force of will she rewove the connections. Breathing heavily—a moment later or ten, she had no idea—she opened her eyes to see the young woman still standing there but clearly ready to run. "I'm fine," she told her through clenched teeth. "Really, I'm fine."

With no choice but to believe, the girl nodded and walked quickly away.

On the corner of College and Spadina, a phone began to ring.

"I will repeat this only one more time," Mrs. Ruth growled in its general direction. "Bite. Me. Mange. Moi."

People moved out of her way as she hobbled toward the Eaton's Center. Most of her scowl came from the pain of a cracked a tooth caused by all the clenching. Most.

In nice weather, he ate lunch on a bench outside the north end of the Center where he watched small children roll past in strollers or dangling from the hands of hurrying adults. These children were too young but he enjoyed speculating on how they would grow. This one would suddenly be all legs, awkward and graceful simultaneously, like

colt. That one would be husky well into his teens when suddenly his
height would catch up with his weight. Her hair would darken. His
dimples would be lost. After his sandwich, his apple, and his diet cola,
he'd go back into the store and later, when school was out, he'd help
the parents of older children buy expensive clothing, clothing the
child would grow out of or grow tired of long before they'd gotten
their money's worth from the piece. The store had a customer appreciation program—every five hundred dollars spent entered the child's
name in a draw for the latest high-tech wonder. Names and ages and
addresses were collected in a secure data base. Where secure meant
accessible only by store staff.

She knew all this when she lowered herself down beside him on
the bench and arranged the layers of her stained black skirts over her
aching legs. "I won't let it happen, bubba."

Knowing what he knew, hiding what he hid, he should have
asked, "Let what happen?" and that question would have given her a
part of him. Every question she drew out after that would have given
her a little more. It was how conversations worked and conversations
could be directed. Direct the conversation, direct the person having it.

But he said only, "All right."

White noise. Nothing given.

"Everyone has limits. I've reached mine."

He said, "Okay." Then he folded his sandwich bag and slid it into
his pocket.

Her presence used to be enough to make them open up. Today,
holding on to her power by will alone, not even leading statements
were enough. Should she release enough power to draw him to her,
she'd lose it all before she had time to deal with what he was.

He stepped on his empty diet cola can, compressing it neatly.
Then he scooped it up and stood.

Mrs. Ruth stood as well.

He smiled.

His smile said, as clearly as if he'd spoken aloud, *"You can't stop
me."*

A sub-conscious statement he had no idea he was making.

"Oh right! You're big man facing down an old lady! I ought to run
over your toes until you can't walk!" He looked startled by her volume, admittedly impressive for a woman her age. More startled still
when she grabbed his sleeve. "How'd you like a little Tabasco sauce
where the sun don't shine!"

"Okay, that's enough." The police constable's large hand closed around her wrist and gently moved her hand back to her side. Fine. Let the law handle it. Except she couldn't just tell him what she knew, he had to ask.

She glared up at him. "Never eat anything with mayo out of a dumpster—all kinds of evil things hiding in that bland whiteness."

She was hoping for: "What the hell are you talking about?"

Or even: "Say what?"

But all she got was: "Words to live by, I'm sure. Now move along and stop bothering people."

Over her years on the street she'd met most of Toronto's finest—a great many of them even were—but this big young man with the bright blue eyes, she didn't know. "Move along? Move along? Listen bubba, I owned these streets while you were still hanging off your mother's tit!"

"Hey!" A big finger waved good naturedly at her. "Leave my mother out of this."

"Your mother . . ." No, better not go there. "I can't leave yet. I have something to do."

When the bright blue eyes narrowed, Mrs. Ruth realized she'd been speaking Hungarian. She hadn't spoken Hungarian since she was nine. The power was unraveling again. By the time she wove things back into a semblance of normalcy, the cop was gone, *he* was gone, she was sitting alone on the bench, and the sun was low in the sky.

"Shit!"

She had no time to find a Hero and the other Aspects were too far away even if they'd agree to help. Which they wouldn't. The Goddess was a part of what kept this world balanced between the light and the dark. She was the fulcrum on which the balance depended. Should the balance shift in either direction, her aspects would come together to right it but this . . . evil was nothing unusual. Not dark enough to tip the scales and with light enough in the world to balance it.

"Business as per bloody usual."

And all very well if only the big picture got considered. One thing the years had taught her—her, not the Goddess—was that the big picture didn't mean bupkas to those caught by the particulars.

Getting a good grip on her shopping cart, Mrs. Ruth heaved herself up onto her feet. She could still see to the point where the dark pattern intersected with her life although she no longer had strength enough to see further. Fine. If she followed the weft to that place, she'd have one more chance.

"The Gods help those who help themselves."

Laughing made her cough but hell, without a sense of humor she might as well already be dead so, laughing and coughing, she slowly pushed her cart north on Yonge Street. She couldn't move quickly but neither could she be stopped.

"After all," she told two young women swaying past on too-high heels, "I am inevitable."

The elder of the two paled. The younger merely sniffed and tossed pale curls.

That made her laugh harder.

Cough harder.

Phones rang as she passed, handing off booth to booth, south to north like an electronic relay.

At Yonge and Irwin, a middle-aged woman held her chirping cell phone up under frosted curls, frowned, and swept a puzzled gaze over the others also waiting for traffic to clear. When Mrs. Ruth pushed between an elderly Asian man and a girl with a silver teardrop tattooed on one cheek, her eyes cleared. She took a step forward as the cart bounced off the curb—boxes rattling, newspapers rustling—and held out her phone.

"It's for you."

Mrs. Ruth snorted. "Take a message."

"They say it's important."

"Do they? What makes their important more important than mine?" When the woman began to frown again, she rolled her eyes. "Hand it over."

The phone lay ludicrously small on her palm. She folded her fingers carefully around it and lifted what she hoped was the right end to her mouth. "She has to pay for this call, you inconsiderate bastards." Then she handed the bit of metal and plastic back and said, "Hang up."

"But . . ."

"Do it."

She used as little power as she could but it was enough diverted she lost another thread or two or three . . . Breathing heavily, she tightened her grasp on those remaining.

At Bloor Street she crossed to the north side and turned west, moving more slowly now, her feet and legs beginning to swell, the taste of old pennies in the back of her throat.

"Could be worse," she found the breath to mutter as she approached Bay. "Could be out in the suburbs."

"Could be raining," rasped a voice from a under a sewer grate.

She nodded down at bright eyes. "Could be."

From behind the glass that held them in the museum, the stone temple guardians watched her pass. Fortunately the traffic passing between them was still heavy enough, in spite of the deepening night, that she could ignore their concern.

By the time she reached Spadina, more and more of her weight was on the cart. When the phone at the station began to ring, she shot a look toward it so redolent with threat that it hiccuped once and fell silent.

"Right back where . . . I started from." Panting she wrestled the cart off the curb, sneered at a street car, and defied gravity to climb the curb on the other side. "Should've just spent the day . . . sitting in the . . . sun."

By the time she turned north on Brunswick, the streets were nearly empty, the rush of people when restaurants and bars closed down already dissipated. How had it taken her so long to walk three short blocks? Had she stopped? She couldn't remember stopping.

Couldn't remember . . .

Remember . . .

"Oh no, you don't!" Snarling, she yanked the power back. "When. I. Chose."

Overhead, small black shapes that weren't squirrels ran along the wires and in and out of the dappled darkness thrown by the canopies of ancient trees.

"Elderly trees," she snorted. "Nothing ancient in this part of the world but me."

"You're upsetting the balance."

She stared down at the little man in the red cap perched on the edge of her cart, twisting the cap off one of the bottles of Tabasco sauce. "Not so much it can't be set right the moment I'm gone. Trust me . . ." Her brief bark of laughter held no mirth. ". . . I know things."

"You're supposed to be gone now," he pointed out, and took a long drink.

"So?"

That clearly wasn't the answer he'd been expecting. "So . . . you're not."

"And they say Hobs aren't the smartest littles in the deck."

"Who says?"

"You know." She thought she could risk taking one hand off the cart handle long enough to gesture. She was wrong. The cart moved one way. She moved the other.

"You're bleeding." The Hob squatted beside her and wrinkled his nose.

"No shit." Left knee. Right palm. Concrete was much tougher than old skin stretched translucent thin over bone. She wouldn't have made it back to her feet without the Hob's help. Like most of the littles, he was a lot stronger than he appeared and he propped her up until she could get both sets of fingers locked around the shopping cart handle once again. "Thanks."

He shrugged. "It seems important to you."

She didn't see him leave but it was often that way with the grey folk who moved between the dark and light. She missed his company, however brief it had been, and found herself standing at the corner of Brunswick and Wells wondering why she was there.

The night swam in and out of focus.

Halfway down the block, a door closed quietly.

Her thread . . .

His thread . . .

Mrs. Ruth staggered forward, clutching the pattern so tightly she began to lose her grip on the power. She could feel her will spread out over the day, stretched taunt behind her from the first phone call to this moment.

This moment. The moment her part of the pattern crossed his.

A shadow reached the sidewalk in the middle of the block, a still form draped over one shoulder. The shadow, the still form, and her. No one else on the street. No one peering down out of a darkened window. A light on in the next block—too far.

This was the reason she'd stayed.

The world roared in her ears as she reached him. Roared, and as she clutched desperately at the fraying edges, departed.

He turned. Looked at her over the flannel covered curve of the child he carried.

It took a certain kind of man to break silently into a house, to walk silently through darkened halls to the room of a sleeping child and to carry that child away, drugged to sleep more deeply still. The kind of man who knew how to weigh risk.

She was falling. Moments passing between one heart beat and the next. Her power had passed. She was no risk to him.

He smiled.

His smile said, as clearly as if he'd spoken aloud, *"You can't stop me."*

It was funny how she could see his smile when she could see so little else.

Then he turned to carry the child to his car.

As the sidewalk rose up to slap against her, curiously yielding, Mrs. Ruth threw out an arm and with all she had left, with the last strength of one dying old woman who was no more and no less than that, she shoved the cart into his heel.

Few things hurt worse than a heavily laden shopping cart suddenly slamming into unprotected bone. He stumbled, tripped, fell forward. His head slammed into the car he'd parked behind, bone impacting with impact resistant door.

The car alarm shrieked.

Up and down the street, cars joined in the chorus.

"Thief! Thief! Thief!"

Their vocabulary was a little limited, she thought muzzily, but their hearts were in the right place.

Lights came on.

Light.

Go into the light.

"In a minute." Mrs. Ruth brushed off the front of her black sweater, pleased to feel familiar substantial curves under her hand, and watched with broad satisfaction as doors opened and one after another the child's neighbors emerged to check on their cars.

Cars had alarms, children didn't. She frowned. Should have done something about that when she still had the time.

He stood. A little dazed, he shoved the shopping cart out of his way. Designed to barely remain upright at the best of times, the cart toppled sideways and crashed to the concrete, spilling black cloth, empty boxes, and bottles of Tabasco sauce. One bottle bounced and broke as it hit the pavement a second time directly in front of the child's face. The fumes cut through the drug and she cried.

He started to run then, but he didn't get far. The city was on edge, it said so in the papers. These particular representatives of the city were more than happy to take out their fear on so obvious a target.

The Crone is wisdom. Knowledge. She advises. She teaches. She is not permitted to interfere.

"She didn't. I did. The power passed before I acted. I merely used the power to get to the right place at the right time. No rules against that."

You knew that would happen.

Not exactly a question. Mrs. Ruth answered it anyway. "Nope, I'd had it. Reached my limit. I had every intention of blasting the son of a bitch right out of his Italian loafers. Fortunately for the balance of power, I died."

The silence that followed filled with the sound of approaching sirens.

But the cart . . .

"Carts are tricksy things, bubba. Fall over if you so much as look at them wrong."

And the Tabasco sauce?

"What? There's rules against condiments now?"

You are a very irritating person.

"Thank you." She frowned as her body was lifted onto a stretcher. "I really let myself go there at the end."

Does it matter?

"I suppose not. I was never a vain woman."

You were cranky, surly, irritable, self-righteous, annoying, and generally bad tempered.

"But not vain."

The child remained wrapped in her mother's arms as the paramedic examined her. The drugs had kept her from being frightened and now she looked sleepy and confused. Her mother looked terrified enough for both of them.

"They'll hold her especially tightly now, cherish each moment. When she gets older, she'll find their concern suffocating but she'll come through her teenage rebellions okay because the one thing she'll never doubt will be her family's love. She'll have a good life, if not a great one, and the threads of that life will weave in and about a thousand other lives that never would have known her if not for tonight."

The power has passed. You can't know all that.

Mrs. Ruth snorted. "You really are an idiot, aren't you? She pulled a pair of sunglasses from the pocket of her voluminous skirt and put them on. "All right, I'm ready. Life goes on."

But you knew it would.

"Not the point, bubba." She turned at the edge of the light for one last look. It wasn't, if she said so herself, a bad ending.

He Said, Sidhe Said

Tam Lin is one of my favorite ballads/poems/stories of all time and I'm not sorry for what I did to it. Well, maybe a little. In case you're curious, it's impossible to find a skateboard magazine in a small town in Canada in the winter. Snowboarding, yes. Skateboarding, not so much. Thank God for the internet.

LAST SUMMER, THEY BUILT THIS new skateboard park down by Carterhaugh Pond; a decent half pipe, some good bowls, a pyramid, couple of heights of rails. Blatant attempt to keep us off the streets, to control the ride, but they put some thought into the design and I've gotta admit that sometimes I can appreciate a chance to skate without being hassled. It was October 24th, early morning, and I had the place to myself. Kids were all in school and a touch of frost in the air was keeping the usual riders away.

I was grabbing some great air off the pipe and I was seriously *in* the moment, so I figured this was the time to try a backside tailslide on the lip. Yeah, yeah, there's harder tricks but for some reason, me and tailslides . . . So, I picked up some serious speed, hit the lip, held the lip, and then WHAM! I was ass over head and kissing concrete.

World kind of went away for a minute or two–you know, like it does–and when I finally got my eyes open, I was staring up at this total babe. I was like "Woo! Liv Tyler!" only without that whole kind of creepy "I look like the lead singer for Areosmith" vibe.

Over the sound of The Bedrockers still jamming in my phones, she said, "Give me your hand!"

I figured she was going to help me up so I put my hand in hers and next thing I knew, the park was gone, the pipe was gone, hell, the whole world was gone. Good thing my other hand was locked on my board.

* * *

The land between the water and the wood has always been ours, one of the rare places where our world touches that of mortal men. The news that it had been defiled came to the High Court with a Loireag who dwelled in the pond. She was a plaintive little thing, wailing and keening as she made her way through my knights and ladies to throw herself damply before me.

The wailing and keening made it difficult to hear her complaint but eventually she calmed enough to be understood. Great instruments of steel and sound were scraping away the earth, crushing and tearing all that was green, driving terrified creatures from their homes and into hiding.

We do not concern ourselves with the world of men and in return we expect that which is ours to be respected. Clearly it was time again to remind them of this.

When I arrived with those of my court I trusted most, I saw that the tale of woe spun to me by the Loireag was true. A great scar had been gouged into the earth and men surrounded it. Large men. Their skins browned by the sun and made damp by their labors. Cloth of blue stretched over muscular thighs and, as I watched, one threw off a gauntlet of leather and tilted back his head to drink.

A lifted finger and I directed a spilled rivulet of water over his chest and down a ridged stomach until it disappeared behind . . .

"Majesty?"

I breathed deeply. "It is overly warm in the world of men," I said as a breeze sped to cool my brow at my command. "We will go and return again another day."

But our days are not the days of men and when we returned, the scar in the earth had been filled with stone sculpted into strange and impossible shapes. In stone cupped into half a moon, a young man rode a winged board.

His hair was dark but tipped with light, his eyes the grey-green of a storm. Loose clothing hid his body from my sight but his hands were large and strong and he moved like water down a mountain side. His smile spoke of earthy joys.

I stepped forward as his head hit the stone.

"Not *again*, Majesty . . ."

Who of my court dared to voice so weary a warning I did not know but for the sake of so enchanting a creature I disregarded it and crossed into the world of men. Admiring the broad shoulders and lean length of my fallen hero, I reached out to him.

"Take my hand," I said.

And he did.

I woke up in what I later learn is called a bower—it was kind of like a bedroom without walls, just this billowy curtainy stuff and I wasn't alone. The babe who wasn't Liv Tyler was with me, we were both totally without clothes, and she was studying this major scabbage I've got all down my right forearm.

"Screwed up a 180 out of an axle stall," I explained trying to sound like this sort of thing happened to me all the time—naked with a strange babe not the scabbage because, you know, sometimes you bail.

She touched it with one finger, all sympathetic.

I probably should have been more freaked but she was naked and I was naked and so . . .

It was a fast ride, but no one did any complaining.

Later, we were lying all wrapped up and worn out when this tall, skinny blonde fem wearing a lot of swishy green just wandered in without so much as a *"Hey, coming through!"*

"Majesty, your husband has sent an emissary. Will you receive him?"

"An emissary?" she asked.

Me, I was kind of fixating on a different word although I totally kept my cool. "You have a husband?"

Once I had him unclothed, I was a little disconcerted to discover that he was damaged. His shins were an overlapping mix of purple and blue and his right arm had been horribly disfigured.

He muttered words I did not understand but I could feel his terror so I touched his arm to calm his fears. His reaction to my touch was unexpected. It had been long since a mortal man had shared my bed and I had forgotten just how impulsive they are. And how quick.

About to suggest a second attempt, my words were halted by the appearance of Niam of the Golden Hair. "Majesty, your husband has sent an emissary. Will you receive him?"

About to ask who my husband had sent *this* time, my words were once again halted.

The mortal threw himself from the bed, hiding his manhood behind a handful of fabric. "Husband?! Oh man, you never said you had a husband!"

As he was the only man in our lands, I had no idea who he was speaking to and would have demanded an accounting had I not caught sight of that infernal Puck hanging about at the edge of hearing. He wore his usual condescending smile that told quite clearly how he would enjoy informing my Lord Oberon of my latest dalliance.

I could hear him now, insinuating that any discontent I felt was a result of my own choices.

As I would not give him the satisfaction, I bound my mortal lover round with cobwebs and as he lay silent and unmoving said, "Tell good Robin that I will speak with him anon. I have matters here to attend to still."

Niam raised a quizzical brow toward the mortal but bowed and left as commanded, sweeping Puck before her.

I drew the mortal him back to the bed and released his bindings. "You need not fear my husband," I told him. "The King has his own Court and does not come to mine."

Now, having heard *husband*, I hadn't paid a lot of attention to the rest of what the blonde chick had said. I mean, I was cool, totally dignified, but a little stunned, you know? I couldn't think of anything to say until we were alone again and the babe was trying to explain about how they were separated and I didn't have anything to worry about.

"He's the King?"

"Yes."

"And that would make you . . .?"

"The Queen."

Of the Fairies as it turns out. No, not those kinds of fairies. Real fairies. Like in fairy tales. We got dressed and she lead me out onto this balcony tree-branch thing and well, it was pretty damned clear I wasn't in Kansas anymore if you know what I mean.

I just did the Queen of the Fairies. Prime!

"What do I call you?" I asked, tearing my eyes away from a whole section of tree that would make a wild ride.

"Majesty."

I knew she was just teasing so I gave her my best *you and me, we're closer than that* smile. "Sure, but you got a name?"

She looked at me for a long moment then she smiled and I knew I had her. "I am also called Tatiana."

"Annie."

"Tatiana!"

"Not to me, babe." I laid my fist against my heart. "Tommy Lane. But I tag with Teal so you want to call me that, I'm cool with it. You know, TL . . . Teal."

"I think I will call you Tommy Lane," I told him. Not that it mattered; he would not be in my realm for very much longer. I would send him home the moment I had dealt with Puck.

"So while you're seeing the dude your old man sent, you mind if I ride?"

As I had no real idea of what he was talking about, I told him I did not.

He raced back into my bower and emerged with his wheeled board—it had merely seemed to have wings so quickly had it moved. Balanced on the edge of my balcony, he grinned with such joy that I felt my heart soften towards him. Then he placed the pieces of sponge upon his ears again and threw himself forward, bellowing out a most impertinent question as he raced along the branch.

"Who's your daddy!"

With any luck he would fall and break his neck and save me the walk back to the place where our lands touched.

"I can't wait for the feast!"

"What feast?" I snapped as Puck dropped down beside me. His manner of perching and appearing and making himself free of my court as though it were my husband's was most annoying.

"The feast you'll be having for your skater-boy."

Tommy Lane was no longer in sight but I could still hear the rasp of his wheels against the tree and the shriek of my ladies as he roared through bower after bower. How unfortunate that none would risk my wrath and stop his ride upon their blade. Birds took wing all around us, protesting so rude a disturbance.

"It's traditional," Puck continued, grinning insolently. "A mortal crosses over and we throw him a feast. You can't send him back without one, not unless you made a mistake bringing him here in the first place."

Oh, he would *like* to go to my husband and say I had made a mistake. They would laugh together over it.

"Moth, Cobweb, Mustard Seed!"

The sprites appeared.

"See that a feast is made ready." As they vanished, I turned to
Puck and said, as graciously as I was able, "You will stay, of course."

Wise enough to recognize the command, he bowed gracefully. "I
wouldn't miss it, Majesty."

After the feast, he would go to my Lord Oberon and tell my husband of the great joy and pleasure I took in my mortal companion
and then my lord could feel the bite of being replaced once again.

I have no idea where the room came from. One minute I was
having the wildest ride of my life and the next I'm landing an ollie
on marble floors. I knew it was marble because Philly used to have
this great park with marble slabs that was prime loc for street skat-
ing. Anyway, there were banners hanging from the ceiling and tables
all down the middle and these little people laying out plates and
stuff.

I saw my Annie up ahead, standing with some short brown dude–
not a brother but brown, hard to explain–and so pushing mongo-foot,
I made my way over. Just before I reached her, I decided to show off
a bit and so did a quick grind along the last of the marble benches that
were up against the wall. Kid's trick but she didn't ride and I could tell
she was impressed.

His *board* left a black mark along the edge of the bench and only
the presence of my husband's emissary kept me from freezing his
blood on the spot.

Flashing my sharpest smile, I planted one on right on the royal
lips. "Hey, babe, what up?"

I did not have the words . . .

Mostly because I hadn't understood the question but also because
of his fearless stupidity. This was truly why we find mortal men so fas-
cinating. Not content merely to die, they spend their short lives court-
ing death in so very many ways. And, in truth, the salutation was a bit
distracting.

"He wants to know what's going on," Puck said helpfully.

I ignored him and graced my unwelcome paramour with my full
attention. "My people prepare a feast in your honor, my love. Rich
raiment befitting one who shares my bower has been laid out for you.
Go and adorn yourself in silk and velvet."

"Silk and velvet? Not my deal. I appreciate the thought but I'm cool."

"You will be warmer in the clothing that has been made ready for you."

He threw back his head and laughed and, to my horror, wrapped an arm around my waist and pulled me tightly against his side. I would have turned him into a newt then and there if not for the irritatingly superior smile on the face of Robin Goodfellow.

"Isn't my Annie the greatest?" Tommy Lane declared once he had his laughter under control.

Puck bowed deeply so that I could not see his expression. "She is indeed," he said.

The food was great. A little gay, you know, with sauces and garnishes and fancy stuff, but there was lots of it and it tasted prime. Unfortunately, the after dinner entertainment totally sucked. One guy with Spock-ears and a harp. I had to ask what the harp was; I thought maybe it was some kind of warped axe. Oh, and the dude was blind but he was no Stevie Wonder. I figured they were all being so nice to him because he was blind and that was cool but the piece he was slaying went on and on and on.

I guess I wasn't too good at hiding what I thought because the little brown dude—name of Robin Goodfellow but he tagged Puck—turned to me and asked what I thought. I could've lied but he didn't look like he was having such a good time either so I told him.

"Too bad you've got no decent tunes with you."

"I do." I tapped the player on my belt. "But I'd need a deck to plug in to."

"I could take care of that."

"Bonus!"

I handed over my player and next thing I knew, The Bedrockers were blasting out at a hundred and twenty decibels.

The queen, *my* queen, whirled around so fast it was all hair and drapery stuff for a minute. Once that settled and I got a look at her face, there was like a second where she looked totally scary. Then Puck told her it was my sound and she chilled although her smile seemed a little forced.

I spent a couple of songs teaching the crowd to move and I gotta hand it to them, for all they looked like they had a collective stick up their butts, they sure could dance.

*   *   *

Worn out by the exertions I would not dignify in calling dance, Tommy Lane spent the night asleep so I did not even gain the small physical pleasure I might have from his presence. When he woke he was annoying insistent upon eating and would not travel until he had broken his fast. Barely concealing my impatience, I had the sprites bring him bread and honey and clear water as much at this time as I would have liked him to have been fed with insects and the dregs of a swamp. Or better still, fed to insects and lost within the swamp.

Although Puck had returned to my husband's court, I did not trust his absence and resolved to keep up the pretense until the boy was gone.

With no intention of traveling to the crossing at a mortal's pace, I took his hand and we were there. Unfortunately, we were not alone.

"Sending him back so soon, Majesty?"

"Why should I not? I have wrung from him all his strength."

At that moment, the boy chose to fling himself down a shear rock face then up and over a bank of earth. Folding himself near in two he clutched at his board, spun about in the air, and landed with a merry whoop.

"Seems to have gotten his strength back. Your husband, my lord Oberon, is pleased you have found amusement. How unfortunate that you find he does not suit."

I could well read the implication between his words. As much as accuse me of a foolish choice. I would not have that. Much angered, my voice sheathed in ice, I said, "Then my husband, the Lord Oberon, will be pleased to hear that I am not sending him back but rather gifting him with passage between our worlds so that he might amuse himself as he will." Masking my fury, I called Tommy Lane to my side and opened the way. "You may go once each day to the place that I found you."

"You trying to get rid of me?"

From his smile I could see that he was making fun and for the sake of our audience, I denied it.

"Her majesty grants you a great gift," my husband's irritating emissary declared. "Do you not, Majesty?"

"Yes," I snapped before I thought.

A Faerie gift once given can not be recalled.

In order for me now to be rid of Tommy Lane, the decision to leave must be his.

* * *

I had it all. A major babe, servants, and great food—after a few
tries they even managed a decent burger and fries—I could ride when
I wanted and some of the fairy dudes were starting to catch on.

"Finvarra, what are you doing?"

He dropped to one knee, his waist length hair wrapping around
him like a silken curtain. "I believe it is called a nollie, Majesty. In
essence, an ollie preformed by tapping the nose of the board instead
of the tail."

My lip curled, almost of its own volition, and my hand rose to
teach him such a lesson as would last the length of an immortal life.
Unfortunately at that moment, Tommy Lane dropped down out of the
trees followed by that nuisance Puck.

"Hey Finvar! Rad move!"

"Your boy's really livening up the place," Puck announced, leaping off a board of his own. With no iron on the original, Faerie magic
had been able to duplicate it easily. No one knew exactly what
aluminum was except that it wasn't iron. "Isn't it great?"

All three waited for my answer.

I locked my temper behind an indulgent smile. "It is."

Tommy Lane waved up toward the line of bark ripped in looping
patterns from the inter-locking branches of the trees. "Did you know
that Disney used boards to work out how Tarzan would move?"

"No."

It seemed my husband had not yet tired of the bothersome Puck's
reports.

I would have to get creative.

Riding the trees was fine but it was hard to keep it real, there were
just some moves I couldn't do on bark. No matter how broad the
branch. And sometimes I rolled right though living space and that was
just whack. Also more danger than I needed in my life; some of those
dudes had really big swords. So, every day, I went back to the skate
park.

I didn't see the girl at first, I saw the flowers. Three big pink roses
sprayed onto the side of the pipe. She wasn't easy to spot because she
was kneeling down at the bottom of the third rose, painting in her tag.
Her green jacket kind of blended in with all the foliage.

I mounted up and carved my way down to the bottom just as she stood. Her tag read Janet. Given that she was at the bottom of the pipe and couldn't get away, she stood her ground.

"Nice work," I said. "I haven't seen you around here before."

"My old man doesn't want me coming here. Says I'll meet the wrong sort." She shrugged. "I come anyway. I've seen you."

"You have?"

"Duh, you haunt this place. Yesterday afternoon, I saw that super high switch heelflip you did."

"Actually, it was switch front heelflip, switch heelflip, backside tailside and a fakie hardflip."

"Wow."

"Yeah." I was good to talk to someone who understood. She was riding an urban assault board, way bigger than most girls like at forty inches and I could see her eyeing my pro model. I have no idea what made me say it but I stepped off and pushed my board over. "Go on. You know you want to."

Her eyes widened. Letting someone else on your ride was more intimate than screwing and I could tell from her expression, she'd never done this before. Finally, she nodded and pushed her ride toward me. "What the hell. The front trucks are a little tight."

She was right and I bailed coming out of a tailslide, trying to carve left across the bowl. Took most of the landing on my right shoulder but still buffed a strip of skin off my jaw. Late afternoon, she came off some air and into a fakie, shifted her weight wrong, hit, and rolled up, blood seeping through the knee of her cargos.

Bonded in blood. Cool.

With her leg locked up, she was done for the day. Using her board like a crutch, she hobble to the edge of the park and turned to stare back at me. "You want to go get some fries or something?"

Actually I did but Annie was expecting me back and . . .

Janet snorted. "You got a girl. I should've known."

While I was thinking of something, anything to say, she limped away.

He was bleeding when he returned to me that night and he stank of mortal company. I would have demanded to know her name but that vexatious Puck was still about and I would not have him carry tales of a mortal lover who dared to cheat on me.

Later, with the nettlesome sprite safely in sight but out of earshot as he sought to annoy me by having Tommy Lane teach him new tricks I got the whole story from the Loireag.

A girl.

I would use her.

That night, as he slept, I cloaked myself in shadow and did what I had not done for many long years–I walked amid the mortal race. The girl was easy enough to find, her blood had mixed with his and his was mine.

She sat by the entrance to her dwelling. Within, raised voices discussed locking her in her room until she told them the name of the boy she was seeing.

In guise of one Tommy Lane would believe, wearing the face of my husband's emissary–which had of late become as familiar to me as my own–I sat down beside her. "They sound angry."

"Who the hell are you?"

Of old, the young were much politer. "I bring you word from Tommy Lane."

"Who?"

Thus I discovered the reason she had not told her elders the name of the boy. "You met him today at the ring of stone by Carterhaugh Pond. You rode his board and he yours."

"Yeah, so?"

"He is in grave danger. Tomorrow night the Queen of Faerie will take his life."

"Where?"

I sighed. "She will end his life."

"Why?"

"Because a tithe to darkness must be paid and she will not sacrifice an immortal knight when a mortal man is close at hand."

"Look, I don't know what you're on, but I got troubles of my own so make like a leaf and get lost."

I drew her gaze around to mine, captured it, and held it. "Do you believe me now?" I demanded when, after many heartbeats, I released her

She drew in a long, shuddering breath. "I guess."

As that appeared to be as good as I would get, I continued. "You must go to the park as the sun leaves the sky and when the Queen arrives to claim him, you must snatch him from his board and hold him tight." A possible problem occurred to me. "Are you afraid of snakes?"

"No."

"Good. Do not fear although he be turned within your grasp into angry beasts or red-hot iron or burning lead or . . ."

"Does this fairy tale have a point? Because if I'm not inside in five minutes my old man's going to come out here and kick my ass."

"If you hold tightly to young Tommy Lane, he will in time become himself again. Then you must wrap him in your mantle green."

"My what?"

"Sorry, wrap him in your green jacket and the spell will be broken."

Annie looked real pleased with herself the next morning and when I went for a quickie before breakfast, she was so into it, it was kind of scary. I mean, I liked her enthusiasm but man . . .

She stretched out on the bed looking all catlike and said, "Wait at the park this evening until I come for you. I have a surprise planned."

Later, everyone I passed on the way to the park said goodbye.

I was making my third run down over Janet's roses, when it was like she suddenly appeared. I looked up on the lip and there she was.

I flipped up beside her. She looked pissed.

"Are you real or what?"

"What?"

"Bastard!" She punched me in the arm.

"What are you talking about?"

And then she told me this bullshit story some short brown dude told her about my Annie and sacrificing me tonight and crap.

"It's a Halloween prank," I told her.

She snorted. "I thought so. The whole thing's a friggin' lie!"

"Not all of it," I admitted. I told her my side of the story and she snorted again.

"Jeez, you are so lame! If that's true than what makes the story I got told not true? It sounds to me like the Queen wants more than your bod. You said she looked pleased with herself. She said she has a surprise planned. Everyone said goodbye to you when you left. Duh! How many times have you bailed on your head?"

When Janet put it that way, it all began to make a horrible amount of sense. Puck. The short brown dude had to have been Puck. He liked me and he didn't seem to like my Annie much. I guess now I knew why.

I stepped onto my board. "I'm so out of here."

* * *

And that was my cue. I could not allow him to merely ride away; the power of the gift I'd given him had to be broken or I would ever live with the nagging feeling that someday he might return.

As I stepped into the mortal world, I was pleased to see the girl wrap her arms around young Tommy Lane and drag him off his board. I wrapped myself in terrible beauty and, as she tried to stare me down, raised a hand.

First I turned him to an adder and Janet held him close, although her language would have withered apples on the tree.

Then I turned him to a lion wild and Janet released one hand and smacked the beast upon the nose.

Then I turned him to a red hot bar of iron and Janet screamed and threw him in the pond throwing her smoldering jacket in after him.

Close enough.

And another wailing visit from the Loireag was little enough to pay.

As I removed the glamour and he was once again Tommy Lane, I cried out, "If I had known some lady'd borrowed thee, I would have plucked out your eyes and put in eyes of tree. And had I known of this before I came from home, I would have plucked out your heart and put in a heart of stone!"

"Possessive much?" Janet snarled from the edge of the pond.

Dragging Janet's jacket behind him, Tommy Lane wadded to the shore, shaking his head. "Babe, we are *so* over."

I had thought that was the point I was making.

When I stepped back into Faerie, it was to find Robin Goodfellow awaiting me.

"Ah yes, the old held by mortal maid shtick." He scratched reflectively beneath one arm. "Funny thing though, I could've sworn that tithe went out after seven years, not seven days."

Had it only been seven days? It had seemed so very much longer. "Shut up," I told him.

"Hey, rules were followed, traditions upheld, I got nothing to say." He bowed, sweeping an imaginary hat against the ground. "If your Majesty has no further need of me."

I forbore to remind him that I never *had* need of him nor ever would. He waved in his most irritatingly jaunty manner and sped through the deepening twilight toward the Lord Oberon's Court, indulging in a series of kickflips as he rode out of sight.

A velvet hush settled over my Court as with stately grace I moved among my knights and ladies. As I settled upon a grassy bank and allowed my ladies to twine starflowers in the midnight fall of my hair, I came to an inescapable conclusion.

It was entirely possible that I had remarkably bad taste in men.

After School Specials

Not only is it often a lot easier to write short stories set in a mythos you've already created in a novel setting but there's the added benefit of exercising that mythos between books—or in this case post-series—so that you can keep dipping back into it at will and maybe, someday, return to novel length without having to start cold. "After School Specials" is set in Tony Foster's Smoke and Shadows, Smoke and Mirrors, Smoke and Ashes *world—which I probably will never go back to but who knows, stranger things have happened. This story may work better for you if you've read the books but it also stands up fine on its own.*

"ASHLEY, YOUR FREAK SISTER IS doing it again."

The drawl was unmistakable; Sandra Ohi, Ashley's only serious competition. Having come back from South Carolina for second term after having actually worked on a movie with her mother, a movie where she had lines and got to cry on camera, a movie shown in class during Black History month, Ashley would have ruled the grade eight girls at The Nellie Parks Academy except for one thing.

Arranging her face in the expression her mother usually saved for her father—somewhere between "Oh, it's you." and "Drop dead."—Ashley turned to face Sandra and the trio of girls currently in her inner circle. "Why so interested in a grade five, Sandra? Oh that's right," she continued too sweetly, "you were told to stop hanging around with the grade threes."

As Ashley's posse snickered, Sandra tossed a perfect fall of blue-black hair back over her shoulder. "As much as I would have preferred to avoid her, the little weirdo is standing in the middle of the atrium talking to the *ceiling*. She's *impossible* to avoid. *Everyone* has noticed her. I'm glad you don't mind that's she's so *noticeable*."

"Well, you'd know about having a sister whose noticeable, wouldn't you?"

"What do you mean by *that*?"

"Last I heard the whole entire senior year of Mackenzie College had *noticed* your sister."

Sandra's eyes narrowed and the nostrils of her extremely expensive made-in-America nose flared. "Your father's show is stupid."

Her father had taught her to never bother arguing an unarguable position. "Yeah, well, that doesn't change the fact that your sister is a slut."

Apparently Sandra's father had taught her the same thing. "At least my sister is a slut in a different school!"

Embarrassing family members might be the norm but they could be denied as long as they weren't sharing the same cafeterias and hallways and extracurricular activity rooms. Unfortunately, until she graduated and moved on to high school at the end of the year, Ashley was stuck with Brianna intruding on her space.

Well aware that she'd scored the final point, Sandra sneered and swept past, trailed by her three acolytes—also sneering.

Ashley took a deep breath, and then another because after a certain age screaming wasn't cool. "I'll be in the atrium," she snarled and stalked off.

Her girls were smart. They didn't follow.

"Ow! You're hurting me, you big cow!"

Ashley tightened her grip on Brianna's arm and dragged her out the front door of the school. "Stop being such a baby."

"I'm telling!"

An extra yank kept the little dweep off balance and unable to kick. "I'm telling first because you promised to stop the freak show at school!"

"I wasn't doing nothing."

"You were staring at the ceiling," Ashley snapped, pulling her sister close and spitting the words right into her face. "And you were talking to yourself."

"I was talking to my *familiar*."

"It's not a familiar; it's a bug in a box!"

"Well it's smarter than you!" Brianna rubbed her arm and scowled up at the older girl. "And better looking too!"

"There's the car." Pushing the brat in front of their father's Lexus would have consequences. They'd so almost be worth it. "Come on!"

"I don't have to do what you say."

"I'll *drag* you."

Brianna glanced down at the pavement and then up at the car, clearly considering it but when Ashley started forward, she hurried to keep up. Once strapped into the back seat she pulled a small gold jewelry box out of the breast pocket of her uniform jacket, opened it a crack and peered inside. Opened it a little wider. "Oh great. My familiar is dead."

Ashley rolled her eyes. "It's a bug!"

"Probably died from having to be in the same car as you." She dumped the dead cricket out on her palm and poked it once or twice. "Hey." Two hard kicks to the back of the driver's seat. "Hey, Theodore, unlock the window. I gotta open it."

"Your father says no. Not after what happened the last time."

"I didn't actually go anywhere!"

"Still no."

"Suit yourself." She flicked the dead cricket at the back of the driver's head. It bounced off his hair and against all odds dropped into the space between collar and skin.

Rubber shrieked against asphalt as he braked.

"Next time let her open the window, dumb ass," Ashley sighed.

"CB Productions, may I help you?" Phone tucked under her chin, Amy continued to sort and staple the next day's sides. "No, the box company is long gone. You've reached CB Productions; home of *Darkest Night,* the highest rated vampire detective show in syndication. What? Well, we've never heard of you either. Ah, the glamour of show business," she muttered as she hung up, slammed in another staple, and added one more set to the finished pile. "There are days . . ." Sort. Staple. Stack. ". . . when I think I should have stuck with NASCAR." Sort. Staple. "Crap!" More and more, this was one of those days. She hurriedly put the stapler away as the boss' daughters came through the front door.

They were better than they used to be. Although it was a DEFCON 4 as opposed to a DEFCON 5 kind of better.

"You're wearing too much black stuff on your eyes," Ashley sneered. "Are you trying to look like a raccoon?"

"Why, yes I am." Amy smiled broadly, insincerely, and threateningly. "Thank you for noticing. Your father is waiting for you on the soundstage and . . ."

"Is Mason there?" Ashley interrupted, having taken a careful step back from the desk.

"He is." And star of the show or not, Mason could be sacrificed for the greater good.

"Then I'm going in to see *him*."

"Happy days. And Tony is in your father's office waiting for you," she told Brianna as Ashley rolled up her uniform skirt another inch and left for the sound stage.

"She thinks Mason likes her but Mason thinks she's a creepy little girl," Brianna snorted.

"Mason's not usually such a good judge of character."

"My familiar died."

"Again? Girl, you're hard on crickets."

"I need something sturdier."

"Why do you need a familiar at all?"

Brianna stared at her for a long moment, brows draw in to a deep vee over her nose. "Because," she said at last.

Amy nodded, a little unnerved by how well she was getting along with CB's younger daughter. "Not a good reason but it'll do."

"Come on, Brianna, concentrate. You have to learn to focus before you can learn to do anything else."

"Why?"

"Because it's the first lesson."

"You never started at the first lesson."

"I'm not eight."

"Nine!"

"Whatever. The point is . . ." Tony cut off his 'I'm a grown-up and you're a little girl' speech as Brianna's eyes narrowed. That was never a good sign. "Look, it's important that you learn this right because someday I may need you to fix something I've screwed up."

"That's what's in if for you. What's in it for me?"

"I won't turn you into a smoking pile of ash and tell your father you did it to yourself by accident."

"Oh. Okay then." She sighed and slumped further down in the chair, kicking one foot against the desk. "My familiar died."

"The bumble bee?"

"That was two familiars ago!"

"Sorry. The uh . . ."

"The cricket!"

"Right." He sent a silent prayer to whatever gods might be listening—and at this point he was pretty damned sure that there were gods listening—that CB keep refusing to get her a cat. "Bri, maybe you're not meant to have a familiar."

"Yes I am. It makes me feel . . ." She closed her lips tightly around what she felt.

Tony didn't need her to tell him that it made her feel less alone. Because after all, he was the grown-up and she was the little girl. "Come on, Bri, focus your power in one spot." He sketched a sparkling blue circle in the air. "You can do this."

"I want a wand."

"You don't need a wand."

"I *want* a wand."

"Use your finger." He sighed. "Use a different finger."

CB had his daughters one weekend a month and three days a week after school. He gave them free run of his studio, had his people supervise their homework—and in Brianna's case the word homework had taken on a whole new meaning—and at some point in there, he saw that they were fed. Sometimes, when Ashley refused to be parted from Mason Reed, they ate from the catering truck. Sometimes, when volume won out over his patience and they swore an oath to never tell their mother, they ate fast food with one of the writers. Sometimes, they went to nice restaurants so he could show his beautiful daughters off to the world.

Over the years he'd learned that enough money excused anything up to and including biting the waiter.

"Tony won't teach me to blow things up," Brianna complained, pushing the last of her smoked salmon and spinach fettuccini around the bowl. "He won't teach me to do anything good."

"Tony's just doing what Daddy tells him," Ashley sniped.

CB winced as his youngest narrowed her eyes. His eldest was obviously still annoyed at having to leave Mason. "I'm sure Mr. Foster will teach you to blow things up when he thinks you're ready."

"I'm ready now!"

"Oh yeah, like you're so ready to be trusted, Cheese. You can't even keep a cricket alive!"

Cooper colored sparks danced on the end of Brianna's fork. "You've got one of Mason's socks in your back pack!"

"Girls, indoor voi . . ."

"Liar!"

"Am not! You're pathetic, Ashes!"

"Girls, don't raise . . ."

"You don't even know what pathetic means, you freak!"

Crushing the linen napkin in her fist, Brianna leaned forward, her eyes barely slitted open. "Mason thinks you're creepy!"

"Daddy!"

"Twenty dollars each to keep your voices down."

Ashley sniffed and Brianna looked mutinous but they held out their hands. As CB passed out the money, he could feel the restaurant staff breath a sigh of relief. Fortunately, they were too early for the crowds and the only other diners had been seated as far away as possible. Over the years, he'd also learned that it was best to show his beautiful daughters off to a little bit of the world at a time.

Ashley sniffed again and stuffed the bill in her pocket. "I'm going to the ladies room."

CB moved to block her way. "What do you do if someone approaches you?"

She rolled her eyes. "Scream blue murder and if it's a guy kick him in the nuts so hard his eyeballs bleed."

"Good girl."

"I'd blow him up if Tony'd teach me," Brianna muttered, as her sister crossed the restaurant, pinging the empty water glasses with a fork as she passed.

"He'll teach you someday."

"Promise."

"Yes." He beckoned the waiter over with the check. Lingering was seldom a good idea.

"My cricket died."

"So my driver informed me."

"It made me very sad."

He pulled out his pen to sign the bill. He usually took the girls somewhere he could run a tab in case of unexpected expenses.

"Very, very sad. Very very very sad."

A tear trembled on her lower lashes and he shuddered. "What will it take for you to feel better?"

Her gaze flickered around the table. "Your pen."

"My pen?" He stared down at it. He'd had it specially carved from Brazilian rose wood, had it made to fit his hand. Most pens were far too small for him to use comfortably. The gold inlay was eighteen carat.

A second tear trembled and her lower lip went out.

Tony Foster couldn't teach her anything more dangerous than that.

He handed her the pen and said, without much hope: "Don't tell your sister."

Teresa Neill hadn't wanted to be a teacher but she hadn't wanted to starve either and teaching paid the bills. She tried not to resent the time it took from her real work, from the great literature she could create if only the world supported talent as it should. She was less successful at not resenting the oh so privileged girls she taught who would always have enough money to follow their muse should any of the spoiled brats ever find a muse willing to allow their . . .

The chalk snapped under her fingers and before she could stop herself she'd drawn a jagged white line across the board.

When she reached for the brush, it fell from the shelf.

When she stepped back to retrieve it, she nearly tripped over her desk chair.

When she threw out a hand to save herself, she knocked a stack of books off the edge of her desk.

When she turned to face her fifth grade math class, all but one of the girls was laughing. Brianna Bane was chewing on the end of an oversized pen and staring at the floor. No, not staring, watching something run along the base of the far wall.

Oh bloody wonderful, she thought as she picked up a fresh piece of chalk and returned to the problem on the board. *The last thing this dump needs is mice.*

"Ashley, your freak sister is at it again only *this* time she's talking to the floor outside the science lab.

"I didn't think you knew where the science lab was."

Sandra's lip curled at that lame evidence that she'd thrown Ashley off her game. "It's right next to your *freak* sister."

The science lab was on the second floor at the front of the building. Brianna was on her knees in the hall outside the classroom door, ear to the floor. Ashley grabbed her arm, yanked her to her feet, and pushed her up against the wall before anyone else saw them. "Now, what are you doing?"

"I can hear something," Brianna told her sulkily after a short, unsuccessful fight for freedom.

"You can what?"

"Hear something in the floor." She looked down at the scuffed tile. "It's a lot easier to hear from up here than downstairs."

"Yesterday, you were listening to something in the ceiling?" When Brianna nodded Ashley gave her a short, sharp, shake. "You said you were talking to your cricket!"

"I was! But I was *listening* to the ceiling!"

"Is it something . . . you know, weird?"

"You mean is it something freaky like me?"

"Yes." A short shake for emphasis. "That's exactly what I mean."

"I think so."

There was, unfortunately, no way she could lift both feet off the floor at the same time. "Is it something bad?"

Brianna shrugged. "I dunno."

"That's it." Still holding her sister, Ashley headed for the stairs. "We're calling daddy."

"What can daddy do?"

"Send Tony."

"Calling the men in the white coats to come and take away your freak sister?" Sandra called across the lawn.

"Calling the newspaper to report a sasquatch roaming around," Ashley yelled back as she pocketed her phone and dragged Brianna over by the sidewalk. "Okay. We wait right here for him."

Brianna's lower lip went out and for a moment, Ashley was afraid there'd be trouble. "She wouldn't call me freak if she knew I was a wizard."

Okay. Different trouble. "Yeah, she would and you know it." Ashley had a hundred cutting replies ready for *"Your sister thinks she's a wizard!"* So far, she hadn't had to use them. "You can't tell people!"

"I know that, stupid-head!" One loafer kicked a muddy swath through the new spring growth. "It doesn't matter, they wouldn't believe me. I'm *nine*! Besides, there's no point in telling people you're a wizard until you can *be* a wizard."

"Frustrating?"

Brianna's sigh sounded a lot older than nine. "You have no idea."

After a moment, Ashley moved closer and bumped the younger girl with her hip. "I'm sorry I called you a freak last night."

"Okay."

"And you're sorry you said that Mason thinks I'm creepy."

"Sure."

From behind the hedge came Sandra's distinctive laugh.

Ashley's lip curled. "The moment you can blow things up . . ."

Brianna nodded. "She's top of the list."

In the final approach to The Nellie Parks Academy, Tony closed out his uplink and began to power down. It was always best to approach CB's daughters with both hands free.

"They're out there waitin' for you, dude."

He leaned around Theo, CB's driver, and sighed. "Yeah. I see them."

"Man, you must've acquired some powerful bad karma in your last life to get stuck babysitting those two in this one."

"I hear you." He snapped the laptop closed and zipped the case shut. "But I'm not the one locked in a car with them."

"Yeah." Theo snorted. "I hear that. I figure I was like a slave trader or something last life and that's why little black girls are making this life a living hell."

"But only three days a week."

"So maybe I wasn't one of them really bad slave traders, you know. Hey!" he called as Tony opened the door. "I can't park here so you call me when you need me to come back."

"And you'll be . . .?"

"Off looking for better karma, dude."

"Good luck with that." Tony slammed the door, slung the computer case off his shoulder, and turned as the car drove away.

"Oh, that's lovely," Ashley sneered.

He looked down at his classic and paint-stained *The Apprentice* sweatshirt.

"Thanks for dressing up," she continued, through an impressively curled lip. "I thought gay guys were supposed to have taste.

"I thought little girls were supposed to be made of sugar and spice." He smiled down at her. "Seems like we were both wrong." And switching a slightly more sincere smile to her sister. "What's up, Bri?"

"Didn't Daddy tell you? She's hearing things in the floor!"

"Is your name Brianna too? That must be really awkward, both of you having the same name."

"Bite me!"

"If only it wouldn't get me fired. Bri?"

Arms folded over her uniform jacket, she rolled her eyes. "I can hear something in the floor."

"What?"

"Muttering and moving and the muttering moves."

CB had been quite clear that he was to deal with whatever it was Brianna had heard. "Well, let's go have a listen shall we?"

"If you don't quit patronizing me, you're gonna be second on the list!"

Tony didn't need to ask what list. Besides, he was impressed by a nine year old using *patronizing* correctly in a sentence. He couldn't have done it when he was nine. "Sorry. Ashley's call upset your dad and you know how he likes to share the joy."

"He yelled."

"He did."

The three of them shared a moment then Brianna sighed. "It's not a big deal or anything. Ashley got all stupid."

"Oh 'cause hearing things in the floor is normal," her sister muttered as they went inside the building.

The school smelled better than Tony remembered schools smelling.

"I sort of know it's there all day," Brianna explained on the way up the stairs. "But I can't really hear it until most everyone leaves."

"Does it sound angry?" he asked.

"More cranky."

"Do things ever happen while you can hear it? Like, if you hear it in a room, do things happen in that room?"

"Things that aren't supposed to happen? Like chalks breaking and books falling and that kind of stuff?"

"Yeah. That kind of stuff."

"You know, if a teacher sees you, they're not going to like it that you're here," Ashley pointed out as they reached the second floor.

"I'll tell them I'm Brianna's tutor." Which was even the truth. When Brianna went to turn right, Tony reached out and turned her in the opposite direction. "No, it's gone this way now."

"You can hear it." She made it more an accusation than a question.

"No. But unless there's a lot going on behind the walls, there's something this way. Come on. Ashley?"

Hands shoved into her jacket pockets, the older girl shook her head. "You guys go wandering. Do that weird stuff you do. I'll wait here."

"You're sure?"

Her lip curled. "I don't do weird."

They walked slowly through the halls, Tony following the feeling that a bit of the world was cock-eyed, and Brianna sticking close by his side. After a while he noticed that their steps were synchronized so perfectly he could only hear one set of foot steps.

"Are you lost?"

"No." He matched Brianna's near whisper. "Reach out. Can you feel it?"

"Reach where? And what am I s'posed to feel?"

"It's hard to describe."

"Totally *not* helpful!"

"Sorry." Trouble was, most of his analogies weren't particularly age appropriate. "Okay, concentrate, and focus. You're groping the world. It's an orange and you're feeling for a seed."

"I'm groping the *whole* world?"

"Not the whole world, just this part of the world."

She frowned, stumbled, and would have fallen had he not grabbed for her. When she looked up at him, she was smiling. "I can feel a seed!"

"Because you focused and you concentrated." A little reinforcement couldn't hurt although it didn't look like she believed him.

The frown returned. "It's really close. What is it?"

Good question. "It might be a Brownie."

"Students aren't allowed to be Brownies. The principal is *always* on a diet."

"What does that . . ."

"The cookies." Brianna interrupted impatiently. "If you have Brownies you have cookies."

It took Tony a minute to work that out. By the time he realized they were talking about two different things, it was past time to mention it.

A sudden burst of noise stopped them outside the music room. Side by side, they carefully peered through the glass at a choir practice.

"It's in there." Brianna muttered as one of the altos reached out to turn a page. Her music stand fell, and the whole row went crashing down.

"I think you're right."

The choir mistress' baton snapped.

Brianna snorted. "I know I'm right."

"Come on, I've seen enough. It's a poltergeist," Tony told her as they headed back to Ashley. "They like to hang around the uh . . . emotional turmoil of young girls."

"So it's not here because of me?"

"It might have come to this school instead of another school because of you. Your power might have attracted it."

"Like you attracted that girl who tried to kill you by sucking your . . ."

"We aren't going to talk about that," Tony interrupted, ears burning. "We, you and me, we aren't *ever* going to talk about that."

"Not even when I grow up?"

"Not even."

They walked in silence for a moment or two then Brianna asked, "Are they dangerous?"

Tony hoped she was asking about poltergeists because, right now, that was all he was willing to discuss with the boss' youngest daughter. "They can be. But mostly they're just trouble makers, not too bright but not actually malicious. Do you know what malicious means?" He took her snort as a yes. "They're hard to get rid of so we'll just let this one be, okay. You keep listening and the moment it sounds actually angry, you call me and we'll deal with it."

"You'll teach me how?"

"Sure." The heat of her regard warmed the side of his face.

"You don't even know how!"

"Not right now, no. But I'll work it out by the time we need to know it." He heaved the computer case back up onto his shoulder. "We're wizards. It's what we do."

In a just world, Ashley thought the next afternoon when once again, Brianna was late meeting her at the curb, *I'd be the wizard and then I could stuff her into a jar and keep her in my pocket.*

"Lose your freak?" Sandra sniffed as she sashayed past, hem of her kilt flipping rhythmically, her posse giggling reinforcement behind her.

Ashley ignored the lot of them as she went back up the stairs and into the school. No Brianna in the atrium. No Brianna in the hall outside the science room. Where the hell was she?

Brianna sat on an overturned bucket in the custodian's closet by the library.

She heard things in the floor and Ashley called daddy. Daddy yelled at Tony. Tony found out about poltergeists on his computer in the car on the way to the school because if he knew what it was she'd heard he wouldn't have brought the computer with him.

She had a computer. And Ashley'd got rid of the Net Nanny about twenty minutes after their mom's last boyfriend had put it in. They'd found out all sorts of good stuff about mom's last boyfriend.

Last night, she'd found out all sorts of good stuff about poltergeists. Even though it took her a bunch of tries to spell it right.

The seed was moving around in the orange but she couldn't get it to come close. Tony said it was attracted to her power. But it wasn't. She frowned and kicked at the side of the metal bucket. Wizards worked things out. Tony said it was what they did.

There were still some other girls in the school being all emotionally turmoiled so maybe she needed more power to make it leave them.

Tony said she needed to learn to focus.

Fine.

And to concentrate.

Whatever.

Tony just pointed and drew blue lines in the air.

She wasn't Tony. Maybe he was right and she didn't *need* a wand. Maybe he was a jerk. Reaching into her backpack, she pulled out the pen. It was wood. And smooth. And it smelled a little like her father's cologne.

She pointed the pen at the floor and she concentrated on being focused. She concentrated as hard as she could but nothing happened.

Because it wasn't a *real* wand! The pen bounced off the wall when she threw it and an instant later a bag of rags bounced off the shelf and landed beside it. The muttering in the walls wasn't muttering now. It was laughing. Laughing at her.

Her lip curled. She kicked the rags aside and snatched up the pen.

A copper colored spark gleamed on the pointy end. By the time she'd carefully spelled poltergeist in sparkling cursive script about an inch above the tiles, it wasn't a pen anymore.

She didn't have to wait very long.

The mops fell over first. Brianna covered her head with her arms as they clattered around the tiny room, biting back a shriek as they whacked against her shoulders. The paper towels flew off the shelf and unrolled. She batted them aside. The lids flew off two bottles of floor cleaner and the contents sprayed toward the ceiling. Cleaner couldn't hurt her.

She felt it touch her pattern.

She gripped her wand, ducked a flying bar of soap, and smiled.

"There you are!" Ashley grabbed her sister's arm and dragged her along the hall toward the front doors. "Mom's going to be here in a minute and you know she throws a total fit when we're late." She glanced down at what Brianna had clutched in one hand. "Tell me you weren't hunting for another bug."

"I wasn't."

"Yay. Why do you smell like floor cleaner? Never mind. Don't tell me." She brushed at Brianna's jacket as they walked. "You've got bits of paper towel all over you."

Narrow shoulders rose and fall. "Some got shredded."

"Were you fighting?" Ashley asked as they emerged out onto the broad stone steps. She stopped on the path and pulled Brianna around to face her. "You'd better tell me."

"Sort of."

"Did you win?"

"Totally."

"Good. You know what Daddy always says . . ."

". . . no point in fighting if you don't win." Brianna grinned up at her.

"I see you found your freak," Sandra called from the lawn. "Maybe you should put a leash on it."

"All right. That's it." Ashley began unbuttoning her jacket. "This school isn't big enough for all three of us. I'm going to rip her hair out and stuff it in her bra with all those socks!"

Brianna's hand on her arm stopped her. "It's okay. Let it go."

Ashley looked from the hand to her little sister. "She keeps calling you . . ."

"I know. But mom's here." As the car pulled up, Brianna pocketed the little gold jewelry box, the new copper clasp gleaming for an instant in the late afternoon sun. "We'll deal with Sandra tomorrow."

Finding Marcus

Sirius: The Dog Star came about because my wife was complaining that there were too many anthologies for cats and not enough for dogs so she emailed our friend Alex Potter who'd done some editing for Tekno Books and suggested he pitch a doggie anthology next time he was talking to anyone in Green Bay, Wisconsin. Okay, not anyone in Green Bay but anyone at Tekno. So Alex did and Martin Greenberg thought it was a good idea and he pitched it to DAW and they liked it. Since the whole thing started in my living room, I kind of had to write a story. I don't often write in first person but trying to think like a dog—albeit a magically enhanced dog—was fun and should there ever be more Sirius books, I'll definitely revisit Rueben and Dawn.

Oh, and the soundstage they end up on, it's where A&E used to shoot Nero Wolfe.

THE RAT WAS FAT, A successful forager, over-confident. It had no idea I was hunting it until my teeth closed over the back of its neck and, by then, it was far too late. As I ate, I gave thanks, as I always did, that some bitch in my ancestry had mated with a terrier. If I'd been all herder or tracker, I'd have been long dead by now. A puddle from the recent rains quenched my thirst and, with my immediate needs satisfied, I took a look around.

The Gate had dumped me in an alley, pungent with the smell of rotting garbage, shit, and stagnant water. There were other rats in the big overflowing bins, roaches under everything, and a dead bird somewhere close. The bins were metal. Never a good sign.

I lifted my head to the breeze coming in from the distant mouth of the alley and sighed. Cars. It's a scent you don't forget. Mid-tech world at least. Although I could already feel the pull of the next Gate, it would be harder to find it in the stink of too many people and too much going on. Still, it wasn't like I had much of a choice.

And sometimes the low tech worlds were worse. A lot worse. It was fear and suspicion on a low tech world that had separated us . . .

Before I left, I marked the place where the old Gate had been. Not so I could find it again—they only worked in one direction—it's just something I've done ever since I got into this mess, sort of saying that the Gates are mine not the other way around. And besides, sometimes I just need to piss on the damn things.

I had a quick roll in the bird as I passed. A guy's got to do some stuff for himself.

At the mouth of the alley, I felt a slight pull to the left so I turned. Nose to the ground, I could smell nothing but the rain. The sky must have cleared just before I showed up. Marcus could be mere minutes ahead of me and I'd never know it.

Suddenly regretting the rat, I started to run.

Marcus could be mere minutes ahead of me.

Minutes.

By the time I stopped running, I'd left the alley far behind. I knew I wasn't going to catch up to him so easily but sometimes it takes me that way, the thought that he could be close, and my legs take over from my brain. I always feel kind of stupid afterwards. Stupid and sad. And tired. Not leg tired; heart tired.

The pull from the next Gate hadn't gotten any stronger so I still had a distance to travel. I had to cross a big water once. Long story. Long, wet, nasty story.

The made-stone that covered the ground was cleaner here. Smelled more of people and less of garbage although I hadn't yet reached an area where people actually lived. At a corner joining two large roads, I lifted my head and sniffed the sky. No scent of morning. Good. It had been nearly mid-dark when I'd entered the Gate one world back, but time changed as the worlds did and I could have lost the night. Lost my best time to travel, lost my chance of catching up to Marcus.

I dove back into a patch of deep shadow as three cars passed in quick succession. Most of the time, the people in cars were blind to the world outside their metal cages but occasionally on a mid-tech world a car would stop and the people spill out, bound and determined to help a poor lost dog. I was hungry enough, hurt enough, stupid enough to let them once.

Only once. I barely escaped with my balls.

When the road was clear, I raced across and, although it made my guts twist to ignore the path I needed to follow, I turned left, heading for the mouth of a dark alley. Heading away from the lights on poles and the lights on building, away from too much light to be safe.

The alley put me back on the path. When it ended in a dark canyon between two buildings, I turned left again, finally spilling out onto another road; a darker road, lined with tall houses. I could follow this road for a while. The lights on the poles were further apart here and massive trees threw shadows dark enough to hide a dozen of me.

As it happened, the shadows also hid half a dozen cats.

Cats are contradictions as far as I'm concerned; soft and sweet and harmless appearing little furballs who make no effort to hide the fact that they kill for fun and can curse in language that would make a rat blush. I took the full brunt of their vocabulary as I ran by. Another place, another night, and I might have treed a couple but with the Gate so far away I needed to cover some serious distance before dawn.

Sunrise found me running along a road between houses so large they could almost be called palaces. Probably, a rich merchant area. High-tech, mid-tech, low-tech—some things never changed. People who suddenly found themselves with a lot of stuff had to show it off. Marcus, who never had anything except me and a blithe belief in his own intellect, used to laugh about it. He used to laugh about a lot of things. He wasn't laughing when they tore us apart, he was screaming my name and that's how I remember him most often.

I couldn't stay on this road much longer, it was beginning to curve away from the direction I needed. But first, breakfast.

Low-tech, high-tech; both were essentially garbage free. But mid-tech—when they weren't piling it in metal bins, people in mid-tech worlds actually collected their garbage up into bags and set it out in front of their houses. It was like they were bragging about how much they could waste. A guy could eat well off that bragging.

Second bag I ripped open, I hit the jackpot. A half circle of flat bread with sausage and cheese crumbled onto a sauce. I gulped it down, licked the last bit of sweet cream out of a container, and took off at full speed as a door opened and a high-pitched voice started to yell.

Over time, I've gotten pretty good at knowing when I'm not wanted.

As I rounded the curve at full speed, I saw that the houses had disappeared from one side of the road. In their place, a ravine—wild and overgrown and the way I needed to go. The spirit pack was definitely looking out for me on this world but then, by my calculations, I was about due. I jumped the barrier and dove through the underbrush.

A squirrel exploded out of the leaf litter in front of me and I snapped without thinking. It managed half a surprised squeal before it died. Carrying it, I made my way down the steep bank, across a path at the bottom, and halfway up the other side. Someone, a long time ago by the smell of it, had scratched out a shallow den under the shelter of a large bush. I shoved my kill between two branches because I don't like the taste of ants and there was no other way to keep them off the squirrel—although it *was* sort of comforting that ants tasted the same on every world. Food safe, I marked the territory as mine and made myself comfortable.

Down on the path, a female person ran by. Nothing seemed to be chasing her. Running beside her was a lovely black and white bitch with pointed ears and a plumy tail. Ears flattened, she glanced up toward me as she crossed my trail but kept running, clearly aware of where her responsibilities lay. I could appreciate that. Resting my chin on my front paws, I went to sleep.

The heat of the sun was warm against my fur when I woke so I knew I'd been asleep for a while. The question: what had woken me? The answer: a sound. A rustling in the bush I slept beneath. I heard it again and slowly opened my eyes.

A small crow sidled toward my squirrel. Only half the size of some crows I'd seen, it's weight was still enough to shake the branch. With one claw raised, it glanced toward me and froze.

"Nice, doggy. There's a nice, big doggy. Crow not tasty. Doggy not eat crow."

"I hadn't intended to," I told her lifting my head. "But I don't intend to allow you to hop in here and eat my kill either."

The crow blinked and put her raised foot down. "Well, you're a lot more articulate than most," she said. "Practically polysyllabic." Head to one side, she took a closer look. "I don't think I know your breed."

"I don't think you do," I agreed. "I'm not from around here."

Left eye, then right eye, she raked me up and down with a speculative gaze. "No, I don't imagine you are. You want to talk about it?"

"No." She took flight as I crawled from the den but after a long, luxurious scratch I realized she'd only flown up into the nearest tree. "What?"

"Where's your . . . what is it you dogs call them again? Your pack?"

I'd have howled except that was a good way to attract the kind of attention I didn't want. Marcus had been the only pack I'd ever had.

"Is that what you're looking for?"

"What makes you think I'm looking for anything," I growled.

"Well, you're not from around here. So . . ." She hopped along the branch. ". . . I'm wondering what you're doing here. You're not lost—you lot are so obvious when you're lost—therefore, you're looking for something. Someone." Crows always looked pleased with themselves but something in my reaction shot her right up into smug and self-satisfied. "I knew it. You have a story."

"Everyone has a story." I started up the bank.

"Hey! Dog! Your squirrel."

"You can have it." Anything to keep her from following me. It didn't work. I heard her wings beat against the air then she landed on a jutting rock just up the path. I don't know why people call cats curious. Next to crows, they're models of restraint.

"Sometimes, it helps to share."

I drew my lips back off my teeth. "Sometimes, I like a little poultry when I first wake up."

"Poultry!" They probably heard her indignant shriek on the other side of the gate. "Fine. Then I'm not going to warn you that the roads are full and you'll never get anywhere unseen. They'll grab you and stuff you into a cage so fast, it'll make your tail curl!"

I nearly got whacked on the nose with a wing as I passed. At the top of the ravine, I peered out between two metal poles and realized the crow had been right. This was another place where no one lived and the roads were full of cars and people.

I marked both posts, hoping that, given enough time, the crow would have flown off and then I started back to the den.

"I told you so."

She was still there. But, on the bright side, so was my squirrel.

"Look, dog, maybe we got off on the wrong foot. Paw. Whatever. You're on your own—and that's not the usual thing with you lot—and I'm on my own and that's not so usual for my lot either. You're probably lonely. I'm not doing anything right now. You've got a story and I'd love to hear it. What do you say?"

I bit the tail off my squirrel's fat little rump, spat it to one side, and sighed. "Do you have a name."

"Dark Dawn With Thunder."

I blinked. "You're kidding?"

She shrugged, wings rising and falling. "You can call me Dawn."

"Rueben." With one paw holding down the squirrel's head, I ripped the belly open and spilled the guts onto the ground. "Here. You might as well eat while you're listening."

"So you'll tell me your story?"

"Why not. Like you said, you're not going away." Neither was I. Talking over the pull of the Gate might help keep me from doing the truly stupid and risking the roads. I'd never find Marcus locked in a cage. And I *was* lonely. Not that I'd admit as much to a crow. "So . . ." I swallowed the last of the squirrel and sat down in the shade. " . . . what do you know about the Gates between the worlds?"

I expected to startle her. I didn't.

She tossed back a bit of intestine. "I know what all crows know. I know they exist. I know the way of opening them has been lost for a hundred thousand memories."

"It's been found again."

"You came through a Gate?"

"And I'm leaving through one."

"You don't say." She searched the ground for any bit she might have missed then folded her wings and settled. "Start at the beginning . . ."

"Marcus."

My beginning. Hopefully, my end.

I'd been with him ever since I'd left my mother's teat and the warm comfort of my littermates. I remember falling over my feet as I chased a sunbeam around his workshop. I remember becoming too big for his lap and sitting instead with my head resting on his knee. I remember the way his fingers always found exactly the right place to scratch. I remember how he smelled, how he sounded. I remember the first Gate.

I think he wanted to prove himself to the old ones in his pack. They believed he was too young to do anything of merit but he only laughed and carried on. He talked to me all the time about what he was doing; I only wish I'd understood more. But understanding came later when, unfortunately, he had a lot less time to talk.

I don't know how he found the Gate. I don't know how he opened it although there were candles lit and a lot of weeds burning and copper wires and a thunderstorm. I'm not embarrassed to admit I yelped when the lightening hit. Marcus laughed and rubbed behind my ears, the sound of my name in his mouth comforting. Then he took hold of the fur on the back of my neck and we walked forward.

Every hair on my body stood on end and for a heartbeat light, sound, and smell vanished. If not for the touch of his hand, I would have bolted. When the world came back, it was different.

The sun was low in the sky—it had been mid-light mere moments before—and we stood on a vast empty plain. No buildings. No smoke. No sign of his pack.

He was happy. He danced around and I danced with him, barking.

And then we found out we couldn't get home.

The Gates only worked one way.

I found the next Gate. And the next. By the fourth world, Marcus had learned to sense their pull—and that was a good thing because it was the first mid-tech world we'd hit and I was in an almost constant state of panic.

By the fifth, I realized that all sounds he made had meaning. The gates were changing me. I remember the first thing he said that I truly understood.

"Well, Rueben, old boy. Looks like we'll have to keep going forward until we get home."

Only the first Gate—the Gate on the world where you belong—fights against being opened. After that, it seems to be merely a matter of knowing where they are. They recognize you don't belong and the next thing you know it's a brand new world. Those first five worlds, when it was just me and Marcus, surviving by our wits, working together, depending on each other's skills the way a pack is supposed to, those were the happiest times of my life.

The sixth world was low-tech and we emerged into a crowded market place. Marcus staggered a little, steadying himself on my shoulder. By the time he straightened, the crowds had begun to scream, "Demon!" I didn't know what it meant but I knew anger and fear when I heard it, when I smelled it, so I braced my front legs and growled.

Marcus tried to soothe me. He thought that laughter and intellect would win the day but I knew he was wrong. If they were going to take him, they'd have to go through me.

I didn't know about crossbows then.

I learned.

It took three to knock me off my feet but I was still snapping and snarling as they dragged us away and threw us in a tiny, stinking, dark hole to wait for the priest.

Marcus begged cloth and water and herbs from the guards. He kept me clean, he kept me alive. I don't know how he convinced them to part with such things but that was when he stopped laughing.

I think he'd begun to realize how much I understood because there were things he didn't talk about.

The priest finally came.

The priests in Marcus' old pack were always good for a bit of something sweet and an absentminded scratch. This was a different kind of priest. The smell of anger clung to him like smoke.

They dragged us out blinking and squinting in the sunlight. Marcus lifted his face to the sky like he'd forgotten what it looked like, like he'd been afraid he'd never see it again. They said we were demons and demons had to die. The priest told us we would burn on top of a holy hill so the smoke would rise into the demon worlds and warn others of our kind to stay away. He said a lot of other things too but none of it made any more sense so I stopped listening.

As we walked to the pyre, I stayed pressed close against Marcus' legs because I think he would have fallen if I hadn't been there. Not that I was in much better shape.

Then we got lucky.

At the top of the hill, I felt a familiar pull and I knew from the noise Marcus made low in his throat that he felt it too. The Gate. And it was close. On the other side of the hill, about halfway down. We should have been able to feel it all along but I think that whatever made the hill holy had blocked it. I didn't think that then, of course, but I do now.

The way things had been set up, there wasn't room for more than one man to hold Marcus as he climbed onto the pile of wood. Why would they need more than one? He was so thin and in so much pain and even I could see that all our time in the darkness had broken something in him. When he wrenched himself free, they froze in astonishment. He grabbed the single rope they had around my neck and we ran.

They hadn't thought we had the strength to escape, you see.

They were right.

They caught us at the Gate. We'd gotten so close that it had opened and they held us so close that it stayed open, waiting for us to leave a world where we didn't belong. Bleeding from new wounds, Marcus tried to explain. The priest refused to listen. He knew what he knew, and nothing anyone could say would change that. As they began to drag us away, I saw my chance and sank my teeth into the arm of the man who held me. He screamed, let me go and I threw my entire weight against Marcus' chest, pushing him and the man who held him back into the Gate. We could deal with *him* on the other side.

Then a hand grabbed the end of the rope tied around my throat and hauled me back.

Marcus screamed my name and reached for me but he was falling too fast. He was gone before my front paws hit the ground.

If the priest thought I'd waste my strength throwing it against the rope, he was very wrong. I took most of his hand through the Gate with me. It took me two worlds to get the taste out of my mouth.

The crow hopped along the branch and stared down at me, head cocked. "So you got away?"

"Obviously."

"Where's Marcus? Wasn't he waiting for you on the other side of the Gate?"

"No." I scrubbed at my muzzle with both front paws to keep myself from howling. "I found out later that you have to be touching for the Gate to send two lives to the same world."

"You're looking for him."

It wasn't a question but I answered it anyway. "I don't know if he's still by that Gate waiting for me to come through or if he's on his way around trying to get back to that world again, but yes, I'm looking for him."

"How long?"

Rolling onto my side, I licked a fall of fur back off an old, faded scar. "This was where one of the crossbow bolts hit. It was open and bleeding when Marcus was thrown through the Gate."

Dawn glided down beside me and peered at my side. If crows knew anything at all, they knew wounds. "A long time."

"Yes. But I *will* find him."

She nodded. "I don't doubt you'll keep trying. It's a dog thing. Hopeless . . ."

My growl was completely involuntary.

"Hopeless," she repeated, clacking her beak. "But romantic. You're lucky crows are a lot more practical."

"Lucky?"

"Because you shared your story, I'm going to help you get to your Gate."

Before I could protest, she took wing, flying toward the upper edge of the ravine. By the time I'd scrambled to my feet and shaken my fur into some semblance of order, she was back. "I don't need your help," I told her walking stiff-legged past her position. "I can find the Gate on my own."

"I don't doubt it. But do you know what traffic is doing? Can you find the fastest route through the buildings? Do you know when it's safe to move on?" She stared at me thoughtfully—well, it might have been thoughtful, it might have been disdainful, it was impossible to tell with crows. "No one will notice me but, if you're not very careful, they'll certainly notice you. Do you have a bear in your ancestry or something?"

"No."

"Pony?"

"No!"

"Marcus fiddle with your DNA?"

"My what?"

She flew ahead and landed on the guard rail. "Not important. What is important though is that, if you hurry, you'll be able to get across the road."

I gave poultry another quick thought then leapt the guard rail.

"Run fast, dog. The light is changing."

Into what? Not important. I started to run. Metal shrieked against metal. As I reached the far side, something big passed so close to my tail that I clamped it tight between my legs and lengthened my stride. Racing along the narrow passage between two buildings, I wondered just what I thought I was doing, listening to a crow.

"You're going to come out into a parking lot. Cross it on a bit of an angle . . . Go to your left. No, your other left . . . and you can use the dumpster to go over the fence."

And why was I *still* listening to the crow?

On the other side of the fence, two cats hissed insults as I went by and a small, fat dog on a rope started barking furiously. I was gone before anyone came out to investigate the disturbance but not so far gone that I couldn't hear them blame the whole noisy situation on the cats. Pretty funny.

Determining this new road went in essentially the right direction, I stopped running full out and dropped into a distance eating trot.

"Aren't you in a hurry?" The crow was on one of the wires that crossed over the street, calling the question down to me. Not exactly unnoticeable to my mind but what did I know of this world? "Shouldn't you be moving faster?"

"I know what I'm doing," I snapped. "Don't you have a flock to join?"

"A murder." She flew ahead and landed again.

"A what?"

"A group of crows are called a murder. A murder of crows."

"Why?" I couldn't stop myself from asking even though I knew any interest would only encourage her to hang around.

Fly ahead. Land. "I don't know."

"I thought crows remembered everything?"

Dawn shrugged philosophically. "Can't remember what I've never been told."

"All right. Fine. Don't you have a murder to join?"

Fly ahead. Land. "Not any more. I left because I'd heard all their stories."

"Stories? What does that have to do . . ."

She clacked her beak. "I get bored easily."

We went on like that until nearly full dark–Dawn flapping from wire to wire and telling me way more crow stories than any dog would ever want to know. A lot of them involved carrion. Then, as the last of the light disappeared, I looked up and she was gone. I shouldn't have been surprised, like most birds, crows prefer not to fly at night. Maybe she should have thought about that before she offered to help. I shouldn't have missed her. But I did.

As the sky began to lighten, the pull of the Gate became so strong that I knew I was close. Using Dawn's dumpster trick, I went over another fence, finding Marcus the only thought in my mind.

Which was why I didn't notice the men until I was in the midst of them.

"Holy fuck! Would you look at the size of that mutt!"

They were all around me. Something hard hit me on the left shoulder and I reacted without thinking. The scent of so many males was too strong a challenge. I whirled to the left, flattened my ears, and snarled.

The man scrambled back. I could smell his fear. A piece of broken brick glanced off my back. The sharp end of a stick jabbed at my haunches. I should have kept running. Should have. Didn't. Now they'd closed in. Too close.

I heard a length of chain hiss past my head.

If they wanted a fight . . .

Then I heard a hoarse shriek of outrage, a scream of pain, and the circle made up of legs and boots and rough weapons opened.

"Where the fuck did that crow come from!"

I don't know how much damage she stayed to do but she found me again after I'd gone to ground. I heard the sound of claws on gravel, looked out from behind the huge wheel on the trailer that sheltered me, and there she was. She snatched up a discarded piece of sugared bread, threw back her head and swallowed, then hopped closer.

"All right, I'm convinced, you really *do* need to find this Marcus of yours because you shouldn't be running around without a keeper. What kind of an idiot picks a fight with seven big burly, cranky, construction workers *before* they'd had their first coffee? You know, if you'd tried the roll-over 'look at me I'm so cute' schtick, you'd have probably gotten a belly rub and a couple of sandwiches. Those kind of guys usually like a dog that's big enough they're not afraid of breaking it. So, you hiding under there?"

As she'd actually paused, I assumed she wanted an answer. "Yes."

"Why?"

I glanced up at the massive trailer. "Because I fit. And because the Gate's in that building."

Dawn turned enough to study the building with her right eye.

It was constructed of the big made-stone blocks. I'd seen windows and a door along the front but neither on the sides. The back of the building, where the trailers were parked, had a set of huge double doors and one smaller one with a light over it.

"So, what do you do now?" she asked.

"I wait." This close to the Gate, I was too jumpy to lie down but there wasn't enough head room to pace. I had to settle for digging a trench in the gravel with a front paw. "I wait until one of those doors open then I run inside."

"And once you're inside?"

"I keep from being grabbed long enough to get through the Gate."

"I like a dog with a plan. But I'm warning you, it's barely daylight and not a lot of people are up at this . . ."

One of the big double doors swung open and slammed back

against the made-stone wall with a crash loud enough to fling Dawn
into the air and raise the hackles on my neck. With the barrier out of
the way, the pull of the Gate nearly dragged me out of my hiding
place but I'd been stupid once this morning and stupid wouldn't help
me find Marcus.

Then the other door opened and men appeared carrying huge
made-things of metal and plastic and glass that I didn't recognize. I
felt the trailer above me shake as they climbed up the ramp.

"Hey, a film crew." Dawn was back on the ground. "I'll let you in
on a secret, Rueben—there's good pickings in the garbage outside the
craft services truck. These guys never seem to have time to finish eating anything."

I had no idea what she was talking about. Nor did I care.

Two of the men were in the trailer. The other two were out of sight
in the building.

My chance.

Marcus.

I was running full out by the time I reached the doors. I leapt a
cart just inside, smelled the sudden rush of fear from the man pushing
it, scrambled along a cloth path on the floor, skidded through a room
with only three walls, found myself outside but not outside, ignored
the yelling, and concentrated on finding the Gate. I'd been in buildings before—once, on a high-tech world, I'd been chased through an
underground structure so complicated ants couldn't have found their
way around—but nothing in *this* building made sense! The ceiling was
too high, the walls didn't reach it, and there were cables everywhere.

I couldn't find the Gate.

My toe nails scrabbling for purchase against a polished stone
floor, I raced around a corner and ended up in a long hall. Three men
ran toward me from the other end, one of them carrying a net. They
were all making soothing sounds, the one with the net repeating, "It's
okay, boy." over and over. I wanted to believe them. I wanted to lay
my head on someone's knee and have him tell me I was home.

I knocked over a row of chairs, jumped a pile of cable, and ran up
a flight of stairs. The stairs ended in another railing and a door. I
threw myself against it.

The wall shook.

The Gate . . . the Gate was on the other side!

I threw myself against the door again. Someone was whining. I
had a horrible suspicion it was me.

So close . . .

Then suddenly, the wall gave way, the stairs shook, and I jumped.

A hand closed around my tail.

The Gate opened.

I braced myself for the pain of my tail being yanked free but it never came. Instead, the grip released and sharp points of pain dug into my back.

This time the Gate dumped me on the edge of a meadow. The sun was shining, birds were singing, and I could smell both rabbits and water on the breeze. My stomach growled and I growled with it.

Ready to move on, I turned to piss on the weed growing closest to where the old Gate had been and discovered I wasn't alone. There was a crow in the grass, lying in a parody of a nest, wings spread and feet in the air. Bending my head, I snuffled her breast feathers. Warm. Alive. The sharp pains in my back suddenly made sense.

Dark Dawn With Thunder had hitched a ride.

I glanced across the meadow, then back at her, then sighed and scratched.

I was napping when she finally opened her eyes but the sound of her flapping awkwardly onto her feet woke me. Her wings looked as though the edges were unraveling and she staggered three paces forward then three paces back before she caught her balance.

"Rather remarkably like flying into a hydro wire," she muttered, caught sight of me and stilled. "Nice doggie. Doggie no yell at crow. Crow have very big headache."

"Crow deserves very big headache," I told her. "What were you thinking?"

Dawn cocked her head and studied me for a moment. "I was thinking you hadn't thanked me for saving your furry ass."

She was right, I hadn't. "Thank you."

"And I was thinking that I'd like to know how the story ends."

"Story?"

"You and Marcus."

"Why do you care?"

"Care?" Twisting around, she poked her tail feathers into alignment. "I don't *care*. I just hate to leave a story hanging. Gives me that unfinished feeling."

I chewed a bit on a paw and when I looked up Dawn was watching me.

"I was also thinking," she said, "that dogs are hopeless romantics and you need taking care of. And besides . . ." Her eyes glittered. ". . . you're certainly not boring."

"You can't go back," I reminded her.

"I'm not going any where until the story ends." She clacked her beak and launched herself into the air. "So, let's get a move on."

I sat and watched her fly for a moment then smiled and shook my head. She was going the wrong way. Not that it mattered, she'd learn to feel the Gates soon enough and for now, she had me. I shook, walked out of the cloud of shed fur, and trotted across the meadow.

After a moment, I heard her wings in the air above my head.

"Any sign of him?" she called as she swooped by.

"Not yet."

The pull of the next Gate was no more than a suggestion so we had a way to travel still and Marcus could be anywhere along the path.

I could tell the crow how the story was going to end.

I *would* find him.

But I supposed it wouldn't hurt to have a little company along the way.

Jack

So I got asked to rewrite a fairy tale into a contemporary fantasy for Little Red in the Big City *and I had no idea of what to write. I'd just finished rearranging Tam Lin into "He Said, Sidhe Said" and I was tapped. And then, one afternoon while* ~~playing Freecell~~ *doing research, my brain said, "Dude, throw me my axe." And just like that, I had the whole story. Well, except for the title which went through half a dozen incarnations before it returned, reluctantly, to the default.*

ONCE UPON A TIME A young man named Jack lived with his band in a dilapidated third floor walk-up on what would have been the wrong side of the tracks had the city actually enclosed tracks. As it didn't, the boarded-up storefronts, uncollected trash, and debris-filled vacant lots were a fairly good indication of the local socio-economic condition.

Not good.

Jack and his band were determined to move up and out and so they practiced day and night. Unfortunately, they were a thrash metal group who didn't so much play as assault their instruments in an era of breathy boy bands and vapid blondes. No one wanted to hear their music: not the producers who signed bands for the major record companies, not the DJ's at the local radio station, not the guy who booked bands at the club on the corner, not even their neighbors . . .

"Would you shut up! It's three in the morning and you suck!"

"Come back to bed, babe. No way they hear you over the damned reverb anyhow."

"They're always fucking practicing; you think they'd get it right occasionally!"

"Word."

Jack slammed his way through the B7th, went back to the E, slid through the Em, and came down hard on the A, really leaning on the strings for all he was worth. They were in the space; his axe was screaming, Gustav's bass was rattling the windows two freaking rooms away, and Maitland was leaving bruises on his skins. They should've been making music but something was wrong.

He stopped playing. After a couple of minutes, he stepped back and turned off Gustav's amp. The bass player kept going for a couple of bars then he frowned, stared down at his fret board, and finally turned toward Jack. Who pointed at Maitland.

Gustav pulled a ball point pen out of his dreads and threw it at the drummer's head.

"Fucking OW!" In the sudden silence, Maitland rubbed at the blue dot in the center of his forehead with the end of a stick. "That hurt."

Jack ignored him. "I couldn't hear Angela."

All three turned to face the skinny blonde in the center of the room. She shrugged bare shoulders, her butterfly tattoo rising and falling. "So?"

"If I can't hear you and I'm standing right next to you, how the hell can they hear you?" He nodded toward the "audience"; on this particular night made up of the usual imaginary crowd and a cockroach investigating the top of the toaster.

"Pretending I care; you got two problems. First, your lyrics blow and second, you play too damned loud."

"Sing louder."

"This is as loud as I sing. Look at this." Angela held out a pale arm Jack could have circled with his thumb and baby finger. "I'm still vibrating. You guys have to play quieter—and when I say play, I mean that in the most general sense."

Maitland stopped scratching down the crack of his ass long enough to frown. "Was that a burn?"

"Yes, you idiot! I am *so* wasting my time here." Heavily kohled eyes narrowed. "Gustav, let's go." As she reached the door, she realized she was alone. "Gustav! I mean it! Me or the band."

"Cheer up man, she wasn't that good."

"Maybe not at the whole singing thing," Gustav allowed. "But she sure looked fine in all that leather underwear."

"Word." Maitland stroked a brush over a cymbal. "What do you call that red thing she had?"

"A corset, man."

"Guys!" Jack cut the reminiscing off cold. "We don't need a skinny fetishist, we need someone with pipes. It doesn't even have to be a chick."

"Dude!"

"For the band, Maitland, you neb. We got the sound, we just need a voice."

"And some food."

"What?"

Gustav stepped back so that the other two could see into the fridge. "The cupboard is bare, Jack."

"That's not a cupboard, man, that's . . ."

"Shut-up, Maitland." Jack stepped carefully through the web of wires spread out over the floor. "What about the packets of plum sauce?"

"Ate them."

"And those three olives?"

"Them too. Man, we are down to tap water and toaster leavings."

Jack glanced over at the cockroach and mentally stroked the toaster leavings off the list. "Tomorrow, we'll buy . . ." His voice trailed off as Gustav slowly shook his head. "We're broke?"

"Totally. And I am not scooping coins out of that fountain again; I almost got pneumonia last time."

"Well, then we can . . ."

"No."

"You didn't even hear . . ."

"I don't want to hear another dumb-ass idea, Jack. Face it, you got to sell the cow."

Jack turned to face the closet and his leather trench coat hanging black and supple over the top of open door. "No."

"You have to."

"I can't." The coat made him feel tough and sexy and powerful and talented and tall.

Gustav draped a supporting arm across his shoulders. "It's all we've got left, man. You don't sell the cow, we don't eat."

And so the next day, Jack set out with the coat over his arm, heading for the pawn shop on 7th. There were pawn shops closer—some days it seemed like they were the only growth industry around—but the pawn shop on 7th was next to the closest store selling food. Besides, Jack wanted to spend as long as he could with the coat. The weather was cool and he could have put it on but he was afraid that if he caught sight of his reflection striding along, if he smelled that distinctive aroma of tanned cow hides, if he felt the leather flapping around his calves one more time, he'd never be able to part with it.

About to walk past the park—because as depressed as he was about pawning the coat, he wasn't suicidal and that's what it would take for a sane man to actually walk into that junkie/mugger-haven-with-trees—he heard the wail of a guitar rising up over the ever present roar of traffic.

Drawn by the sound, he stepped off the sidewalk.

Jack found the axe-man under the skeletal remains of a swing set; a barrel-chested dude with long grey hair and a short grey beard, he was just standing there, pulling the most amazing music out of an old Martin. It was an acoustic, a folkie guitar, but it sounded like Eddie Van Halen, and Joe Satriani and Chris Impellitteri all rolled up in one. Incredible sounds. Impossible sounds.

With the coat over his arm and his mouth open, Jack stood and listened. The music pounded through him, vibrating blood and bone.

After a final, amazing chord progression—chords Jack couldn't even identify the sausage-sized fingers moved so fast—the old man stopped playing, looked up and frowned. "What?"

"That was like wow. And loud. Like, really really loud! I never heard a guitar played like that. I never knew anyone *could* play like that!"

The old man snorted. "You don't get out much, do you? What's your name, boy?"

"Jack. I play. Not like that; but you know. I have a band."

"Of course you do."

"I got a demo disc!" He pulled the tiny MP3 disc out of his back pocket. "We already pawned the player but I got a disc. I carry it everywhere because, like, you never know."

"You never know what?"

"What?"

The old man sighed. "Never mind."

"Man, if I could play like you . . ."

"You'd sound like a crap imitation." He let the guitar slide around on its strap until it hung upside down along his back, tangling with the long grey pony-tail. "Play like yourself," he growled turning away.

"Don't go! I need to know how you do that! Please . . ."

The scuffed motorcycle boot, raised to step away, settled gently back onto the packed sand. "Ah, the magic word. You really want to know how I play like I play?"

"Yes!"

"It's these." And the old man reached into the pocket of his faded jeans and pulled out three neon green picks.

Jack looked down at the plastic triangles and then back up at dark eyes.

"Picks?"

"Magic picks."

"Are you shitting me?"

"I wouldn't think of it. These picks will let you pull the music in your soul out of your axe."

"I don't do soul. Or country or R&B. I do metal, man."

"And does anybody actually listen to you? I thought not," he continued, raising a hand to cut off Jack's sputtering rationalization. "Use these picks and I guarantee people will listen. You give me that coat you're carrying, and you can have all three of them."

"The coat?"

"Yes."

"That I'm carrying?"

"Yes."

"For three magic picks?"

"Yes."

"Totally a deal, Dude!"

So Jack ran back to the dilapidated third floor walk-up, past the boarded up storefronts, and the uncollected trash with the magic picks clutched tightly in one hand. He couldn't wait to hear what the rest of the band would say.

"Are you fucking nuts, man?" Disbelief—and possibly hunger—made Gustav's voice more than a little shrill. "We sent you out to buy food and you came back with fucking guitar picks?"

"Magic guitar picks," Jack explained, holding out his hand, the three picks piled on his palm.

"Can we eat them?"

"No, but . . ."

"Then I don't care if they make you sound like Mike Fucking Nesbit. You traded the only thing we had that was worth anything for them and they're crap!" Gustav slapped Jack's hand aside.

Frustration added force to the slap.

The picks flew up, turned slowly through a beam of late afternoon sunlight, and disappeared out the open window.

Jack searched until long after dark but the picks had disappeared into the debris that filled the vacant lot.

They didn't practice that night. They went to bed early listening to the rumblings of their empty stomachs and Maitland complaining about having to return to work for the finance department of the municipal government.

Jack usually woke up when the beam of sunlight spilling in through the curtainless window had moved far enough across the room to fry his face. On cloudy days, he slept in. On this particular day, after having rolled over and gone back to sleep twice, he finally sat up and peered across the room at the window. Either his internal clock was way, way off or the pollution levels over the city had gotten seriously out of hand.

He scrambled into the clothes piled on the floor beside his mattress, and, holding his shoes, padded barefoot across the room. If he turned on the lights he'd wake the guys and considering how pissed they already were about the whole food thing, he decided he'd just do a little checking first.

The window opened almost quietly.

The total lack of light beginning to seriously freak him out, he leaned through the opening and almost immediately cracked his head against another building–a building that definitely hadn't been there when he went to sleep.

A building about fifty stories tall and exactly the shape of the vacant lot, Jack discovered standing out on the sidewalk a few moments later. It looked like it had been made from sheets of gold-colored glass and, gleaming in the sunlight, it seemed to promise that, inside, dreams could come true. Written in shiny black on the big front doors were the words, B. Stalk Productions.

He could see a security guard sitting at a desk in front of a pair of doors. One was the elevator the other bore a sign saying EMER-GENCY EXIT. On the wall between them were about a hundred gold records. At least Jack assumed they were records; he'd never actually seen one up close and personal. After scraping a bit of crusty plum sauce off his t-shirt with the edge of his thumb nail, he pushed open the door and shuffled across the polished marble floor.

"Dude?"

The guard looked up from his monitors, dark eyes locking on Jack's face. "Yes?"

Jack opened his mouth, closed it, and opened it again. "Do I, like, know you?"

Inside his short, grey beard, the guard's lip curled. "No."

"Are you sure because . . ."

"I'm sure. What do you want?"

"What do I want?"

"What. Do. You. Want?" the guard asked again, very slowly.

And Jack remembered why he'd come into the building. "What does B. Stalk Productions, like, produce?"

"Music, boy. Mr. Stalk is a giant in the music business. Sitting up there in his offices at the top of this tower, he decides what gets heard."

"I've never heard of him."

"Has he ever heard of you?"

"Not yet but . . ."

"Then I'll have to ask you to leave the property."

"Yeah but . . ."

"Now, boy, or I'll . . ."

Jack never found out just what the guard was about to do because at that very moment a stretch limo pulled up outside the building and four faceless minions in suits herded a girl out of the back and into the lobby. She wasn't the kind of girl he'd ever expected to see coming out of a car like that. She amply filled both jeans and tank, an electric pink mouth seemed curled up into a permanent sneer, and a tattoo on one rounded arm read, "BITE ME!"

She looked angry.

Jack loved that about her. He loved everything about her. He really loved the way she'd totally drawn the attention of the guard. Backing up slowly, he headed for the emergency exit and slipped through as his new love used some very, very bad language and was even more distracting.

And what a voice! It sounded just like Jack had imagined it would. It sounded the way she looked, strong and edgy and different.

He hated to leave her but this was his big chance.

He'd climb all the way up to B. Stalk if he had to and force him to listen to the demo.

He reached back into his pocket, touched the disc for luck, and started climbing.

By the sixth floor, his knees hurt.

By the tenth floor, he started singing to keep up his spirits.

By the twelfth floor, he stopped singing because all those bottles of beer falling off the wall were making him thirsty.

On the twenty-third floor, a skeleton wearing a white jumpsuit and rather a lot of tacky jewelry leaned against the door. Jack had seen freakier art on discs so no real big. "Dude, I guess you never *did* leave the building," he said thoughtfully as he passed.

He felt as if he'd been climbing for days when he finally staggered up the last flight of stairs and stood staring at the gold number 50 stenciled onto it. For a moment, he didn't realize what it meant then, his heart beating like a double drum kit, he very carefully pulled open the door.

He was standing at one end of a long hall. At the nearer end, a huge window let in the light. At the far end was a double door, the right half slightly open. To his immediate left was the elevator. Along the other side of the hall, were half a dozen closed doors. He could hear voices and, logically, they could only be coming from one place.

His shoes sinking deep into the plush beige carpet, he made his way toward the open door.

The cream colored walls were covered in laminated posters of half a dozen interchangeable boy bands—where the word boy had been stretched to its limit and beyond—and three different blondes. The 'oh look at me I'm a bad girl but not really' poses were all slightly different so Jack *assumed* they were different blondes. He'd never considered himself overly imaginative but he could've sworn the eyes on the posters followed him as he passed.

"Look, I don't know about this, Mr. Stalk."

It was the voice of the girl. She sounded like she was still angry although a hint of uncertainty had begun to soften her edged tone.

"But I do know, my dear. I've handled a hundred young women, worked them like clay, made them into what they are."

"I guess but . . ."

"You want to be a star don't you?"

"Yeah, but . . ."

"Trust me."

Trust him? Jack shuddered as he peered around the edge of the door. He'd trust that deep oily voice about as far as he'd trust Maitland to maintain a certain minimum standard of personal hygiene. Which was to say: not very.

The room behind the door was incredible. The desk, the leather sofa, the book cases, the poster of the current flavor of the month covering the wall behind the desk; they all looked like they'd been supersized. The minions looked dwarfed by the furnishings. In the center of the room, perched in a chair so overwhelming the thick, ridged rubber soles of her boots barely touched the floor was the love of Jack's life. The moment he saw her, all thoughts of having B. Stalk listen to his demo fled.

She was . . . blonde!

And somehow, she looked . . . thinner!

"Packaging, my dear, is everything."

Jack's gaze jerked over to the music mogul. He was kind of a little guy actually; short, and skinny, and going bald. The cigar clenched between his teeth was probably bigger than his . . .

"We'll work the tattoo into the design of something a little more marketable. Something like a butterfly or a unicorn. Won't be any trouble at all, will it boys?"

"No, sir, Mr. Stalk!"

Given the harmonies in their unison answer, Jack had a horrible suspicion he knew what happened to boy bands when maturity won out over marketing.

She chewed on her lower lip, no longer electric pink but softer, glossier, and said, "I . . . I . . . I need to take a piss."

"Tinkle."

"What?"

"From now on, you tinkle."

Jack shuddered.

Her fingers gripped the arms of the chair so tightly the leather squeaked a protest. "Whatever. I gotta go."

"First door on the left."

Jack flattened against the wall as she came out into the hall remaining hidden safely behind the open door and exposed again as it closed. Fortunately, she didn't look back.

"The girl's got potential."

"Yes, sir, Mr. Stalk."

"As soon as we change the way she sings, and pierce that navel, we'll have ourselves another . . ."

As the bathroom door closed behind him it cut off the name of the blonde they were planning to copy. Jack was just as happy not knowing.

He'd never been in a girl's bathroom before. It was cleaner and it smelled better and instead of a condom dispenser there was a . . .

Eww.

"Hey! What the hell are you doing in here?"

Oh yeah. That was the rage he loved! He ducked her swing, backed up against the sink, and raised both hands in surrender. "I'm here to rescue you!"

"Are you tripping?"

"No! This Stalk guy, he's trying to . . ."

"To make me a star, fuckwad."

"OW!" Hopping sideways, rubbing his shin, Jack tried to watch her fists and her feet simultaneously. This wasn't easy given that he was being to feel a little faint with hunger. "He's not trying to make you a star. He's trying to make you a *pop* star."

"That's a lie!"

"Don't take my word for it, look in the mirror."

Straightening cautiously, he watched her face as understanding dawned.

She reached out one trembling finger and touched her reflection. "Oh my god. I'm almost . . . cute."

Grabbing the hem of her tank, she hauled it up, bent forward and scrubbed the soft glossy coloring off her mouth. Just as Jack began to wonder what she was going to do next, she reached into the depths of her cleavage and pulled out a silver tube. In half a heartbeat, her lips were electric pink again.

"Man, that's better."

And it was, although Jack was too busy watching her put the lipstick away to say anything.

"Well don't just stand there with your thumb up your ass, let's haul it!"

"Right." A raised hand held her back as he peered out into the hall. The coast was clear and the elevator was still at the top floor. "Come on!"

Holding his breath, Jack led the way. The door to B. Stalk's office was still open and something about the music mogul suggested his life would not be pleasant if they were caught. Fortunately, the carpet muffled two sets of footsteps as easily as one. Jack had begun to breathe normally again when, suddenly, the posters lining the walls cried out, "Master! Master!"

Jack froze. The girl froze. They looked at each other. They looked at the walls.

"Okay," Jack muttered. "Didn't expect that."

"Master! Master! A dirty metal head is helping the new girl escape!"

From the far end of the hall came an enraged roar. "Fe, Fi, Foe, Justin! After them!"

"Yes, sir, Mr. Stalk!"

All at once, standing still seemed like a bad idea. "Run!"

The posters were shrieking, the minions were yelling but they were at the elevator and Jack jabbed the button. The door whooshed open. He dove in, hit the close door, grabbed his love by the arm, and dragged her inside.

"That's for bleaching my hair, dipshit!" she screamed back at the minion sinking slowly to his knees, both hands clutching his crotch.

Then the door closed and they were moving. It took a few floors for that final word to stop echoing within the stainless steel enclosure.

Mouth open Jack stared in admiration. "Man," he said when there was a chance of being heard, "have you got a set of pipes."

She spread her hands, the gesture somehow taking in not only the tower but her reason for being in it. "Well, duh."

"I'm uh, Jack. Jack Grimm."

Her eyes narrowed. "Stage name?"

"Yeah. But not the Jack part." He waited.

After a long moment, she sighed. "Lyra Gold. Not a stage name. Dumbass parents."

He nodded sympathetically. "Rough."

"No shit."

They watched the numbers fall on the digital display.

"So now what?" Lyra asked as they passed the halfway mark.

"Well, there's only the one elevator so the minions'll have to take the stairs."

"Yeah, but there's a security guard on the first floor; they'll just call down and he'll be waiting for us."

Jack had a strong suspicion that one elderly security guard would be no match for Lyra's boots but he kept it to himself and pressed the button for the third floor. "I flop next door," he explained. "The building's three stories high but the stories, they're not so high. Not so high as here, I mean. Because they're high enough for themselves. Anyway, that oughta put the window on the third floor hall right over the roof."

"What?"

"We're going to jump out the window to the roof of the building next door."

"Right."

The elevator chimed softly and the door opened to an empty hall; plainer than the hall on the fiftieth floor and poster free but otherwise, identical.

Jack listened at the stairwell door. He could hear the minions descending, moving fast. "Oh sure," he muttered, joining Lyra at the window. "You guys get to come *down* the stairs."

He could see his roof, his peeling tar paper, his fine patina of pigeon shit, only an easy four foot jump away.

"It doesn't open!"

"No problem." Taking a deep breath, Jack moved back a dozen paces and ran at the window as hard as he could. The noise he made on impact wasn't quite splat, but it was close.

"Move your skinny ass out of the way," Lyra snapped.

It seemed like a plan, so he did and then watched amazed as Lyra took a deep breath—he was definitely in love now—and sang. One note. One very high, sustained note.

The window shattered.

"You okay?" she asked as the glass fell to the roof below.

"Thrash metal band," he told her. "I got calluses on my ear drums an inch thick."

"Sweet." She gestured out the jagged opening. "Age before beauty."

"Pearls before swine."

"Together?"

Her hand was warm and dry.

"Together."

They stood shoulder to shoulder on the roof and stared up at the tower. As impossible as it seemed they could clearly hear the footsteps of the minions still pounding after them, prodded on by screams from the fiftieth floor.

"YOU BELONG TO ME, LYRA GOLD! WE HAVE A CONTRACT!"

"You signed a contract?"

"I was desperate!"

Jack raised both hands. "Say no more. Been there."

"I'LL GET YOU! I'LL GET YOU AND YOUR LITTLE BAND TOO!"

"I think he's confused," Lyra muttered as Jack ran for the door leading down into his building. "Hey, where you going?"

"I've got an idea."

The door was never locked but then again the wood was so rotten there wouldn't have been much point. Jack ripped it open and stuck his head into the moldering stairwell. "Gustav!"

Down below, the door to the apartment opened and Gustav peered out into the hall. "Dude?"

"Up here!"

"Dude!"

"My axe, man. Throw me my axe!" After a moment he added, "And an amp and an extension cord!"

The tower threw the first note back at him. Jack smiled. He was just warming up. By the third note, Gustav was plugged in and playing beside him. By the . . . well, after a while, Maitland had his set up and was pounding out a rhythm on his skins. Chording right up at the base of his fret board, Jack turned to Lyra and nodded.

"Dude!" Gustav bellowed into his ear. "She doesn't know the words!"

"Yeah, she does!"

"But . . ."

"Trust me!"

And Lyra sang. They weren't the words as written but that didn't matter.

Two angry verses later, nothing had happened.

Jack threw everything he had at the lead in to the chorus. Knew the guys were doing the same. He watched Lyra draw in a deep breath—worth watching regardless.

Last verse.

The tower began to shimmer.

The gold coloring in the glass began to pick up an oil slick on a puddle kind of iridescence. It began at the edge of the broken window and worked its way out. It shimmered and moved faster, growing brighter, chasing itself from floor to floor until it finally caught itself and . . .

Jack had been on stage at the community center once when they were testing the lights. This was a thousand times brighter. This wasn't community center lighting or bar lighting–this was stadium lighting!

Although they couldn't see, they played on to the end of the song, Lyra's final note hanging in the air until it became the distant sound of a police siren over on Harris Street. Clutching his guitar, blinking away after images, Jack shuffled to the edge of the roof; pretty much exactly as far as his cord would let him go before he tipped over his amp.

He wasn't surprised to see that the tower was gone.

The grocery store with the bins of fresh fruit out front, that surprised him a bit.

As Lyra joined him, an old grey haired guy with a guitar hanging down his back stopped in front of the apples, picked up a granny smith, and tossed a coin to someone just out of Jack's line of sight.

"Thang you, thang you very much."

The old man didn't look up; he just shoved the apple in his pocket and walked on.

Except that Jack was ninety percent certain it wasn't an apple by the time it reached the pocket. He was ninety percent certain it had become a handful of bright green picks.

He was ten percent certain he'd suffered irreparable brain damage at some point over the last couple of days.

"Dude?"

He turned to face the band. Maitland was scratching his ass but Gustav seemed to have a few questions. One question, actually.

"What the hell just happened?"

Lyra slipped her hand into his and Jack smiled. "We just made music."

Continuing to make music, they all lived happily ever after.

"Dude! I said no red M&M's! What kind of a dumbass stage manager are you? Man, this show's been a total crap fest since Carson Daly left!"

More or less.

Slow Poison

This is one of the other stories that I'm proud of and it's a very close second to "I Knew a Guy Once" as my favorite bit of writing ever. To a certain extent, looking at it from a purely thematic point, it's the same story. Sort of.

The anthology request was to write a story from the point of view of the conquered. The bad guys have won; what do you do now? And I thought to myself, who is left to rebel when the war is over? When the war is lost? Who is left to fight when swords have failed?

You'd probably better eat something before you read this.

SHE LOOKED NEITHER TO THE left nor right as they escorted her up to the small audience chamber. No need to look, she knew what she'd see. The tapestries that had bracketed the broad corridor for hundreds of years had been torn down, ripped apart for the gold thread they contained. The walls beneath bore the marks of hammers and pry bars as the invaders searched for the treasure they knew the Citadel contained. The air that had once carried the scent of perfumes and fine foods stank of blood and fire and despair.

No guards in ceremonial armor, sunbursts gleaming on enameled breastplates, stood outside the double doors. The doors themselves had been reduced to thousand year old kindling for this was where the Citadel's defenders had made their last stand. Her shoes stuck to the red-brown pattern on the marble floor—still too wet to be called stains. There were women in this room she recognized, their fate over the day and night since the fall evident on faces and bodies.

Some of them watched her as she crossed to the dais. Some of them had retreated too far the deep corners of their own minds to even know she was in the room. She didn't blame them but this was no time to retreat; not if they wanted to defeat the darkness. Strength of arms had failed. Other strengths were needed now.

The men on the dais wore looted silks and brocades as well as the stained linens and rough furs that had been under their crude but ultimately effective armor. The man they surrounded had slipped a wide-skirted, peacock-blue jacket embroidered with golden suns over a leather covered torso. She had seen the jacket last on one of the younger princes. The cuffs were stained the same color as the floor.

He was that indeterminate age between young and old—those few years when skill and physical ability briefly matched. The flesh along his jaw was still firm and his clothing covered heavy, functional muscle.

She was at the edge of the dais before he noticed her, preoccupied as he was with the elderly man dangling from one scarred hand. Eyes the brown of sugar cakes just off the fire turned toward her, and widened slightly as she calmly met his gaze.

A heavy hand landed on her left shoulder. The deep voice of her escort commanded her to kneel as he shoved her toward the floor.

She turned her head enough to meet his gaze in turn and snapped, "You'll be there to help me back to my feet will you?"

When he hesitated, visibly confused by both her response and her immobility, she shook her head. "Never mind, I expect I'll manage."

Gathering up her kirtle in both hands, she shifted her weight to one leg and lowered the other knee cautiously to the floor. Once she had her bulk settled more of less comfortably, she looked back to the dais. And waited.

The man with the sugar cake eyes waited as well. His name was Arwed. If there was more to his name than Arwed, she hadn't heard. His men called him the warlord when they spoke of him and Warlord when they spoke to him—all things considered an unremarkable designation. He and his horsemen had ridden out of the west, conquering everything before them until they reached the Citadel and the sea and could go no further. Turning north would take them up into the mountains, turning south to battles they could not win. Unless they learned to sail, this was where they would stay. She wondered how far back along the path of destruction they'd left their women and children or if these were the men without either and that was why they'd thrown themselves so entirely into war.

If Arwed expected her to fidget or show some other sign of fear he was doomed to be disappointed. At her size fidgeting required too much energy and at her age there were no fears remaining she hadn't faced. At this new angle, she recognized the man he held. The Duc of Arn—a man who had fresh brown bread and honey every morning with his coffee when the sun touched the edge of his office window—the King's chancellor. The *late* king's chancellor. The king, or parts of him, were hanging over the central gate.

After a long moment, the man who had removed the king's head smiled. He had, she noted, good strong teeth. "They say you cook." His accent was thick but understandable.

She had been in charge of the Citadel kitchens. "I do."

"Did you cook for your useless dead king?"

"I did."

"They say you are the best."

"I am." The simple truth.

"Then you will cook for me." Arwed swept the arm not holding the chancellor around the room. "And these my conquering warriors!"

The men roared their approval. One of the women screamed, the sound cut short by the impact of flesh on flesh.

"Bring us food," he continued, "as the sun sets!"

Another roar. The sun had been the symbol of the defeated.

"I'll need to find those of my kitchen workers still alive," she pointed out once the roaring stopped.

"You need what I tell you you need."

Her voice could have dried apples. "I'm not as young as I once was. If you want food fit for eating for this number, I'll need help."

"You need a hand?" Almost too fast to follow he drew his sword and swung. A heartbeat later, the chancellor's pale hand lay twitching on the dais. He tossed the limp body aside—if not a body now, soon enough, she thought—and kicked the hand toward her. "How about this?"

It smacked against her hip. She looked down, looked up, and sighed. "Not particularly useful even had you left it attached."

Arwed frowned, looked at her as though he were seeing her for the first time, and laughed. It was a man's laugh. A hale fellow well met let's slaughter a few innocents laugh. His men laughed with him although only the few actually on the dais could have known why.

"I am pleased to see my men did you little harm."

There were bruises, dried blood crusted around a cut just above the steel grey cap of her hair. "Perhaps I reminded them of their mothers."

He laughed again. "A terrifying thought! Find the people you need, Cook. When we eat, I'll decide if you can keep them."

When the Citadel fell the conquerors were more interested in treasure rooms than the pantries. Armed men had come reluctantly to the kitchens and stayed only long enough to make sure the new order was understood. They'd searched for hidden warriors, had thrown some flour about—the greatest mess for the least amount of effort—had killed the head baker, and had taken away the three young girls who'd worked in the scullery.

She got one of the girls back—Brigatte, the youngest, wobbling on unsteady legs like a new-born calf, the purple imprint of large hands on both her arms. Three middle-aged women, two from the kitchens, one from the laundry, she found cowering and bloody in a corner. A little water showed the damage superficial—slit noses and notched ears. Cruelty for cruelty's sake. She could find none of the men. The odds were very good they had joined the baker in death. With time running out, these four would have to be enough.

"Get fires lit in both roasting ovens and in the larger stove." As her head emerged from behind the bib of a clean apron—the linens had been undisturbed—she noticed none of the four had moved from their huddle just inside the door. This wouldn't do. Food didn't cook itself. "Swords fail," she told them, her voice as matter-of-fact as it had ever been, her words chosen carefully to slide past the bored young man appointed her personal guard, "*that* fight is over but people still have to eat."

The woman from the laundry moved first. She stepped forward, her eyes narrowed, searching. After a long moment, tight lines around her mouth and eyes relaxed. "My name is Anna," she said. "I'll get your fires lit."

"Thank you, Anna." She set Brigatte back in her familiar place with a pile of vegetables to deal with. Before she left, she cupped the child's chin with her hand and gently lifted her head. The girl sniffed once then met her gaze. After a long moment, she nodded. "Good girl. You'll do." It was as close to comfort as she could afford to express. Her smile evoked a tremulous smile in return. "Exactly." A nod to the vegetables. "Now, we do what must be done because there is no one to do it but us."

As Anna, the laundress, tended the fires, she put the other two women—Rose and Molly—to seasoning joints of meat. A man designated the warlord would expect meat but this would be meat as he had never eaten it before. Seared dark and blood red and each mouthful bursting with subtle flavor; he didn't have to notice the subtlety but it was imperative he eat.

This would be the bait.

With the familiar sounds of the kitchens rising over the distant sounds of fire and pain, she set two large scoops of cornmeal to soak in milk from the one stone crock that had not been spilled. The Warlord's men had recognized bread, if nothing else, and there was no time to make more. It would have to be cornbread but, fortunately, there would be plenty of rendered fat from the joints.

When the cornbread, rich with dripping was slid into the oven, she began the desserts. The cream had already sat in the cold room for two days, no point in wasting it.

And this would set the hook.

The smell of cooking food had brought another three of her people and one of the wine stewards to the kitchen. She tore linens into bandages, set the steward's broken arm and put them to work, hoping for more. The dumb waiter had been destroyed in the fighting and actually getting the food from the kitchen to the warlord would require more hands than she had.

Then half a dozen noble women, too old to be used in more pleasurable ways, arrived prodded by the sword points of three young warriors. She didn't think for a moment that the warlord had anticipated her need, only that he had found another way to humiliate the conquered. His reasons didn't concern her, only that there were now hands enough to carry the food.

She gave them tea and slices of an apple cake she'd found protected by an upturned bowl. When their guards protested, she pointed out that they needed strength enough to carry the food.

"They drop; we kill!"

"Suit yourself, but your warlord will object to his supper bouncing down the hall. If I feed them," she added slowly and deliberately when they looked confused, "they'll carry the food, your warlord will eat, you will eat, everyone will be happy. If I don't feed them, they'll drop the food and they'll be killed but no one will get any supper. You want your supper don't you?"

They did. The smell of cooking food was very nearly overwhelming. They salivated but the warlord's dogs were too well trained to pull meat from his table.

In the end, she gave them apple cake as well.

Three of the women were sunk deep in shock but she thought they would emerge in time. Two of them were frightened but angry. One had nothing but anger remaining.

Arwed frowned as only five of the women returned to the small audience chamber with his meal.

"Where is the other, Cook?"

"The Lady Adelade objected to serving you." She reached out and with the edge of her apron swept an assortment of nasty bric-a-brac to the floor then stepped aside to allow Molly and Rose to place the first joint on the table. One of your warriors killed her."

"And what did you do, Cook?"

She beckoned Anna forward and showed her where to place the dish of new onions and peas glistening with butter. "I objected to the mess."

The smell of the food was almost enough to mask scent of death in the room.

The warlord pulled at a braided cord around his neck and from behind the peacock-blue and linen came a gleaming ivory spiral about as long as his thumb. "Do you know what this is?" His smile suggested he was about to win whatever contest of wills they had been involved in.

"Yes." So this was why, in spite of the guard, he hadn't been worried she would poison him. "It's the point of a unicorn horn."

Leaning forward he touched the tip of the horn to the nearest joint. "If there is poison in my food, I will make these women eat it."

Of course he would. She wasn't stupid.

There was no poison.

Still smiling he indicated she should approach him and when she was near enough, he placed the point of the horn between her eyes. It was warm and sticky with juices. "Don't you want me dead, Cook?"

She'd never heard that a lie was a type of poison to a unicorn but her days of attracting unicorns were far behind her. Not that it mattered, she had no intention of lying to him—particularly not a lie he would never believe. "Of course I do."

Of course she did.

"Your food is getting cold," she added. "It's a lot better tasting if you eat it hot."

Tucking the bit of horn back against his skin, he shook his head watching her through narrowed eyes. "What makes you so fearless, Cook?"

She shrugged. "People have to eat."

Later, as he devoured large bowl of crème brulee, crunching his way through the caramelized crust, he graciously allowed she could keep the people she had.

The next morning she brought him eggs and sausage—her own recipe—and fresh baked biscuits and two kinds of jam and coffee thick and dark and sweet. Two hours later, a bowl of sugared almonds and a fresh pot of coffee. Two hours after that, a whole chicken golden brown filled with truffles and chestnut stuffing and more coffee.

As people died and history burned and chaos moved out from the Citadel, it was business as usual in the kitchens, an island of calm amidst the spreading destruction.

"Damned that unicorn horn,"Anna growled as she yanked the last feathers from a goose and threw it down on the table. "You could have killed him a dozen times by now!"

The kitchen guard stopped chewing long enough to laugh derisively.

The goose had been fattening for the king. Oblivious to the battle passing by its crate it had merely gone on eating.

She reached into the cavity and carefully freed the swollen liver. She would season it with paprika and ginger and sugar then sauté it in hot goose fat before serving it to the warlord with sautéed onions and apples and bottle of the king's best dry sherry.

"The food has changed, Cook." The warlord stared at her suspiciously, tapping the unicorn horn against his palm. "I did not say you could change the food."

She shrugged. "I can only cook what I have. I have no milk. I have no cream. I have no butter."

"Then get milk and cream and butter," he snarled, threat implicit in his tone.

She waited. To ask *and if I don't?* aloud would challenge his authority and force him to respond. She wasn't so foolish. .

"Where did you get these things when you cooked for your useless dead king?" he demanded at last.

"The Citadel had a dairy but the cows have either been slaughtered or driven off and the dairy maids . . . well, they also have either been slaughtered or driven off.

"Get cows. Get dairy maids. Get out and cook!"

The dairy was under the warlord's protection. The calm spread from the kitchen.

At first Arwed rode out everyday to terrorize what was left of the town. With the thick walls of the Citadel to retreat to, he feared no reprisal. The Citadel had stood, dressed-stone anchored deep in high rock, for over six hundred years. It had only ever been taken once.

"This food stinks of rot!"

Wiping the contents of the thrown apricot dumpling off her face with a corner of her apron, she rolled her eyes. "It's not the food, it's the room." Flies hung over the darker corners.

"So fix it."

"In order for the food to smell and taste as it did, this room will have to be cleaned. Daily."

"My men . . ."

"Do not need to piss where you eat."

He thought it was funny to see those who had been ladies scrubbing up the filth of their conquerors so he kept them at it. His men taunted them; deliberately made more mess for them until they were so overwhelmed and exhausted they had no time to clean the small audience chamber where he took his meals.

"I killed the sniveling one but the rest work no harder or faster." Arwed wiped his blade on the skirt of the peacock blue coat.

She set a tray of lemon-ginger tarts on the table, the sweet glaze glistening golden in the afternoon sunlight. "Then they're working as hard and as fast as they can. If you want them to finish, have your men leave them alone."

"My men do as they please, Cook."

"My mistake. I thought they did as you pleased."

The taunting continued but the women were left to clean in peace.

She cooked him pork ribs—huge racks glistening with fat, basted with sugar and tomato sauce and dried chilies—and got permission to rebuild the pigpens and find some stock.

"I'll need swineherds."

"For what?"

"Swine also have to eat or they'll come skinny and tough to the table."

"You can have two." He wiped grease from his mouth and pointed. "Those two."

One of them had been a Lady of the Chamber, one a Duchess whose lands were to the west and had been overrun. She had come to the citadel for safety. Now they were swineherds.

Another ripple of calm.

The few chickens she had been able to round up were being kept in a room that had been used for the cutting and arranging of flowers, a small door that had once lead to a cutting garden now lead to a chicken yard.

She threw the mangled chicken down in front of him. "That was to have been your supper but one of your men thought it would be funny to let the dogs in with them."

The warlord laughed. "It is funny. Kill another chicken for my supper."

"Very well. Then there will not be enough chickens to supply you with eggs for your breakfast." Eggs scrambled with sautéed garlic and mushrooms. Eggs poached and perched on thick slices of last year's ham, covered in a white sauce fragrant with rosemary. Thick slices of fine white bread dipped in egg and fried in butter then dusted with flour or drowned in sweet syrup.

"Fine. Who let the dogs in?"

"He did." His name was Chouin, a scared and grizzled veteran of the warlord's ride to the coast. He had followed her to the audience chamber, laughing, secure in the knowledge that he was one of the conquerors and she merely a cook.

Arwed's hand flicked out and a knife buried itself in the man's throat. He looked astounded, gurgled and pitched forward, hitting the floor with a wet thud. "The rest of you, stay away from the birds." And to her. "Happy, Cook?"

One less chicken. One less warrior. "Yes."

A small vegetable garden, small because the warlord had begun with little use for vegetables and desired them even less as time went on and she tempted his palate. The pigpen. The chicken run. The dairy. The kitchen. All to provide food for the warlord and his men. Food and as much of the sweet rich coffee as she could get them to drink.

Seven cleaners kept the marble halls gleaming so that filth did not over-whelm the food.

The laundry reopened when the peacock-blue coat began to carry a scent more pungent than the roasted garlic and apple that accompanied the roast goose. Anna moved from the kitchen and found three women to help her.

More workers were needed in the kitchen to feed those who worked to keep the warlord and his men fed.

There were those who said she betrayed her people by serving the conquerors but her people were safe under her eye. They ate scraps and leavings and food that once would have gone to the Citadel's pig-pens while the warlord ate braised liver cockaigne with wine, crown roast of pork stuffed with sausage and chestnuts and parsley and cream, potato chunks pan-fried in lard and dusted with dried chili, fried potato cakes with sour cream and paprika, , buttermilk rolls and honey biscuits served thickly spread with butter, jelly rolls, seven egg puddings with a chocolate maple glaze, and cornstarch custards with sweet cheese crumble toppings.

The king's wine cellars were emptying.

A man who came to be called the warlord was not in the habit of denying himself.

She cooked.

He ate.

"I'm almost out of flour."

"So?"

"No flour, no baking."

"Get more."

"The nearest market town still standing is four days ride, north up the coast road."

"Then I'll send some men; they can use the exercise. All this good food is making them weak." Flesh moved with the back of his hand as he swiped at the grease dribbling down his chin.

"If your men ride up to the town the people will disappear. They won't get any flour."

He snorted. "So what did your useless dead king do?"

"There were carters who went to the market towns and came back with food but they're gone. Your men killed them, took the horses, and burned the carts."

Carmel bubbled up thick and sweet down as he shoved a spoon into an apple raison cobbler. "One of the rats scrabbling in the ruins around this drafty hunk of stone can drive a horse and cart. Find that rat," he told the room at large. "And a horse and a cart. And someone they care about to make sure they come back. Two of you," he added grinning, "accompany the cart. There are dangerous men about."

"They'll need money to buy the flour," she reminded him when the laughter died.

"So take what you need!"

" I'm a cook." A nod toward an elderly woman on her hands and knees scrubbing the marble floor. "She used to work for the chancellor. She knows money."

"You!"

The woman started and lifted her head. Her own left ear hung on a chord around her neck.

"Deal with this!"

Then the kitchen needed fuel. And then sugar. And then as the days turned, strawberries for pies, new potatoes to be fried with spring onions, and peaches for cobblers.

The carters started rebuilding, protected because they brought supplies for the warlord's table. Those of the warlord's men who rode out with them wore the colors of the Citadel so that the people in the market towns wouldn't run from them.

Word spread. A thin girl with bruised eyes brought a basket of oysters to the kitchen door. After feeding the girl and giving her loaves of heavy brown bread to take home to her family, she prepared deep fried oysters with seasoned bread crumbs and andalouse sauce.

The warlord wanted more.

And the oyster harvesters came under the warlord's protection.

The woman who used to work for the chancellor came so many times to the warlord for coin, he gave her access to the treasure he had taken with the Citadel.

"And you will die if you can not account for every copper," he snarled through a mouthful of thick sliced beef.

Clean hair dressed neatly over the ruin of her ear, she bowed her head.

* * *

Arwed continued to test everything she served him with the unicorn horn certain he would, at some point, be poisoned. He tested the meat through thick rinds of crispy golden brown fat. He tested the potatoes roasted in their skins then drenched in sour cream and sprinkled with chopped chive. He plunged the horn into the gleaming white heart of the bread then in turn into the jams and flavored honeys he spread thickly over it. He tested each nut in its crunchy sugared coating. He dipped it into the coffee and the cream. She was commanded to stand by at every meal until the test was done.

He no longer rode out and his leathers had been replaced by loose silks and velvets plundered from the wardrobes of the Citadel. But he was still the Warlord and warlords needed armor that fit. Armor needed blacksmiths and leather workers. Drawn by the gold from the Citadel, some of those who had fled before the destruction returned to the town.

Those of his men who still preferred to wear their armor guarded the carters and the oyster harvesters lest the bounty for the warlord's table be taken from them. They guarded the gates of the Citadel and every day a different warrior stood guard in the kitchen. The warlord had no wish for his men to have closer access to his food than he did. As she chopped and rendered and sautéed, she noted which ones of her guard asked what and noted especially the fewer who asked why.

"I am out of coffee and nearly out of chocolate."

He rolled his eyes, nearly hidden now in pouches of flesh and spat, "Get more."

"These things come from the south, on ships. The trade is complicated."

"Then I will make it simple for you, Cook." The point of his blade buried in the table top, he leaned toward her, breathing heavily, his face flushed. "I rule here. If I say get more, get more!"

There were women in the Citadel who understood trade, who had sat silent beside fathers and husbands. Some now worked cleaning the halls, some in the kitchens, one in the dairy. She was just as glad to set them to work they understood because every single one of them had at one time or another let the meat over-cook and the potatoes boil dry. The less said about their experiences with eggs and cream, the better. The women from the town, who replaced them, rolled up their sleeves and did as they were told.

* * *

She finally put the aconite–carefully distilled from tincture of monkshood–in a crème brulee. It had been, since that very first meal, his favorite desert and he demanded she prepare it two or three times a week.

Arwed stared at the piece of unicorn horn as the black climbed slowly up the spiral. His eyes widened, his jaw dropped, and, after a long moment, he leaped from his chair.

"You thought you were safe!" he roared. "A hundred of these I have eaten! A thousand!" He jabbed the now ebony horn toward her. "You dared to think I would not check because of that? Ha!" Dark circles of red appeared on each cheek and began to spread. "Am I a fool? Am I?" he roared at the watching men and women. "No! I have conquered and I have killed and I taken what I please!" The red of his face had begun to purple and his eyes bulge alarmingly. "You have made a fatal mistake, Cook! I will have you roasted in your own ovens! Turned on your own spit! Salted and boiled and . . ."

His mouth opened. Closed. Opened again but no sound emerged.

The fingers of his left hand curled and as he clutched at the peacock-blue fabric over his breast with his right, the horn fell and cracked through the praline crust of the brulee to protrude over the side of the custard dish like a stick of fluted licorice.

He stumbled back and just before he fell, she caught his gaze and held it.

Swords had failed.

Gasping for breath that wouldn't come, he crumbled to the floor.

The small assembly room was silent for a long moment and she began to worry she would have to do this as well. Then the woman who had worked for the chancellor of the old king, who now commanded the treasury of the captured Citadel, rose to her feet and snapped, "Don't just sit there! You and you, carry him carefully to his bedchamber! You! Find a healer! Cook!"

She waited.

"Return to the kitchen."

Arwed was dead by nightfall but the structure held.

She wasn't surprised; she had never had a soufflé fall.

The new Warlord was one of the men who asked why. By his side was a woman of the Citadel, her belly round with new life. When that child came in time to rule, he would not be a warlord but a king. Perhaps there would even be sunbursts on the breastplates of his guard.

She busied herself preparing the funeral feast.
After all, people had to eat.

Tuesday Evenings, Six Thirty to Seven

I will readily admit that I'm not the most organized person in the world and, sometimes, with two authors under one roof things get a little . . . confused. A while ago, my wife was asked to be in an anthology about fantasy concepts gone wrong—or close enough to that as makes no real difference—while at the same time I was asked by the same editor to be in an anthology about assassins. Then I lost my email, remembered only that Fiona was asked as well, checked hers and wrote this story.

Which confused the heck out of the editor. I apologized and wrote the assassin story. As it happened, Eeriecon, where I was to GOH, publishes a chapbook for sale at the convention and I had nothing on file to send them. I'd have to write something new. Oh wait! I'd just written something new. Life is good.

SHE SAT IN THE CHURCH hall basement on the old wooden chair just like she'd sat for a thousand Septembers where a thousand equaled thirty-seven but seemed like so many more.

In the old days, she'd sat with other women—Tawny Owls, Grey Owls, Brown Owls—chatting and laughing and joyfully waiting for the new girls. Some girls raced down the stairs, leaving mothers or older sisters behind, thrilled to finally be old enough. Some descended slowly, deliberately, holding onto an adult hand, shy and unsure.

For the last eight years, she'd waited alone but the girls still came. Less of them, sure but she didn't need many—three or four eight year olds to join her nine year olds to replace those girls who had flown up. But both of last year's eight year olds had moved away so, this year, there were no nine year olds.

She watched the clock, watched eight o'clock come and go and she stayed just a little longer. Sometimes parents got off work late. Or the girls might have school functions they needed to attend.

Eight thirty came and went.

She knew; she could feel the certainty catching at the back of her throat every time she swallowed. No one was going to come. What few girls the right age there were among the graying population of this small town had too many other enticements. Five hundred channels. A hundred gigabytes. Baseball. Ballet. Soccer. Music lessons.

They'd wanted her to fold the troop last year.

Maybe they'd been right.

She reached out a hand to scoop up the paperwork and brochures spread out on the scarred desk in front of her.

"Oi, missus! Is this where we sign up?"

Decades of dealing with little girls had given her nerves of steel. Although she'd thought herself alone in the basement and could, in fact, see no evidence to the contrary, she neither started nor shrieked, merely leaned forward and peered over the edge of the desk.

Five men peered up at her. The tallest had to have been less than a meter high or she'd have been able to see the top of his head from her chair. All five wore old fashioned clothing in varying shades of brown: waistcoats and jackets, loose trousers and cotton shirts, handkerchiefs knotted loosely around tanned necks. All five had brown hair and brown eyes. In fact, they looked remarkably like . . .

She leaned out a little further, half afraid she'd see hairy feet.

Thank God. Brown shoes.

"Take a picture," grumbled one. "Lasts longer."

The other four seemed to find that very funny but even during all the sniggering, not one expectant gaze had left her face. They were clearly waiting for her to say something.

All right.

"Sign up for what?" she asked.

The tallest little man sighed. "We're Brownies, ain't we? We heared this is where you sign up."

Suddenly, sitting down seemed like an excellent idea.

"Oi! Where'd she go?"

"I'm thinking she fainted like. Took one look at your ugly puss and fell right . . . OW!"

"Don't be daft. If she was on the floor we could see her."

They had accents; a soft burr on voices that rose and fell like her

Uncle Dave's after an evening at the Legion. A clattering that a part of her brain translated as wooden soles against tile—she'd worn clogs back in the seventies—and all five came around the corner of the desk. Only four of them were in wooden soled shoes, the fifth wore modern trainers although she'd never realized they came in brown.

"Right then, there you are." The tallest folded his arms. "Let's get on with it, we ain't got all night."

"Yes, we do."

"Shut it!" he snapped without turning or unlocking his gaze from her face. "You the Brownie leader then?"

She had to clear her throat to find her voice. "Yes, but . . ."

"So what's the problem?"

"You're not . . ." A rudimentary sense of self-preservation cut her off before she could finish with *the right kind of Brownies.* " . . . the kind of Brownies I usually deal with."

Their spokesman folded his arms belligerently, his action mirrored by the other four. "So?"

"This organization is for little girls."

"Little girls?"

"Yes."

"But we're *Brownies!*"

She spread her hands in the universal gesture for *that's not really relevant and there's nothing I can do about it anyway.*

"But, but . . ."

A small but hoary fist smacked him on the shoulder. "I told you this'd never work you great git!"

"Little girls," snorted another.

"It'll never happen for us," sighed a third.

Raised fists fell. Feet lifted to kick settled back onto the ground. A mouthful of damp sleeve was spit slowly out. What had clearly been about to descend into violence became instead five dispirited little men.

Shoulders slumped, they turned away.

"Sorry for bothering you, Missus."

"Wait!" Not until they started to turn did she realize she'd been the one to call them back. After a moment's silent panic, she figured she might as well be hung for a sheep as a lamb and a moment later decided that might not be the best simile she could use as a couple of the little men looked like they'd rustled a sheep or two in their day. "If you're already Brownies . . ."

"If?" A bit of the belligerence returned.

"Sorry. *Since* you're already Brownies, why do you want to join my troop?"

"Why?"

"Yes, why."

"Right then." A gnarled finger indicated she should hold that thought and the Brownies huddled up.

"If she can't help, she doesn't need to know."

"If she knows, maybe she can help."

"But then she'll know too much."

"We could kill her."

"Sure and what century are you living in? We'd have CSI all over us before we could say Killicrankie."

"You know, I've never understood why we'd say Killicrankie. It's daft. Totally bloody daft."

"Oh shut your pie hole."

She wondered if they knew or cared she could hear every word. A short scuffle later, the vote to tell her went four to one. After the forceful application of a clog to the dissenter's nether regions, it ended five votes in favor. As they jumped up to sit on the edge of the desk . . .

"Right then, that's a mite easier on the back of the neck."

. . . she handed out tissues and fished a box of last season's classic cookies out of her bag. All hands were still busy blotting bloody noses and minor bites so she left the open box on the desk, took a chocolate and a vanilla and sat back in her chair.

The tallest Brownie gave her a thoughtful look—his shiner already beginning to fade—took a cookie of each flavor, and passed the box along. "It's like this, Missus," he said, "we're tired of being Brownies . . ."

"All the cleaning."

"And the serving."

"And the not being appreciated."

"Or believed in."

". . . and we heard you can make us something else."

"Something else?"

"That's what we heard." He tapped a fingertip to the side of one hirsute nostril.

"Well, my girls fly up to be Guides but . . ."

"Guides!" Unsurprisingly, his smile was missing a couple of teeth. "Then that's what we'll be. We'll be Guides."

Agreement from the others emerged slightly muffled by the cookies.

She thought she was taking this remarkably well, all things considered. "You don't understand; Guides are another level in a worldwide organization."

"Aye. And we're Brownies."

"You'll be making us Guides," added the Brownie in the running shoes.

They really weren't getting it. "It's not *Guides* the same way that you're Brownies. It's more a name given to acknowledge that the girls are ready to move on."

"Aye." The tallest Brownie nodded. "And so are we."

"Past ready."

"Way past."

"Long past."

"Oi, Missus! Got any more cookies?"

"No. You've eaten the whole box, any more and you'll make yourself sick." When they accepted that without argument, she took a deep breath and tried again. "Brownies are part of an all female organization. They're eight and nine year old girls. You're not girls and even if you were, you'd be too old."

"But we *are* Brownies."

"Yes, but . . ."

"Que Sera."

"He starts to sing I'm for stuffin' my fist down his gullet."

"That'd improve things."

"What's he gotta use them fancy foreign words for anyways?"

"Too big for his bloody britches."

"Stop it." To her surprise, they did—if not immediately, after only some minor bruising. "That kind of behavior is not good citizenship."

"What does that mean when it's home?"

But the tallest answered before she could. "It means she's taken us on; doesn't it, Missus?"

The clock showed twenty past nine. They were alone in the basement, just her and five Brownies.

"Yes," she told them. "That's what it means." After all, the latest Strategic Plan listed increasing the diversity of membership as a key priority.

* * *

Their names were Big Tam, Little Tam, Callum, Conner, and Ewan. There was a reason they sounded like her Uncle Dave.

"Have you looked in your phone book lately," Big Tam snorted. "Two pages of Mc's and near three of Mac's plus Campbells and Buchanans and Browns and Kerrs. We came across the big pond with them, didn't we. Course Ewan's working for a Singh now, his last Campbell married over."

Ewan grinned. "I'll take a nice curry over a bloody bowl of milk and a bannock any night."

When she pointed to the curse cup, he sighed and dropped in a coin. She didn't ask where he got the money. She suspected she didn't want to know.

Only Callum, the Brownie in the running shoes, could read and write. The others thought he was full of himself and too quick to take up new fangled ideas. After three fights and a small fire no one would admit to setting, she'd taken the registration forms away and told them she'd fill them in herself. It was important to register them. If they weren't registered then they weren't *real* Brownies and it would mean nothing when they flew up. She'd feminized their names and added Scottish family names for everyone except for Ewan–who became Eula. He was a Singh. Over the years, she'd helped fill in enough of these forms that the lies came easily.

Too easily considering that honesty was a part of the Brownie law. *I'll sell extra cookies to make up for it.*

The registration fee was $75 dollars, each.

"Bugger that!"

Big Tam grabbed Conner by the collar and hauled him back into the circle. "You want to be serving 'til the end of time then? You want to spend eternity cookin' and cleanin' and muckin' out their shite and grinding their flour? Well, there's not much flour grinding of late but you take my meaning." He shook the smaller Brownie so hard a confused looking squirrel fell out of his pocket. "Hand it over," he commanded as Conner grabbed the squirrel and tucked it back out of sight.

She had to drive into the city to sell some of the registration money at a rare coin store. Even considering that half of what they'd offered her had disappeared when the sun hit it, she had more than enough to cover the fees for all five and order each of them a badge vest. Back in her day, they'd have been wearing skorts and knee socks and, as imagination supplied the visuals, she thanked God that uniform choices had become more flexible.

They met every Tuesday evening in the church hall basement. She intended to run this troop the way she'd run every troop–well, except for the curse cup. That was an idea she'd picked up from a Guide leader who dealt with a very rough group of inner city tweens.

"Oi, Missus! What's with the sodding mushroom?"

She waited until his coin hit the curse cup before she answered. "It's not a mushroom, it's a toadstool and it's very old."

"Old?" Conner scoffed, right index finger buried knuckle deep in his nose. "I got boogers older than that there."

"It's old," she repeated. The toadstool had spent every Tuesday evening in the basement for as long as she had. It had been the focus of thousands of circles of girls.

Big Tam stared at her for a long moment. "It's no old to us."

"But you don't want to be you anymore, do you?"

His brows dipped so deep they met over his nose. "You're daft, Missus."

"Probably." But she was going to turn these Brownies into Guides. That's why they'd come to her and that's what she did. "Each of you take a cushion and sit in a circle around the toadstool. Oh, and stop calling me Missus. Address me as Brown Owl."

Their reactions put another seventy five cents, two doubloons, and a farthing in the curse cup although she'd had to guess that Little Tam's tirade was obscene since she was unfamiliar with all of the words and half the gestures.

It was a small circle, she realized when they were seated, the smallest she'd ever had.

"Don't be worrying about that, Missus," Callum told her reassuringly when she voiced the observation. "Size don't matter."

"You'd say that, would you?" Big Tam snorted, leaping to his feet and reaching into his trousers. "Them what says that, they ain't got size enough to matter. Now, me, what I got . . ."

"Put it away."

"But . . ."

"Now."

"Fine. Still bigger," he muttered sitting down.

Never let them know they'd flustered you. Little girls reacted to weakness like wolves–which was not particularly fair to wolves who were, on the whole, noble creatures. But saying that little girls react-ed to weakness like chickens who were known to peck their compan-ions to death just didn't have the same kind of mythic power behind it even though it was more biologically accurate.

"Missus?"

Right.

She cleared her throat and dried her palms on her thighs. "We'll start with the Brownie law."

"Well," Conner said thoughtfully, "we ain't allowed to be reward-ed for our services."

"Though that's really more of a guideline than an actual law," Ewan pointed out.

Little Tam nodded. "You're supposed to be leaving stuff out for us."

"Good stuff," Callum qualified. "No shite."

"And a little appreciation for services rendered, that don't go amiss," Big Tam added to a chorus of: "Oh aye."

She absolutely was not thinking of what service Big Tam could render. "This is a different Brownie law, for the kinds of Brownies who become Guides."

"Let's have it then, Missus. Owl. Missus Owl."

Close enough.

They learned the law and the promise and could soon recite them both.

"Honest and kind? This lot?" Conner pulled his finger from his nose and stared at the tip. "That's a laugh."

"You calling me a liar, you miserable little shite?"

"You want kind? Have a knuckle sandwich!"

"I'm gonna feed you my friggin' boot!"

"Up yours, asswipe!"

She got the toadstool back in essentially one piece and, as she dis-infected it before repainting, figured first aid had better be the initial Key Badge.

The curse cup already held enough money for various bandages, analgesic creams, and cold packs. It took three weeks for them to stop using the slings to tie each other into anatomically impossible posi-tions and a week after that to stop eating the creams but eventually they learned how to deal with black eyes, bloody noses, scraped knuckles, wrenched shoulders, and swollen genitalia–the later a necessary addition to the basic course material.

"Who'd have thought that frozen water'd feel so fine nestled up against the nads," Little Tam sighed, adjusting the ice pack.

They sold the Classic Cookies in the fall–the chocolate and vanilla center cream cookies stamped with the Guide trefoil. She had regular customers who'd bought boxes for years and didn't care if they came from smiling little girls or scowling little men as long as they got their fix.

New customers found themselves holding boxes in one hand and an empty wallet in the other without being entirely certain how it had happened. She was pleasantly surprised to find that although a few people were over cookied, no one was ever short changed.

"Brownies are honest," Ewan reminded her, as the entire troop looked a bit insulted by the surprised part of her reaction.

She made it up to them by presenting *Money Talk* badges all around.

They were heading for a record year when she realized they were in danger of attracting too much attention. "You've done remarkably well," she said, choosing to ignore the baby swapped for a doll made of cookies that she'd managed to swap back just in time. "But record numbers will bring us to provincial attention, maybe even national, and Brownies are supposed to be secretive folk who keep out of sight."

"No one saw us, Missus Owl."

"But they'll know something is going on and some one will come to investigate."

"Ah," Little Tam nodded. "CSI."

They all watched too much television but she'd dealt with that before. The best way to counteract it was to lead them into the limitless worlds of imagination that came with books.

Half and hour of every meeting was devoted to teaching four of her five brownies how to read; unfortunately, without much success.

"It's not that they don't want to learn, Missus Owl," Callum confided after the other four had vanished from the basement muttering about just what they'd like to do to Dick and Jane. "It's just you gotta teach them from stories they're interested in."

"Myths and legends."

He snorted. "Not quite."

*   *   *

"Dear Penthouse forum. Last night when my girlfriend and I were getting . . ."

"Sound it out, Little Tam."

"Int. I. Mate. Intimate!"

"Very good."

"Hey! Let's see them pictures!"

"Back off! It's my turn to read!"

"Git!"

"Arse!"

"Who remembers how to apply the ice pack?"

For the Halloween meeting she dressed as an Indian Princess. She always dressed as an Indian Princess; the costume had moved past traditional some years earlier and was currently approaching legendary. This year the beaded buckskin dress felt restrictive and uninspiring but it was too late to change.

Big Tam dressed up as a Boggart, Little Tam as a Hobgoblin, Conner as a Bodach, Ewan as a Red Cap and Callum, always a bit more progressive than the others, as Liza Minnelli. His story about her comeback concert was terrifying.

In November they used the kitchen upstairs in the church hall to bake a Sugar Pie.

"Or as the Acadians call it," she told them as Big Tam sprinkled cream on the maple sugar, "*la tarte au sucre.*"

The old oven was a bit temperamental and she had to call the minister's wife over to help get it going. The Brownies stayed out of sight—she explained they were down in the basement working on a project—and didn't reappear until the minister's wife was gone and the pie was in the oven.

While it baked, they traced the route of the dispossessed Acadian exiles out on a map.

She cut the pie into small pieces but that hardly mattered when everyone had seconds. And thirds.

That night, persons unknown repaved the parking lot behind the town hall causing incidental damage to five pigeons and 1988 Buick. The pigeons recovered, the owner of the Buick found a bag of assorted coin worth twice the blue book value of the car in his trunk, and she resolved to be more careful with sugar in the future.

* * *

By mid-December the curse cup held three hundred and twelve dollars and forty-two cents as well as three wizened black beans Conner swore were magic and should cover his contributions well into the new year.

"Oi! None of that ya cheap bastard!"

Later, after a review of first aid basics, she suggested they use the money to help under-privileged children celebrate Christmas.

"We don't do Christmas," Big Tam pointed out. "We're older than that, ain't we."

"Aren't we. And I'm not asking you do Christmas. I'm asking you to help children. Think of it as service to the community."

"We're all about service to the bleedin' community, Missus Owl."

"Workin' our arses off in the background, never getting no recognition."

"Aye, and we're right tired of it."

She could understand that.

"Still," Callum added a moment later, "it ain't the kiddies fault."

Three in the backseat, two with her in the front and she could fit all five into her car for a trip to the big toy store in the city.

"Big Tam, take your hand off my thigh."

"Sorry Missus Owl. Ewan's shoving like."

"Bugger I am!"

"Brownies, what did we discuss about seatbelts?"

"No one gets punched." five voices responded. "No one gets bit. Seatbelts stay on and no one gets hit."

"But . . ."

"No, Ewan."

"Not fair, Missus Owl! He sodding started it."

They had three hundred and twenty-seven dollars to spend by the time they reached the store.

She ran into the minister's wife as she emerged from a painfully pink aisle, her arms piled high with boxed baby dolls.

"Are you here on your own?" the minister's wife asked as she helpfully adjusted the pile.

"No, I'm here with my Brownies."

"I'd love to meet them." Smile tight and official, the minister's wife peered around the store. "Where are they?"

From three aisles away she heard, "Sod off you cheap bastard, we're buying the web slinging set what comes with Doc Octopus."

"Oh, they're around."

Little Tam was the hit of the talent show in January. The other four stomped and shouted and whistled, applauding long and loudly when he finished his song. Unfortunately, it was in Gaelic and she didn't understand a word of it.

"It's about a shepherd," Big Tam explained, glaring around the circle as though daring the others to contradict him. "A shepherd what really, really loves his sheep."

In February, on the Tuesday evening closest to the full moon, they made snow men—one large and five small—out behind the church hall. She provided carrots for noses but each of the Brownies had been told to bring enough small stones to create eyes and mouth.

"What's so funny mate," Callum muttered, finishing his snow-man's smile. "I'm freezing my bloody bollucks off out here."

"This is a part of your Winter Outside badge," she reminded him, uncertain if bollucks was a cursing or slang.

"Is there an icicle up the arse badge? Because I've got that one nailed."

The minister's wife appeared as she was unlocking her car.

"I've missed them again have I?"

"Only just." She smiled and checked to make sure that she'd obliterated the distinctive prints made by hobnailed boots.

"I could see you from my upstairs window." The minister's wife gestured toward the old stone house that went with the church. "I couldn't see your Brownies though."

"I expect the angle was wrong. And that pine tree's in the way."

"I've never seen them." The light over the parking lot made her eyes look a little wild. "I see you park here every Tuesday evening but never them."

"They come in through the other entrance." She didn't know what entrance they came through, they arrived every week a few minutes after she did. The *other* entrance was therefore no lie. "You've come out without your boots and hat. You do know you lose forty-five percent of your body heat through an uncovered head, don't you? You should get back inside before you get a chill."

Her first year as a leader, she'd brought in pictures of John Glenn, her Great Aunt Rose who'd raised eight children on her own after her husband had been killed in the first world war, and Superman. She'd talked about what it meant to be a hero and then had the girls come up with heroes of their own. Over the years, she'd added many of their heroes to her portfolio. This year, it took her nearly an hour to carefully tape them all to the painted concrete walls.

She hadn't been snuck up on in thirty-seven years and so she turned, smiling, when she heard the faint sound of footsteps behind her. The tall, dark haired woman with the minister's wife came as a bit of shock but she didn't let it show. It helped that over the last little while she'd become used to seeing the minister's wife pop up at odd moments. "Good evening. May I help you?"

The dark haired woman held out her hand. "Hello, my name is Janet O'Neill." Under her coat, a blue and white striped shirt, a dark blue sweater, a prominent pin . . ."I'm from the provincial office."

Of course she was.

"I was in the area visiting Samantha Jackson . . .

The name threw her for a moment and then she remembered. Samantha Jackson was the minister's wife; who was looking less nervous than usual now she had backup.

". . . and I thought I'd drop in and visit your troop."

"My troop."

"Your Brownies."

Oh dear.

"I see you're studying heroes tonight. Why don't you run us through the pictures while we wait for the girls to arrive?"

It took forty-five minutes. It would have taken longer but after forty-five minutes, Janet raised her hand and said, "They're not coming are they?"

"Well, of course they . . ."

"Aren't!" the minister's wife finished dramatically. "I've never seen these Brownies of yours. No one has. I've asked around and no one in town has enrolled their daughter in the program."

"You've spoken to everyone in town?" She was honestly curious. Who knew the minister's wife had that much free time.

"Not everyone. A lot of people though. It's a small town!"

Janet pulled five familiar registration forms from her briefcase. "I just want to ask you a few questions about these forms. You filled them in yourself didn't you?"

"Yes, but only because they couldn't."

"There is no they!" The minister's wife jabbed a shaking finger at her. "No one came to register that night but you've been a Brownie leader since the beginning of time and you couldn't bear not having a troop. So you made them up, didn't you? They're total figments of your imagination!"

"They are not!"

"Then where are they?"

"They won't come when you're here!"

"Why not?"

"Why should they? You don't believe in them."

Janet cleared her throat.

She stepped back, took a deep breath and apologized for shouting.

"I need to meet these girls," Janet said firmly. "I need to know that our organization hasn't been . . ."

"Used by a crazy lady!" the minister's wife finished.

"I swear to you," she spoke directly to Janet, "my Brownies may be a little rough around the edges but they're trying and isn't that what this we're about? They're doing their best and they understand about duty . . ."

"Duty hasn't been a part of the promise for years," Janet reminded her gently.

"Well, maybe it should be. The point is, they want to be more than they are and they came to me for help and I helped them because that's what we're about too. Helping."

"I need to meet these girls," Janet repeated. "Or I'm afraid that..."

"Oi, Missus. Sorry we're late."

Hobnailed boots coming down the stairs. In front as usual, Big Tam held out a gnarled hand to Janet O'Neill. "Tammy McGregor," he said. "Pleased to meetcha, Missus. This here's my younger sister Tina." Little Tam grunted, still apparently annoyed he'd had to change his name. "Our Da gives us all a ride into town but he had a cow in calf and we couldn't go until the bugger popped."

"Oh, I didn't realize you were all from farms."

She blinked. If that was the provincial leader's only concern she was adding a new picture to her wall of heroes.

"Well, Eula here ain't . . ."

Ewan waved.

". . . but Da picks her up on the edge of town. We'd all been part of 4-H but we had to keep Karen away from the sheep if you know what I mean; wink-wink, nudge-nudge."

"Oi, none of that you lying bastard!"

She cleared her throat. Callum stopped his charge, sighed, and tossed a coin in the curse cup, muttering, "Knuckle sandwich later, boyo."

Conner sidled up to Janet and tugged on her sleeve. "I learned to read here."

"Well, good for you."

"I got a badge for it."

"Congratulations." Her pleasure seemed genuine.

"But there's no one there!"

Everyone turned to stare at the minister's wife who had collapsed into a chair and was visibly shaking.

"She takes a header, dibs on mouth to mouth!"

"I'm for CPR me!"

"You just wants ta grab her boobies."

"Brownies!"

The rush toward the minister's wife stopped cold.

"With me, please. Let Guider O'Neill handle this."

They muttered but they fell in behind her as Janet eased the minister's wife up out of the chair.

"Come on, Mrs. Jackson. I'll just take you home now and maybe we'll make a few phone calls, all right?" Half way up the stairs, the smaller woman supported against her shoulder, she turned and smiled. "It was lovely to meet you all. And I'm sorry for the misunderstanding."

"Nice lady that," Ewan announced as the outside door closed.

"It's called a glamour," Big Tam explained before she could ask. "The dark one, for all she was here to check you out, truly wanted to see Brownies so that's what she saw and heard—wee girls. The other, well, she'd convinced herself that there were no such thing as Brownies hadn't she? So that's all she saw."

"It's not quite a lie," Callum added.

They watched anxiously for her reaction.

"You're not responsible for people's expectations but," she added as they began to preen, "it is important that people not have low expectations of you and I don't think you can get lower than Mrs. Jackson's."

Little Tam nodded. "No expectations at all, I'd say that's lower than an ant's arse."

"I think it would be a good troop project to raise those expectations."

By summer, the minister's wife had gotten used to a spotless house, clean clothes, cooked meals, and landscaping the envy of the neighborhood. She started a pilates course, had an affair with UPS driver, and seemed a lot happier.

The Brownies picked up two more badges.

They couldn't go to camp . . .

"Glamour a great group of little girls? No offense, Missus, but are you daft?"

. . . so they learned about the wonders of nature by hiking together in the woods outside of town.

She learned there were unicorns in the woods.

"Why is it they won't come to you, Missus Owl?"

"That's none of your business, Big Tam."

They gathered to watch the Perisis Meteor shower for their *Key to Stem* badge.

"Make a wish, Missus Owl."

"It's not a falling star, Ewan. It's a piece of rock burning up in the atmosphere."

"Aye, but make a wish anyway."

So she did.

They got their *Key to the Living World* badge by joining the fall Trash Bash and cleaning up a full five kilometers of road.

"It doesn't count as trash if it's parked in someone's garage, Conner."

"But it's a Lada, Missus Owl."

"Put it back."

Callum got his *Pet Pals* badge by directing the dump rats in a performance of West Side Story. It was the best amateur theatre she'd seen in years.

That Halloween she dressed as a Gypsy. Big Tam was leprechaun. Little Tam a Fianna. Conner as Jack-in-Irons. Ewan a Phouka. And Callum came as Britney Spears.

* * *

At Christmas, they delivered gift baskets to the seniors at Markam Manner. The Brownies picked out the contents themselves. Since the seniors seemed to appreciate being treated as adults instead of grey-haired children, she decided to consider the baskets a success. The staff of the nursing home were less accepting but then they were the ones dealing with the aftereffects.

By spring, all five vests were covered in badges—all the key badges and all but two of the interest badges. There were no Sparks for them to help—not necessarily a bad thing—and as they'd tried and failed to hack CSIS on her laptop, she'd refused to give them their *Information Technology* badge on principal.

Most leaders kept their troops intact until the end of summer so the girls could have one more visit to camp but since that was still out of the question she decided they should fly up in the spring.

She liked the symbolism better; new growth, new life, and the same ceremony her old Brown Owl had used when she'd flown up.

The Brownies appeared as they always did a few moments after she'd set the toadstool in place. They recited the Law and the Promise and, with a minimal amount of insults and no profanity at all, sat down.

She had a whole speech prepared dealing with what it meant to be a Brownie and what it meant to leave that behind and move on but looking around the circle, from face to face, all that seemed somehow presumptuous. They knew more about what it meant to be a Brownie than she ever would.

So all she said was, "It's time."

They looked a lot like her girls then, a little scared, very excited—quite a bit hairier.

She'd built a three step platform, shallow steps so that to the top was no more than a foot off the ground. Two posts—broom handles really—wrapped in sparkly ribbon and attached to the platform with more ribbon strung between them made a low door. Hanging from the ribbon were five sets of construction paper butterfly wings.

"Big Tam."

He started, stood, and walked to the first step, tugging his vest into place. She smiled reassuringly and he nodded.

"Do your best to be honest and kind." A light touch on his shoulder.

One step.

"Be true to yourself."

Two steps.

"Help to take care of the world around you."

He was on the platform now.

"Take your wings and fly."

She'd written their names on the construction paper in lavender glitter ink. A little girly maybe but old habits were hard to break.

Big Tam reached for his wings, took a deep breath, and without looking back, jumped through the door.

The way he disappeared into a soft white light that smelled of fresh mown hay came as no great surprise. The brass band playing *She'll be Coming Round the Mountain*, well, that was a little unsettling but she coped.

Little Tam. Callum. Conner. Ewan. Who paused on the platform and said, "Thank you."

"You're welcome."

Alone in the basement of the church hall, she reached up to take the ribbon down and shrieked as Big Tam's head appeared between the broom handles, the first time in thirty-seven years she'd been taken by surprise.

"Oi, Missus. You comin'?"

"I'm not . . ."

Over the sound of a euphonium solo, she heard: "Oi! Get yer flamin' mitts of me wings!"

"I'll wing you, ya skeezy pervert!"

"You'd best bring the ice pack," Big Tam sighed as he disappeared.

She scooped it out of the cooler, picked up the curse cup, and climbed to the top of the platform. As she ducked under the ribbon, she wondered if her old wings still worked . . .

Blood in the Water

This is actually the second story I started for Army of the Fantastic. The request was for military fiction using fantastical creatures and the examples given seemed to suggest that what was wanted was actual military battle rewritten with those creatures—dragons as air force, centaurs as cavalry . . . that sort of thing. I knew early on I was going to use The Battle of the St. Lawrence—I cleared the naval thing with the editor who actually wanted Military of the Fantastic but thought that kind of sucked as a title—but I couldn't decide if I was going to do what would be WWII era contemporary fantasy or shift the whole battle to a fantasy world. Eventually, I decided on the later and ended up liking the story and the characters so much I'm thinking of expanding it into a novel. Also, the whole Navy Seals thing is damned clever if I do say so myself.

"Mister Trynt! Get that anchor line on the lateen moved aft!"

"Aye, sir!"

With the line moved and more of the sail engaged, Captain Harl shaded his eyes and searched for the shadow against the horizon that meant land. Cut off from the mainland by the Catlaine Strait, the island of Barravista had always depended on the sea—on the fish that silvered the water over the coastal shoals, on the ships that brought in the food the rocky, windswept soil couldn't produce. When the war had threatened to cut them off, when privateers backed by the enemy's treasury had swept in from the south stripping schooners and caravels bare, Queen Isabella had called in Admiral Buryl and commanded him to take control of the sea lanes . . ." . . . *hold against all Navareen aggression. I will not have the edges of my empire starved into surrender."*

So the Admiral had pulled the *Dawn Arrow* out of the battle in the gulf, loaded its hold with grain and wine and oil and sent it to Barravista. After the *Arrow's* heavy catapult had sent the third privateer to the bottom in flames, the rest had cut their losses and headed south for easier pickings. Unfortunately, the Admiral had decided to maintain the show of force and Harl continued to ply the merchanter's route, the only danger the monotony of an easy passage.

"Land ho!"

The cry from the crow's-nest, jerked him out of his reverie.

"Tighten up those lines; let's put some wind in those sails! I want to clear that headland by . . ."

Impact threw him against the helmsman. He swore and grabbed for a ratline, hauling himself back up onto his feet.

"Heading?"

"We're dead on course, sir." The helmsman hauled the wheel around. 'It's no reef."

"Debris?" There'd been enough merchant ships taken down in these waters to add the hazard of floating timbers to the trip.

"Nothing on the surface, sir!" the bow lookout called. She hooked her legs around the bowsprit and leaned out over the water. "And nothing just be . . ."

"Serpent!"

"In these seas?" Harl snarled as he turned toward the call. "Don't be . . ."

Its head was already a tall man's height above the waves and still rising. Glistening green and gold and blue, the color of sunlight on the sea, it blinked onyx eyes and tasted the air with a forked tongue. The only sound was the lap of water on wood and the hum of the wind in the lines as the crew stood frozen in shock. The great serpents were rare even in the south and never seen this far north.

It rose above the starboard rail.

Almost up the lowest spar.

"Archers!" The Weapons Master's voice shattered the silence and jerked the crew into action.

Harl clamped his teeth shut on commands of his own. They were already running full out and had no hope of out-distancing the serpent even should he find more wind.

"Fire at will!"

As the serpent continued to rise, a rain of arrows bounced off iridescent scales and fell into the sea.

"Aim for the eyes!"

But the eyes had risen past the upper spar, the folds and ridges of the creature's muzzle making it an impossible shot from below. As Harl watched in horror, the great head dove forward between the masts and arced down over the port side. Between one heartbeat and the next, a belt of flesh constricted around the ship.

"Blades!"

The belt tightened unmarked by weapons. Ends of broken lines whipped around the masts. A body tumbled shrieking from torn rigging to the water. The upper rail splintered.

"All hands!" Harl bellowed pulling his long knife and charging forward. "Use your points! In behind the lap!"

They drew blood then but not enough. It had barely splashed against the deck when the deck boards shattered. Curses and prayer came mixed from the sailors chancing the sea and the monster within it rather than be caught in the dangerous mess of wreckage.

As the masts toppled and the weight of the sails pulled the halves apart, Captain Harl went down with his ship, still driving his knife between the serpent's scales. Finally, lungs screaming for air, he kicked toward the surface.

Felt sharp teeth close around his waist.

"So there's a sea serpent in the Catlaine Strait destroying ships and then devouring the crews."

"Yes, sir. One of my people was on the *Sea Shepard*. Given his report I believe the *Lord Ryden* and the *Dawn Arrow* suffered the same fate."

Admiral Buryl peered out from under heavy brows at his head of Naval Intelligence. "If this serpent is devouring the crews, how did your man escape?"

"My people are very fast swimmers when motivated, sir."

"No doubt," muttered the admiral's aide. "Your people excel at getting away."

Gaison NcTran ignored her and, with an effort, kept from rubbing the stump of his left arm. His people gathered intelligence, they didn't fight battles they had no hope of winning nor did they die trying to save lives already lost.

"The moment we knew the *Arrow* was lost, I would have put one of your people on the *Ryden*. We wouldn't have lost the *Shepard* if we'd had word earlier."

He turned to the nearer of the two Captains who'd accompanied the admiral to the briefing. "Our assumption was that the privateers had returned more heavily armed. Until we had confirmation this wasn't so, my people were better deployed elsewhere. Our numbers are limited and we need to go where we can be best used."

"You need to be used where you're most needed!"

They locked eyes. The captain looked away first. Unlike the admiral's aide who had all the prejudices of a fisher family toward shapeshifters who were not only their competition in the boats but had the unfair advantage of becoming seals in the water, the captain spoke from distress at loss of ships, of life.

"And you're sure, NcTran, you're sure this serpent is being used by the enemy?"

"As sure as I can be, sir." Gaison turned his attention back to the admiral. "They hate the cold and the Catlaine Strait is never warm. Even in the south, they rarely bother with ships because the food value isn't worth the effort expended. And, more tellingly, the Navareen fishing fleets have left the Empire Banks."

"They're paying the serpent in fish?"

The Navareen were paying the serpent the way all those who brought a tactical advantage to war were paid - it had been deeded its own estate, sole access to one of the richest fishing areas in the West Sea. But as that essentially meant they were paying it in fish, Gaison nodded. "Yes, sir."

"Wonderful." Admiral Buryl sighed and stared down at the map table. "It's not enough we're fighting them on the sea, now we have to fight them under it as well. Can you talk to it?"

"It, sir?"

"The serpent, man, the serpent! If it was convinced to fight for the Navareen, maybe you can convince it to change sides."

"Unfortunately, Admiral, even if we had something to offer it . . ." And there was no need to add that they didn't. ". . . none of my people speak serpent. The Navareen have to have paid for the services of a Mer."

"A Mer?"

"It's the only way they could make the deal, sir."

Buryl sighed. "They must really want to win this war if they're willing to dump that much of their treasury into the sea. All right, we can't talk to it and we can't out run it. Can we go around it? Stay in water too shallow for it maybe."

"Unfortunately, there's no way to get to Barravista without crossing deep water. Miles of deep water," he added, turning enough to the side that he could trace a large area out on the map with his remaining hand. "The serpent could be anywhere in this area."

"Wonderful. What's left?"

Gaison shrugged. "We destroy it, sir."

"Of course we do. How?"

"The Mer . . ."

"Too expensive." The second captain, the Admiralty's member on council raised her hand, cutting him off. "Even if the council would allow the expenditure, this war's left bugger all in the treasury. You'll have to think of something else."

Buryl reached out and picked the wooden ship representing the *Dawn Arrow* off the table. "Think of it soon, McTan, or we lose Barravista. Make stopping this serpent your first concern."

"Sir, my regular duties . . ."

"Can be handled by your second. The Queen refuses to lose that island which makes it our job to hang onto it. Go. And I don't want this to get out," he continued, his voice stopping Gaison with his hand on the door. "People find out Navareen's sent a sea serpent into our waters and we'll have panic in every village up and down the coast. Every idiot who lives by the sea will be assuming the serpent's come for them. No offense."

All of Gaison's people lived by the sea. "None taken, sir."

No point in being offended at an accurate observation.

"Gaison!"

Closing the admiral's door behind him, he turned to see Jeordi NcMarin, his Second and a cousin on his mother's side, hurrying along the corridor, a sheaf of paper in one hand.

"We had a bird from outpost seven." Jeordi thrust the paper toward him. "Mirag made landfall day before yesterday. She says there's a new design being built in the Navareen shipyards. Shallow draft, lean and fast. She thinks they're planning a run up the coast."

Gaison nodded, ignoring the paper. "Makes sense. What with our attention on deep water right now. What about the second bird confirming?"

"Not yet. Weather's been unsettled. It may have run into trouble."

"It may have been shot and eaten," Gaison snorted. "Wouldn't be the first time. Take the report into Admiral Buryl."

"Me?" Jeordi's dark eyes widened.

"He's got me dealing with the trouble in the Catlaine Strait." No need to be more specific, not within the Admiralty wing.

"Dealing? How?"

"Damned if I know."

When the war with Navareen escalated from a border conflict into out and out conquest, Queen Isabella had conscripted all the mages within her borders into her service. Since four of the six were already in her service and the fifth had just celebrated his 107th birthday while the sixth had barely passed his 17th, this made very little impact on either the mages or the nation.

They'd been given the top floor of the palace's old south range and told to direct their studies toward winning the war. Their only contribution to date had been a spell that delayed the ignition of fireballs until the impact with the target shattered the glass ball containing the spell. When it worked, when the cork remained in the ball and the catapult operators hit the target, the results were impressive–but only the glassblowers were completely happy with it.

The way Gaison saw it, enlisting the wizards might not help but considering what they were facing, it couldn't hurt.

"Preposterous." The middle-aged woman peered at him from under an impressive tangle of bright red hair. "Sea serpents don't come this far north."

Gaison sighed and tried again. "This one's working for the Navareen. They've sent it north into our shipping lanes to cut off Barravista. It's attacking our ships from below."

"Well of course it's attacking from below. It would hardly be attacking from above, now would it? You're one of the seal people, aren't you? Got your skin put away safe do you? Have you been to a Council meeting? This palace is a den of thieves, you know that right? I imagine you'd be lost if it was stolen wouldn't you? Couldn't change then, could you?"

"What do you want *us* to do about this serpent?" asked another wizard while Gaison still reeled under the spate of questions from the first.

He turned away from the redhead faster than was strictly polite. "I need to destroy it and I was hoping you might have some ideas."

"As a general rule when the great serpents begin hunting in

shipping lanes, it's easier to move the shipping than the serpent." The youngest wizard looked up from the massive book in front of him and Gaison caught a glimpse of an illustration of a ship split in two—very much like what had been reported happening in the Caitlaine Strait. "Is that possible?"

"Not this time. Her Majesty doesn't want to lose Barravista."

"I imagine Barravista doesn't want to be lost, does it?" snorted the red head.

"No. But neither," Gaison added pointedly, "do we want to lose more ships or more lives. They're going down with all hands and I have orders to stop it. It seems the only way to stop it is to destroy the serpent."

"The only way? The only way?" A wizard wrapped tightly about with strips of blue cloth rolled her eyes. "Isn't that just like the army."

"Navy."

She ignored him. "The only way is destruction! Typical. Honestly. It takes your arm, you take its life."

"What?' He glanced down at his pinned sleeve then up at the wizard. "I lost the arm in the last war. The serpent had nothing to do with it."

The redhead snorted again. "So you say."

Nodding and grumbling, four of the six wizards returned to what they'd been doing when he arrived. The fifth continued snoring and the sixth squared his shoulders.

"I'll see what I can do," the youngest wizard said. "I had an uncle on the *Dawn Arrow.*"

Gaison had almost reached the shipyard when he realized the wizards had given him an answer.

"What do you mean we don't have to destroy it?" Admiral Buryl growled.

"It's the ultimate solution, sir, but until we can work out how, what we really need to do is get ships through to Barravista and home again."

"You're trying my patience, NcTran."

"Sorry, sir." Gaison straightened involuntarily, as though he were back on board ship being chewed out by the mate. "If the great serpents don't normally attack shipping because there's so little food return for the effort they put out, what we need to do is draw the serpent away from the ship with food that won't require much of an effort. Decoy food."

"Decoy food?"

"Yes, sir. When the serpent is spotted, half a dozen of my people will hit the water and lure it away from the ship, they'll lose it in the shallows off the west end of Barravista, follow the shoals around to the harbor and pick up the ship for the trip back where they'll do the same thing."

Heavy brows drew in. "You can order your people to be sea serpent food?"

"Decoy sea serpent food, sir. I'm pulling six of my best off intelligence work. After all, we excel at getting away." He glanced over at the admiral's aide, who colored.

Buryl stared at the map, at the blocks of wood that represented three ships lost with all hands, at the outline of the island cut off from desperately needed supplies. "They're *sure* they'll be fast enough?"

That was the question, wasn't it? Gaison rubbed at the stump of his left arm. "Unfortunately, there's only one way to find out."

"There's another problem. Your report mentioned that the lookout didn't see the serpent until it surfaced for the attack. That's too late to decoy it away."

"It is well camouflaged, sir but I think I have a solution. It doesn't go deep because it doesn't like the cold and so it tends to stay just under the surface where there's some warmth from the sun . . ."

"Wait."

Gaison fell silent while the admiral gathered his thoughts.

"If it can swim that shallow," Buryl asked after a moment, "how can your people lose it in the shoals?"

"Shallow's not the same as just under the surface, sir. Something that big needs a lot of water around it."

"Yes, well, you'd know," The admiral grunted, his gaze flicking over the other man's bulk. "Carry on then."

"The lookouts couldn't see the serpent because of their angle . . ." He sketched it in the air. ". . . and the reflection of light on the water but if we brought in some aerial support . . ."

"What did you have in mind, NcTran?"

"We borrow a couple of Hawk-eyes from the army."

The waves remained ever changing, no section of the sea the same twice, but Donal NcAylo was positive they were nearly at the point the *Dawn Arrow* had gone down. "Anything yet?"

"No. Nothing. There was nothing half a second ago and there's nothing now." Somehow the Hawk-eye managed to glare even through her feathered blindfold. "When I see something, you'll be the first . . ."

"What?" he demanded in the pause.

"I see something."

Donal stepped away from the scout and peered up at her hawk—a black spec growing larger as it broke off its search pattern and dove toward the sea.

"It's the serpent." The Hawk-eye cocked her head. "Damn, that thing's huge."

"Starboard side, people! Let's move!" He slipped out of his breeches as his team joined him. "Remember we're going to draw it as deep as we can. The cold water will slow it down."

"Big snakes don't like the cold," his brother Eryc muttered as he stripped.

"That's not what I'd call a big snake," a cousin snorted, glancing at his crotch as she tossed her clothes onto the pile.

"Keep your attention on the job," Donal reminded them. "Maintain formation as long as possible; we want it to think it can get us all in one mouthful." Scooping up his skin, he went over the rail, aware of his team hitting the water behind him even as he changed to seal-shape.

A quick surface to check position—no mistaking Eryc, he was a big man and a bigger seal—then a deep breath and, digging at the sea with his flippers, Donal led his team toward the serpent.

When he heard the hawk scream a warning, he rose just far enough to fill his lungs then, nostrils clamped shut, he slid down into the trough of a wave and dove. Felt the others dive behind him. Felt currents shift and eddy as death changed course.

Donal tipped the whole formation deeper—left flippers up, right down, powerful tails beating against the sea—and felt the water begin to cool. The serpent followed.

So far, so good.

"Well, it's not stupid, I'll say that much for it but it *is* hungry so the plan worked." Donal accepted the mug of sweet tea with thanks and all but gulped it down. "Worked better on the way there than the way back though, Gaison. If Kytlin hadn't rolled back and slammed it in the eye, Eryk's rear flippers would have been a mouthful shorter."

"She damage it?"

The younger man shook his head. "Startled it is all, threw it off its stroke. Fortunately, we know these waters and it doesn't so we worked the currents and got clear." He held out his empty mug.

Gaison took it, refilled it, then walked over to the window. He could see the tops of masts in the harbor, smell the salt, hear the gulls and wanted nothing more than to swim away and leave the serpent for someone else to deal with. "Can you do it again?" he asked without turning.

"What, now?"

"We've had information that Navareen is planning to send two ships out and around to attack Barravista from the west." Gaison turned then, his hand falling to stroke the seal skin lying on the end of his desk. "Her Majesty is sending two of the new warships out to defend the island."

Donal's dark eyes narrowed. "They'll be stationed there? With full war crews?"

"Yes."

"That'll mean . . ."

"Supply ships will have to run more frequently, yes." He waited while Donal thought it through, weighing the condition of his team against need.

"Will the army let us keep the Hawk-eye?"

"The army has volunteered another two pairs."

"Really?"

"No." Donal's expression forced out the first smile Gaison had managed in weeks. "But the admiral convinced the queen that we needed the air support so the army had no choice." Then he sobered. "I'm putting together another two teams but it'll take time to pull people from the water and replace them with . . ."

"The young and the old," Donal filled in the pause.

"Younger and older," Gaison corrected, praying the war wouldn't last long enough to make Donal's words true. "Next time you're in, you'll get leave, but this time . . ."

He scooped up the bag that held his seal skin and stood. "Duty calls."

Eyrk's luck ran out on the return trip. They lost two members of the second team the trip after that. The next trip ran clean. The next they lost another two and Donal lost a back flipper when he turned to help a cousin caught but not dead. The serpent had slid further up onto the shoals than it ever had before. It *wasn't* stupid. It was learning and it was losing interest in the decoys. The last team practically had to feed themselves to it to get it to follow. The only good news was that with the serpent in the strait the sharks stayed away, even when there was blood in the water.

Gaison finished his report for the admiral and worked the stiffness out of his hand. The ships were safe, but at what cost? His people, their numbers never large, were dwindling. His family mourned. They were not the only family mourning of course, this war with Navareen was being fought and men and women were dying in places other than the Strait of Catlaine, but there were damned few among his people not family by blood or marriage so every death swept past them all like an icy current.

The serpent had to be destroyed.

Unfortunately, all the information he'd been able to gather suggested the serpent couldn't be destroyed. They had no way to attack it under water and it only surfaced when it attacked a ship. Conventional weapons were useless until it was close enough to drive blades up under its scales and by then it was far too close for blades to matter.

It had no natural predators and poison enough to kill it would destroy everything else living in the strait. Gaison had even asked the herbalist about poisoning himself and then diving into the sea to poison the serpent. She'd shaken her head and said, *"If this creature is as large as you tell me, you could not swallow enough poison to kill it. Seven, maybe eight of your people yes, provided it got you all down before it noticed how nasty you tasted."*

Seven or eight to save the rest. They hadn't come to that yet, but they might . . .

A tentative knock brought him back to his office. He waited for Jeordi to open the door, remembered Jeordi had gone to the strait, and barked, "What is it?"

A thin, almost familiar young man stuck his head into the room. It looked as though bits of his hair had been burned away. "Commander NcTran?"

No one used his rank as a title. "What it is?" he asked again, beckoning the young man in.

"I think I know how we can destroy the serpent."

Gaison frowned as he shoved back his chair and stood. "You're the sixth wizard."

"Alaster Grant."

Of course he had a name. And, apparently, a solution.

"It's a variation on the time delay spell we set up for the catapults. We tuck it into a heavy load, something that'll sink fast, and, at the same depth as the serpent swims, it'll explode."

"Explosions under water?"

"Yes. It's the depth that sets the spell that blows the charge."

"What if the serpent changes depth?"

"Each spell can be set before it's fired."

"The explosions will disorient it," Gaison allowed. "Might give the ships time to get clear."

Alaster straightened thin shoulders. "Pack the load with nails. It may do more than disorient it."

Gaison grinned and grabbed the young wizard's arm. The scorch marks on his robe matched his hair. "I like the way you think. Come on."

"No! I couldn't find anyone to get you! I'm not supposed to be out of the workshop!"

"Workshop be damned, lad. You're going to sea."

"I'd feel better about this if we could take a few practice shots," the Weapons Master on the *Dark Dancer* grunted, glaring at the wizard once again bending over the rail.

Jeordi shrugged, tugging the heavy fleece robe tighter around his shoulders. He was too old to stand in a north east wind wearing nothing but breeches. "Alaster says the spells are hard to set and this . . ." A nod toward the row of eight depth charges. "This is all we have."

"Better be enough or your lot'll be freezing your tails off in the water."

"We'll be warmer in sealskins," Jeordi told him. "And the colder the water gets, the better our odds of out swimming the serpent."

The Weapons Master turned his scowl on the four men huddled around the Hawk-eye, their bulk shielding her from the worst of the wind. "No women in this group."

"No." Just younger and older men. Young and old men soon enough if the serpent wasn't stopped.

"Are we there yet?" Alaster moaned, staggering back, wiping his mouth.

Before either Jeordi or the Weapons Master could answer, the Hawk-eye stiffened and cried, "Serpent!"

Jeordi grinned. "That would be a yes."

Firing coordinates came from the bird struggling to maintain position in the chill wind, to the Hawk-eye, to the Weapon's Master. There was no need to reset the first spell; unsuspecting, the serpent cruised at its usual depth.

The explosion to larboard was muffled but near enough to the surface that a geyser of water shot up tying sea to sky.

"It didn't like that!" the Hawk-eye called, as someone cheered from the forecastle. "It's turned. New coordinates left about twenty degrees, maybe three meters deeper . . ."

Brow furrowed, Alaster laid his hands on the charge.

The second shot drove it deeper still. The third . . .

"I can't tell for sure," the Hawk-eye cocked her head as her bird barely skimmed the tops of the waves, "but I think it took damage!"

The fourth went off close enough to the ship that there were a series of small thuds below the water line and the fifth blew another geyser.

Then a long silence as half the crew of the *Dark Dancer* watched the bird, wheeling against low grey cloud, and half the crew watched the Hawk-eye.

"I can't see it," she said at last.

"Is it dead?" the captain called from her place by the helm.

"I don't think so. But it's gone!"

"What if it comes back before we get clear of the strait," Jeordi asked under the cheers.

The Weapons Master shrugged. "Then we hit it again."

"And on the return trip?"

They looked together at the three remaining charges and then went to rescue Alaster from the enthusiastic congratulations of the crew.

Injured or cautious, the serpent stayed well away for the remainder of the voyage into Barravista. For the five days in port Jeordi's team escorted the wizard from one celebration to another. Feted by sailors and locals both, Alaster was so overwhelmed by the attention that Jeordi was amused to note he actually welcomed their return to the *Dark Dancer* even if it meant a return to hanging over the rail.

When the Hawk-eye spotted the serpent on the trip back to the mainland, everyone watched and waited, breath held, as Alaster laid shaking hands on the first charge and reset the spell.

"It's turning. Heading aft!"

The second charge arced over the stern, disappeared beneath the waves, and blew a column of water nearly the serpent's height into the sky.

"It's not coming any closer!"

"Hold that last charge!" the Weaponsmaster bellowed. "Keep it in reserve until that monster comes closer in!"

A day and a half later, they sailed into the harbor with the last charge still loaded but unfired. The serpent had followed at a cautious distance to the edge of the deep water. Once or twice it lifted its head above the waves and fixed the ship in an onyx gaze as thought trying to work out just how exactly it's intended prey was connected to the noise and pressure and pain but it came no closer.

The captain had sent a bird when they reached safety and Gaison was waiting on the pier.

"Not dead, but definitely discouraged," Jeordi called as his commander came aboard. "Alaster's done it. The strait is ours again."

"Glad to hear it." Gaison gripped his cousin's shoulder then turned his attention to the wizard. "The admiral wants you with him when he speaks to the queen. Her Majesty will be well pleased with what you've accomplished, your Wisdom." He grinned as Alaster looked startled at the honorific. "I expect she'll want to reward you before you head back to Barravista."

"Back?"

"Well, I imagine her Majesty will eventually order at least one of the other wizards shipboard but for now, you're it."

"Me?"

"The *Sea Vixen* leaves tomorrow on the late tide."

Eyes wide, Alaster clutched at Gaison's sleeve. "But we've only one charge remaining!"

"Here."

"No. Well, yes, but here is all there is. I only had ingredients to make the eight before we left."

Gaison stared at the wizard, at Jeordi, and just because he needed a few moments more to gather his thoughts, up into the rigging. "All right," he said at last. "I'll tell the Admiral you need more time and he can delay the *Vixen* until she can be armed. While you're building new charges, you'll put together a workshop so that while you're at sea everything but the final spell can be reconstructed ready for your return. How much time do you need?"

"Two of the elements are very rare . . ."

"You'll have access to all the manpower you need," Gaison told him. "How much time?"

"Six or seven months."

"What?"

"Five," Alaster squeaked, taking a step back. "Five, if the army has retaken Harstone and reopened the mines."

"Six or seven months!"

The army had not retaken Harstone.

Alaster ducked behind Jeordi as Admiral Buryl stomped around his office growling curses under his breath. The admiral had gone to sea at fifteen and he had a wide variety of profanity to work through. Finally, he wound down, took a deep breath and glared at his head of Naval Intelligence. "Now what?"

Gaison glanced at his cousin. "My people go back in the water, sir," he said.

"Will that even work?" the admiral demanded. "Suppose the serpent thinks aha, those seals are in the water again. There were no explosions when they were in the water before so there'll be none now and I can go after that ship. You said it was already losing interest in the decoys."

"Yes, but I don't think it thinks like that." Gaison half shrugged as the admiral's brows rose dramatically. His job was to know, not to think, and to find out if he didn't know. Unfortunately, in this situation they had theories but no facts.

"It was hanging back on the return trip," Jeordi offered. "Maybe that last charge might discourage it permanently."

"Maybe. Might." the admiral grunted. "I can't risk crews on a maybe or a might. The only way to permanently discourage that monster is to destroy it."

"If the serpent would swallow a charge . . ." Alaster began, flushed and fell silent as the other three turned to stare.

"Go on," Gaison prodded.

The youngest wizard looked as though he wanted to run but he cleared his throat, and finally managed to keep talking. "Well, if it would swallow a charge it's possible that at a certain depth, when the spell went off, its physiognomy would react violently."

"Its what?"

"Its um . . . its physical construction."

"How violently?"

"Ka boom. Where the ka refers to the charge blowing and the boom to the serpent."

"How possible?"

Alaster cleared his throat again. "Fairly."

"Would you risk your life on it?" Admiral Burl demanded.

After a long moment, Alaster nodded.

"If we could get it to open its mouth," Gaison began.

"It would be easy enough to slap it in before the spell went off," Jeordi finished.

"Easy," the admiral snorted. But he didn't argue. "I assume this puts your people back in the water, NcTran." He drummed his fingers against his desk. "One question, if its lost interest in the decoys, how do your people get it to open its mouth?"

Gaison rubbed the stump of his left arm. "We make it an offer too good to ignore."

"I can't believe Admiral Buryl agreed to let you do this," Jeordi muttered, head sunk deep within the high collar of his robe. "Setting yourself up as bait is completely insane. You're in no kind of shape to be doing this."

"If I was in shape," Gaison reminded him, "this wouldn't work. And besides, it's not like I'll be swimming alone—there'll be others in the water."

"And a sea serpent!"

Feet braced against the movement of the deck, Gaison ignored his cousin's protest the way he'd been ignoring his protests ever since he'd floated the plan. He'd always been among the larger of his people and the last decade of relative inaction had helped to pack on more bulk. The serpent would not only see a large, meaty seal, it'd see a large meaty seal missing half a front flipper. Food that had no chance of getting away.

"What if it sees the charge?"

"What? With me there to snack on? I doubt it."

"All right, what if you can't get clear? What if it takes you as well as the charge? What if Alastar's wrong and there's just ka, not ka boom?"

"Then it looks like you get my job." When no response was immediately forthcoming, Gaison clapped the younger man on the shoulder. "Look at the bright side; we're almost in sight of land with no sign of the serpent."

And right on cue from the crow's-nest: "Land ho!"

Jeordi peered toward the low smudge of grey on the horizon. "Do you think it's gone?"

"Serpent! Starboard side!"

Gaison tightened his grip as the Hawk-eye tightened her bird's pattern. "Actually, no."

"This is insane," Jeordi repeated when Gaison dropped his robe.

Gaison ignored him as Alaster handed over a slightly scaled down charge hammocked in a length of net.

"It's set to go about six meters down," the wizard told him, pointedly not looking toward his stump. "You need to . . . it's just . . . I mean . . . Good luck."

"Thank you." Sealskin in his hand, net in his teeth, he waited until the others were all in the water and moving into position before he followed.

He missed the sea when he wasn't in it and he wasn't in it much these days. When this was over, one way or another, he'd spend more time in the water. Net still clenched in his teeth, charge dangling below him, Gaison pushed himself forward and down with his tail, right flipper sculling back hard to keep him swimming in a straight line.

He could feel the serpent drawing closer and every instinct screamed at him to turn and swim for his life. Down as far as he needed to be—below the serpent but above the depth to set the spell—he paused, hanging in the water, the charge hanging down by his tail, his single front flipper driving him around in a flailing aimless circle.

Sharks would find the performance irresistible. What large predator could resist prey already maimed?

Maimed undeniably but he'd had years to practice and adapt. When he finally came around to see the serpent diving for him, mouth gaping, he stopped his spin, flipped back and, releasing the net, slapped the charge right into the serpent's mouth. If he also emptied his bladder, no one needed to know.

The charge clanged off a row of serrated teeth and bounced down the creature's throat. Gaison knew that for a fact because he was staring right down that throat. Then two lithe forms slammed into his from below, driving him toward the surface. One of the longer teeth dug into his side as he twisted to clear the upper jaw. He rose in a haze of blood as the serpent continued down, too big to change direction immediately.

Two more dark shapes darted past, wedge shaped shadows in the deep and the serpent, cheated of a sure meal, followed.

Gaison knew it the moment Alaster's charge went off, knew it because with his two minders moving him toward the ship, he was free to twist his head back in time to see the great tail come whipping up toward the surface. He pushed the boy on his right hard away and rolled with the one on his left tight against his body. They fought turbulence sucking them under and down and had no idea how close they were to the ship until they slammed into it, his wound darkening the water with another cloud of blood.

Nostrils still clamped shut, he struggled to the surface pulling the stunned young seal with him. Heaving the limp body up onto his shoulders, he rolled it into the net and found himself rolled in turn by the second boy. By the sailors pulled them on board, the serpent had stopped writhing.

"I don't see it," the Hawk-eye announced.

Gaison shrugged out of his skin and stood, blood dripping to the deck as he counted his people. His two, one of them not happy but alive. One of the two who'd lead the serpent deeper. Two short.

Barking from the larboard side drew everyone across the deck and the two uninjured seals went back into the water to help roll a bleeding body into the net and then roll in after it.

"This isn't a wound I can treat a on a seal," the ship's medic protested so they pulled Jeordi out of his skin and wrapped a leather belt lightly around the stump of his leg.

"The serpent?" he gasped.

Gaison shook his head and turned toward the wizard.

"There was no boom," Alastar said, miserably. "There should have been a . . ."

The water on the larboard side of the ship suddenly erupted. Chunks of scaled meat slammed into the deck.

A moment later, there was only an oval of white foam bobbing on blue-green waves.

"I suspect that was your boom," Gaison said dryly, lifting the wizard back onto his feet.

Alaster stared down at the bloody mark where a fist-sized piece of meat had slammed into his chest. "Ow."

"You're lucky it wasn't a bigger piece."

"I know but . . ." He lifted his head, eyes suddenly widening. "It worked."

Gaison nodded, suddenly very, very tired. "It worked."

The wizard frowned as he counted the hunks of meat. "But the serpent was huge. Enormous. This can't be all of it."

"The rest of it sank," the Hawk-eye told them, holding her arm out for her bird. "Three, maybe four big sections heading for the bottom."

"It's dead then?"

"Idiot," Jeordi hissed through clenched teeth.

The cheering started then and continued into Barravista. This time, without an escort to run interference, Alaster lasted three days before he staggered back to the ship and hid out with the injured. Gaison sent a sloop out with birds to carry the message to the admiral and the queen.

A week later, after a heavily laden caravel came into port, the *Vixen* started home. Standing at the rail, watching the waves, Gaison realized that the serpent had gone down close enough to the *Dawn Arrow* that its body probably rotted on the seabed within sight of the first ship it had destroyed.

He couldn't help but feel that Captain Harl would enjoy the view.

Not That Kind of War

So the publisher decided that an anthology about women at war needed a woman co-editing at the very least. Because I'd just finished the second Torin Kerr space Marine novel, Better Part of Valor, *I was asked. I'd never edited anything before but since Alex Potter, the other editor, was going to be there to hold my hand and since I was going to be able to also write a story, I agree.*

It seemed obvious to pretty much everyone that I'd write a Torin Kerr story. This is a prequel to first book, Valor's Choice.

"WE STILL HAVE ONE HELL of a lot of colonists to get off this rock before we can leave." Captain Rose frowned out at Sho'quo Company's three surviving 2nd Lieutenants and the senior NCO's. "And every ship going up is going to need an escort to keep it from being blown to hell by the Others so we're on Captain Allon's timetable. Given the amount of action up there . . ." He paused to allow the distant crack of a vacuum jockey dipping into atmosphere to carry the point. ". . . we may be down here for a while. Bottom line, we have to hold Simunthitir because we have to hold the port."

"The Others have secured the mines," 2nd Lieutenant di'Pin Arver muttered, her pale orange hair flipping back and forth in agitation, "you'd think they'd be happy to be rid of us."

"*I'd* think so. Unfortunately, they don't seem to." The captain thumbed the display on his slate and a three dimensional map of Simunthitir rose up out of the holo-pad on the table. "Good news is, we're up against a mountain so, as long as our air support keeps kicking the ass of their air support, they can only come at us from one side. Bad news is, we have absolutely no maneuvering room and we're significantly out-numbered even if they only attack with half of what they've got on the ground."

In Staff Sergeant Torin Kerr's not inconsiderable experience, even the best officers liked to state the obvious. For example: *significantly out-numbered.* Sho'quo Company had been sent off to this mining colony theoretically to make a statement of force to the Other's scouts. They'd since participated in a rout and now were about to make one of those heroic last stands that played so well on the evening news. No one had apparently told the enemy that they were merely doing reconnaissance and they had, as a result, sent two full battalions—or the Other's equivalent—to take the mines.

"Lieutenant Arver, make sure your remaining STA's . . .

And what fun, they'd already lost two of their six surface to air missiles.

". . . are positioned to cover the airspace immediately over the launch platform. See if you can move one of them up here."

A red light flared on the targeting grid overlaying the map.

"Yes sir." The lieutenant keyed the position into her slate.

"Set your mortars up on level four. I want them high enough to have some range but not so high any return fire they draw may damage the port. You're going to have to take out their artillery or we are, to put it bluntly, well and truly screwed. Staff Sergeant Doctorow . . ."

"Sir."

Doctorow's platoon had lost its 2nd Lieutenant in the first exchange.

". . . I want all accesses to the launch platform in our hands ASAP. We don't need a repeat of Beniger."

With the Other's beating down the door, the civilians of Beniger had rushed the ships. The first had taken off so over-loaded it had crashed back, blown the launch pad and half the port. Granted, any enemy in the immediate area had also been fried but Torin figured the dead of Beniger considered that cold comfort.

"Lieutenant Garly, I want one of your squads on stretcher duty. Get our wounded up into port reception and ready to be loaded once all the civilians are clear. Take position on the second level but mark a second squad in case things get bad."

"Sir."

"Lieutenant Franks . . ."

Torin felt the big man beside her practically quiver in anticipation.

". . . you'll hold the first level."

"Sir!"

Just on the periphery of her vision, Torin saw Staff Sergeant Amanda Aman's mouth twitch and Torin barely resisted the urge to smack her. Franks, Torin's personal responsibility, while no longer a rookie, still had few shiny expectations that flared up at inconvenient moments. He no longer bought into the romance of war—his first time out had taken care of that—but he continued to buy into the romance of the warrior. Every now and then, she could see the desire to do great things rise in his eyes.

"You want to live on after you die, Staff . . ." He danced his fingers over *his touchpad, drawing out a martial melody. ". . . do something that makes it into a song."*

Torin didn't so much want Lieutenant Franks to live on after he died as to live on for a good long time so she smacked that desire down every time she saw it and worried about what would happen should it make an appearance when she wasn't around. The enemy smacked down with considerably more force. And their music sucked.

The captain swept a level stare around the gathered Marines. "Remember that our primary objective is to get the civilians out and then haul ass off this rock. We hold the port long enough to achieve this."

"Captain." First Sergeant Chigma's voice came in on the company channel. *"We've got a reading on the unfriendlies."*

"On my way." He swept a final gaze over the Marines in the room and nodded. "You've got your orders people."

Emerging out of the briefing room—previously known as the Simunthitir Council Chamber—the noise of terrified civilians hit Torin like a physical blow. While no one out of diapers was actually screaming, everyone seemed to feel the need to express their fear. Loudly. As if maybe Captain Allon would send down more frequent escorts from the orbiting carrier if he could only hear how desperate things had gotten.

Captain Rose stared around at the milling crowds. "Why are these people not at the port, First?"

"Port Authorities are taking their time processing, sir."

"Processing?"

"Rakva."

Although many of the Confederation's Elder Races took bureaucracy to a fine art, the Rakva reveled in it. Torin, who after twelve years in the Corps wasn't surprised by much, had once watched a line of the avains patiently filling out forms in triplicate in order to use a species specific sanitary facility. Apparently the feathers and rudimentary beaks weren't sufficient proof of species identification.

"They're insisting that everyone fill out emergency evacuation forms."

"Oh for the love of God . . . Deal with it."

Chigma showed teeth—a distinctly threatening gesture from a species that would eat pretty much anything it could fit down its throat and was remarkably adaptable about the later. "Yes sir."

"Captain . . ." Lieutenant Franks' golden brows drew in and he frowned after the First Sergeant. "Begging your pardon, sir, but a Krai may not be the most diplomatic . . ."

"Diplomatic?" the captain interrupted. "We've got a few thousand civilians to get off this rock before a whole crapload of Others climb right up their butts. If they wanted it done diplomatically, they should-n't have called in the Corps." He paused and shot the lieutenant a frown of his own. "Shouldn't you be at the first level by now?"

"Sir!"

Torin fell into step at his right shoulder as Franks hurried off the concourse and out onto the road that joined the seven levels of Simunthitir into one continuous spiral. Designed for the easy transportation of ore carriers up to the port, it was also a strong defensive position with heavy gates to close each level off from those below and the layout ensured that Sho'quo Company would maintain the high ground as they withdrew to the port. If not for the certain fact that the Others were traveling with heavy artillery—significantly heavier than their own EM223's—and sufficient numbers to climb to the high ground over the piled bodies of their dead, she'd be thinking this was a highly survivable engagement. Ignoring the possibility that the Others' air support would get off a lucky drop.

"Well, Staff, it looks like we've got the keys to the city. It's up to us to hold the gates at all costs."

And provided she could keep Lieutenant Franks from getting them all killed—but *that* was pretty much business as usual.

"Anything happen while I was gone?"

Sergeant Anne Chou shook her head without taking her attention from the scanner. "Not a thing. Looks like they waited until you got back."

Torin peered out over the undulating plain but couldn't see that anything had changed. "What are you getting?"

"Just picked up the leading edge of the unfriendlies but they're packed too close together to get a clear reading on numbers."

"Professional opinion?"

The other woman looked over at that and grinned. "One fuk of a lot, Staff."

"Great." Torin switched her com to command channel. "Lieutenant, we've got a reading on the perimeter."

"Is their artillery in range?"

"Not yet, sir." Torin glanced up into a sky empty of all but the distant flashes of the battle going on up above the atmosphere where the vacuum jockeys from both sides kept the other side from controlling the ultimate high ground. "I imagine they'll let us know."

"Keep me informed."

"Yes, sir."

"You think he's up to this?" Anne asked when Torin tongued off her microphone.

"Since the entire plan is that we shoot and back up, shoot and back up, rinse and repeat, I think we'll be fine." The lieutenant had to be watched more closely moving forward.

Anne nodded, well aware of the subtext. "Glad to hear it."

The outer walls of Simunthitir's lowest level of buildings presenting a curved stone face to the world about seven meters high, broken by a single gate. Running along the top of those buildings was a continuous line of battlement fronted by a stone balustrade about a meter and a half high.

Battlements and balustrades, Torin thought as she made her way to the gate. *Nothing like getting back to the basics.* "Trey, how's it going?"

The di'Taykan Sergeant glanced up, her hair a brilliant cerulean corona around her head. "She's packed tight, Staff. We're just about to fuse the plug."

They'd stuffed the gate full of the hovercraft used to move people and goods inside the city. Individually, each cart weighed about two hundred kilo's, hardly enough to stop even a lackluster assault, but crammed into the gateway—wrestled into position by the heavy gunner's and their exo-skeletons—and then fused into one solid mass by a few well placed demo charges, the gate would disappear and the city present a solid face to the enemy.

As Trey moved the heavies away, Lance Corporal Sluun moved

forward keying the final parameters into his slate.

"First in Go and Blow, eh?" Lieuentant Franks said quietly by Torin's left shoulder.

"Yes sir." Sluun had kicked ass at his TS3 demolition course.

A trio of planes screamed by closely followed by three Marine 774's keeping up a steady stream of fire. Two of the enemy managed to drop their loads—both missed the city—while the third peeled off in an attempt to engage their pursuers. The entire tableau shrieked out of sight in less than minute.

"I only mention it," the lieutenant continued when they could hear themselves think again, "because there's always the chance we could blow not only the gate but a section of the wall as well."

"Trust in the training, sir. Apparently Sluun paid attention in class."

"Firing in five . . ."

"We might want to step back, sir."

". . . *four* . . ."

"Trust in the training, Staff?"

". . . *three* . . ."

"Yes sir. But there's no harm in hedging our bets."

". . . *two* . . ."

They stopped four meters back.

". . . *one. Fire in the hole.*"

The stones vibrated gently under their feet.

And a moment later . . . "*We've got a good solid plug, Lieutenant.*" Trey's voice came over the group channel. "*They'll need the really big guns to get through it.*"

Right on cue: the distinctive whine of incoming artillery.

This time, the vibrations underfoot were less than gentle.

Four, five, six impacts . . . and a pause.

"Damage?"

"*Got a hole into one of the warehouses, Staff.*" Corporal Dave Hayman's voice came over the com. "*Demo team's filling in the hole now.*"

"Good." She tongued off the microphone. "Everything else hit higher up, sir. I imagine we've got civilian casualties."

Franks lips thinned. "Why the hell isn't Arver pulsing their targeting computers?" he demanded grimly.

Shots seven, eight, and nine missed the port entirely.

"I think it took them a moment to get the frequency, sir."

Ten, eleven, and twelve blew in the air.

Confident that the specialists were doing their jobs, the Marines on the wall ignored the barrage. They all knew there'd be plenty to get excited about later. Electronics were easy for both sides to block, which was why the weapon of choice in the Corps was a KC-7, a chemically operated projectile weapon. Nothing disrupted it but hands-on physical force and the weighted stock made a handy club in a pinch. Torin appreciated a philosophy that expected to get pinched.

Eventually, it would come down to flesh versus flesh. It always did.

As another four planes screamed by, Torin took a look over the front parapet and then turned to look back in over the gate. "Trey, you got any more of those carts down there?"

"Plenty of them, Staff."

"All right, lets run as many as will fit up here to the top of the wall and send those that don't fit up a level."

"Planning on dropping them on the enemy?" Lieutenant Franks grinned.

"Yes sir."

"Oh." Somewhat taken aback, he frowned and one of those remaining shiny patches flared up. "Isn't dropping scrap on the enemy, I don't know . . ."

Torin waited patiently as, still frowning, he searched for the right word.

"UnMarinelike?"

Or perhaps he'd needed the time to make up a new word.

"Look at it this way sir, if you were them and you thought there was a chance of having two hundred kilos dropped on your head, wouldn't you be a little hesitant in approaching the wall?"

"I guess I would . . ."

He guessed. Torin, on the other hand, knew full well that were the situations reversed, Lieutenant Franks would be dying to gallantly charge the port screaming *once more into the breach!* And since her place was beside him and dying would be the operative word, she had further reason to be happy they were on this side of the wall. If people were going to sing about her, she'd just as soon they sang about long career and a productive retirement.

The Others came over the ridge in a solid line of soldiers and machines, the sound of their approach all but drowning out the scream of the first civilian transport lifting off. Marine flyers escorted it as far as the edge of the atmosphere where the Navy took over and the Marines raced back to face the bomber the Other's had sent to the port. One of Lieutenant Arver's sammies took it out before it had a change to drop its load. The pilot arced around the falling plume of wreckage and laid a contrail off toward the mountains, chased away from the massed enemy by two ships from *their* air support.

According to Torin's scanner, these particular soldiers fighting for coalition the Confederation referred to as the Others were mammals; two, maybe three, species of them given the variant body temperatures. It was entirely possible she had more in common physically with the enemy than she did with at least half of the people she was expected to protect–the Rakva were avain, the Niln reptilian and both were disproportionately represented amongst the civilian population of Simunthitir.

The odds were even better that she'd have an easier time making conversation with any one of the approaching enemy than she would with any civilian regardless of species. Find her a senior non-com, and she'd guarantee it. Soldiering was a fairly simple profession after all. Achieve the objective. Get your people out alive.

Granted, the objectives usually differed.

Behind her in the city, in direct counter-point to her thoughts, someone screamed a protest at having to leave behind their various bits of accumulated crap as the remaining civilians on the first level were herded toward the port. It never failed to amaze her how people hung on to the damnedest things when running for their lives. The Others *would* break into the first level. It was only a question of when.

She frowned at an unlikely reading.

"What is it, Staff Sergeant?"

"I'm not sure . . ." There were six, no seven, huge inert pieces of something advancing with the enemy. They weren't living and with no power signature they couldn't be machinery.

The first of Lieutenant Arver's mortars fired, locked on to the enemy's artillery. The others followed in quick succession, hoping to get in a hit before their targeting scanners were scrambled in turn. A few Marines cheered as something in the advancing horde blew. From the size of the explosion, at least one of the big guns had been taken out–along with the surrounding soldiers.

"They're just marching into an entrenched position," Franks muttered. "This won't be battle, this will be slaughter."

"I doubt they'll just keep marching, sir." Almost before she finished speaking, a dozen points flared on her scanner and she switched her com to group . . ." It's about to get noisy people!" . . . and dropped behind one of the carts. Lieutenant Franks waited until the absolute last moment before joining her. She suspected he was being an inspiration to the platoon. Personally, she always felt it was more inspiring to have your lieutenant in one piece, but hey, that was her.

The artillery barrage before the battle—any battle—had one objective. Do as much damage to the enemy as possible. Their side. The other side. All a soldier could do was wait it out and hope they didn't get buried in debris.

"Keep them from sneaking forward, people!" It wasn't technically necessary to yell, the helmet coms were intelligent enough to pick up her voice and block the sound of the explosions in the air, the upper city, and out on the plains but there was a certain satisfaction in yelling that she had no intention of giving up. She pointed her KC-7 over the edge of the wall. "Don't worry about the artillery—they're aiming at each other not at you!"

"Dubious comfort, Staff!"

Torin grinned at the Marine who'd spoken. "It's the only kind I offer, Haysole!"

Ears and tourquise hair clamped tight against his head, the di'Taykan returned her grin. "You're breaking my heart!"

"I'll break something else if you don't put your damned helmet on!"

The di'Taykans were believed to be the most enthusiastically non-discriminating sexual adventurers in known space and Private Haysole di'Stenjic seemed to want to enthusiastically prove he was more di'Taykan than most. While allowances were made within both branches of the military for species specific behavior, Haysole delighted in stepping over the line—although in his defense he often didn't seem to know just where the line was. He'd made corporal twice and was likely never going to get there again unless casualties in the Corps got much, much worse. Given that he was the stereotypical good-humored, well-liked, bad boy of the platoon, Torin was always amazed when he came out of an engagement in one piece.

"Staff." Cpl. Hollice's voice sounded in her helmet. His fireteam anchored the far end of the wall. *"Picking up unfriendlies approaching our sector."*

Torin glanced over at the lieutenant who was obviously—obvious to her anyway—fighting the urge to charge over to that sector and face the unfriendlies himself, mano a mano. "Mark your targets people, the official number seems to be one fuk of a lot and we're not carrying unlimited ammo."

"Looks like some of them are running four on the floor. Fuk, they can really motor!"

"What?"

"Uh, sorry Staff, old human saying. One group has four legs and they're running really fast."

"Thank you. I'm guessing they're also climberers or they wouldn't be first . . ." And then she was shouting in the sudden silence. ". . . at the wall," she finished a little more quietly. "Stay sharp."

"Artillery seems to have finished smashing things up," Franks murmured as he cautiously stood and took a look around.

The two lower levels were still more or less intact, the upper levels not so much. The question was, had the port survived. And the answer seemed to be yes as a Marine escort screamed in and another civilian carrier lifted off.

The distinct sound of a KC-7 turned Torin's attention back to the plains.

"Our turn," Franks murmured. "Our turn to stand fast and say you shall not pass."

Had that rhymed? "Sir?"

His cheeks darkened slightly. "Nothing."

"Yes sir."

All Marines qualified on the KC-7. Some of them were better shots than others but every single one of them knew how to make those shots count. The problem was, for every one of the enemy shot, another three raced forward to take their place.

"I hate this kind of thing." Franks aimed and fired. "There's no honor in it. They charge at us, we shoot them. It's . . ."

"Better than the other way around?" Torin suggested.

He shrugged. Aimed. Fired. "I guess so."

Torin knew so.

The enemy wore what looked like a desert camouflage that made them difficult to see against the dead brown grasses on the plains. Sho'quo company was in urban camouflage—black and grey and a dirty white—that hopefully made them difficult to see against the walls of Simunthitir. Most were on foot but there were a scattering of small vehicles in the line. Some the heavy gunners took out—the remains of these were used as cover at varying distances from the wall. Some kept coming.

Torin pulled the tab on a demo charge, counted to four, leaned over the wall and dropped it. The enemy vehicle blew big, the concussion rattling teeth on the wall and windows behind them in the port.

"I suspect they were going to set a sapper charge."

"Odds are good, sir."

"Why didn't you drop a cart on them?"

"Thought we'd best leave that to the end, sir. Get a few carts stacked up down there and they'll be able to use them to get up the . . . Damn!"

The quadrupeds were climbers and they were, indeed, fast. One moment there were only Marines on the wall, the next there was a large soldier with four heavily clawed legs and two arms holding a weapon gripping the edge of the parapet. One of the heavies went down but before the quad could fire again, Lieutenant Franks charged forward, swung his weapon so that the stock slammed in hard between the front legs, and then shot it twice in the air as it fell backwards off the wall.

He flushed slightly as Marines cheered and almost looked as though he was about to throw himself off the wall after it to finish the job. "I was closest," he explained, returning to Torin's side.

He wasn't. She hid a smile. Aimed. Fired. Hid a second smile as the lieutenant sighed and did the same. He wanted deeds of daring and he got target practice instead. Life was rough. Better than the alternative though, no matter how little the lieutenant might think so. *Do or die* might have more of a ring to it but she much preferred *do and live* and did her damnedest to ensure that was what happened for the Marines under her care.

Another civilian carrier lifted off. So far they were three for three.

"Artillery seems to have neutralized each other," Franks murmured, sweeping his scanner over the plain. "That's some nice shooting by Arver's . . . What the hell?"

With the approaching ground troops dug in or pulling back, Torin slaved her scanner to the lieutenant's. The inert masses she'd spotted earlier were being moved forward—no, *pushed* forward, their bulk shielding the pushers from Marine fire.

"Know what they are, Staff?"

"No idea, sir."

He glanced over at her with exaggerated disbelief, as he activated his com. "Anyone?"

"I think they're catapults, sir."

"*Cat*–apults, Corporal Hollice?"

"Yes sir, it's a pre-tech weapon."

"And they're going to what? Throw cats at us?"

"No sir. Probably rocks."

Franks glanced at Torin again. She shrugged. This was new to her. "They're going to throw rocks at us?"

"Yes, sir."

"I'm not reading a power source, Hollice."

"They use, uh, kind of a, uh, spring thing. Sir."

"You have no idea, do you Corporal?"

"Not really, sir. But I've read about them."

Franks took another look through the scanner. "How do the mortars target something with no energy read?"

"Aim and fire, sir. They're not that far away."

"Not so easy with an emmy, Staff." Franks mimed manually aiming one of the mortars and Torin grinned.

Then she stopped grinning as the first of the catapult things fired and watched in disbelief as a massive hunk of ore laced rock arced overhead and slammed into level five. The wall shattered under the impact flinging debris far and wide.

"Cover!"

Then BAM! BAM! BAM! BAM! Not as deafening as artillery but considerably more primal.

Most of the rock screamed over their heads, aimed at the remaining emmies now beginning to return fire from level four.

Most.

One of the rocks grew larger, and larger, and . . .

The wall bucked under foot, flexed and kicked like a living thing trying to throw them off. A gust of wind blew the rock dust clear and Torin saw that a crescent shaped bite had been taken out of the top of the wall. "Chou?"

"Two dead, three injured, Staff. I'm on it."

What if they gave a war and nobody died . . . Never going to happen. "Listen up, people, next time you see a great hunk of rock sailing toward you, get the fuk out of the way! These things are moving a lot slower than what we're used to!"

Only one emmy spat back an answer, blowing one of the incoming rocks out of the sky.

"Oh for . . . COVER!" A piece of debris bounced off Torin's helmet with enough force to rattle her teeth and a second slammed into her upper back, fortunately moving fast enough that her vest absorbed most of the impact.

"Arver!" Spitting out a mouthful of blood from a split lip, Franks screamed the artillery lieutenant's name into his com. "You want to watch where you're dropping that shit!"

"You want to come up here and try and aim this thing manually?"

"I don't think you're going to have time for that, Sir." Torin nodded out over the wall. Under cover of the rocks, which were probably intended to be as much of a distraction as a danger, the Other's had started a second charge, the faster quadrupeds out front once again and everyone else close behind.

The odds of deliberately hitting a randomly moving object were slim. The Marines switched to full automatic and sprayed rounds into the advancing enemy. Bodies started hitting the dirt. The enemy kept coming.

"As soon as you can take out multiple targets, start dropping the carts!"

Out of the corner of one eye, Torin saw Juan Checya, one of the heavy gunners, sling his weapon, flick on a hovercraft, and, as it lifted on its cushion of air, grab the rear rail with both augmented hands and push it to the back of the wall. As soon as he had the maximum wind-up available, he braced himself and whipped around, releasing the cart at the front of the arc. It traveled an impressive distance before gravity negated the forward momentum.

The quadrupeds closest to the casualties keened at the loss of their companions and seemed to double their speed. Torin found it encouraging, in a slightly soul deadening way, that they grieved so obviously. Grief was distracting. Unfortunately, not only distracting for the enemy. "Sir . . ."

Franks rubbed a grimy hand over his face, rock dust mixing with sweat and drawing vertical grey streaks "I'm okay, Staff."

"Never doubted it, sir."

Above and behind them, a fourth civilian carrier rose toward safety.

"One carrier remaining." Captain Rose's voice on the command channel. Torin almost thought she could hear screaming in the background. She'd rather face a well armed enemy than civilians any day.

"Lieutenant Franks, move your platoon back to level three and take over stretcher duty from Lieutenant Garly who will hold level two!"

"Captain!" Lieutenant Franks slid two steps sideways and blew a biped off the wall. Although it might be a new species, Torin missed any other distinguishing features—after a while, the only thing that registered was the uniform. "Unfriendlies have broken the perimeter!"

"That's why we're moving the perimeter, Franks. Fall back!"

"Yes, sir! Staff . . ."

"Sir! Fall back by numbers, people! You know the drill! Keep low so the second level has as clear a shot as possible! And Amanda, I want that covering fire thick enough to keep out rain!"

"You got it, Torin!"

The word retreat was not in the Corps vocabulary. Marines fell back and regrouped. In this particular instance it wasn't so much back as down. The heavies leapt off the wall into the city and then joined in providing covering fire so that those without exo-skeletons to take up the impact could come off the wall a little more slowly. And then it was a fast run up the lowest level of the spiraling street, squads leapfrogging each other as Lieutenant Garly's platoon swept the first level wall, keeping the enemy too occupied to shoot down into the city.

Given the fire from the second level, a number of the enemy decided that the safest thing to do was to follow the Marines down to the street.

Also, without Marines on the outside wall to keep the sappers away . . .

The explosion smelled like scorched iron and filled the street with smoke and dust. Swearing for the sake of swearing, Torin ducked yet another rain of debris.

"They're in!"

Squad one made it through the second level gate. Torin and the lieutenant crouched behind a rough barricade as squad two followed. As a clump of the enemy rounded the curve of a building, a hovercraft sailed off level two, plummeted downwards, and squashed half of them flat.

"I think that's our cue, Staff."

"Works for me, sir."

They moved back with the squad, Torin keeping herself between the lieutenant and the enemy. The largest part of her job was, after all, keeping him alive.

They were no more than four meters from the gate when a pair of the quadrupeds charged over the wreckage of the hovercraft, keening and firing wildly as they ran. Their weapon was, like the KC, a chemically powered projectile. The rounds whined through the air in such numbers that it almost seemed as though they were being attacked by a swarm of angry wasps. No choice but to dive for dirt and hope the distinctly inadequate cover would be enough.

Shots from the second level took the quad's out just before they reached the squad.

Torin scrambled to her feet. "Let's go before more show up."

No one expected the quads to have riders; smaller bipeds who launched themselves from the bodies. One of them died in the air, the other wrapped itself around Haysole and drew its sidearm. Haysole spun sideways, his helmet flying off to bounce down the street, and got enough of an elbow free to deflect the first shot. Between the frenzied movement, and the certainty that taking out the enemy would also take out Haysole, no one dared shoot. Torin felt rather than saw Franks charge forward. He was big man—because he was a second lieutenant she sometimes forgot that. Large hands wrapped around the enemy's head and twisted. Sentient evolution was somewhat unimaginative. With very few exceptions, a broken neck meant the brain was separated from the body.

Turned out, this was not one of the exceptions.

"You okay?" Franks asked as he let the body drop.

"Yes, sir."

"Then let's go . . ."

They stepped over the body which was when pretty much everyone left on the street noticed that harness strapped to the outside of the uniform was festooned with multiple small packets and what was obviously a detonation device.

Rough guess, Torin figured there were enough explosives to take out the gate to the second level. The high ground didn't mean much if you couldn't keep the enemy off it.

Franks gave Haysole a push that sent him stumbling into Torin. "Move!" Then he grabbed the body by the feet and stood, heaving him up and into the air. The explosion was messy. Loud and messy.

It wasn't until Franks slumped onto her shoulder as she wrestled him through the gate that she realized not all the blood soaking his uniform had rained down out of the sky.

He'd been hit in the neck with a piece of debris.

As the last squad through got the heavy metal gate closed and locked, he slid down her body, onto his knees, and then toppled slowly to the ground.

Torin grabbed a pressure seal from her vest but it was too late.

The lower side of his neck was missing. Veins and arteries both had been severed. He'd bled out fast and was probably dead before he hit the ground. There were a lot of things the medics up in orbit could repair; this wasn't one of them.

"Damn, the lieutenant really saved our asses." Sergeant Chou turned from the gate, ignoring the multiple impacts against the other side. "If they'd blown this sucker we'd have been in a running fight to the next level. Is he okay?"

Torin leaned away from the body.

"Fuk." Haysole. The di'Taykan had a way with words.

Chou touched her shoulder. "Do you . . .?"

"I've got it."

A carrier roared up from the port, its escort screaming in from both sides.

"That's it Marines, we're out of here!"

"Staff . . ."

"Go on, I'm right behind you."

They still had to make it up to the port but, holding the high ground as they did, it shouldn't be a problem. She spread the body bag over Second Lieutenant Franks and sealed the edges as Lieutenant Garly's platoon started spending their heavy ordinance. From the smell of things, they'd dropped something big and flammable onto the street behind the gate.

This wasn't the kind of war people made songs about. The Confederation fought only because the Others fought and no one knew why the Others kept coming. Diplomacy resulted in dead diplomats. Backing away only encouraged them.

But perhaps a war without one single defining ideology was exactly the kind of war that needed an infinite number of smaller defining moments.

Torin smoothed out the bag with one bloody hand then sat back and keyed the charge.

Maybe, she thought as she slid the tiny canister that now held Lieutenant Franks into an inner pocket on her combat vest, maybe it was time they had a few songs . . .

Under Summons

A few years ago, I wrote a series call "The Keeper Chronicles." In the end, there were three books, Summon the Keeper, The Second Summoning, *and* Long Hot Summoning. *If I had to call them something, I'd call them humorous contemporary fantasy—where the humor was one of the main points rather than incidentally included. I'd always intended to write more in this mythos but two of the main characters, Sam and Austin were based on two of my cats and when Austin died while I was writing* The Second Summoning *and then Sam died just after book three, the funny kind of went out of it for me and I doubt there'll be more books.*

But there might be more stories . . .

EYES SQUINTED AGAINST THE EARLY morning sun, Diana Hansen walked down the lane toward the Waupoos Marina listening to the string of complaints coming from the cat in her backpack.

"The boat is leaving at seven-thirty," she said when he finally paused for breath. "If we'd gotten up any later we'd have missed it."

The head and front paws of a marmalade tabby emerged through the open zipper and peered over Diana's shoulder toward the marina. "I thought need provided for Keepers during a Summoning?"

"Need has provided, Sam. There's a boat leaving for Main Duck Island this morning."

He snorted. "Why can't need provide a boat at a reasonable hour?"

"It doesn't work that way. Besides, cats do that hunt at dust and dawn thing—you should be happy to be up."

"First of all, I'm not hunting. And second," he added ducking

158

down into the backpack as a car passed them, "I'd rather have sausages for breakfast than a damp mouse."

"Who wouldn't."

Another car passed bouncing from pot hole to pot hole.

"You'd better stay down," Diana told him, hooking her thumbs under the padded shoulder straps. "It's starting to get busy."

"Oh yeah," the cat muttered as a pickup truck followed the two cars. "It's a real rush hour. I'll be napping if you need me."

The Ministry of Natural Resources trawler was tied up at the nearer of the big piers out behind the marina. Pausing at the southwest corner of the big grey building, Diana scoped out the crowd. Most of the twenty-four other travelers were older couples, sensibly dressed in long pants wearing both hiking boots and hats. Half a dozen women were obviously together and just as obviously part of a club—unless they'd all accidentally worn the same lime green t-shirt. There was a sprinkling of younger adults and three teenagers. Two girls, probably sisters, and a boy. They were the only ones in shorts. The boy caught her gaze and smirked. He was a good looking kid—and he knew it.

"Okay, everyone, listen up!" A forty-ish man wearing Ministry khaki, climbed up on wooden crate and waved a clipboard. "Some you already know me but, for the rest, I'm Gary Straum and I'll be your guide this trip. The young man driving the boat, is Jamie Wierster. He knows almost as much as I do about the island so if I'm not available he'll do his best to tell you anything you need to know."

A ruddy cheeked young giant leaned out of the tiny cabin and waved.

"I just want to remind you of a few things before we get started," Gary continued as the two girls giggled. "Main Duck Island is part of the St. Lawrence Islands National Parks system and is a nature sanctuary. You may not take samples of the plant life away with you—this means no picking, no digging, no collecting seeds. The wild life is to be left strictly alone. If there's a disagreement of any kind between you and any creature living on that island, I will rule in favor of the creature. Anything you carry in must be carried out. If you can't live with that, I suggest you leave now." Gary smiled as an older man grabbed the back of the teenage boy's skater shirt and hauled him back by his side. "All right then. When I read your name, come and pick up your life jacket . . ." He gestured at the open steel locker beside him. ". . . put it on, and board. The sooner we get going, the more time we'll have to spend on the island."

Diana's name was the last on the list. She hadn't put it there and she felt a little sorry for the actual twenty-fifth person who'd been bumped to make room for her but there was a hole in the fabric of reality out on Main Duck Island and it was her job as a Keeper to close it.

Feeling awkward and faintly ridiculous in the life jacket, Diana sat down on a wooden bench and set her backpack carefully at her feet.

"I saw the cat. When we passed you in the lane."

She answered the teenage boy's smile with one of her own as he dropped onto the bench beside her. According to the boarding list, his name was Ryan. Ryan, like everyone else on the boat, was a Bystander and, given the relative numbers, Keepers were used to working around them. "Of course you did, Ryan. *Please* forget about it."

It really was a magic word.

He frowned. Looked around like he was wondering why he was sitting there, and, after mumbling something inarticulate, moved across the boat to sit back down in his original seat. The girls, Mackenzie and Erin, sitting on the bench in front of him, giggled.

"I get the impression you're not the giggling type."

It was one of the older women, her husband busy taking pictures of Gary casting off and jumping aboard.

"Not really, no."

"Carol Diamond. That's my husband Richard. We're here as part of an Elder Hostel program." Her wave took in the rest of the hats and hiking boots crowd. "All of us."

"Great."

"Are you traveling on your own, dear?"

"Yes, I am."

Carol smiled the even, white smile of the fully dentured and nodded toward the teenagers. "Well, how nice you have some people of your own age to spend time with."

Diana blinked. Two month shy of twenty, she did not appreciate being lumped in with the children. Fortunately, between the motor and the wind it was difficult to carry on a casual conversation and Carol didn't try, content to sit quietly while her husband took pictures of Waupoos Island, Prince Edward Point, waves, sky, gulls, the other people in the boat, and once, while he was fiddling with the focus, his lap.

The three pictures with Diana in them would be mysteriously over-exposed.

So would at least one of the shots south across Lake Ontario but Diana had nothing to do with that.

"Hey!" Ryan managed to make himself heard over the ambient noise. "What's that?"

Everyone squinted in the direction he was pointing. A series of small dark dots rose above a sharp edged horizon.

"That's our first sight of the island; we're about five miles out." Gary moved closer to the teenager. "Well done."

Ryan turned just far enough to scowl at him. "Not that. Closer to us."

Also a series of small dark dots rising and falling with the slight chop. Then, suddenly, they were gone. The last of the dots rose up into a triangular point just before it disappeared.

"That looked like a tail!"

"Might be a loon," Gary offered.

"Fucking big loon!"

"Ryan!"

Ryan rolled his eyes at his father but muttered an apology.

"It's probably just some floating junk." A half-turn included the rest of the group in the discussion. "You'd be amazed at the stuff we find out here." His list had almost everyone laughing.

Lake monster wasn't on it, Diana noted.

As Main Duck Island coalesced into a low solid line of tree tops joined by land with a light house rising off the westernmost point, Gary explained that it had been acquired by the park service in 1998 having been previously owned by John Foster Dulles, a prominent lawyer who became American secretary of state in the Eisenhower administration. The island was 209 hectares in size and except for the ruins of some old fishing cabins—which were posted—none of it was off limits.

"The lighthouse?" one of the lime-green t-shirt group asked.

"Is unmanned and closed to the public but you can go right up to it and poke around."

Mention of the lighthouse started the shipwreck stories. There were a lot of them since the area around the island was known as the graveyard of Lake Ontario and contained the wrecks of a number of two and three-masted schooners, brigantines, barges and steamers dating back to the sinking of a small French warship enroute to Fort

Niagara with supplies and a pay chest of gold for the troops that went down in late fall around 1750.

Diana was beginning to get a bad feeling about the location of the hole she had to close.

As Jamie steered the trawler into School House Bay, Gary told the story of the *John Randall*. She'd anchored in the bay for shelter back in 1920 only to have the wind shift into the north and drive her ashore. Her stern hit a rock and her engine lifted up and she broke in two.

"The crew of four scrambled up onto the bow and remained there for ten hours washed by heavy seas and lashed by November northeaster. They finally made it ashore on a hatch cover and stayed with the lighthouse keeper nine days before they were picked up. You can still see the wooden ribs and planks of the ship in the bay."

"So no one died?" Ryan asked.

"Not that time." With the dock only meters away, Gary moved over the port side of the boat and picked up the rear mooring line. "But a year and eight days later, the Captain of the *Randall* went down while in command of the *City of New York*. His wife and his ten month old daughter went with him."

"So sad," Carole sighed as Gary leapt out onto the dock. "But at least they were together." She twisted on the bench to look back the way they'd come. "I bet those waves hide a hundred stories."

"I bet they hid a hundred and one," Diana sighed, hoisting her backpack. She was not going to enjoy explaining this to Sam.

"In the water?"

"Essentially."

Sam's ears saddled. "How *essentially*?" The echoed word dripped with feline sarcasm.

"Under the water."

"Have a nice time."

Down on one knee beside him, Diana stroked along his back and out his tail. "There's a lake monster out there too. Looked like a sea serpent. Probably came through the hole."

"And that's supposed to make me change my mind?" the cat snorted. He peered off the end of the dock into the weedy bay. "Frogs pee in that water you know."

"That's not . . ." She probed at the Summons, trying to narrow it down a little. ". . . exactly the water we're going into."

He sat back and looked up at her, amber eyes narrowed. "What water are we going into, exactly? If *we* were going that is?"

"South-west." She straightened. "Toward the lighthouse."

"I'll wait here."

"Come on. The nature hike went through the woods. We'll take the beach and avoid an audience." About to lift the backpack, she paused. "You want to walk or ride?"

Tail tip twitching, he shoved past her muttering, "What part of 'I'll wait here' did you not understand."

The beach consisted of two to three meters of smooth gravel trimmed with a ridge of polished zebra mussel shells at the edge of the water. As Diana and Sam rounded a clump of sumac, they saw Ryan, a garter snake wrapped around one hand, moving quietly toward the two girls crouched at the ridge of shells.

"You think we should get involved?" Sam wondered.

Before Diana could answer, Ryan placed his foot wrong, the gravel rattled and both girls turned. Although he no longer had surprise on his side, he waved the snake in their general direction.

"Look what I have!"

Braced for shrieking and running, Diana was surprised to see both girls advance toward Ryan.

"How dare you!" Mackenzie snapped, fists on her hips. "How would you like it if someone picked you up by the throat and flailed you at people?"

"The poor snake!" Erin added.

"I'm not hurting it," Ryan began but Mackenzie ran right over his protest with her opinion of the kind of people who abused animals for fun while Erin gently took the snake from him and released it.

"In answer to your question," Diana snickered as they started walking again, "I don't think we're needed."

A little further down the beach, two even larger snakes lay tangled together in the sun on a huge slab of flat rock. The female hissed as they went by. Sam hissed back.

"Don't be rude, Sam, it's their beach."

"She started it," Sam muttered.

About half way to the lighthouse, with the teenagers out of sight behind them, Diana headed for the water.

"Is it here?"

"No, it's farther west but these shoals go out over half a mile in places and I'd rather not be visible from shore for that long. I don't want to have to maintain a misdirection when we're wading waist deep."

"When *we're* wading?" Sam sniffed disdainfully at the mussel shells. "Lift me over this would you."

"Actually," she bent and picked him up, settling his weight against her chest, "why don't I just carry you until we're in the water."

"Yeah, yeah." He sighed and adjusted his position slightly. "It's going to be cold."

"It's Lake Ontario, I don't think it ever gets warm. But don't worry, you won't feel it." As the water lapped against the beach gravel a centimeter from the toes of her shoes, Diana reached into the Possibilities and wrapped power around them. Then she stepped forward. "There's a nice wide channel here," she said, moving carefully over the flat rock. Sam would be completely unbearable if she missed her footing and a wave knocked them down. "We can follow the rift out to deep water and . . ."

The bottom dropped out from under her feet.

She stopped their descent before the channel grew uncomfortably narrow. The last thing she wanted was to get her foot stuck between two rocks while under three meters of Lake Ontario with a cranky cat. Well, maybe not the *last* thing she wanted—being forced to sit through a marathon viewing of Question Period ranked higher on the list but not by much.

Thanks to the zebra mussels, the water was remarkably clear—the one benefit of an invasive species that blocked intake pipes up and down the Great Lakes. Enough light made it down from the surface that they could easily see their way.

"Of course I could see anyway," Sam reminded her as she let him go. He swam slowly around her, hair puffing out from his body. "Cats see much better than humans in low light levels." A little experimentation proved he could use his tail as a rudder. "You know, when you don't have to get wet, swimming is kind of fun. Hey! Is that a fish!"

Since the fish was moving in the right direction and Sam didn't have a hope of catching it, Diana merely followed along behind, half her attention on the Summons and the other half on the cat.

"Sam, come on! This way! We've got to go deeper."

"How deep?" he demanded, scattering a small school of herring.

"Right to the bottom." She slipped one arm out of her backpack and swung it around so she could pull out her flashlight. "Now come on and stop bothering the fish."

"Something has them freaked."

"They probably don't get a lot of cats down here."

"I don't think it's me. Mostly, I seem to be confusing them."

"Welcome to the club."

"What?"

"Never mind." The water was definitely getting darker. Jade green now and, finally, a little murky. "If not you, what?"

"Something big."

"The sea serpent?"

He was back at her side so quickly that the impact sent her spinning slowly counter-clockwise. "Maybe."

Diana stopped the spin before her third revolution. A Keeper spinning three time counter-clockwise near an open accident site could have unpleasant—or at the very least unlikely—consequences.

"How can you have a sea serpent in a lake?" Sam snorted in a tone that said very clearly, *I wasn't scared so don't think for a moment I was.*

Diana shrugged. "I don't know. I guess because lake serpent sounds dumb."

"What's that?"

She turned the beam of the flashlight. A small piece of metal glinted on a narrow shelf of rock. "We should check it out."

"Is it part of the Summons?"

"Yes . . . No . . ." She started to swim. "Maybe." Feeling the faint tug of a current nearer the rocks, she half turned. "Stay close. I don't want you swept away."

He paddled at little faster and tucked up against her side. "Good. I don't want to *be* swept away."

"We're lucky it's so calm today. On a rough day with high waves, there's probably a powerful under-tow through here."

"Don't want to be eaten by an under-toad," Sam muttered.

"Not under-toad. Under-tow."

"You sure of that?"

Glancing down into the dark depths of the lake, Diana wasn't, so just to be on the safe side, she stopped thinking about it. The older Keepers got unnecessarily shirty about the accidental creation of creatures from folklore. As a general rule, the creatures weren't too happy about it either.

"It's the clasp off a chain purse." The leather purse itself had long rotted away. "Hang on . . ." Slipping two fingers down into a crack in the rock, she pulled out a copper coin, too corroded to be identified further.

"You should put that back."

A second coin. She tucked them both into the front pocket of her jeans.

"Okay, fine. Don't listen to the cat."

"I need them."

"What for?"

Good question. "I don't know yet. Come on."

"Come on?" Sam repeated, paddling with all four feet to keep up. "You say that like I was the one who paused to do a little grave robbing."

"First of all that wasn't a grave, and second," she continued before Sam could argue, "I haven't actually robbed anything since the coins are still here. In the water."

"In your pocket."

"That only counts if I take them away with me."

"So you've borrowed them?"

"More or less."

"Less," the cat snorted.

Diana let him have the last word. It was pretty much the only way to shut him up.

By the time they reached the bottom, the only illumination came from the flashlight. The water was a greenish-yellow, small particulates drifting through the path of the beam.

"Are we there yet?"

"A little further west."

The bottom was still mostly rock but there were patches of dirt supporting a few small weeds in spite of the depth. They followed a low ridge for close to half a kilometer, stopping when it rose suddenly to within a few meters of the surface.

"This is the place," Diana said, sweeping the light over the rock. "Somewhere close and . . . Sam, what are you doing?"

He was floating motionless, nose to nose with a good sized herring. "Staring contest."

"You can't win."

"Cats always win."

"I don't think fish have eyelids."

Sam's tail started to lash, propelling him forward. "You cheater!"

Diana couldn't be sure but she thought the fish looked slightly

sheepish as it turned and darted away. "Never mind that!" she yelled
as Sam took off in pursuit. "We're right on top of the Summons so I'm
thinking–given where we are–that we've got to find a wreck."

"In a minute!" Sam disappeared around the edge of the shoal.
"I'm just gonna teach that cheating fish a . . ."

"Sam?"

"Found it."

"Found what?" Diana demanded as she swam after the cat. "Oh."

Much like Main Duck Island itself, the shoal rose almost into a
nearly vertical underwater cliff on the north side but fell off in layers
to the south. On one layer, about a meter and a half up from the bottom the skeletal prow of an old wooden ship jutted out from the ridge,
huge timbers held in place in the narrow angle between two slabs of
canted rock and preserved by the cold of the water.

"Well this is . . ."

"Obvious," snorted Sam. "Big hunk of rock rising toward the surface. Exposed wreck. Probably been a hundred divers down here
every summer."

"Probably," Diana agreed swimming closer. "But this is where the
hole is, I'm sure of it. Somebody did something sometime recently."

"Oh that's definitive," Sam sighed following her in.

The hole she'd been Summoned to close was not part of the wreck
but in the rock beside it where a narrow crevice cut down into the lake
bed.

"Isn't the word hole usually more of a metaphorical description,"
Sam wondered as Diana floated head down and feet up, peering into
the crevice.

"Usually. Still is mostly." The actual opening between this world
and the nastier end of the Possibilities stretched out on both sides of
the crevice but it was centered over the dark, triangular crack in the
rock. "There's something down here."

"I'm guessing fish poo."

"And you'd be right."

"Eww."

"But something else too." Tucking the flashlight under her chin,
Diana grabbed onto a rock with her left hand and snaked her right
down into the crack. "Almost . . ."

"If you lose that hand, are you still going to be able to use a can
opener?"

"I'm not going to lose the hand!"

"I'm just asking."

Sharp edges of rock dug into her arm as she forced her hand deeper, her jacket riding up away from her wrist. One finger tip touched . . . something. Even such a gentle pressure moved whatever it was away. A little further. Another touch. She managed to finally hook it between her first two fingers.

"Uh, Diana, about that sea serpent . . ."

"What about it?" She'd have to move her arm slowly and carefully out of the crack or she'd lose whatever she was holding.

"It's either heading this way from the other side of the wreck or the Navy's running a submarine in the Great Lakes."

"I pick option B."

"And you'd be wrong."

Time to yank; she could always pick the thing up again. Unfortunately, a sharp tug didn't free her arm. Upside, she managed to hang onto the thing. Downside, approaching sea serpent.

Wait! If her arm was stuck then she didn't need to hold the rock and if she didn't need to hold the rock . . .

She grabbed the flashlight and aimed the beam toward the wreck, hoping it would be enough. Pulling power from the Possibilities over a hole would not be smart, not considering where that hole lead. There were worse things than lake monsters out beyond the edges of reality.

Framed between two rotting timbers, green eyes flashed gold in the light. Mouth gaping, the sea serpent folded back on itself, and fled, the final flick of its triangular tail knocking a bit of board off the wreck.

"Looks bigger up close," Diana noted, trying to remember how to breathe.

"Ya think!" Sam snarled, paws and tail thrashing as he bobbed about in currents stirred up by the creature's passage.

"Maybe it was just curious."

"Sure it was. Because you get that big eating plankton!"

"Whales do."

"*Some* whales do and that was not a whale! That was a predator. I know a predator when I see one!"

Diana tucked the flashlight back under her chin and reached out to stroke the line of raised hair along Sam's spine—the Possibility that allowed them to move and breathe underwater granting the touch. "You're shouting."

He speared her with an amber gaze. "I don't want to be eaten by a sea serpent."

"Who does?"

"Who cares?" he snapped. "The point is, I don't. Let's get that hole closed and get back on dry land before I'm a canapé."

Diana had to admit he had a point, although she admitted it silently rather than give him more ammunition for complaints. The serpent was better than ten meters long and almost a meter in diameter. A five kilo cat would be barely a mouthful. The sooner she got the hole closed, the better.

Carefully, but as quickly as she could, she worked her right hand out of the crack and when it was finally free, dropped a fragment of bone into the palm of her left.

"The graveyard of Lake Ontario," Sam noted solemnly, his cinnamon nose nearly touching her hand. "There's more than just ships at rest down here."

"Not every body washed ashore," Diana agreed with a sigh. "I'm betting there's more of this body down in that crevice."

"You think it got smashed and that's what made the hole?"

"I think someone—probably someone diving around the wreck—smashed it, deliberately, and *that's* what made the hole."

"You need to get the rest of the bone out."

It wasn't a question but she answered it anyway. "I do."

"Great. Considering how long the first piece took, we're going to be down here forever and that serpent's going to come back and it's going to be kitties and bits. You're the bits," he added.

"Thanks, I got that. You're not usually this fatalistic."

"Hello? Lake monster. Cat at the bottom of Lake Ontario."

"You worry too much. Now that I've got one piece out I can call the rest to it. It'll be fast." She held the hand holding the bone out over the crack and Called. Other fragments floated up, danced in the water, and after a moment or two, formed most of a human jaw.

Suddenly conscious of being watched, Diana whirled around to see a herring hanging in the water. "What?"

Silver sides flashing, it swam about two meters away then stopped, turned and continued staring.

"Is that your friend from before?"

"We're not friends," Sam snorted. "Get on with it."

Diana studied the jaw. "There's a tooth missing."

Sam looked from the curved bone to the Keeper. "*A* tooth?"

"Okay, a bunch of teeth and the rest of the skeleton but right here . . . see where the reformed jaw is a different shade?" She touched it lightly with the tip of one finger. "There was a tooth in there until recently. Who ever did this, cracked the jaw and took the tooth."

"Why?"

"People'll notice if you come up from a dive with most of a jaw but you can hide a tooth."

Sam licked his shoulder thoughtfully, frowned when his tongue made no impression on his fur thanks to the Possibilities keeping him dry, and finally said, "Cats don't care about the things we leave behind."

"People do. Disturbing a body—even one this old—in order to get a souvenir is illegal, immoral, and kind of gross. So, now we have a problem."

"The lake monster."

"No."

Before she could continue, Sam shifted so he was almost vertical in the water and pointed upwards with one front paw. "Yes!"

A long line of undulating darkness passed between them and the surface, turned and passed again a little closer.

"Okay, problems. I need the tooth to close the hole."

"Great." Sam kept his eyes on the serpent, one pass closer still. "So call it."

Diana reached out and grabbed him as the lashing of his tail propelled him upwards. "Two problems with that. One, it might be locked away and not able to move freely and two we don't know how far away it is and staying down here indefinitely's really not an option. We need to go to it."

"And?"

"And that's not a problem given that we've got the rest of the jaw, we'll just follow it. The problem is, I can't pull from the Possibilities this close to the hole."

"So we leave and come back another day. And when I say we come back," Sam amended as he wriggled free and started swimming toward shore, "I mean you."

Diana grabbed him again. "Did I mention that the serpent has to go back through the hole before I close it? If we leave and come back, the serpent could be anywhere, not to mention that another serpent—or worse—could come through."

"You're just full of good news."

"But I have a plan."

"Oh joy."

"You won't like it."

He sighed. "Why am I not surprised?"

"I'm going to use the Possibilities that are keeping us dry and breathing."

"There's a problem with that." He squirmed around until he was looking her in the face. "They're keeping us dry and breathing."

"We take a deep breath and the next instant we'll be standing by the missing tooth."

"That doesn't sound so bad."

"We'll just be a little wet."

"When you say a little, you mean . . ."

"Completely."

He locked his claws in her jacket. "No."

"Would you rather be eaten by the lake monster?"

A glance toward the surface. The serpent was close enough that the broad band of lighter brown around its neck was visible. It seemed to be picking up speed with each pass, confidence growing as nothing opposed it.

"Sam?"

"I'm thinking."

There were teeth visible just inside the broad mouth. Rather too many teeth in Diana's opinion. Rather too many teeth suddenly facing them. And closing fast. Really, really fast. "Take a deep breath Sam."

"I don't . . ."

"Now!"

And they were standing, dripping, in a basement workshop, the room barely lit by two low windows.

"I'm wet!" Claws breaking through denim to skin, Sam leapt out of Diana's arms and raced around the room spraying water from his sodden fur. "Wet! Wet! Ahhhhh! Wet!" Tail clamped tight to his body, he disappeared under the lower shelf of the workbench.

"Oh for . . ." Far enough from the hole that all Possibilities were open to her, Diana reached. "There. Now you're dry."

"I'm still sitting in a puddle," came a disgruntled voice from under the bench.

"So move." Taking her own advice, Diana stepped out of a puddle of her own and held out the jaw. "Can you hear that?"

"I have water in my ears."

"Sam!"

"Fine." He crawled out from under the bench, shook, and sat, head cocked. "I hear tapping."

"Can you find it?"

The look he shot her promised dire consequences.

"I'm sorry. *Would* you find it? Please." Not a compulsion, just a polite request. Compelling cats had much the same success rate as Senate reform, which was to say, none at all.

The tooth was in a small plastic box, tucked inside a red metal tool box, shoved to the back of an upper shelf.

"What's the point of having a souvenir no one can see?" Sam wondered as the tooth settled back into the jaw with an audible click.

"I guess the point's having it. Let's go."

"In a minute." He walked over to where a full wet suit hung on the wall, neoprene booties lined up neatly under it. Tail held high, he turned around.

"What are you doing?"

He looked up at her like she was an idiot and she supposed it was a pretty stupid question.

"Good aim," she acknowledged as he finished. "I just hope they don't have a cat that can be blamed when he puts that boot on next."

"They don't."

"You really got upset about him taking that tooth," she murmured bending and scooping him up.

"Please," he snorted settling into the crock of her arm. "I got *wet!*"

"Who are you?"

They stared at each other for a moment, and then Diana turned toward the piping voice.

A little girl, no more than five stood in the open doorway, half hanging off the door knob. Behind her, a rec room empty but for a scattering of brightly coloured toys.

Diana glanced down at the jaw and smiled. "I'm the tooth fairy," she said, reached into the Possibilities and allowed the bone to pull them back to the wreck.

The serpent was no where in sight but since they hadn't been gone long, she figured it hadn't gone far. The trick would be getting it to come back.

"Sam! Now what are you doing?"

He paused, up on his hind legs, front claws embedded in a squared piece of timber. "Is that a trick question?"

"Just stop it."

"Fine." Sighing, he swam back over beside her. "Now what?"

"We need to lure the serpent back through the hole before I can close it."

"I refuse to be bait."

"I wasn't going to ask."

"Good."

She nodded at the lone herring watching from the shelter of the wreck. "I need you to talk to your friend."

"It's a fish."

"So?"

"It's not a friend, it's food."

"So you can't talk to it."

Whiskers bristled indignantly. "I didn't say that!"

"I need you to ask it to get a school together, get the serpent's attention, lure it back here, and peel away at the last minute so that the serpent goes through the hole rather than hitting the rock."

Sam stared at her. "You want me to convince fish to be bait? Why don't I just convince them to roll in breadcrumbs and lie down under a broiler?" The darker markings on his forehead formed a 'w' as he frowned. "Actually, that's not a bad idea."

"If they do this, the serpent will be gone and they'll be a lot safer."

"Provided he doesn't catch them and eat them."

"I'm not saying there isn't a risk. Just try."

As Sam swam over to the herring, Diana slid her back pack around onto her lap and undid the zipper. She needed something that would write under water on slippery, algae covered rock. Pens, pencils, markers, bag of biodegradable kitty litter, litter box, six cans of cat food, two cat dishes, box of crackers, peanut butter, pajamas, clean jeans, socks, underwear, lap top; nothing that would work. The outside pockets held her cellphone, a bottle of slightly redundant water, and . . . a nail file. Possibly . . .

"She wants you to sweeten the deal."

"She does?" Diana glanced over at the herring. "How?"

"She wants you to get rid of the fish that suck the life out of other fish."

"There's vampire fish in this lake?" All at once, the dark corners under the rocks looked a little darker.

"Get real. They're called sea lampreys and they came into the lake after World War II and decimated the native populations. TVO special on the Great Lakes," he added when Diana blinked at him.

"Decimated?"

"It means ate most of."

"I *know* what it means."

"Hey, you asked," he snorted. "What do you say? They're not supposed to be here, no one would miss them, and you can't lure the serpent without herring co-operation. She just wants her fry to be safe." He paused and licked his lips.

"You're thinking about fried fish, aren't you?"

"Yeah."

"Well, stop." If she gave the herring what she wanted, Diana knew there'd be consequences. More healthy native species of fish in the lake for one thing. Actually, more healthy native species of fish in the lake was about the only thing. She couldn't see a down side—which was always vaguely unsettling.

"You can't do it, can you?"

"Of course I can do it." It was disconcerting that her cat was using the same argument on her that she'd used on him. "Technically, as a Keeper, if I'm asked for help to right a wrong, I can't refuse and sea lampreys in the lake seem to be definitely a wrong."

"So what's the problem?"

"I'm not sure fish were included under that rule."

"Very anti-ichthyoid of you."

"Anti what? Never mind." She waved off his explanation. "You're watching way too much television. Okay, tell her I'll do it but it has to be after the hole is closed, I can't access the Possibilities until then."

"She wants to know why she should trust you."

Diana glanced over at the herring. "Because I'm one of the good guys."

"She only has your word for that."

"Sam!"

"Okay, okay, she didn't say that. You get to work; I'll convince her you're trustworthy."

"Thank you." Setting the jaw bone carefully aside, Diana began to scratch the definitions of the accident site onto the rocks around the hole with the point of her nail-file, the algae just thick enough for it to leave a legible impression.

"Incoming!"

"I'm almost done."

"Maybe you don't quite understand what incoming means," Sam shouted as the first herring whacked into her shoulder.

Diana scrambled to get the last definition drawn in the midst of a sliver swirl of fish and dove out of the way in the instant of clear water that followed.

Given a choice between diving face first into rock or returning back where it had come from, the serpent choice the second, less painful, option.

The instant the tip of its wedge shaped tail disappeared, Diana grabbed the definitions and slammed the hole closed. When she looked up, three dozen silver faces stared back at her, all wearing the same expectant expression. Well, probably expectant; it was surprisingly hard to judge expression on a fish.

"Okay, okay, give me a minute to catch my breath." She tested the seal on the hole and reached into the Possibilities. Turned out there were a lot of sea lamprey in the lake and over half of them had to be removed from living prey.

"Where'd you put them?" Sam spun around in a slow circle, lazily sculling with his tail.

"I dropped them in the Mid-Atlantic."

"There are sharks in the Mid-Atlantic."

"So?"

"Sharks eat lampreys."

"Sharks eat Volkswagens. What's your point?"

"We've been down here for hours, we missed lunch, and I'm hungry. Can we go now?"

"In a minute, I have one more thing to do."

It was only a part of a jaw bone but once it had been a part of a man who'd sailed the lake.

Diana set the bone down beside the wreck and waited.

He hadn't been very old. Under his knit cap, his hair was brown, long enough to wisp out over his ears and there was a glint of red in his bad teenage moustache. He was wearing blue pants with a patch on one knee. His heavy sweater looked a little too big for him but that may have been because he was wearing it over at least one other sweater, maybe two. At some point, not long before he'd died, he'd whacked the index finger on his left hand, leaving the nail black and blue.

Pulling the two copper coins from her pocket, Diana bent and laid one on each closed eye. "To pay the ferryman," she said feeling Sam's unasked question. "He's been in the water long enough, I think he'd like to be back on it."

A heartbeat later, there was only the wreck and the rocks.

The coins and the jaw bone were gone.

"Now can we go?"

Diana slung her backpack over one shoulder and picked up the cat with her other hand. "Yes. Now we can go."

Carol Diamond was standing on the shore when she came out of the water. Her eyes were wide and her mouth worked for a moment before any sound emerged. "You went . . . you were . . . in the . . ."

"I went wading."

"Wading?"

"Yes. You saw me wading. Then I came out of the water . . ." Diana stepped over the ridge of zebra mussel shells and set Sam down on the gravel. ". . . and I rolled down my jeans and put my shoes and socks back on."

White curls bounced as she shook her head. "You were under the water!"

"Couldn't have been. I'm completely dry."

"But you . . ."

"But I what?" Diana held the older woman's gaze.

"You went wading?"

"Yes, I did."

"But that water must be freezing!"

"I hardly felt it."

"Well," Carol laughed a little uncertainly, "it must be nice to be young. Doesn't that rock look just like an orange cat?"

"You think? I don't see it."

Sam sighed and headed for the dock.

Ryan sat between the two girls on the way back to the mainland. There was a fair bit of giggling from all concerned.

The lake was calm, the silvered blue broken only by the wake of the boat and a small school of herring rising to feed on the water bugs dimpling the surface.

Sam had eaten then curled up and gone to sleep in her backpack. Dangling a bottle of water from one hand, Diana leaned back against the gunnels and listened to Gary Spraum list just some of the more than fifty ships that had gone down between Point Petre and Main Duck Island. She didn't know which ship her sailor had been from, but it didn't really matter.

He was home now.

"The Metcalfe, the Maggie Hunter, the Gazelle, the Norway, the Atlas, the Annie Falconer, the Olive Branch, the Sheboygan, the Ida Walker, the Maple Glenn, the Lady Washington . . ."

A Woman's Work . . .

The premise for this anthology was the If I were an Evil Overlord *lists that are all over the internet. The basic list is pretty old but it's been added to and up-dated and adapted for* Star Trek *and* Star Wars *and minions and heroes and sidekicks and the evil overlord's accountant and the damsel in distress. Authors were to consider the list as inspiration and deal with at least one of the points in their story. I've always been a bit of an overachiever and I think I used over a dozen but the first scene, the queen's reaction to the challenge, that came from watching* Troy. *Seriously, if Hector's mother had been on the wall when Achilles showed up, this is how it would have gone down. Women are infinitely more practical about things like that than men—it's why they make such excellent evil overlords.*

IT WAS OBVIOUS THAT THE man outside the city wall was a Hero. His plain but serviceable armor—armor that had obviously seen several campaigns—did nothing to hide the breadth of his shoulders, the narrowness of his hips, or the long and muscular length of his legs. His hair gleamed gold under the edges of his helmet and even from her viewing platform on the top of the wall, Queen Arrabel could tell his eyes were a clear sky blue with the direct, unwavering gaze of an honorable man.

Over his left arm, he wore a simple unadorned shield, designed to deflect blows not support his ego by announcing his family ties to the world. In his right hand, he carried a sword. It looked like a hand and a half, double-edged broadsword although he was so mighty a warrior he made it seem small. She could just make out a heavy gold ring on the second finger of his right hand. It was the only jewelry he wore.

"Prince Danyel!" He called, his voice clear and carrying. "Come out and face me. Let you and I settle the animosity between our two peoples! There is no need for war; we will fight, man to man! He who wins our conflict will decide all!"

The queen raised her own voice enough to be heard by her people standing along the wall. "A gold coin to the archer who puts one in his eye."

For an instant there was a sound like the buzz of a thousand angry wasps.

Then a sound like a sudden hard rain on a state roof.

Then silence.

Leaning a little past the battlement to get a better line of sight, the queen smiled. "Nice grouping, archers. Well done. Wallace!"

"Majesty!" Her personal aide leapt forward.

"Go down and check the fletching on those arrows—it looks like we have at least three winners." Her archers were her pride and joy, even though she knew she shouldn't have favorites among her extensive armies. "Take a wizard with you and make sure he hasn't been magically booby-trapped then strip the body. Bring the armor and the ring to me, have the body cremated."

"And his horse, Majesty?"

The beautiful black stallion standing just to the right of the gate stared up at her with intelligent eyes.

"Archers!"

"Mother! I wanted that horse!"

Arrabel sighed, turning to her son as the stallion whirled to escape and crashed dead to the ground looking remarkably like a horse-shaped pin cushion. "Horses don't have intelligent eyes, Danyel. Nor are they able to determine who, in a group of people standing on top of a wall twenty feet over their heads, is in charge."

Danyel frowned, dark brows almost meeting over his nose. "So the Hero knew I'd win and take his horse and the horse was to kill me later. The horse was enchanted and the Hero was a sacrifice."

"I suspect the horse was no more than a back-up plan. Heroes never think they're going to lose."

"I could have taken him." At nearly twenty he was too old to pout but his tone was distinctly sulky.

She patted his arm as she passed. "Of course you could have. Captain Jurin."

Almost overcome by adoration, clearly astounded that the queen knew his name, the Captain stepped forward and saluted. "Majesty!"

"Send out a couple of patrols to make sure this Hero didn't leave one of those annoying side-kicks skulking about in the bushes."

"Yes, Majesty."

On the way back to the palace, she smiled and waved and noted how pleased everyone her son's age and younger was to see her. The free schooling she provided for her subjects until the age of twelve was paying off—it was so much easier to teach children how to think than it was to change their minds as adults. A strong apprenticeship program helped too. Idle hands found time for mischief and nothing straightened out a young troublemaker faster than twelve hours of hauling stone. City walls didn't build themselves.

It pleased her too to see so many babies around. Young men who tried to get out of the responsibilities of fatherhood were sent to the mines and their very fair wages paid entirely to the mother of their child. Fatherhood seemed a good deal in comparison. And the sort of man that might succeed at rebellion thought better of it when they became responsible for the care and feeding of six or seven screaming children who were guaranteed schooling and employment should the status quo be maintained.

"Mother."

One child had certainly done his best to sap her energy.

"Mother!"

"What is it, Danyel?"

"There's a girl standing on your statue."

"That's nice, dear." Arrabel blew a kiss to a strapping young man and smiled to see him blush. "Which statue?"

"The one with your hand on the head of the beggar brat. Mother, you'd better pay attention to this!"

Sighing, she turned, and glanced toward the statue in question. "Don't point, Danyel, it's common."

He dropped his arm with a sullen clank of van brace against breastplate. "Well, do you see her?"

It was hard to miss her. "Andrew, stop the coach." As the six archers in her escort moved into new defensive positions, the queen shifted over to stare out Danyel's window.

The girl had a head of flaming red hair and stood with one booted foot on the beggar child's stone head and the other tucked into the queen's bent elbow. Gesturing dramatically, she pitched her voice to carry over the ambient noise of the streets and shrieked that the queen cared nothing for her subjects.

"That would go further if she wasn't standing in front of the hospital you had built," Danyel muttered.

The people loved the hospital. Arrabel loved it more. With all healers working for the crown at salaries too good to walk away from, the crown controlled who got healed and how.

"The queen has turned you into mindless drones in her glittering hive!"

People who might not have noticed the girl, noticed the queen and the crowds began to quiet, half their attention on the flamboyant redhead and half on the royal coach.

"The queen has taken away your freedoms!" The last word fell into a nearly perfect silence and the girl's eyes widened as she stared over the heads of the crowd and realized who was in her audience.

"Like their freedom to starve?" Arrabel asked. "Do go on with what you were saying," she added, adjusting the paisley shawl more securely around her shoulders, "but I'm afraid I can't stay to listen, I have a country to run."

The crowd roared its approval as she gestured for her driver to go on. Had they not been well aware of her opinion on wasting food, she felt sure the girl would have been wearing a variety of produce in short order.

"It's weird how those types keep showing up," Danyel snorted, settling back into the velvet upholstery. "Each of them more ridiculous than the last. No one even listens to them any more."

"I'm glad to hear that." She already knew it.

"Still . . ." He scratched under the edge of his van-brace until he caught sight of her expression then he stopped. "This one seemed to really believe what she was saying."

"Did she? I didn't notice." Mirroring her son's position, minus the scratching, Arrabel made a mental note to have Wallace arrange a 'tour of the provinces' for the young actress when she showed up at the palace to be paid. If even Danyel had noticed a certain conviction in her performance, then the girl had become a liability. The last thing Arrabel wanted was for the people to start thinking.

Wallace was waiting for her in her private receiving room, the Hero's armor and ring on the table.

"The wizards have checked it thoroughly, your Majesty. It's nothing more than the well-made armor it appears."

"And the ring?"

"Also free of magical taint." He picked it up and handed it to her with a slight bow. "It bears the eagle crest of Mecada."

It was heavy and so pure a gold she could almost mark it with her thumbnail. "A gift to the Hero from King Giorge?"

"It seems likely, Majesty."

"He's really beginning to annoy me. This is what, the third attempt at myself or my son this month? Send this to the mint," she continued tossing the ring back to her advisor before he could respond. "It'll just cover what I paid those three archers to kill him."

It was only chance that a fortnight later the queen was inspecting new recruits in the outer courtyard near enough to the palace gate to hear a voice raised in protest.

"Oh come on, mate, what I get for this here load's gonna feed my family this coming cold. You're not after burning up the food in my family's mouths are you?"

In the courtyard, Arrabel smiled at the twenty young men and women who had just been congratulated on having passed the stringent physical and mental tests required to wear the Queen's Tabard, reminded them to write their mothers weekly, and then dismissed them into the care of her Captain of Recruits. He was a genius with young people. Once he got their training well under way, they'd protect her with their lives. By the time he finished, even death wouldn't stop them.

Moving quickly, her escort falling into place around her, she arrived at the gate in time to hear a second protest.

"But I'm from all the way out in New Bella! How would I have heard that her Majesty wants all hay delivered in tight bales?"

"Are you suggesting that my word has not reached New Bella?" she asked in turn, stepping out of the shadows. "Because if that's the case, I can repeat it more emphatically."

Very early on in her rule, she'd discovered that nothing spoke with quite so much emphasis as a troop of light cavalry armed primarily with torches and accelerant.

The carter paled as the pair of gate guards clanged to attention. "I'm sure I was the only one who didn't hear, Majesty!"

"Good. Unharness your . . ." She raised a brow at the animal, which rolled its eyes so that the whites showed all the way around and fought the reins trying to shy away from her.

"Mule, Majesty."

"Is it? Well, get it away from the cart, I'd hate for it to be injured."

To his credit, the carter had the mule away from the cart in record time.

"Burn it."

One of the gate guards dropped a lit torch into the hay which burst into flames and ejected a medium-sized nondescript man who leapt toward her, smoldering slightly. The six arrows that suddenly pounded into his torso knocked him back into the fire.

"Mercy, Majesty!" The carter dropped to his knees at her feet and laced rough, work-reddened fingers together. "He threatened my family, said he'd slit their throats in the dark if I didn't help him."

The queen sighed, ignoring the screaming as the wounded assassin burned. "How could he slit their throats if he was hiding in the back of your cart?"

"Majesty?"

"Once you took him away from your family, he couldn't slit their throats and all you had to do was drive-up to anyone in a Queen's Tabard and tell them what you had hidden in the hay. Since you didn't do that, I can only assume one of two situations apply. The first is that you were delivering him of your own free will. The second is that you are too stupid to live." Twitching her skirts aside, she raised her hand. "Since the end result is the same for either," she told the body as it fell, bristling with arrows. "It's not particularly relevant which applies. Now then . . ." She turned to the gate guards. ". . . this is exactly why we don't allow carts filled with loose hay into the city. Do you understand?"

"Yes, Majesty!"

"I'm pleased to hear that. We'll let this incident stand as an object lesson . . ." The assassin had finally stopped screaming. ". . . but I'm disappointed in both of you—a rule is a rule and although you didn't allow the cart through the palace gate, you did let the carter argue. That might have given the assassin time to slip inside and then how would you have felt?"

"Terrible, Majesty," admitted the guard on the left.

"Terrible," agreed the guard on the right, his eyes watering a little from the smoke.

"I certainly hope so. If you want to make it up to me, you can find out who let this cart into the city because I'm *very* disappointed in them. Wallace!"

"Majesty!" Her aide stepped over a bit of burning wheel.

"I don't imagine there's enough left of the body to identify but check his weapons. Let me know as soon as you have something. Oh, and Wallace?" Arrabel paused, her escort pausing in perfect formation with her. "See that the mule is given a good home. Something about it reminds me of my late husband."

"His knives are Mecadain, Majesty." Wallace laid all four blades in a row on the table. "As were what was left of his boots."

There was no point in asking if he were sure. He wouldn't have told her if he wasn't. "King Giorge again."

"Yes, Majesty."

"I was planning to invade Mecada next spring."

"I think that's why he was trying to remove you, Majesty."

"Yes, well, you'd think that someone who didn't want me to invade would put a little more effort into making friends and a little less effort into annoying me." The queen walked around the table slowly, her heels rapping out a piqued beat against the parquet floor. She stared down at the knives and shook her head. "When I look at these, I'm *very* annoyed." A slight, almost inaudible sound drew her attention to her aide. "Oh, not at you, Wallace. At King Giorge. Tell General Palatat that I'd like to see him and his senior staff. And then find me a few bards who wouldn't mind a new wardrobe and an all expense paid trip to Mecada."

"A new wardrobe, Majesty?"

"I think we should let the people of Mecada know what their King has gotten them into and the bards will be able to reach more people if they're not so obviously mine."

Arrabel was the sole patron of the Bardic College. It was amazing how many bards preferred to sing warm and well fed, permitted to travel freely about the land wearing the Queen's colors. Of course, there were always a few who insisted on suffering for art's sake so Arrabel saw to it that they did.

The queen accompanied her army into Mecada, turned a captured border town into a well fortified command center, and stayed there.

"You won't be riding at the front of your army, Mother?"

"No, Danyel. When the ruler rides at the front of the army, she only gets in the way."

"And there is also the great danger you would be in, Majesty!"

She glanced across the war room at Captain Jurin standing a mid a group of staff officers and sighed. "Thank you for considering that, Captain."

He blushed.

"I'm not afraid," Danyel declared.

Arrabel settled her shawl more securely around her shoulders and stared at her son for a long moment. He squared his shoulders and raised his chin. "I'm sure you aren't," she said at last. "Chose then whether you stay here or ride into battle."

"I will ride into battle!"

She sighed again. "You're beginning to remind me so much of your father. You'll be treated as nothing more than a junior officer, say . . ." Her eyes fell on Captain Jurin. ". . . a captain. Wallace."

"Majesty?"

"Have a captain's uniform made for my son."

"Yes, Majesty."

Danyel stared at her, appalled "But . . ."

"Billy goats butt, dear. You'll obey your commanders because their orders come from General Palatat . . ."

"But, Mother, I'm a prince!"

". . . and General Palatat," Arrabel continued mildly, "speaks for me." She took his silence for assent and smiled. "Don't grind your teeth, dear. Of course you'll keep the lines of communication open between the battle and this command center," she told the General. "But I trust you and your staff to do their job." Which went without saying really because they wouldn't have their jobs if she didn't.

Queen Arrabel's army had the advantage of numbers, training, and motivation. King Giorge's people, invaded because they were next on the list, had only the moral high ground.

"Free bread and beer, Mother?" Danyel, back in full royal regalia, rubbed at a smudge on his van-brace as he rode beside his mother through the conquered capital.

"It doesn't take much to make the people like you, dear. It's worth making a bit of an effort."

"But you just conquered them."

"Most people don't care who's in charge as long as someone is."

"And the people who do care?"

"Are easy enough to replace." Arrabel stared out at the city–many

of its buildings damaged by her siege engines during the final battle–
and began working out the amount of stone it would take to rebuild
it. And, of course, there were schools to be built. Some of the more
recalcitrant nobility could start hauling blocks in as soon as possible.

She let Danyel emerge first at the palace, waiting until her escort
was in place before she stepped out of the carriage. She wore her
usual neat clothing over sensible shoes and was well aware that next
to her more flamboyant son she looked like a sparrow next to a peacock.

People tended not to shoot at sparrows.

"Mother, why didn't you wear your crown?" Danyel asked her as
they stepped carefully over the shattered remains of the palace gate.

"Everyone who needs to know who I am, knows." Tucking a
strand of hair behind her ear, she stopped in the outer courtyard and
glanced over at a group of Mecadian soldiers–prisoners now–huddled next to the smoking ruin of what had probably been a stable.

"Wallace."

"Majesty?"

"Make sure they let their mothers know they survived."

"Yes, Majesty. And the ones who didn't survive?"

"Well, they'll hardly be able to write home, now will they?"

General Palatat met them outside King Giorge's throne room in
front of the enormous brass-bound doors. "The door's been spelled,
Majesty, we can't break it down. But, they're still in there–King
Giorge, Queen Fleya, both princes, both princesses."

"Personal guards?"

"They died out here, Majesty, covering the royal family's retreat."

"All of them?" She glanced over at the liveried bodies piled out of
the way. "My, that was short-sighted."

"Yes, Majesty. One of the princesses has been talking through the
key hole. She says her brothers want to negotiate a surrender but
they'll only speak to you. Royal to royal as it were."

"They could speak to me," Danyel muttered.

His mother ignored him. "Do you think the princes will negotiate
in good faith?"

"They are considered to be honorable men," the general told her.
"They will do what they feel is right regardless of the consequences."

"They take after their father then." The queen stared at the door
to the throne room. The smart thing for King Giorge to have done
would have been to get his family out of the country when it became

obvious he'd lost–which would have been about half an hour after the first battle had been joined. Arrabel assumed he'd refused to leave his people or some such nonsense. "Well, tell them I'm here."

At the general's signal, one of the Queen's Tabards banged on the door with a spear butt.

"Is she there?" Interestingly, the girl sounded more annoyed than distressed.

"I am."

"There's a secret exit at the end of the hall, by a statue of my father. Do you see it?"

"The statue?" There were ankles on a plinth and rather a lot of rubble. A bit of the rubble seemed to be wearing a stone crown. "No but I can see where it was."

"My brothers will come out, stripped to their breaches so you can see they're weaponless. You approach them alone and they'll give you our father's terms of surrender."

"I'm to approach alone?" A raised hand cut off the general's protest. "At two to one odds?"

"We know you have archers with you. You always have archers with you!"

"True enough. Very well, given that I have archers, I will meet you at the end of the hall." She sighed and smoothed a wrinkle out of her skirt. "Wallace?"

"Yes, Majesty?"

"Am I getting predictable?"

"Only in the best of all possible ways, Majesty."

Arrabel glanced over at him and when he bowed, she smiled but before she could compliment his answer, a section of the wall at the end of the hall slid back and a half naked young man emerged. And then a second.

Both princes were in their mid-twenties not quite two years apart in age and, given that very little was left to the imagination, in obviously fine condition. Muscles rippled everywhere muscles could ripple. One wore his golden hair loose, the other tied his darker hair back but except for that they could have been twins. That she had an appreciation for handsome men was no secret so she suspected Giorge had sent out his sons because he expected they'd get better terms.

"Mother, I could take them."

"Not now dear, mother's going to go negotiate." She walked

purposefully forward and stopped a body-length and an equal distance from both princes. "Well?"

The blond cocked his head, grey eyes narrowed. "You don't look like I imagined."

"Is there any reason I should?"

Before he could respond, the brunette charged at her, screaming.

At least one, maybe two of the arrows passed so close she felt the breeze. As the prince hit the floor, she rolled her eyes. "That was stupid."

"No," the other prince snarled. "That was a sacrifice. Your archers can not save you now; my brother's death has disarmed them. For what you have done to my people, I will kill you with my bare hands and yes, I expect to die just after but . . ." He stopped and stared in astonishment at the half dozen arrows suddenly protruding from his chest, one of them adorned with a small piece of fabric. "But . . ."

"My archers can reload, aim, and fire in under seven seconds," Arrabel told him as he dropped heavily to his knees. "Never pause to gloat, dear," she added, patting his cheek as he sagged back.

"Mother! Are you all right?"

"Of course I am."

"But what if he'd grabbed you and used you as a shield?" Danyel grabbed her arm to illustrate and a long, thin knife slid out from under her neat, lace-trimmed cuff, scoring a line along the enamel on his van-brace.

"Then I'd have dealt with it myself," she said, pulling free of his slackened grip. "Although I'm just as glad I didn't have to." The knife disappeared. "I'm quite fond of this dress and I'd hate to have gotten blood all over it. And speaking of this dress . . ." she turned to face her archers, brandishing the hole in her full skirt. "Who took the shot that went through here?"

A very pale young man stumbled forward and dropped to one knee. He was shaking so hard it sounded as though he was tapping his bow against the floor.

"Conner Burd isn't it? Your mother runs a small dairy on the outside of the capital."

The young archer managed part of a nod.

"Let that be a lesson to you all, if my life is in danger, don't worry about my clothing and don't feel you're redundant just because another five arrows are heading for the target. Those arrows could miss. Good shot, Conner. General Palatat."

"Majesty!"

"Stop trying to break through the door and go through the wall."

"Majesty?"

"No one ever thinks to have a wizard spell more than the door. Get a few strapping young men up here with sledge hammers and go through the wall." Her tone suggested she'd better not have to repeat herself a third time.

The queen was not the first to step through the breech in the wall. The queen was the sixteenth to enter, after fourteen soldiers, General Palatat and her son. The first soldier through the breech took a tapestry pole to the back of the head.

The throne room was empty except for the royal family. King Giorge sat slumped in his throne, head on his chest. Queen Fleya sat at his feet, sobbing. One of the princesses, her hair a mass of tangled mahogany curls and showing just a little too much cleavage for the situation, stood snarling by her father's side, the tapestry pole having been taken away from her with only minor damage. The other princess, blonde hair neatly tied back, arms folded over her sensible cardigan, stood just behind her sister, frowning slightly.

"You can't touch him now," Queen Fleya cried as Arrabel approached the throne. "He's gone beyond your control!"

Arrabel cocked her head and studied the king, his lips and eyelids were a pale blue-green. "Took poison has he?"

Eyes red with weeping, Fleya's lip curled. "He knew he could expect no mercy!"

"It's hardly practical to leave live enemies behind me, now is it?" she answered switching her attention to the queen. "I wonder what he thought I'd do with you."

"You will force me into exile with my daughters and the body of my dead husband and we will live out our lives torn from the country we love." She wiped her eyes and straightened her shoulders. "It's what is done."

"Really? The upholstery on the throne—it's expensive is it?"

Fleya looked up at the embroidered gold velvet under her husband and back at Arrabel, confused. "Yes but . . ."

"Hard to keep clean?"

"I expect so but . . ."

"General Palatat."

"Majesty."

"There's no reason to make things more difficult than we have to for the staff. Have King Giorge's body dragged down to the floor then behead him."

The queen and the dark-haired princesses screamed out versions of "You can't!"

The second princess said nothing at all.

When Giorge's head came off there was rather a lot of blood, enough to partially obscure an impressive mosaic map of the kingdom set into the throne room floor. Released by the soldier who held her, Queen Fleya ran to her husband's side.

Danyel said, "But Mother, he was already dead."

"Dead men don't bleed like that, Danyel." Arrabel stepped back as the blood spread. "The poison only feigned death. After the three of them reached exile it would wear off and Giorge would rise from his supposed grave to seek vengeance."

"But how did you know?"

"It's what I would have done, dear. Wallace."

"Majesty?"

"Make sure he's cremated."

"Noooooooooooooo!" Fleya's wailed protest drew everyone's attention. Sitting on the floor, her silk skirts soaking up the king's blood, she held his headless body clasped tight in her arms. "You will not take him from me! I will not go into exile without my Giorge!"

Arrabel sighed. "Of course you won't." She raised her hand. Because of the late king's body, four of the arrows went into Fleya's upper torso, the other two went one into each eye. "All right, who risked the eye shots?" When two of the archers admitted as much, she smiled at them and pointed a teasing finger. "There's no need to show off, I know how good you are. Now then . . ." Lifting her skirts, she walked around the growing puddle. "This is taking far too long. You." The same finger pointed at the dark-haired princess, held struggling between two Tabards. "You'll marry my son, giving his claim to rule this kingdom validity."

"Never!"

She raised a hand. "I expected as much," she sighed as the body hit the floor and pointed at the second princess. "*You'll* marry my son and give his claim to rule this kingdom validity."

The girl stared into Arrabel face for a moment then shrugged. "All right."

"Don't shrug, dear. It's common." A slight frown as recognition dawned. "That was your voice at the door."

"Yes."

"The poison was your plan."

"Yes."

"And your brother's attempt?"

"My plan."

"Really? What's your name?"

"Mailynne."

"How old are you Mailynne?"

"Seventeen."

"I imagine you have some ideas about how the kingdom should be run."

Mailynne's grey eyes narrowed. "Yes."

"Good."

"Mother, I don't want to be married." Danyel reached to grab her arm, noticed the gouge on his van-brace and thought better of it.

Arrabel and Mailynne turned together. "That's not really relevant, dear."

"But ..." He paused, mouth open. "Wait. I'm to rule this kingdom?"

"Under my guidance."

"But you'll be at home?"

"Yes."

Dark brows drew in. "And I'll be here?"

"Yes."

"Oh." His smile showed perfect teeth and an enchanting dimple. "Well, that's different then."

His mother placed her hand in the center of the princess' back and gently pushed her forward. The girl was wearing some kind of harness under her sweater that probably held at least one weapon. "You will rule Mecada with Mailynne at your side."

"As you say, Mother." Danyel bent and kissed the princess' hand. "I want an enormous wedding," he announced when he straightened.

"Don't be ridiculous, dear. You don't bankrupt a county that's recently lost a war just so you can have a party. Wallace."

"Majesty?"

"We'll need someplace central with good security but high visibility."

"And somewhere we can release a hundred white doves!"

"Doves aren't really relevant right now, Danyel."

"The surviving nobility that served my father should be there," Mailynne suggested as her future husband pouted.

Arrabel turned a maternal smile on the girl. "That's not really relevant either, dear."

The wedding was short but beautiful. As a wedding present, Arrabel left a regiment of the Queen's Tabards in Mecada to help keep the peace. Her new daughter-in-law narrowed her eyes but accepted the gift graciously.

Because there was correspondence to go over, Wallace rode with her in the carriage on the way home.

"Wallace?"

"Yes, Majesty?"

"How long do you figure Danyel will last?"

"Majesty?"

"I expect she'll keep him around until she has an heir. And I expect that will happen as soon as possible."

"But Majesty . . ."

"As much as he adored me, he was becoming a distraction. Mother this and mother that and eventually he'd distract me at a bad time. This girl was a good choice, Wallace, I won't live forever and I'd like to think—on that very distant day—that I was leaving my people in good hands. Hands that won't undo all the work I've done."

"She does remind me a little of you, Majesty."

"Yes." Arrabel picked up the wrapped slice of wedding cake from the seat beside her and tossed it out the window. "She does, doesn't she."

The Things Everyone Knows

Way back in the bright beginning, or many years ago at least, I had an idea for the ending of a short story but no story to attach it to. And then Stephen Pagel asked me to write a story for an anthology of gay, lesbian, bi fantasy called Swords of the Rainbow *and hey, suddenly I had a place to put the ending if only I could come up with a beginning and a middle. To make a longish story short, I did and thus the first Terizan story, "Swan's Braid," was published.*

Terizan is a thief in a vaguely Middle-Easter city called Oreen and I had more fun building her world than should be legal. I'd love to do something with her and Swan and Poli and the rest at novel length but, so far, no plot that will carry the weight. Still, not dead yet.

This is the fifth Terizan story.

"But I'm a thief."

"Why so you are. It's interesting that never occurred to us, what with this being the Thieves Guild and all."

Terizan's lip curled in spite of all efforts to keep her expression neutral. Tribune One's lip curled in return. Tribunes Two and Three shuffled their seats out of the direct line of fire as surreptitiously as only master thieves could shuffle. Gaze locked on One's face, Terizan's right brow flicked up.

One laughed.

When that was it for confrontation, Two and Three exchanged nearly identical expressions of chagrin.

What they'd missed, and what One hadn't, was that Terizan had no intention of becoming part of the Thieves Guild Tribunal, at least not yet. Granted, she'd been taking reading lessons on the Street of

Tales but she wasn't ready to make an irreversible challenge to the Tribunal's authority. Besides, the thought of spending any significant amount of time in close proximately to Tribune Three and the scent of sandalwood oil he'd recently started rubbing all over his not inconsiderable bulk, turned her stomach.

Terizan hoped he was doing the rubbing himself because the alternative just didn't bear considering.

"The job you're talking about," she continued, scratching her nose to keep from sneezing, "is a job for a spy."

"And what is a thief but one who steals in and then steals out again holding something belonging to another. In this instance, the something is information. Otherwise there is no difference." Tribune Two sounded more emotionless than usual—probably in an effort to make up for the earlier reaction.

"It's simple," Tribune One sighed, lacing ringless fingers together. "If the rumors are true and there actually is a conspiracy to overthrow the Council, you steal into one of their meetings then you steal out with the names of those involved."

"If," Tribune Three snorted.

"The Council is convinced . . ." Two began.

"The Council has its collective head so far up its collective ass that it's run out of air," Three interrupted.

"Tribune Three has a point," Terizan noted. "What if the Council's wrong? What if there is no conspiracy?"

"Then bring them proof of that."

"Proof of nothing?"

"That should be no problem for a thief of your skills," One said, not bothering to hide her smirk. "Unless your failure at the wizard's tower has shaken your confidence."

Oh yeah. She was never going to live *that* down. That she'd succeeded at the wizard's tower was beside the point since no one could know of it. "I'm not questioning my skills; I'm questioning the Council's requirements."

Two's pale eyes narrowed. "Rumors of conspiracy make the Council understandably paranoid. If this matter isn't settled conclusively, they will begin making random arrests. They've already hired another two dozen constables."

"We don't need to tell you that increased security will adversely affect our membership," One added. "Of course, you may refuse the job . . ."

Terizan held up a hand and slid off the pile of stolen carpets that seemed to be a permanent fixture in the Sanctum. "If I turn down the job, you'll offer it to a thief with lesser skills who'll get caught and probably killed and I'll be responsible and blah blah blah. We've been through this all before."

"If you turn down the job," Two told her, voice cold, "we'll offer it to a thief who might be less than scrupulous about the names he or she offers the Council. Who might add names to the list for personal reasons."

The pause after this declaration was triumphant.

"Did the council give you any idea where I should start looking for this conspiracy?" she sighed.

"They've heard rumors of meetings in the Necropolis. You have three days."

The Necropolis was haunted. Everyone knew that. From all reports, the winding paths that lead from the gate to the top of the hill were as busy with the restless dead as Butcher's Row was with the living on market day. Only the lowest plateau down by the river where the very poor were buried in trenched graves remained untouched by ghostly activity.

Terizan figured the very poor were probably glad of a chance to finally rest.

She'd never seen a ghost. Mostly because she never went to the Necropolis, a decision of a very early Council having made sure the dead had nothing worth stealing.

"When it has been decided by a physician of Oreen that in death the citizen shall pose no danger to the city, then the body shall be wrapped in an unbleached cotton shroud and laid to rest in that part of Oreen designated for the dead."

The City of the Dead; where the wealthy built mausoleums like mansions and everyone else marked their family's place with as much ornately carved stone as they could afford. The Thieves Guild, like many of the city's professional organizations, had an area in the catacombs for their members without family although, for obvious reasons, thieves' funerals were seldom well attended.

If an organization intent on overturning the Council *was* meeting unseen in the Necropolis, they were probably meeting in the catacombs. Cut into the lowest level of the hill, the narrow passageways and chambers carved out of the rock would provide a perfect hiding place for any number of secret societies—underground in more ways than one.

As the wall around the perimeter was low enough that any reasonably determined adult could easily get over it, and the Necropolis was large enough that there wasn't one place to watch all access points, Terizan decided she might as well go directly to the catacombs. Where she found the black, iron-bound doors securely locked.

They were the kind of locks a merely competent thief like Balzador could get through but even by fitful moonlight it was obvious to Terizan no one had. Not for some time. If this rumored organization was meeting in the tunnels under the Necropolis, it was getting in another way. She peered up toward the crest of the hill, past the hundreds of tombs cut into the walls of each terrace. Any one of them could be a secret entrance to the catacombs below. She couldn't break into all of them. Well, she could, but there was no time and less need.

Moving to a less visible position while she considered her options, she crouched in the velvet shadow cast by the cracked sandstone box that held the remains of Hanra Seend, Wife, Mother, Weaver and something else too worn to be read in the moonlight. She could climb to a better vantage point and hope she spotted one of the conspirators skulking about the graves, waiting to be followed. Or she could just pick these locks and go through the front door then decide on her next step once she got inside.

"He'll let her use my loom!"

Terizan pivoted slowly in place to find her nose barely a finger's width away from the nose of the pale, distraught, and translucent woman crouched beside her.

"He'll let her use my loom," the woman repeated. "She won't take care of it, I know she won't. You have to tell him not to let her use my loom."

". . . and then she touched my arm and I bolted."

Poli raised a delicate arched brow higher still. "Everyone knows the Necropolis is haunted, Sweetling."

"That's not the point." Terizan paced across her best friend's bedchamber and back again to stand at the foot of the bed. "She was dead, Poli and she was talking to me. She wasn't just moaning and wafting about, she was interacting. And when she touched me, I could feel this flash of despair."

One elegant shoulder lifted and fell. "Well, as you said, she was dead. That's a valid reason to be depressed."

"Poli!"

He sighed. "So the poor woman carried the concerns of life over into death; you just got in her way, stop taking it personally." Moving a fringed cushion aside, he patted the edge of the bed. "Come and sit and tell me why you were in the Necropolis after dark. You know you're going to anyway so you might as well get it over with. That way we can both get some sleep."

"It was Guild business . . ."

"Anything said in my bed, stays in my bed—or *my* guild wouldn't *have* much business." He patted the blanket again. "Come on."

So she told him how The Council had heard rumors of a conspiracy and how rumor had placed the conspiracy in the Necropolis. She told him how The Council had come to the Thieves' Guild and how she was to steal into a meeting and out again with the names of those involved. "Although how I'm supposed to get the names of those I don't recognize, I have no idea. I doubt they do a role call before every meeting." She deepened her voice. "Ajoe the Candle-maker?" And up again. "Aye."

"Don't tell me Ajoe the Candle-maker's involved!"

"I was just using him as an example because I was at the Necropolis and his wife's just died and that's not the point," she sighed. "The point is, I have no idea how I'm supposed to steal these names."

"You'll think of something. You always do." He spent a moment staring at his reflection in the hand mirror he'd taken from the tiny table by the bed. "What will The Council do with the names when you get them?" he asked at last, tucking a strand of hair behind his ear.

She shrugged and plucked at the blanket. "They'll arrest everyone involved, probably execute them."

"People are always complaining about the Council." He lifted a thoughtful gaze up off the mirror. "Taxes are too high, the constables are never there when you need them, there are holes in my street deep enough to swallow a donkey—but it's never come to action before. I wonder why now. This lot's certainly no worse than any other."

"Better than some," Terizan allowed. It hadn't been that long ago that the Council had executed three of their own who'd been taking bribes from a bandit chief.

"The rumors could be wrong."

"Could be." Rumor moved through Old Oreen faster than weak beer through the Fermentation Brotherhood. "But then they want proof of that."

"Proof of nothing?"

"That's what *I* said," she snorted. "What do you think I should do, Poli?"

"I think you should have sex more often, let your hair grow out, and wear brighter colors."

Her hand went involuntarily to her cap of short dark hair. "I have to get into the catacombs," she said. "But I think I'd best check the place out in daylight first."

"Well if you knew," Poli sighed. "Why did you ask?"

The maintenance of the Necropolis was handled by acolytes of Ayzarua, the Gateway. She wasn't exactly a death goddess–two hundred years ago, after trouble with competing death cults, the Council had made the worship of Death illegal. Ayzarua represented the passage from life to death, a definition just vague enough to get around the law. She had no temple; her followers believed that all living creatures carried her temple within them.

Terizan thought the whole thing was kind of creepy but she had to admit the Ayzaruites took good care of the Necropolis. The paths were raked, the cracks in the rock were weed free, and the small amount of vandalism she could see appeared to be in the process of being either repaired or removed. The Ayzaruites were a definite presence in the Necropolis. Something to remember.

In daylight, the locks on the catacombs looked no more difficult than they had by moonlight and just as infrequently used. Shooting a nervous glance toward Hanra Seend's resting place as she passed, Terizan started along the first terrace trying to look fascinated. Apparently, the City of the Dead, was a popular destination for visitors to Oreen. Took all kinds, she supposed.

The basic design of the wall tombs included four shelves on each of three walls with a stone crypt in the center for when bare bones were ready to be removed and the shelf refilled. Tombs in the Necropolis were used for generations and they were all variations on the theme. Individuality showed up in the ornately carved facades and in the narrow gates that lead through them. Steel gates, stone gates, wooden gates; bolted, mortared, chained in place; every one of them, even the most solid, with a small horizontal window just at eye level.

The reason for the window had long been forgotten but as newer tombs copied the oldest tombs everyone knew it was supposed to be there so the window remained. It reminded Terizan of jail cells.

Approaching the first tomb, she hesitated, afraid that when she looked in, something would look out. Bodies, were no problem, she'd seen plenty and robbed a couple but Hanra Seend's ghost had prodded her imagination.

Terizan rubbed at her arm. It was just turned noon. Ghosts, like thieves and traitors worked under cover of darkness. Of course, *she* was here now so . . .

Just look!

It took a moment for her eyes to adjust to the faint spill of sunlight past her head but eventually she managed to make out the vague outlines of cloth wrapped bodies. There was a faint smell of rot, a stronger smell of incense, and nothing at all to suggest either a secret entrance into the catacombs or a restless spirit. Relieved, she kept moving.

By mid-afternoon, her legs ached from the constant climb. With about a third of the Necropolis examined, she'd seen nothing out of the ordinary. Trying to ignore how hungry she was, she crossed to a particularly ornate tomb and peered through the opening in the big double gates.

Years of practice kept her from shrieking. She leapt back, the heel of her sandal came down hard on something soft and yielding and she leapt forward again as it moaned.

Too close to the tomb for comfort, she whirled to see one of Ayzarua's acolytes hopping in place, rake forgotten, both hands wrapped around one bare foot. Well, she knew what she'd stepped on. That was a start.

Heart pounding, she managed a fairly coherent, "Sorry, I didn't see you."

"I know!"

"Are you hurt?"

"Pain is transcendental," he gasped.

Terizan figured that was a yes. She watched as he put the injured foot down and shifted his weight.

"But I'll live," he concluded after a moment. He studied her in turn. "What frightened you?"

"I wasn't," she began, saw his eyebrows rise, and surrendered bravado. "There's something in there," she told him, nodding toward the tomb. "It grabbed for me."

"Did it now?" He limped past her and peered through the gate. "Ah, I thought so. Pardon her ignorance, Gracious Lady. It is my Lady," he explained turning toward Terizan with a smile. "Her likeness at least. She reaches out to help the recently dead through the gate."

Dared by his smile, Terizan leaned forward, eyes narrowed. Even knowing it was a statue, her heart still jumped at the sudden sight of a hand nearly at her nose. The Goddess herself, back in the dim depths of the tomb was barely visible. Terizan thought she could see friendly eyes and a gentle, welcoming smile within the depths of a stone hood then suddenly . . .

"Okay." She jumped back again. "Skull."

"The best images of my Lady recognize she stands between life and death," the acolyte explained. "This particular image, commissioned by the Harl family and sculpted by Navareen Clos, has a spell attached. If you look long enough into the darkness beyond the Goddess, you'll see the Gateway open. There are only two other tombs like it in the entire Necropolis, up on the crown of the hill in crypts of the two of the oldest families in Oreen—the Aldaniz and the Pertayn. Unfortunately the Aldaniz didn't specify . . ."

Terizan let his voice wash over her, paying only enough attention to nod where it seemed appropriate. The sort of person who'd spend the day methodically climbing the Necropolis peering into tombs was the sort of person who'd actually listen to this kind of lecture. It had obviously been a long time since this particular acolyte had found an audience and he seemed determined to make the most of it. Fortunately, he wasn't trying to convert her, he was just talking.

And talking.

Terizan kept nodding and amused herself by watching the shadows move across a particularly ornate carving on the next tomb over. She frowned slightly as the shadows caressed the edge of the highest bolt holding the gate to the tomb. That bolt had been removed and, from the raw look of the surrounding stone, both recently and frequently. Why bother to unlock the gate when it could be lifted, locked, away from the stone. Not the oldest trick on the scroll—she seemed to remember it was actually number eleven or twelve—but useful.

"And what brings you to my Lady's city?"

"Me?" Jerked from her reverie, Terizan searched for an answer that didn't involve conspiracy or the Thieves Guild. "It's uh, peaceful." Disturbingly peaceful. Uncomfortably peaceful.

The acolyte nodded. "There are few places more peaceful than the grave."

Hard to argue with that, Terizan acknowledged. She needed to find out if he'd seen anything. But just in case he was in on it, she needed to do it subtly. "So, do many people come here at night?"

His brows rose. Poli was right. She really sucked at subtle.

"The gates are locked at sunset."

Everyone knew that. "And your lot makes sure other people stay out?"

"There's no need. The Necropolis is haunted."

Conscious of the Ayzaruite's attention, she went out the gate just before sunset and back over the wall shortly after. Moving quickly from shadow to shadow on a path that took her well around the weaver's crypt, she finally climbed into a hiding place on top of the tomb with the loosened bolts. Everyone knew that conspirators met in the dark of night when cloaked figures scuttling about empty streets were likely to be noticed and they'd have no plausible excuse if they got caught. If she was running a conspiracy, she'd have them meet in the late evening and have them head home with the crowds when the cantinas closed, hiding them in plain sight. Of course, she *wasn't* running this conspiracy and that became obvious as time passed and she saw no one but a few translucent figures wafting by, moaning.

She determinedly ignored them and they ignored her.

Finally, after the bells of Old Oreen rang midnight, the sound strangely muffled in the City of the Dead, Terizan saw two cloaked figures approaching. They opened the tomb, exactly the way she'd know they would—the bolts whispering out of the stone—and slipped inside, replacing the gate behind them. She'd have never noticed the faint spill of lantern light a moment later if she hadn't been waiting for it.

Hanging upside down over the gate, she could just make them out as they crouched by the rear wall and together slid the shrouded body from the lowest shelf. Setting it carefully to one side, Conspirator number one lay down in its place and crawled into darkness. Conspirator number two passed the lantern through and followed.

Terizan waited a moment for her eyes to readjust to full dark, checked that there were no more cloaked conspirators approaching, and flipped down to the ground. The gate was heavy for one person but she didn't need to open it very far. She slipped through, closed it, and keeping her fingertips on the center crypt made her way to the back wall. By the time she reached it, she was in total darkness. She knew she was holding her hand in front of her face but she couldn't see it.

Fortunately, it was impossible to get lost.

There was room to stand on the other side of the corpse shelf but just barely. Her fingertips danced over rough stone; a crack in the rock, a natural fissure. She counted twelve paces, felt the air currents change, and stopped. Barely an arm's length from her face, the fissure opened up into a much wider passageway.

When she held her breath she could hear a quiet hum of sound. When she crept silently forward and peered out of the crack, she could see a faint graying of the dark off to her right.

The conspirators were meeting in one of the catacombs' square tomb-within-a-tomb areas and enough light spilled out the entrance that Terizan could just make out the Carters' crest carved over the arch. As she came closer, the sound fractured into a number of voices all making the kind of anticipatory small talk that suggested the meeting had yet to start. Since there were more people present than the two she'd followed, there were clearly other routes in.

She could lie down and peer around the corner into the tomb well below where most people would even think of looking for intruders but there was no way of telling how many more conspirators were still to arrive and that would leave her exposed. Provided this was the meeting of conspirators the Council had hired the Thieves Guild to find. For all Terizan knew, she'd stumbled on a social club for necrophiliacs.

Pressed up against the stone niches that lined the passageway, she glimpsed a line of grey at the edge of her vision. Peering over the shrouded body on the shoulder-level niche, she could see a crack in the rock as wide as her thumb. Moving quickly, she scooped up the corpse—breathing through her teeth at the intensified smell of rot—and stuffed it in with the body in the niche below. Any small sounds she made were covered by the sudden rhythmic rise and fall of a single voice inside the tomb. It sounded like . . .

Poetry?

Not surprising, given the venue, images of death were prevalent.

The niches were narrow and not easy to get into but Terizan had been in more difficult places and with a minimum of bruising, she managed to get her right eye lined up with the crack. There were seven cloaked figures in the tomb. Not a large conspiracy but she supposed seven motivated people could do some damage. After all, she'd managed to destabilize the throne of Kalazamir all by herself.

As she watched, the poet finished, slid the scroll into a pocket, and blew his nose, clearly overcome. She could see three faces clearly and didn't recognize any of them. Then a fourth raised both arms, the cloak sliding back as he gestured for silence and with some surprise Terizan recognized the heavy gold links he wore around one wrist. She'd had her eye on that bracelet for a while. It seemed as though Ajoe the Candle-maker *was* involved and not only involved, but in a position of some authority. Maybe grief at the death of his wife and infant son had addled his brains and turned him from law-abiding artisan to . . .

Poet?

"We ask justice for the dead," Ajoe declared, his voice rough with grief.

Terizan hoped the next couple of lines would rhyme. She liked Ajoe and didn't want him involved in anything that would result in his head on a spike in the Crescent.

"Overcrowded streets slow the arrival of what few healers there are. The high taxes paid by the apothecaries keep medicines too expensive. The rulings of the Council kill those we love. Those who lead have failed us and must be removed."

Not poet.

"Who will lead us to justice?"

The other six mirrored his position, arms up. "Who will lead us?" they repeated.

Terizan had assumed the question was rhetorical, the sort of thing secret organizations chanted to get in the mood for conspiracy, but as she watched a translucent figure floated down from the ceiling in the far corner of the room. Pride kept her from bolting this time. Pride and well, it seemed there was some truth in familiarity breeding contempt.

It took her a while to recognize the ghost but, in her own defense, the last time she'd seen Councilor Saladaz his head had been on a spike in the Crescent after he'd been executed for betraying caravans to the bandit chief Hyrantaz for a percentage of the stolen goods.

He seemed to have gotten his head back.

His voice a distant whisper, he began to speak of how the Council had been responsible for countless deaths in Oreen. Men, women, and children all lost to life and love because of the actions or inactions of the Council. "We all know the Council is corrupt. We all know the Council must be stopped before more loved lives are lost." Thought about rationally, nothing Saladaz said made much sense but it was obvious to Terizan watching the seven people listening that they weren't thinking rationally. Like Ajoe, these men and women were lost in grief and that grief was being expertly manipulated by the dead councilor. He'd always been able to work a crowd into near hysteria and while death had lowered his volume it had focused his skill.

In a weird way, she admired Saladaz's ability to hold a grudge beyond the grave. The Council had him executed and now he was using what he had—grief stricken visitors to the Necropolis—to exact his revenge. It was probably a good thing he didn't know she'd been the one who'd exposed his dealings with Hyrantaz.

"The Council must be removed," Saladaz whispered, moving about the tomb and touching each of the conspirators in turn.

They shuddered and chanted, "The Council must be removed."

Terizan shuddered with them, remembering the weaver's touch. It was a small step from grief to despair.

"The dead must have justice."

"The dead must have justice!"

Terizan would have bet serious coin that when Saladaz spoke of the dead, he meant only himself.

"We must take action to avenge our dead."

"We must take action to avenge our dead!"

"When the time of mourning is done, we will take action," Ajoe the candle-maker added in a tone as definite as the dead councilor's had been suggestive.

Saladaz's face twisted as the other six repeated, "When the time of mourning is done." Throwing off their cloaks, they began to wail and beat at their chests. His mouth moved but it was impossible to hear his rough whisper over the grieving and finally he surrendered to the inevitable and wafted back up through the tomb's ceiling.

Leaving seemed like a good idea to Terizan. Besides Ajoe, she'd recognized another of the seven by the silver and lapis clasp that bound her thick grey hair. She didn't yet know the woman's name but she knew she worked on Draper's Row and that was enough. Sliding silently out of the niche, she waited a moment for her eyes to adjust and then, fingertips stroking the stone, moved into the dark of the catacombs, counting her footsteps back to the crack in the tomb wall.

The name of the woman who'd owned the silver hair clasp was Seriell Vanyaz, her eldest son had recently died in a construction accident in the new city, crushed under a load of stone. Terizan settled the clasp in her pocket and crossed the bridge into the Necropolis. It would be easy enough now to find the other names, all she had to do was ask an acolyte for the names of those who'd been interred over the last few months and match the faces of the mourners to the faces of the conspirators.

She could hand the names to the Tribunal a day early. The Tribunal would hand them to the Council and then, probably before Terizan had even counted her share of the payment, the Council would add another seven bodies to the City of the Dead.

She'd thought about telling the Tribunal that Councilor Saladaz was the only actual conspirator.

"A dead Councilor? Not only dead but beheaded? You saw him then? Conspiring? Alone?"

Council might believe that Saladaz wanted revenge, they'd known him in life after all, but they'd never believe a dead man was working alone. Ajoe and the others might be grief-addled puppets but they *were* conspiring.

Of course, now she wanted an acolyte there were none around.

She stood for a long moment outside the tomb that held the entrance to the catacombs and, frowning slightly, traced on the surface the path of the underground passage, climbing up and over terraces and tombs. When she was fairly certain she was as close to the meeting room as she could get, she began to read the names carved into the stone.

Councillor Saladaz's family name was Tyree. Terizan knew it because she'd robbed his townhouse once. Well, twice actually but it hadn't been his townhouse the second time because he was already dead.

The rear wall of the Tyree family tomb was directly over the part of the catacombs where the meeting had been held.

"The carving of the colonnade is thought to be exceptionally fine."

Terizan had often been accused of walking silently but the

Ayzaruites could give her lessons. Heart pounding, she turned to find the same older man who'd spoken to her the day before. At least she assumed it was the same man; one acolyte looked pretty much like another and besides, she was better with jewelry. "The what?"

"The decorative columns." He gestured helpfully.

"I was wondering . . ."

"About the mason?"

"No!" She didn't think she could cope with another lecture on stone carving. "I was wondering about the recently . . ." She paused and stared into the Tyree crypt. Saladaz had been dead for nearly a year. "I was wondering why the ghosts of the Necropolis don't move out into the city."

"They are tethered to their bodies by my Lady's will. They are not alive and she will not give them the freedom of life."

"She won't?" That was interesting. "She seems a little annoyed about it."

The acolyte shrugged. "My Lady is the Gateway and she would prefer the dead accept her assistance."

"But if the body was moved out of the Necropolis . . ."

"If a body with an active spirit was removed from her influence then it could go where it would." His tolerant smile suggested he didn't know why he was bothering to explain what everyone knew. "Except back into the Necropolis of course."

That answered the one question that had really been bothering her. None of the seven conspirators were violent people. Violent in their grief, maybe, but not the sort to start whacking Councilors even with the encouragement of a dead politician. She couldn't believe it of Ajoe the Candle-maker and she doubted the others were much different. So what was Saladaz actually working them up to?

He wanted them to remove his body from the Necropolis.

Once he got them to commit, they probably wouldn't bother being subtle; they'd crowbar the gate off the tomb, bundle him up, and bury him secretly in the city somewhere. After that, he could haunt whoever he wanted to.

Terizan rubbed her arm. If forced to chose, she'd take Ajoe and company over the Council in a heartbeat. Unfortunately, unless they were going to move Saladaz tonight she didn't have that option. The Council would have either the names of the conspirators or proof there was no conspiracy by tomorrow or they'd begin to implement their extreme new security measures. As a thief, Terizan wasn't fond of the idea of extreme new security measures.

Nor, as it happened, did she particularly care for the idea of someone like Saladaz wafting about Oreen.

If she gave the names to the Council, they'd deal with both the living and the dead and things in Oreen would continue on the way they had been. No extreme security. No dead councilors being a bad influence on the grieving. No Ajoe the Candle-maker. No Seriell Vanyaz. She reached into her pocket and stroked the silver and lapis hair clasp.

Good thing the Council had given her another option.

The acolyte cleared his throat, breaking into her reverie. "It is, of course, a crime to steal a body from the Necropolis," he declared.

"How do you prevent it?"

He stared at her as though she was out of her mind. "We are a presence in the day and no one comes into the Necropolis at night. The Necropolis is haunted."

Terizan sighed. "Trust me, that's not the deterrent you think it is."

"He'll let her use my loom!"

Terizan backed away from the crypt. Hanra Seend followed.

"He'll let her use my loom!"

And a little further away.

"She won't take care of it. I know she won't."

And further still.

"You have to tell him not to let her use my loom!" Between *my* and *loom*, Hanra stopped following.

And that gave Terizan the rough length of Ayzarua's tether.

Terizan moved quickly between crypts and tombs touching nothing. Unfortunately, there was one ghost she couldn't avoid but she did her best to delay the inevitable by waiting until she saw a pair of cloaked figures slip into the catacombs and then humming all twelve verses of *Long Legged Hazra*. If tonight's meeting followed the same pattern as last night's that would give Saladaz time to appear and begin talking.

Motivated, Terizan got through the three locks on the Tyree tomb in record time. Once inside she carefully lit her tiny lantern and swept the narrow beam around the shelves. It wasn't hard to find the councilor's corpse; he was the only member of the family to have been beheaded.

Breathing through her mouth, she wrapped the shrouded body in

waxed canvass and tied off the ends, leaving a length of rope just a little longer than Ayzarua's tether. Then holding the end of the rope, she
dragged the body out of the tomb.

"The dead must have justice!"

Apparently, she'd pulled him away from his rant. She kept moving and didn't look back.

"Thief! Stop thief!"

He could yell all he wanted. Unless there was a horde of dead
constables around, there was no one to stop her. A quick, nervous
glance from side to side determined that there were *no* hordes of dead
constables.

"Do you know who I am, little thief? I am Councilor Saladaz
Tyree!"

"You were," Terizan muttered, picking up speed on the raked
gravel off the path. The ranting turned to threats behind her until she
stopped by the tomb with the loosened bolts.

"Fool! I learned the secrets of the City of the Dead. I gathered
those who would hear my voice. Everyone knows you can not stop
the dead! I will have my revenge."

Terizan ignored him and moved one tomb past the tomb with
entrance to the catacombs. Her arm barely fit between the bars but
she managed to put the end of the rope in Ayzarua's outstretched
hand. The moonlight extended just far enough for her to see the
Goddess' welcoming expression turn to grinning bone.

A little unnerved by the sudden quiet behind her, she turned to
come face to face with Saladaz. He roared and reached for her. With
the rope in the Goddess' hand, his body was now close enough that
she was just within the limit of his tether.

Oh that was clever!

She spun around, pressed hard against the bars, and stared into
the darkness behind the Goddess. The acolyte had said that if she
stared long enough, the gateway would open.

She needed that gateway open.

Goddess. Skull.

Skull. Goddess.

Five lines of icy cold down her back. Again. And again. Overcome by a despair so deep she wanted to die, Terizan sagged against
the bars and reached to take the Goddess' hand.

When flesh touched stone, the darkness behind the statue light-
ened. A tiny circle of grey growing larger and larger until the Goddess

was silhouetted against it. Only the cold wind roaring past her into the grey kept Terizan on her feet.

One last glimpse of Saladaz's face. Not a cold wind roaring past her then but his spirit being assisted through the gate. His translucent form stretched into caricature, he howled, "The dead must have justice!" as he disappeared.

Terizan lifted her other hand just far enough to flash a rude gesture.

She dropped to her knees as the gateway closed. Dragged her tongue over dry lips. Realized with the clarity that came from nearly dying, that it was the despair brought on by Saladaz's touch that had opened the Gateway. Without it she could have stared into the darkness until she starved and nothing would have happened.

Well, if she'd starved to death the Gateway would have opened but she didn't have that kind of time.

She took a moment to convince herself that she'd meant to do it that way.

As soon as she could stand, she'd put the body back in the tomb. Without Saladaz, there was no conspiracy, just seven grieving men and women.

Unfortunately, the Council had asked for proof of nothing but even she wasn't that good. She'd have to bring them proof of something else.

In the morning, she needed to have a word with an acolyte and get those names.

"There is no secret organization meeting in the Necropolis and conspiring against the Council."

One steepled her fingers and smiled over them. "Prove it."

Terizan threw a small crumpled scroll on the table. She'd picked the poet's pocket when he left his shop to get some lunch.

Two snatched the scroll from Three's fingers before it could get covered in scented oil. Unrolled it. Frowned. "This is a ballad mourning a dead love."

"And not a good one either," Three muttered reading over Two's shoulder.

"Poets?" One asked, lip curled. "There are poets in the Necropolis?"

"Dressing in black. Wearing silver jewelry. Rhyming *into the darkness* with *broken hearted*. And I'm not going back in there for another poem, I barely escaped as it was." Lines of cold across her back. Her shudder was unfeigned. "You can send someone else if you need more proof."

"We will."

"Go ahead."

She meant it and that convinced them. After all, if there was a conspiracy, and she turned down the job, it would go to a thief who might be less than scrupulous about the names he or she offered the Council. Terizan would never be responsible for something like that.

And every one knew it.

We Two May Meet

The first story of mine I ever sold (not including the two poems to the Picton Gazette *when I was ten) was called "Third Time Lucky," it came out in* Amazing Stories, *the November 1986 issue under the byline T.S. Huff, and it was about Magdelene, the most powerful wizard in the world. This, the 7ᵗʰ Magdelene story, was written for the DAW 30ᵗʰ anniversary anthology. It was due September 30ᵗʰ, 2001– which means I started writing it right after 9/11. At about the three quarter mark, I realized I was writing a story about survivor's guilt.*

MAGDELENE WAS BESIDE HERSELF WHEN she woke that first morning home from Venitcia –which wasn't really surprising as she'd never been much of a morning person. If truth be told, she was more of a mid-afternoon, heading into cocktail hour kind of a person.

What *was* surprising was that the self she was beside, appeared to be snoring.

"Mistress?" Kali's red eyes widened as two wizards walked into the kitchen–identical but for the fact that one had her thick chestnut hair pulled back into a tight bun and seemed to be wearing an outfit in which all the items not only complimented each other but covered her from neck to knees. The demon housekeeper turned to the other wizard, whose hair fell in the usual messy cascade and who was wearing a vest and skirt in virulently opposing shades of green. "Mistress, there are two of you."

"No." Magdelene crossed the kitchen and pulled a mug embossed with the words, *the most powerful wizard in the world* off the shelf. "There's still only one of me. I just seem to have gone to pieces."

Kali sighed, but said, as was expected, "Well, pull yourself together."

"Not without a cup of coffee."

"Very funny," the second Magdelene snorted. "But neither misplaced humor nor your unseemly addiction to that beverage is getting us any closer to solving our problem!"

"We've managed to determine that she's my unfun bits," the first Magdelene informed the demon, sinking into a chair and reaching for a muffin.

"I hope you're not having butter on that!"

"Also my nagging, uptight bits."

"Mistress, how did this happen?"

The first Magdelene shrugged, spreading butter liberally on the muffin. "Beats the heck out of me. She was there when I woke up; large as life and twice as tidy."

"And I can't seem to get her to care," growled the second through clenched teeth. "We must find out who did this to us and why."

"It's too hot to care." The first stuck her foot out into a patch of sunlight and grinned down at the shadow of her bare toes on the tile floor.

"Mistress, if there is a wizard powerful enough to do this . . ."

"What difference does it make? I mean, really? It's been done."

"You see? You see what I've had to put up with?" The second glared down at her double. "Well, fine. I don't need you–I was only including you in the process to be thorough. I can get the answers on my own." Pivoting on one well-shod heel, she stomped out of the room, the door slamming behind her.

"What a bitch," the first snorted.

Mistress, if she is a part of you . . ."

"Then I'm well rid of her."

The door swung open hard enough to crash against the wall. "What have you done to my house!"

Magdelene-one sighed, reaching for another muffin. "What do you mean, your house? Try, my house.

"The tower is *missing!*"

"Is not."

Shaking her head, Kali went out into the hall. Not only was the tower missing but two of the hall's four doors opened into the garden and the door that should have returned her to the kitchen lead sequentially to the sitting room, the bathing room, Joah's old room, and a room the demon didn't recognize although from the piles of debris it appeared to be a storeroom of sorts. A half-grown calico cat meowed indignantly down at her from a stack of crates.

"I have no idea," she said, closing the door again. If the house was causing the cat's problems, things were even more serious than they appeared.

A fifth attempt finally took her back to the kitchen. Magdelene-one was licking the jam spoon while Magdelene-two made notes on Kali's recipe slate.

"The house," she announced, "is out of control."

"That's just so unlikely," Magdelene-one scoffed stickily.

"Never-the-less, Mistress, it is the case."

Sighing heavily, Magdelene-one heaved herself up out of the chair and sauntered over to the door, Magdelene-two following close behind, arms folded and lips pressed into a thin line. They walked out of the kitchen and stood in a square hall, warmly lit by the large skylight overhead.

"Sitting-room, bathroom, stairs to the Netherhells . . ." The doors opened and closed showing the rooms behind them as they were named. ". . . stairs to the tower." Magdelene-one rolled her eyes and headed back to the kitchen. "You guys make such a fuss over nothing."

As the door closed behind her, the house shifted and the green and gold lizard who had moments before been sunning himself in the garden stared up at Magdelene-two in shock.

"You're right," she told it. "The situation is completely unacceptable. Fortunately, a reasoned analysis finds a simple solution." Opening a door, she reached into the kitchen, grabbed her other self by the back of the vest and hauled her into the hall. The lizard disappeared, the doors returned. "Clearly, we must stay together in order to maintain the house."

"Clearly," Magdelene-one mocked. "Why?"

"Let me think . . ."

"Oh, you're thinking. I can smell the smoke."

Magdelene-two ignored her. "As you observed previously, there is still only one of us, we have merely been separated into pieces. It's therefore logical to assume that our power has been equally divided between us. Together, we remain the most powerful wizard in the world. Separate, we are merely powerful—and not powerful enough to mindlessly support old magics."

"That sort of sucks."

"Indeed. We need answers." Clutching her other self's elbow, Magdelene-two threw open a door and marched them both up the steps to the cupola on the top of the tower.

"Stairs; what was I thinking?"

From the outside, the turquoise house on the headland seemed to be only one story tall. From the copula, the two wizards had an uninterrupted view of the surrounding countryside from fifty feet in the air.

Magdelene-one gazed down at the cove and the fishing village that hugged the shore. "Nothing much happening there. Wait a minute, that's Miguel working on his boat. Would you look at the shoulders on the man. And the ass—you could bounce clams off that ass." Leaning forward, she whispered something in Miguel's ear. The fisherman turned and waved. Even at such a distance, they could see his broad smile.

"What did you say to him?" Magdelene-two demanded suspiciously.

One giggled. "I told him that if the kaylie weren't running I knew something else he could spend the morning spearing."

"Have you no concern for your dignity? And if not," she continued before her double could reply, "have you no concern for mine? We are the most powerful wizard in the world and we have a position to maintain!"

"Prude."

"Slut."

Magdelene-one stuck out her tongue, flickered once, and glared across the room. "You stopped me! How dare you stop me!"

Hands on her hips, Two returned the glare. "Have you forgotten why we came up here?" A half turn and a sharp wave toward the large oval mirror in the rosewood stand. "We must discover who did this to us!"

"Why?"

"So that we can undo it."

"Why?" One asked again, dropping down onto the huge pile of multicolored cushions that filled most of the floor space. "Personally, I think I'm better off without you dragging me down."

"Me dragging you down?" the other Magdelene snorted turning to the mirror. "Oh, that's a laugh."

The mirror—an expensive replacement after a wizard wannabe

had broken her original trying to use the demon trapped inside—
showed nothing but a reflection of both Magdelenes.

"You've broken it!"

"I haven't done anything."

"Oh, you never *do* do anything do you?"

"At least I know how to enjoy myself," Magdelene-one pointed
out. She flashed her double a sunny smile and vanished.

"At least *I* won't end up with sand in unmentionable places," Two
sneered to an empty room.

"Where . . .?"

"The village," Magdelene-two snorted as she crossed the kitchen.
"She is such an embarrassment, Kali." Lowering herself into a chair,
legs crossed at the ankles, she quivered with indignation. "I shudder
just thinking of how she's perceived."

"The villagers have always treated her—you—with respect,
Mistress."

"But she's so . . ." Manicured nails beat out a staccato beat against
the polished wood of the table as she searched for a description that
managed to be both accurate and polite and managed only: ". . .
enthusiastically athletic."

"From what I have heard, they respect that as well and I have
received the impression on a number of occasions that some are
rather in awe." Kali set a lightly steaming cup of tea on the table by
the wizard. "Did you discover who is responsible for this division?"

Magdelene-two took a ladylike sip of tea and sighed. "I'm afraid
not. The mirror is non-functional and showed only our reflections.
Whoever divided us in two must have disabled it in order to cover
their tracks."

The demon nodded thoughtfully.

"What's this?" Magdelene-one blinked down at the lightly
steamed vegetables and the poached fish on her plate.

Kali placed a pitcher of water and a glass on the table. "Lunch,
Mistress. High in fibre, low in fat. Your double ordered it."

"Then why isn't my double here eating it?"

"She remains in the workshop, delving in eldritch realms to discover the cause of your affliction."

"Hey, it's nothing a little salve won't cure. Oh, *our* affliction.
Right. Well, she's going to get us into trouble with that whole

eldritch realms thing–it's likely to bring on an angry crowd of villagers with torches and pitchforks. And hang on, I don't have a workshop."

"She has added one on, Mistress."

"And you just let her?"

"I am her housekeeper as much as yours, Mistress. If you are unhappy with her decision, perhaps you should confront her yourself."

"Yeah, probably, but I don't really feel much like doing it now. Maybe later." A lazy flick of a knife point teased apart two translucent flakes of white flesh. "Any chance of getting some tarter sauce with this?"

"What are you doing?"

"What does it look like I'm doing?" Magdelene-two demanded. She dropped a cushion onto the ground, dropped to her knees on the cushion and began inscribing runes in the fresh earth. "I'm laying out protective wards around the house."

"Didn't there used to be cat mint there?"

"Do you want what happened last night to happen again?" Magdelene-two sniffed ignoring the actual question.

Magdelene-one settled back down in the hammock and scratched at her bare stomach. "Don't see how it can. We're already in two pieces."

"And what would you say to four pieces?"

"Five card draw, monkey's wild, it'll cost you a caravan to open."

Magdelene-two sniffed again. "You're making absolutely no sense."

"With four," her double sighed, "we'd have enough for poker."

"You think you're very funny, don't you? You're just lucky you have me to take care of things."

A tanned hand waved languidly in the hot afternoon air. "Whatever makes you happy, sister."

"Don't call me that!" two protested, vehemently tucking an escaped strand of hair back behind her ear. "I'm not your sister, I'm *you!*"

"Then I really need a nap. I'm not usually this cranky."

"Kali, what is this?"

"Supper, Mistress." Thankful that the kitchen was one of the more anchored rooms, Kali put down the plate of spiced prawns in garlic butter. "Your double ordered it." When faced with the inevitable, she felt she might as well just say the lines assigned.

Magdelene-two's lip curled. "Then why isn't my double here eating it?"

"There was a delivery from the village this afternoon."

"A delivery of what?"

"I do not know. He never reached the house."

"Why not?" Kali opened her mouth to answer but a raised hand and a scarlet flush on the wizard's cheeks cut her off.

"Never mind. How can she take a chance like that? He might not be a mere delivery boy, he could easily be our enemy attempting to take us unawares. He could be the wizard who divided us, arriving to check on our weakened condition." Magdelene-two leapt to her feet. "He could have weapons designed to destroy us!"

The demon placed her hand on the wizard's shoulder and pushed her back down into the chair. "I believe he was searched quite thoroughly," she said.

Magdelene-two looked up from placing her folded clothing neatly into a chest and clutched at her voluminous nightshirt. "What do you think you doing here?"

"This is my bedroom."

"Excuse me, I believe that it's my bedroom."

"Whatever." Magdelene-one shrugged. "It's a big bed." She began to work at the laces on her vest.

"I am not sharing this bed with you."

"You're not my first choice either but . . ." The vest hit the floor, quickly followed by the skirt. ". . . so what. It's late. I'm sleepy. And this is my bed."

"You can sleep in one of the spare rooms."

"I don't want to." She kicked her crumpled clothes into a corner. "Besides, I have dibs. I'm clearly the original."

"And how do you figure that?"

"I have all the dominant character traits."

"You're a lazy, lecherous, slob!"

"I rest my case." Triumphant, she dropped onto the bed. "And you're only angry because you know I'm ri . . . HEY!"

Releasing her double's ankle, Magdelene-two stepped back and pointed toward the door. "Out. Now."

Magdelene-one scrambled up off the floor. "You shouldn't have done that."

"Really? What were you planning to d . . . AWK!" Pressed up against the back wall, she struggled to get an arm free.

"I plan to get some sleep if you'd just shu . . . OW!"

For every offense, an equal defense. For every spell, a counter spell. For every pillow slammed into a face or across the back of a head, there was a pillow slammed in return. The pillows were, by far, getting the worst of it.

The villagers stared up at the lights and noises coming from the house of the most powerful wizard in the world and they wondered. Some wondered what fell enchantments were afoot. Most wondered why they hadn't been invited to the party.

One wondered why the ground seemed to be shaking slightly . . .

The impact shook the house and knocked both Magdelenes to their knees, hands buried in each other's hair.

"Now what have you done," Magdelene-two demanded, eyes wild.

"Wasn't me," her double denied hurriedly. "It must have been you."

"Well, it wasn't. Unlike some people, I maintain perfect control at all times."

"So, if I didn't do it and you're maintaining perfect control," Magdelene-one mocked. "Who's doing all the bang . . ."

The second impact was more violent than the first.

The wizards' eyes widened simultaneously and together they raced for the hall.

Unencumbered by the tangled ruin of a nightshirt, Magdelene-one reached the door first and threw it open, peering down the long, long flight of stairs that lead to the Netherhells. Swinging free, the door began to tremble.

"DUCK!"

After impact the two wizards lifted their heads to peer wide-eyed at the object embedded in the wall. It was a large bone, almost five feet long and a handspan in diameter. Crude sigils had been carved around the curve of the visible end.

"That can't be good," Magdelene-one observed, standing.

Gaining her feet a moment later, Magdelene-two crossed to the bone. "It appears that one of the demon princes is attempting to breach the door. This sigil here is the sign of Ter'Poe, and this the sign of conquest, and this . . ." She tapped her finger lightly against another. ". . . this is what appears to be a corrupted version of my name with certain Midworld influences apparently creeping into the actual line and curves."

The other wizard gave an exaggerated yawn. "Even facing potential disaster you're boring."

"Potential disaster, Mistresses?"

They turned together to face the housekeeper.

"You don't think an invasion by the Netherhells where we all end up murdered in our beds and all manner of evils like sloth and gluttony . . ." Magdelene-two paused long enough to glare at her double. ". . . run loose in the world is a disaster?"

"I merely question your use of the word potential, Mistress. If their missile was able to reach the house, they are already through the door."

On cue: the distant sound of pounding footsteps rose from below.

Magdelene-one scratched thoughtfully. "At the risk of repeating myself, that can't be good."

"You idiot!" Magdelene-two charged across to the open door and lifted both hands to shoulder height, palms out, fingers spread. "And while the darkness from the deep doth into this world try to creep, I raise my powers from their sleep . . ."

"What are you doing?"

"Stopping an invasion by the Netherhells!"

"With bad poetry?" Accepting a dressing gown from Kali, Magdelene-one belted it then pointed down the stairs. "Go home."

"Ow!" The exclamation was distant but unmistakable. The footsteps paused.

And then they began again.

"That can't be . . ."

"Yes, we all know. That can't be good. Stop repeating yourself and start throwing things at them before we're horribly killed and responsible for the deaths of thousands."

"I don't think . . ."

"Fortunately for the world, I do."

"I can think of someone's death I'd like to be responsible for," Magdelene-one muttered.

"That . . . was close," Magdelene-two gasped, sagging back against the now closed door.

"Too . . . close," Magdelene-one agreed from where she lay panting on the floor.

"As long as your power remains divided, I very much doubt you could stop a second assault," Kali pointed out. "And there will be a second assault, Mistresses. You may count on that as a certainty."

"She has . . . a point."

"Two. They're horns."

"She has a point about the two of us not being able to defeat the demon-kind a second time," Magdelene-two ground out through clenched teeth. "We have to do something before we're all destroyed. Before we're chopped into pieces and devoured. I'll return to the workshop and attempt to find the strongest spells we can perform with our reduced power."

"Good on you. I'll have a nap."

"No," Kali sighed. "You will both come with me to the tower."

"Kali, lest you forget I . . ."

"We," amended Magdelene-one.

". . . are mistress here."

Kali ignored them both and started up the stairs. After a moment, they exchanged identical expressions of confusion, and followed.

"The mirror is not functioning properly," Magdelene-two reminded the demon.

"Yes, Mistress, it is. Ask it other than who divided you from yourself."

After a moment spent working out demonic syntax, and another moment spent jockeying for position, the wizards took turns asking questions they knew the answers to. The mirror performed flawlessly.

"Now," prodded the demon, "ask it who is responsible for this division."

Magdelene-one shrugged, leaned past her double and asked.

The mirror continued to show only the reflection of the two Magdelenes.

"See? It's busted."

"No." Kali shook her head. "It is not. Think, both of you, who is strong enough to do this to the most powerful wizard in the world? You did it to yourself," she confirmed as understanding began to dawn. "The mirror has been giving you the correct answer from the beginning."

"We did this to ourselves?"

"Bummer."

"How? When?"

"When? It happened in the night as you slept. How?" Scaled shoulders rose and fell. "I do not know. Only you know."

"I don't know." Magdelene-one flopped down on the pillows. "Do you know?"

Magdelene-two pushed back a straying strand of chestnut hair and shook her head. "I'm forced to admit that I have no memory of doing any such thing."

"But clearly, it was done. And it must be undone before the world is overrun with others of my kind who are less . . . nice." Kali folded her arms. "For reasons only you can know you have brought this division upon yourself. Only you are powerful enough to undo what you have done."

"Granted, but we don't know what we've done."

"It is in your heads, Mistresses. It must come out."

"Eww." One's lip curled. "Look, I have an idea, let's just stay like we are."

"I want you back as a part of me as little as you want me in you," Two snorted, "but we have a responsibility to everyone in the world. We must save them from the encroachment of the Netherhells."

"Why? We've been saving them from that encroachment for a very long time. I say let someone else take the responsibility so I can have some fun."

"You've been having fun!" Magdelene-two reminded her sharply, arms folded over the ruins of her nightshirt. "In fact, you've been having everyone who's come within twenty feet of this house and it's GOT. TO. STOP."

"Bitch."

"Tramp."

"Mistresses, enough. You must pull yourselves together before disaster overcomes us all! There is a man," Kali continued, shooting a warning glare toward Magdelene-one, "a Doctor Bineeni, in Harmon, a town three days travel inland. I have heard he attends to problems of the mind."

"Heard from who?"

"The baker's husband has a nephew whose friend had very good things to say about the man."

"The baker's husband's nephew's friend?" One shook her head in disbelief. "Oh, yeah, that's a valid recommendation."

"Do you have a better idea?" Two demanded.

"Sure. I leave and the demon princes do what they want to you."

"Fine. Two can play at that game."

"It is not a game and no one is playing." Kali's crimson eyes glittered. "If you have no consideration for the peoples of this world, then consider this: the demon princes have vowed vengeance for the death of their brother. They will not care how many pieces you are in when they begin but I guarantee you will both be in many more pieces when they finish. You may continue arguing and die or go to Harmon and live."

The only sound in the tower was the soft shunk, shunk, shunk of Magdelene-one stroking a silk tassel.

"Live?" she said at last, glancing up at her double.

"Live," Magdelene-two agreed.

"We have to walk?"

Kali rolled her eyes, white showing all around the red. "You have never been to Harmon, Mistress. You can not go by magic to a place you have never seen."

"What about borrowing Frenin's donkey and cart?"

"You may not be seen in the village like this. It will cause them great distress."

Magdelene-two looked pointedly at her companion who was wearing wide-legged, purple trousers, an orange vest, and yellow sandals. "I can fully understand why."

"Ice-queen."

"Sleaze."

Kali stared up at the huge wrought iron gate over-filling the break in the coral wall and sighed. Deep and weary exhalations weren't something demons indulged in as a rule but over the last day she'd become quite accomplished. Had she ever stopped to anticipate their current situation, she might have expected two Magdelene's would be twice as much trouble as one. She would have been wrong. Twice as much trouble was a distinct underestimate.

"What the Netherhells have you got in that thing?" Magdelene-one drawled poking a finger at her companion's carpet bag.

"Clean handkerchiefs, water purification potion, bug repellent, extra sandal straps, desiccated dragon liver, a comb, one complete change of clothes, soap, a talisman for stomach problems . . . What?"

Two demanded, the list having raised not one, but both eyebrows to the hairline of her listener.

"You do remember you're a wizard?"

"Your point?"

Magdelene-one held up a small belt pouch. "I have everything I need in here."

"And if we're unable to use our powers?" Two demanded.

"I still have everything I need."

"There's not enough room in there for a pair of clean underwear."

Rubbing at a rivulet of sweat, Magdelene-one grinned. "Good thing I don't wear them then. I still don't see why we can't take the carpet," she complained to Kali before her double could respond.

"With your powers divided it would take both of you working in concert to keep the carpet aloft," the demon explained again. "Should your attention wander, even for a moment, it could be fatal."

"Three days on the road with Ms. Knettles-in-her-britches here could be fatal too."

"No one ever died of boredom, Mistress. Or embarrassment," she added as the second Magdelene caught her eye. "And the sooner you begin, the sooner we can put all this behind us. Remember what is at stake." She all but pushed the wizards through the gate and onto the path. As they rounded the first turn, already squabbling, she sighed again and closed her eyes.

Which was how she missed the black shadows slinking around the corner behind them.

soon soon
at their weakest
away from home
away from help
soon soon

Harmon was a largish town, four, maybe five times, the size of the fishing village nestled under Magdelene's headland. It boasted a permanent market square, three competing inns, two town wells, a large mill, four temples, a dozen shrines, and one small theater that had just been torched by the local Duc who'd objected to having his name and likeness appear in a recent satirical production.

In its particular corner of the world, Harmon was about as cosmopolitan as it got.

Which could have been why no one gave the two identical wizards a second glance—although, it was more likely they passed unnoted because no one knew they were wizards and they weren't, after three days travel, particularly identical.

The shifting shadows of early evening hid the bits of darkness that entered the town on their heels.

soon

"Excuse me, we'd like a room."

'Two rooms," Magdelene-one corrected. "A dark, narrow uncomfortable room for her." She nodded toward her companion. "And a big, bright, comfortable room for me." Smiling her best smile, she leaned toward the barman. "With a big, bright, comfortable bed."

Totally oblivious to the beer pouring over his hand, the barman swallowed. Hard.

Magdelene-two gestured the tap closed. "One room," she repeated, her tone acting on him with much the same effect as a bucket of cold water. "The one at the end of the hall with the two beds will do and we will not . . ." A pointed look at her sulking double. "be sharing it with any other travelers." As four coins of varying sizes hit the counter, she swept the common room with an expression icy enough to frost mugs and drop curious eyes down to the table tops. "First night's payment plus payment for use of the bathing room. I want the water hot and clean linens—clean, mind you, not just turned clean side out. And don't bother telling me you never do that," she cautioned, spearing the barman with a disdainful snort. "I know you do."

"How?"

"We're the most powerful wizard in the world," Magdelene-one told him brightly while being dragged toward the stairs. A shower of coin hit the bar. "I'll get the first rou . . . OW!"

Maintaining her grip, Magdelene-two leaned in close to what should have been a familiar ear. *Except that one never sees ones own ear from that angle*, she reflected, momentarily nonplussed. "Don't you think we should be keeping a low profile?" she asked quietly, dropping her voice below the sudden noise of fourteen people charging toward the bar, tankards held out. "We shouldn't be letting the whole world know we're at half strength. That's just asking for trouble!"

"You worry too much." Rolling her eyes, Magdelene-one pulled her arm free. "Look, you have the first bath while I hang out here. I'll be fine." She sighed at the narrowed eyes and thin lips. "What? You don't trust yourself?"

"You are not the parts of myself that I trust!"

". . . so he said, *Are you waiting to see the whites of his eyes?* and I said, *Not exactly!*" Magdelene's gesture made it very clear just what, exactly, she'd been waiting to see. As the crowd roared its approval of the story, she upended her tankard and finished the last three inches of beer.

Before she could lower it, a hush fell over the room.

By the time she set the tankard on the table, the hush had become anticipation.

"Rumor has it, you're a wizard."

A quick inspection proved her tankard was definitely empty. Since no one seemed inclined to fill it, she sighed and turned. There were three of them. Big guys, bare arms; attitude. Since this particular tavern didn't cater to the "big guys with bare arms and attitude" crowd, they'd clearly dropped by to make trouble.

"You don't look like a wizard," the leader sneered. "You don't act like a wizard." He leaned forward, nostril's flaring over the dangling ends of a mustache adorned with blue beads. "You don't smell like a wizard."

His companions grunted agreement.

"We wanted to see a wizard and we get pissed right off when we don't get what we want." A booted foot kicked the end of a bench; two people toppled to the floor.

Magdelene knew how to deal with this sort. One way or another she'd been dealing with these kinds of idiots her entire life. Unfortunately, she couldn't remember what she usually did. And the bi-colored codpiece worn by the man on the right wasn't helping her concentration.

The bath was helping. Deep, hot water to soak away the road and the indignities. How could she even consider becoming one again with that low minded, badly dressed hussy?

On the other hand, how could she consider allowing the Netherhells to visit death and destruction on the Midworld?

Vigorously exfoliating an elbow, Magdelene wondered how she'd gotten herself into a situation with no viable alternatives.

The sound of raised voices caught her attention. One of the voices sounded familiar, although the language left much to be desired and nothing at all to the imagination.

"Oh, for the love of . . ." The water sluiced off skin and hair as Magdelene climbed from the tub and by the time she reached her neat pile of clean clothes, she was completely dry. Dressing quickly as the noise level rose, she opened the bathing room door, stepped out into the hall, paused, and returned to hang the mat neatly over the side of the tub. Some things a wizard had to do to retain her self-respect.

She wasn't surprised to see herself as the center of attention in the common room. After pushing through the crowd, she *was* a bit surprised to see that the man who had her double by the vest was standing on chicken legs under the multi-colored arc of a rather magnificent tail. There were two others, also half-man half-chicken and a couple of dozen onlookers who seemed uncertain if they should be amused or appalled. Whatever her other half had done, it had only half worked.

In the midst of being shaken, Magdelene-one caught her double's eye and croaked, "Little help here?"

Two rolled her eyes. "Were you going up the scale, or down?" she asked pitching her voice under the roars of the chicken-man.

"D . . . d . . . down."

The three roosters, the largest marked with blue dots on the ends of its wattles, made a run for the door and the wizards found themselves alone in the center of the room. The noise building in the surrounding crowd began to sound like an angry sea.

In Magdelene's experience, crowds became mobs very quickly.

Familiar fingers interlocked, left hand to right.

One voice from two mouths murmured, "Forget."

"Why roosters?" Two asked as they climbed the stairs.

One rubbed at a beer stain on her trousers. "Well, all three were acting like pricks and pricks are another word for co . . ."

"I get it. You have to be more careful. Just because it's on your body, doesn't mean I want some over-muscled idiot rearranging my face. The world can be a nasty, brutal place and you must be prepared for that at all times."

"I don't think I want to live in your world," One snorted, pushing open the door to their room and slouching inside.

Two glared down at the handprint on her double's right cheek. "I know I don't want to live in yours." Closing the door with more force than was necessary, she walked over to the window, and reached out for one of the shutters. Frowning, she stared down into the inn yard. "The shadows are roiling."

"Yeah, yeah whatever that means."

"They're excited about something."

Magdelene-one dropped onto the nearest bed and belched. "Probably not about the beer."

together
not now
not when together
when apart

"You Doctor Bineeni?"

The elderly man slumped over the scroll jerked erect so quickly his glasses slid down to the end of his nose. Half turning, he glared at the chestnut haired woman standing in the door to his inner sanctum. "Here now, you can't just barge in unannounced!"

A second woman joined the first. "That's what I said, but she never listens to me."

Magdelene-one jerked a finger toward her companion. "Thinks she's my better half. What a laugh, eh?"

Pushing his glasses back into position, Doctor Bineeni stared. "Twins? But at your age even identical twins would be less than identical as differing experiences would write differing histories on the face."

"At our age?" Two bristled.

"You look . . ." He frowned. "But you're not young."

One sighed. "You don't know the half of it sweet cheeks. We're the most powerful wizard in the world."

His eyes widened, strengthening his resemblance to a startled lizard. "You're Magdelene?"

Waving a bundle of dried herbs onto the top of the tottering pile across the room, One dropped into a chair. "He's heard of us."

"That should make this easier," Two agreed. She ran her finger along the edge of a shelf and clucked her tongue at the accumulated dust.

"But . . . you're a legend. You don't really exist."

"Oh, I exist. You can touch me if you like. Ow!" Shooting a steaming look at Two, she muttered. "I meant he could touch my hand."

"Sure you did."

Wide-eyed the doctor looked from one to the other. "*You* are the most powerful wizard in the world?"

"Yes."

"Both of you?"

"That's correct."

"There should only be one of you."

"Also correct." Two dusted off her hands, tucking them into the sleeves of her robe. "It appears that in the split, we both got half the power . . ."

"And she got the really shitty bits of the personality."

". . . and we need you to put us back together before the Netherhells make another try for the stairs."

"The stairs?" Dr. Bineeni asked, looking from one to the other.

"Yes, the flight of stairs in my house that descends into the Netherhells."

He smiled and raised an inkstained finger, shaking it in their general direction. "Almost you had me, ladies. I can help with your delusion but you'll need to make an appointment."

"Under other circumstances, I'd be more than willing to follow protocol but we need to see you now."

"Ladies, I'm sorry . . ."

"Not as sorry as you will be if Ter'Poe gets up those stairs," One snorted. "We're not leaving until you help us."

The smile gone, Dr. Bineeni turned toward a back door. "Evan. Petre."

Two burly young men pushed their way into the room past the piles of books.

"Not bad." Magdelene-one fluffed out her hair and undid the top fastener on her vest. "One each."

Two stared at her in disbelief. "Is that all you ever think about?"

"No!" One's brows dipped in. "Well . . ."

"Slattern!"

"Anal-retentive!"

Evan, or possible Petre, reached for Magdelene-two's arm.

"Oh, go to sleep!" she snapped.

Both men fell to the ground.

"Horizontal. Very nice."

"Slut!"

"Ha! You're repeating yourself."

Two gestured. One countered. Power sizzled against power in the center of the room.

now

Darkness rose out of the shadows, divided an infinite number of times, took form and substance.

"Imps?" Two stared at the swarm of tiny figures scuttling toward her."They dare to send imps against me?"

"Whatever." One didn't bother standing. She waved a languid hand and several imps imploded. The rest kept coming. Chestnut brows drew in. "That can't be good."

"Would you quit saying that!" Two shrieked as the first imps reached her.

They climbed into mouths and ears and noses. They tangled in hair. They tried to fit themselves into every bleeding wound they made. And for every dozen Magdelene destroyed, another dozen rose from the shadows.

Driven out of the chair, Magdelene-one staggered around the room, flailing power at her attackers. Stumbling over a muscular body, she began to fall and grabbed hold of the closest solid object: Magdelene-two's hand. As their finger tightened, the wizard looked herself in the eye and smiled.

An instant later, the only sign that a battle had been fought and nearly lost, was the tangled mess of Two's hair.

"I can't believe they'd send imps after us," she growled, her hair rearranging itself back into a tight bun.

"I can't believe the imps almost kicked ass," One added.

A whimper turned them to face Dr. Bineeni who was kneeling on the floor, staring up through the bars of his stool. "You're actually her!"

Yawning, One dropped back into the chair. "Yeah, we actually are."

"And we need your help. You saw what happens when we try to fight the darkness as two separate wizards."

"Yes. I saw." Drawing in a long, shuddering breath, the doctor seemed to come to a decision as he slowly stood. "Who did this to you?"

"Well, it's like, uh . . ."

"Are you blushing?" Two demanded taking a disbelieving step

toward her double. "I wouldn't have thought you still knew how to blush!"

"Up yours."

"You know what your problem is? You're not willing to face reality." Straightening her robe, Two speared Dr. Bineeni with a irritated glare."We did it to ourself. Ourselves."

"And you want me to . . .?"

"Put us back together."

Brushy gray brows rose above the rims of the glasses. "You want to be back together?"

"It doesn't matter what we want," Two explained over One's gagging noises. "We have a responsibility to the world to be back together before the Netherhells attack again."

"Not to mention a responsibility to not be personally sliced and diced."

"I see. You held hands to defeat the smaller darkness," he added thoughtfully.

"We can't keep doing that."

"Why not?"

"We can't stand each other."

"Again, why not?" He spread his hands. "Are you not both you? Do you dislike yourself so?"

"I like myself just fine," One broke in before Two could answer. "It's her can't stand. Bossy, up-tight, neat freak!"

"Lazy, lavicious—you don't care about anything but yourself!"

"Lady Wizards, please." Stepping over a sleeping body guard to stand between them, the doctor looked from one to the other and sighed. "What happened to make you dislike yourself so?"

Dr. Bineeni's consultation room was as full of books and scrolls and candles and jars as his inner sanctum but it also held a wide chaise lounge. Magdelene-two created a second and the wizards—wearing identical apprehensive expressions—laid down.

"All right." Settling himself down into the room's only chair, the doctor picked up a slate and a piece of chalk. "Let's start with some stream of consciousness. I'll begin a phrase and you will finish it with the first thing that comes into your head. You . . ." A finger pointed toward Magdelene-one. ". . . will respond first and then you will alternate responses. Are you ready?"

"Sure. I guess."

"With great power comes great . . .?"

"Sex!"

Her chaise lounge collapsed.

"Hey! It was the first word that came into my head!"

"No surprise!"

"Lady Wizards! Please. Let's try something else. What is the last thing you remember before this happened."

"I went to bed."

"Alone?"

"Yes. I just gotten back from Venitcia and I was tired."

"Venitcia?"

"A city." Two frowned, trying to remember.

"And you were there because?"

"I don't know."

The doctor turned to One, who shrugged. "You got me, Doc."

"This is important." Dr. Bineeni pushed his glasses up his nose. "I will begin the thought, I want you to finish it. I went to Venitcia because . . .?"

"Someone asked for my help."

"Our help."

Right hand gripping the rail with white knuckled fingers, Magdelene straightened and wiped her mouth on the back of her left. "Did I happen to mention how much I hate boats?"

"You did." Trying not to smile, Antonio handed her a water skin. "And then you called a wind to speed our passage, and then, if I'm not mistaken, you mentioned it again." He waited until she drank then reached out and gently caressed her cheek. "Did I happen to mention how grateful I am that you would not allow this hatred to keep you from helping my people?"

"You did." Leaning into his touch, Magdelene all but purred. Not even the constant churning of her stomach could dull her appreciation of a beautiful, dark-eyed man. She liked to think that she'd have agreed to help regardless of who the Venitcia town council had sent to petition her but she was just as glad that they'd hedged their bets by playing to her known weakness.

Until he'd climbed the path to the turquoise house on the hill, Antonio had thought he'd been sent on fool's errand—that the most powerful wizard in the world was a legend, as story told by wandering bards. Told enthusiastically by bards who'd wandered in the right direction. Magdelene had always been partial to men who made music. And to those who actually made an effort to seek her out.

"My village was built many, many years ago on the slopes of an ancient volcano, a volcano that has recently begun to stir. My people can not leave a place that has been home to them for generations."

"Can not?"

"Will not," Antonio had admitted smiling and Magdelene was lost.

"We're close," he told her, tucking her safely in the curve of his arm as the boat rolled. "That is the smoke of the volcano. When we round this headland, we'll see Venitcia . . ."

When they rounded the headland, they saw steam rising off the water in a billowing cloud as a single lava stream continued to make it's way to the sea. There was no town. No terraced orchards. No temples. No wharves. No livestock. No people.

The captain took his vessel as close as he dared then Magdelene and Antonio took the small boat to shore. It took them a while to find a safe place to land and then a while longer to walk back to the town. Antonio said nothing the entire time.

Magdelene laid her palm on the warm ground, on the new ground, so much higher than it had been. "It happened just days after you left. Long before you found me. It was fast—ash began to fall and then the rim of the crater collapsed. The town was buried."

"How . . .?"

The lava told me." It had been bragging actually. She left that part out.

Antonio walked to the edge of the crust and stared down into the last river of molten rock. "Is everyone dead?"

"Yes."

He sighed, brushed a fall of dark hair back off his face, and half turned; just far enough to smile sadly at her. "It wasn't your fault," he said.

Before Magdelene could stop him, he fell gracefully forward and joined his people in death.

Until that moment, she hadn't even considered that it might be her fault.

"I didn't take it seriously enough."

"I should have hurried."

"You called a wind to fill the sails of the boat," Dr. Bineeni reminded them gently.

"That was for my comfort," Two said bitterly. "Not for Venitcia."

Sitting with her back against the wall, legs tucked up against her chest, One wiped her cheeks on her knees. "I was too late."

The doctor shook his head. "It wasn't your fault. Antonio was right."

"Antonio is dead."

"Yes. But he made his choice. You have to let that go." Looking from one to the other, he spread his hands. "You can't raise the dead."

"Actually, I can."

Dr. Bineeni blinked. Then he remember to breathe. "You can?"

"If the flesh is still in a condition for the spirit to wear it," Two amended.

"Although I sort of promised Death I'd stop," One sighed. "It screws up her accounting."

"So, given the manner of his death, you couldn't bring Antonio back."

"No."

"Nor any of his people."

"No."

"But if I'd known," Two insisted, "I could have stopped it."

"So many things I could stop if I knew," One agreed.

"But I don't know. Because all I do is lie in the sun and have a good time."

The doctor's brows rose at Two's declaration. "All *you* do?"

"All I did." Two lips were pressed into a thin disapproving line as she nodded toward her double. "All she does. I recognize my responsibilities."

"But without her, you can't fulfill them." He rubbed his upper lip with a chalk stained finger as he studied his slate. "I have one final question."

One scooted forward to the edge of the lounge. "Then you can fix us?"

"No. Then you can fix yourself."

"If I'm going to fix myself," One muttered, "why'd I have to come see you."

Dr. Bineeni ignored her. "You have to learn to like yourself again."

"Myself, yes. Her . . ."

". . . no." Two finished, lip curled.

"We'll see." He sat back, glanced from one to the other, and said quietly, "You have, in your house, a flight of stairs that descends to the Netherhells. Why?"

One snorted. "It's convenient."

"Convenient? To have demons emerge out of your basement?"

"Well, it's more of a sub-basement, but yes."

"Why?"

"So that I know where they are," Two interjected before One could answer. "The demon princes gain power by slaughter. You don't want them running around the world unopposed."

"No, I don't." As the silence lengthened, he added, "Legends say there were once six demon princes but the most powerful wizard in the world stood between the mighty Kan'Kon and the slaughter he craved and now there are five. Mourn for Antonio, mourn for his people, but do not define the rest of your life by his loss."

Although she had the boiling oil ready at the top of the stairs, Kali stepped gratefully aside as a single pop of displaced air heralded the return of her mistress. The clothing suggested that only Magdelene-one had returned but then she noted the purposeful stride and the light of battle in the wizard's eyes and the demon-housekeeper gave a heavy sigh of relief.

Even given that the light of battle was more accurately a light of extreme annoyance.

"Mistress, they are very close."

"I can see that," Magdelene noted as the bone spearhead came through the door. Grasping the handle, she flung it open and smiled at the demon attempting to free his weapon. "Hi. I'm back."

It froze. Those members of the demonic horde pushing up the stairs behind it who were within the sound of her voice, froze as well.

From deep within the bowels of the earth, a fell voice snarled, "What's the hold up!"

"She's back."

Silence. One moment. Two. Then: "Oh, crap."

The demon at the top of the stairs curled a lipless mouth into what might have been a conciliatory smile.

"If it's any consolation," Magdelene told it, raising a hand, "you'll be at the top of the pile."

A moment later, the stairs were clear—although the bouncing continued for some time. Magdelene waited until the moaning and the swearing and the recriminations died down, then she leaned out over the threshold. "Don't make me come down there."

The lower door slammed emphatically shut, the vibration rocking her back on her heels.

"Temper, temper," she muttered, stepping back into the hall.

"I am pleased you are yourself again, Mistress." Lifting the vat of oil, Kali carried it into the kitchen. "I am happy the doctor was able to heal you."

"He got me moving forward again," Magdelene allowed, following her housekeeper. "Although I am the most powerful wizard in the world and I probably could have figured it out eventually on my own."

"We had time for neither probably or eventually, Mistress."

"True. I guess I needed someone to get into my head."

Kali stared at the wizard for a long moment then surrendered to temptation. "That's a change," she said.

The Demon's Den

Way back after I sold my first book, Child of the Grove, *and I was looking for an agent, I called Mercedes Lackey who had two books out with the same publisher and was still able to take calls from people she didn't know. Long story short(er) we became friends and started sending each other our manuscripts on fanfold paper. This lead to me reading a number of the Valdemar books sitting on the floor in my living room while drifts of paper billowed around me because I was too caught up to actually separate the pages.*

Which is a long way of saying I was honored to have been asked to be a part of the Valdemar anthologies.

This story, by the way, is the third in this collection that I'm proud of. Mostly because it's so very much a Valdemar story and it's not as easy as you many think writing in someone else's world, especially such a well-loved world, and actually nailing the characters, and the story and, most importantly, the feel right.

THE MINE HAD OBVIOUSLY BEEN abandoned for years. Not even dusk hid the broken timbers and the scree of rock that spilled out of the gaping black hole.

Jors squinted into the wind, trying and failing to see past the shadows. :*Are you sure it went in there?*:

:*Of course I'm sure. I can smell the blood trail.*:

:*Maybe it's not hurt as badly as we thought. Maybe it'll be fine until morning.*: His Companion gave a little buck. Jors clutched at the saddle and sighed. :*All right, all right, I'm going.*:

No one at the farmstead had known why the mountain cat had come down out of the heights—perhaps the deer it normally hunted had grown scarce; perhaps a more aggressive cat had driven it from its territory; perhaps it had grown lazy and decided sheep were less work. No one at the farmstead cared. They'd tried to drive it off. It had retaliated by mauling a shepherd and three dogs. Now, they wanted it killed.

Just my luck to be riding Circuit up here in the great white north. Jors swung out of the saddle and pulled his gloves off with his teeth. :How am I supposed to shoot it when I won't be able to see it?: he asked, unstrapping his bow.

Gervis turned his head to peer back at his Chosen with one sapphire eye. :*It's hurt.*:

:*I know.*: The wind sucked the heat out of his hands and he swore under his breath as one of the laces of his small pack knotted tight.

:*You wounded it.*:

:*I know, damn it, I know!*: Sighing, he rested his head on the Companion's warm flank. :*I'm sorry. It's just been a long day and I should never have missed that shot.*:

:*No one makes every shot, Chosen.*:

The warm understanding in the mind-touch helped.

The cat had been easy to track. By late afternoon, they'd known they were close. At sunset, they spotted it outlined against a grey and glowering sky. Jors had carefully aimed, carefully let fly, and watched in horror as the arrow thudded deep into a golden haunch. The cat had screamed and fled. They'd had no choice but to follow.

The most direct route up to the mine was a treacherous path of loose shale. Jors slipped, slammed one knee into the ground, and somehow managed to catch himself before he slid all the way back to the bottom.

:*Chosen? Are you hurt?*:

Behind him, he could hear hooves scrabbling at the stone and he had to grin. :*I'm fine, worrywart. Get back on solid ground before you do yourself some damage.*:

Here I go into who-knows-what to face a wounded mountain cat and he's worried that I've skinned my knee. Shaking his head, he struggled the rest of the way to the mine entrance and then turned and waved down at the glimmering white shape below. :*I'm here. I'm fine.*: Then he frowned and peered down at the ground. The cart tracks coming out of the mine bumped down a series of jagged ledges, disappeared completely, then reappeared down where his Companion was standing.

:I don't like this.:

If he squinted, he could easily make out Gervis sidestepping nervously back and forth, a glimmer of white amidst the evening shadows.
:Hey, I don't like this either but . . .:

:Something is going to happen.:

Jors chewed on his lip. He'd never heard his usually phlegmatic Companion sound so unsettled. A gust of wind blew cold rain in his face and he shivered. *:It's just a storm. Go back under the trees so you don't get soaked.:*

:No. Come down. We can come back here in the morning.:

Storm probably has him a bit spooked and he doesn't want to admit it. The Herald sighed and wished he could go along with his Companion's sudden change of mind. *:I can't do that.:* As much as he didn't want to go into that hole, he knew he had to. *:I wounded it. I can't let it die slowly, in pain. I'm responsible for its death.:*

He felt a reluctant agreement from below and, half wishing Gervis had continued to argue, turned to face the darkness. Setting his bow to one side, he pulled a small torch out of his pack, unwrapped the oil-skin cover and in spite of wind and stiff fingers, got it lit.

The flame helped a little. But not much.

How am I supposed to hold a torch and aim a bow? This is ridiculous. But he'd missed his shot and he couldn't let an animal, any animal die in pain because of something he'd done.

The tunnel slopped gently back into the hillside, the shadows becoming more impenetrable the further from the entrance he went. He stepped over a fallen beam and a pile of rock, worked his way around a crazily angled corner, saw a smear of blood glistening in the torch light, and went on. His heart beat so loudly he doubted he'd be able to hear the cat if it should turn and attack.

A low shadow caught his eye and against his better judgement, he bent to study it. An earlier rock-fall had exposed what looked to be the upper corner of a cave. In the dim, flickering light he couldn't tell how far down it went but a tossed rock seemed to fall forever.

The wind howled. He jumped, stumbled, and laughed shakily at himself. It was just the storm rushing past the entrance; he hadn't gone so far in that he wouldn't be able to hear it.

Then his torch blew out.

:Chosen!:

:No, it's okay. I'm all right.: His startled shout still echoed, bouncing back and forth inside the tunnels. *:I'm in the dark but I'm okay.:* Again,

he set his bow aside and pulled his tinderbox from his belt pouch with trembling fingers. *Get a grip, Jors,* he told himself firmly. *You're a Herald. Heralds are not afraid of the dark.*

And then the tunnel twisted. Flung to his knees and then his side, Jors wrapped his head in his arms and tried to present as small a target as possible to the falling rock. The earth heaved as though a giant creature deep below struggled to get free. With a deafening roar, a section of the tunnel collapsed. Lifted and slammed against a pile of rock, Jors lost track of up and down. The world became noise and terror and certain death.

Then half his body was suspended over nothing at all. He had a full heartbeat to realize what was happening before he fell, a large amount of loose rock falling with him.

It seemed to go on forever; turning, tumbling, sometimes sliding, knowing that no one could survive the eventual landing.

But he did. Although it took him a moment to realize it.

:*Chosen! Jors! Chosen!*:

:*Gervis . . .*: The near panic in his Companion's mind-touch pulled him up out of a grey and red blanket of pain, the need to reassure the young stallion delaying his own hysteria. :*I'm alive. Calm down, I'm alive.*: He spit out a mouthful of blood and tried to move.

Most of the rock that had fallen with him seemed to have landed on his legs. Teeth clenched, he flexed his toes inside his boots and almost cried in relief at the response. Although muscles from thigh to ankle spasmed, everything worked. :*I don't think I'm even hurt very badly.*: Which was true enough as far as it went. He had no way of telling what kind of injuries lurked under the masking pressure of the rock.

:*I'm coming!*:

:*No, you're not!*: He'd landed on his stomach, facing up a slope of about thirty degrees. He could lift his torso about a handspan. He could move his left arm freely. His right was pined by his side. Breathing heavily, he rested his cheek against the damp rock and closed his eyes. It made no difference to the darkness but it made him feel better. :*Gervis, you're going to have to go for help. I can't free myself and you can't even get to me.*: He tried to envision his map, tried to trace the route they'd taken tracking the cat, tried to work out distances. :*There's a mining settlement closer than the farmstead, just follow the old mine trail, it should take you right to it.*:

:*But you . . .*:

:*I'm not going anywhere until you get back.*:

I'm not going anywhere, he repeated to the darkness as he felt the presence of his Companion move rapidly away. *I'm not going anywhere.* Unfortunately, as the mountain pressed in on him and all he could hear was his own terror filling the silence, that was exactly what he was afraid of.

It was hard to hear anything over the storm that howled around the chimneys and shutters but Ari's ears were her only contact with the world and she'd learned to sift sound for value. Head cocked, tangled hair falling over the ruin of her eyes, she listened. Rider coming. Galloping hard. She smiled, smug and silent. Not much went on that she didn't know about first. Something must've gone wrong somewhere. Only reason to be riding so hard in this kind of weather.

The storm had been no surprise, not with her stumps aching so for the past two days. She rubbed at them, hacking and spitting into the fire.

"Mama, Auntie Ari did it again."

"Hush, Robin. Leave her alone."

That's right, leave me alone. She spat once more, just because she knew the child would still be watching, then lifted herself on her palms and hand-walked towards her bench in the corner.

"Ari, can I get you something?"

Sometimes she thought they'd never learn. Grunting a negative, because ignoring them only brought renewed and more irritating offers, she swung herself easily up onto the low bench just as the pounding began. Sounds like they didn't even dismount. *I can't wait.*

"Who can it be at this hour?"

Her cousin, Dyril. *Answer it and find out, idiot.*

"Stone me, it's a horse!"

The sound of hooves against the threshold were unmistakable. She could hear the creak of leather harness, the snorting and blowing of an animal ridden hard, could even smell the hot scent of it from all the way across the room—but somehow it didn't add up to horse.

And while the noises it was making were certainly horse-like . . .

From the excited babble at the door, Ari managed to separate two bits of relevant information; the horse was riderless and it was nearly frantic about something.

"What color is it?"

It took a moment for Ari to recognize the rough and unfamiliar voice as her own. A stunned silence fell, and she felt the eyes of her extended family turned on her. Her chin rose and her lips thinned. "Well?" she demanded, refusing to let them see she was as startled as they were. "What color is it?"

"He's not a it, Auntie Ari, he's a he. And he's white. And his eyes are blue. And horses don't got blue eyes."

Young Robin was obviously smarter than she'd suspected. "Of course they don't. It's not a horse, you rock-headed morons. Can't you recognize a Companion when you see one?"

The Companion made a sound that could only be agreement. As the babble of voices broke out again, Ari snorted and shook her head in disbelief.

"A Companion without a Herald?"

"Is it searching?"

"What happened to the Herald?"

Ari heard the Companion spin and gallop away, return and gallop away again.

"I think it wants us to follow it."

"Maybe its Herald is hurt and it's come here for help."

And did you figure that out all on your own? Ari rubbed at her stumps as various members of the family scrambled for jackets and boots and some of the children were sent to rouse the rest of the settlement.

When with a great thunder of hooves, the rescue party galloped off, she beat her head lightly against the wall, trying not to remember.

"Auntie Ari?"

Robin. Made brave no doubt by her breaking silence. Well, she wouldn't do it again.

"Auntie Ari, tell me about Companions." He had a high-pitched, imperious little voice. "Tell me."

Tell him about Companions. Tell him about the time spent at the Collegium wishing her blues were grey. Tell him how the skills of mind and hand that had earned her a place seemed so suddenly unimportant next to the glorious honor of being Chosen. Tell him of watching them gallop across the Companion's field, impossibly beautiful, impossibly graceful—infinitely far from her mechanical world of stresses and supports and levers and gears.

Tell him how she'd made certain she was never in the village when the Heralds came through riding circuit because it hurt so much to see such beauty and know she could never be a part of it. Tell him how after the accident she'd stuffed her fingers in her ears at the first sound of bridle bells.

Tell him any or all of that?

"You saw them, didn't you, Auntie Ari. You saw them up close when you were in the city."

"Yes." And then she regretted she'd said so much.

:*Chosen! I've brought hands to dig you out.*:

Jors released a long shuddering breath that warmed the rock under his cheek and tried very, very hard not to cry.

:*Chosen?*:

The distress in his Companion's mind-touch helped him pull himself together. :*I'm okay. As okay as I was, anyway. I just, I just missed you.*: Gervis' presence settled gently into his mind, and he clung to it, more afraid of dying alone in the dark than of just dying.

:*Do not think of dying.*:

He hadn't realized he'd been thinking of it in such a way as to be heard. :*Sorry. I guess I'm not behaving much like a Herald am I?*:

A very equine snort made him smile. :*You are a Herald therefore this is how Heralds behave trapped in a mine.*:

The Companion's tone suggested he not argue the point so he changed the subject. :*How did you manage to communicate with the villagers?*:

:*When they recognized what I was, they followed me. Once they saw where you were, they understood. Some have returned to the village for tools.*: He paused and Jors had the feeling he was deciding whether or not to pass on one last bit of information. :*They call this place the Demon's Den.*:

:*Oh, swell.*:

:*There are no real demons in it.*:

:*That makes me feel so much better.*:

:*It should,*: Gervis pointed out helpfully.

"Herald's down in the Demon's Den." The storm swirled the voice in through the open door stirring the room up into a frenzy of activity. All the able bodied who hadn't followed the Companion ran for jackets and boots. The rest buzzed like a nest of hornets poked with a stick.

Ari sat in her corner, behind the tangled tent of her hair, and tried not to remember.

There was a rumble, deep in the bowels of the hillside, a warning of worse to come. But they kept working because Ari had braced the tunnels so cleverly that the earth could move as it liked and the mine would move with it, flexing instead of shattering.

But this time, the earth moved in a way she hadn't anticipated. Timbers cracked. Rock began to fall. Someone screamed.

Jors jerked his head up and hissed through his teeth in pain.

:*Chosen?*:

:*I can hear them. I can hear them digging.*: The distant sound of metal against stone was unmistakable.

Then it stopped.

:*Gervis? What's wrong? What's happening?*:

:*Their lanterns keep blowing out. This hillside is so filled with natural passageways that when the winds are strong they can't keep anything lit.*:

:*And it's in an unstable area.*: Jors sighed and rested his forehead against the back of his left wrist. :*What kind of an idiot would put a mine in a place like this?*:

:*The ore deposits were very good.*:

:*How do you know?*: Their familiar banter was all that was keeping him from despair.

:*These people talk a great deal.*:

:*And you listen.*: He clicked his tongue, knowing his Companion would pick up the intent if not the actual noise. :*Shame on you, eavesdroppers never hear good of themselves.*:

Only the chime of a pebble, dislodged from somewhere up above answered.

:*Gervis?*:

:*There was an accident.*:

:*Was anyone hurt?*:

:*I don't . . . no, not badly. They're coming out.*:

He felt a rising tide of anger before he "heard" his Companion's next words.

:*They're not going back in! I can't make them go back in! They say it's too dangerous! They say they need the light! I can't make them go back in.*:

In his mind's Jors could see the young stallion, rearing and kicking and trying to block the miners who were leaving him there to die. He knew it was his imagination for their bond had never been strong enough for that kind of contact. He also knew his imagination couldn't be far wrong when the only answer to his call was an overwhelming feeling of angry betrayal.

The damp cold had crept through his leathers and begun to seep into his bones. He'd fallen just before full dark and, although time was hard to track buried in the hillside, it had to still be hours until midnight. Nights were long at this time of the year and it would grow much, much colder before sunrise.

Ari knew when Dyril and the others returned that they didn't have the Herald with them. Knew it even before the excuses began.

"That little shake we had earlier was worse up there. What's left of the tunnels could go at any minute. We barely got Neegan out when one of the last supports collapsed."

"You couldn't get to him."

It wasn't a question. Not really. If they'd been able to get to him, they'd have brought him back.

"Him, her. We couldn't even keep the lanterns lit."

Someone tossed their gear to the floor. "You know what it's like up there during a storm; the wind howling through all those cracks and crevasses . . ."

Ari heard Dyril sigh, heard wood creak as he dropped onto a bench. "We'll go back in the morning. Maybe when we can see . . ."

Memories were thick in the silence.

"If it's as bad as all that, the Herald's probably dead anyway."

"He's alive!" Ari shouted over the murmur of agreement. Oh sure, they'd feel better if they thought the Herald was dead, if they could convince themselves they hadn't left him there to die, but she wasn't going to let them off so easily.

"You don't know that."

"The Companion knows it!" She bludgeoned them with her voice because it was all she had. "He came to you for help!"

"And we did what we could! The Queen'll understand. The Den's taken too many lives already for us to throw more into it."

"Do you think I don't know that!" She could hear the storm throwing itself against the outside of the house but nothing from within. It almost seemed as though she were suddenly alone in the room. Then she heard a bench pushed back, footsteps approaching.

"Who else do you want that mine to kill?" Dyril asked quietly. "We lost three getting you out. Wasn't that enough?"

It was three too many, she wanted to say. If you think I'm grateful, think again. But the words wouldn't come. She swung down off her bench and hand-walked along the wall to the ladder in the corner. Stairs were difficult but with only half a body to lift, she could easily pull herself, hand over hand, from rung to rung–her arms and shoulders were probably stronger now than they'd ever been. Adults couldn't stand in the loft so no one bothered her there.

"We did all we could," she heard Dyril repeat wearily, more to himself than to her. She supposed she believed him. He was a good man. They were all good people. They wouldn't leave anyone to die if they had any hope of getting them out.

She was trapped with four others, deep underground. They could hear someone screaming, the sound carried on the winds that howled through the caves and passages around the mine.

By the time they could hear rescuers frantically digging with picks and shovels, there were only three of them still alive. Ari hadn't been able to feel her legs for some time so when they pried enough rubble clear to get a rope through, she forced her companions out first. The Demon's Den had been her mine and they were used to following her orders.

Then the earth moved again and the passage closed. She laid there, alone, listening to still more death carried on the winds and wishing she'd had the courage to tell them to leave her. To get out while they still could.

"Papa, what happened to the Companion?"

"He's still out there. Brandon tried to bring him into the stable and got a nasty bite for his trouble."

Ari moved across the loft to the narrow dormer and listened. Although the wind shrieked and whistled around the roof, she could hear the frenzied cries of the Companion as he pounded through the settlement, desperately searching for someone to help.

"Who else do you want that mine to kill?"

She dug through the mess on the floor for a leather strap and tied her hair back off her face. Her jacket lay crumpled in a damp pile where she'd left it but that didn't matter. It'd be damper still before she was done.

Down below, the common room emptied as the family headed for their beds, voices rising and falling, some needing comfort and absolution, some giving it. Ari didn't bother to listen. It didn't concern her.

Later, in the quiet, she swarmed down the ladder and hand-walked to where she'd heard the equipment dropped and sorted out a hundred foot coil of rope. Draping it across her chest, she continued to the door. The latch was her design; her fingers remembered it.

The ground felt cold and wet under the heavy callouses on her palms and she was pretty sure she felt wet snow in amongst the rain that slapped into her face. She moved out away from the house and waited.

Hooves thundered past her, around her, and stopped.

"No one," she said, "knows the Den better than I do. I'm the only chance your Herald has left. You've probably called for others–other Heralds, other Companions–but they can't be close enough to help or you wouldn't still be hanging around here. The temperature's dropping and time means everything now."

The Companion snorted, a great gust of warm, sweetly scented breath replacing the storm for a moment. She hadn't realized he'd stopped so close and she fought to keep from trembling.

"I know what you're thinking. But I won't need eyes in the darkness and you don't dig with legs and feet. If you can get me there, Shining-one, I can get your Herald out."

The Companion reared and screamed a challenge.

Ari held up her hands. "I know you understand me," she said. "I know you're more than you appear. You've got to believe me. I will get your Herald out.

"If you lie down, I can grab the saddle horn and the cantle and hold myself on between them." On a horse, it would never work, even if she could lift herself on, she'd never stay in the saddle once it started to move; her stumps were too short for balance. But then, she wouldn't be having this conversation with a horse.

A single whicker, and a rush of displaced air as a large body went to the ground a whisker's distance from her.

Ari reached out, touched one silken shoulder, and worked her way back. *You must be desperate to be going along with this,* she thought bitterly. *Never mind. You'll see.* Mounting was easy. Staying in the saddle as the Companion rose to his feet was another thing entirely. Somehow, she managed it. "All right." A deep breath and she balanced her weight as evenly as she could, stumps spread. "Go."

He leapt forward so suddenly he nearly threw her off. Heart in her throat, she clung to the saddle as his pace settled to an almost gentle rocking motion completely at odds with the speed she knew he had to be travelling. She could feel the night whipping by her, rain and snow stinging her face.

In spite of everything, she smiled. She was on a Companion. Riding a Companion.

It was over too soon.

:*Jors? Chosen!*:

The Herald coughed and lifted his head. He'd been having the worse dream about being trapped in a cave-in. *That's what I get for eating my own cooking.* And then he tried to move his legs and realized he wasn't dreaming. :*Gervis! You went away!*:

:*I'm sorry, heart-brother, please forgive me but when they wouldn't stay . . .*: The thought trailed off, lost in an incoherent mix of anger and shame.

:*Hey, it's all right.*: Jors carefully pushed his own terror back in order to reassure the Companion. :*You're back now, that's all that matters.*:

:*I brought someone to get you out.*:

:*But I thought the mine was unstable, still collapsing.*:

:*She says she can free you.*:

:*You're talking to her?*: As far as Jors knew, that never happened. Even some Heralds were unable to mind-touch clearly.

:*She's talking to me. I believe she can do what she says.*:

Jors swallowed and took a deep breath. :*No. It's too dangerous. There's already been one accident. I don't want anyone dying because of me.*:

:*Chosen . . .*: The Companion's mind-touch held a tone Jors had never heard before. :*I don't think she's doing it for you.*:

When they stopped, Ari took a moment to work some feeling back into each hand in turn. *Herald's probably going to have my finger marks permanently denting his gear.* Below her, the Companion stood perfectly still, waiting.

"We're going to have to do this together, Shining-one, because if I do it alone, I'll be too damned slow. Go past the mine about fifty feet and look up. Five, maybe six feet off the ground there should be a good solid shelf of rock. If you can get us on to it, we can follow it right to the mouth of the mine and avoid all that shale shit."

The Companion whickered once and started walking. When she felt him turn, Ari scooted back as far as she could in the saddle, and flopped forward, trapping the coil of rope under her chest. Stretching her arms down and around the sleek curve of his barrel, she pushed the useless stirrups out of her way and clutched the girth.

"Go," she grunted.

He backed up a few steps, lunged forward, and the world tilted at a crazy angle.

Ari held her uncomfortable position until he stopped on the level ground at the mouth of the mine. "Remind me," she coughed, rubbing the spot where the saddle-horn had slammed into her throat, "not to do that again. All right, Shining-one, I'll have to get off the same way I got on."

His movement took her by surprise. She grabbed for the saddle, her cold fingers slipped on the wet leather, and she dismounted a lot further from the ground than she'd intended.

A warm muzzle pushed into her face as she lay there for a moment, trying to get her breath back. "I'm okay," she muttered. "Just a little winded." Teeth gritted against the pain in her stumps, she pushed herself up.

Soft lips nuzzled at her hair.

"Don't worry, Shining-one." Tentatively she reached out and stroked the Companion's velvet nose. "I'll get your Herald out. There's enough of me left for that." She tossed her head and turned towards the mine, not needing eyes to find the gaping hole in the hill-side. Icy winds dragged across her cheeks and she knew by their touch that they'd danced through the Demon's Den before they came to her.

"Now then . . ." She was pleased to hear that her voice remained steady. ". . . we need to work out a way to communicate. At the risk of sounding like a bad Bardic tale, how about one whicker for yes and two for no?"

There was a single, soft whicker just above her head.

"Good. First of all, we have to find out how badly he . . ." A pause. "Your Herald is a he?" At the Companion's affirmative, she went on. "How badly he's hurt. Ask him if he has any broken bones."

:I don't know. I can't move enough to tell.:

Ari frowned at the answer. "Yes and no? Is he buried?"

:Only half of me.:
:Chosen, I have no way to tell her that.:
:Then yeah, I guess I'm buried.:

"Shit." There could be broken bones under the rock, the pressure keeping the Herald from feeling the pain. Well, she'd just have to deal with that when she got to it. "Is he buried in the actual mine, or in a natural cave?"

:She seems to think it's good you're in a natural cave.:

Jors traced the rock that curved away from him with his free hand. His fingers were so numb he could barely feel it. *:Why?:*

:I can't ask her that, Chosen. She wants to know if you turned left around a corner, about thirty feet in from the entrance to the mine.:

:Left?: He tried to remember but the cold had seeped into his brain and thoughts moved sluggishly through it. *:I, I guess so.:*

"Okay." Ari tied one end of the rope around her waist as she spoke. "Ask him if the quake happened within, say twenty feet of that corner."

:I don't know. I don't remember. Gervis, I'm tired. Just stay with me while I rest.:

:No! Heart-brother do not go to sleep. Think, please, were you close to the corner?:

He remembered seeing the blood. Then stopping and looking into the hole in the side of the tunnel. *: Yes. I, I think no more than twenty feet.:*

"Good. We're in luck, there's only one place on this level where the cave system butts up against the mine. I know approximately where he is. He's close." She reached forward and sifted a handful of rubble. "I just have to get to him."

A hundred feet of rope would reach the place where the quake threw him out of the mine but, after that, she could only hope he hadn't slid too deep into the catacombs.

Turning to where she could feel the bulk of the Companion, Ari's memory showed her a graceful white stallion, outlined against the night. "Once I get the rope around him, you'll have to pull him free."

He whickered once and nudged her and she surrendered to the urge to bury face and fingers in his mane. When she finally let go, she had to bite her lip to keep from crying. "Thanks. I'm okay now."

Using both arms at once then swinging her body forward between them, Ari made her way into the mine, breathing in the wet, oily scent of the rock, the lingering odors of the lanterns Dyril and the others had used, and the stink of fear old and new. At the first rock-fall she paused, traced the broken pieces and found the passage the earlier rescue party had dug.

Her shoulder brushed a timber support and she hurried past the memories.

A biting gust of wind whistled through a crack up ahead, flinging grit up into her face. "Nice try," she muttered. "But you threw me into darkness five years ago and I've learned my way around." Then she raised her voice. "Shining-one, can you still hear me?"

The Companion's whicker echoed eerily.

"You don't need to worry about him running out of air, this place is like a sieve, so remind your Herald to keep moving. Tell him to keep flexing his muscles if that's all he can do. He's got to keep the blood going out to the extremities."

:*What extremities?*: Jors heard himself giggle and wondered what there was to laugh about.

:*Chosen, listen to me. You know what the cold can do. You have to move.*:

:*I know that.*: Everyone knew that. It wasn't like he hadn't been paying attention when they'd been teaching winter survival skills, it was just, well, it was just so much effort.

:*Wiggle your toes!*:

Gervis somehow managed to sound exactly like the Weapons-master and Jors found himself responding instinctively. To his surprise, his toes still wiggled. And it still hurt. The pain burned some of the frost out of his brain and left him gasping for breath but he was thinking more clearly than he had been in some time. With his Companion's encouragement, he began to systematically work each muscle that still responded.

The biggest problem with digging out the Demon's Den had always been that the rock shattered into pieces so small it was like burrowing through beads in a box. The slightest jar would send the whole crashing to the ground.

Her eyes in her fingertips, Ari inched towards the buried Herald, not digging but building a passageway, each stone placed exactly to hold the weight of the next. Slowly, with exquisite care, she moved up and over the rock-fall that had nearly killed Neegan. She lightly touched the splintered end of the shattered support, then went on. She had no time to mourn the past.

Years of destruction couldn't erase her knowledge of the mine. She'd been trapped in it for too long.

"Herald? Can you hear me?"

Jors turned his face towards the sudden breeze. "Yes . . ." :*Gervis, she's here!*:

:*Good.*: Although he sounded relieved, Jors realized the Companion didn't sound the least bit surprised.

:*You knew she'd make it.*:

Again the strange tone the Herald didn't recognize. :*I believed her when she said she'd get you out.*:

"Cover your head with your hands, Herald."

Startled he curved his left arm up and around his head just in time to prevent a small shower of stones from ringing off his skull.

"I'm on my way down."

A moment later he felt the space around him fill and a rough jacket pressed hard against his cheek.

"Sorry. Just let me get turned."

Turned? Teeth chattering from the cold, he strained back as far as he could but knew it would make little difference. There wasn't room for a cat to turn let alone a person. To his astonishment, his rescuer seemed to double back on herself.

"Ow. Not a lot of head room down here."

From the sound of her voice and the touch of her hands, she had to be sitting tight up against his side, her upper body bent across his back. He tried to force his half frozen mind to work. "Your legs . . ."

"Are well out of the way, Herald. Trust me." Ari danced her fingers over pile of rubble that pinned him. "Can you still move your toes."

It took him a moment to remember how. "Yes."

"Good. You're at the bottom of a roughly wedge-shaped crevasse. Fortunately, you're pointing the right way. As soon as I get enough of you clear, I'm going to tie this rope around you and your Companion on the other end is going to inch you up the slope as I uncover your legs. That means if anything's broken it's going to drag but if we don't do it that way there won't be room down here for me, you, and the rock. Do you understand?"

"Yes."

"Good." One piece at a time she began to free his right side.

:*Gervis, she doesn't have any legs.*:

:*I know.*:

:*How did she get here?*:

:*I brought her.*:

:*That's impossible!*:

The Companion snorted. :*Obviously not. She's blind too.*:

"What!" His incredulous exclamation echoed through the Demon's Den.

Ari snorted and jammed a rock into the crack between two others. It wasn't difficult to guess what had caused that reaction, not when she knew the silence had to be filled with dialogue she couldn't hear. She waited for him to say something Herald-like and nauseating about overcoming handicaps as though they were all she was.

To her surprise, he said only, "What's your name?"

It took her a moment to find her voice. "Ari." .

"Jors."

She nodded, even though she knew he couldn't see the gesture. "Herald Jors."

"Are you one of the miners?"

Why was he talking to her when he had his Companion to keep him company? "Not exactly." So far tonight, she'd said more than she'd said in the five years since the accident. Her throat ached.

"Gervis says he's never seen anyone do what you did to get in here. He says you didn't dig through the rubble, you built a tunnel around you using nothing but your hands."

"Gervis?"

"My Companion. He's very impressed. He believes you can get me out."

Ari swallowed hard. His Companion believed in her. It was almost funny in a way. "You can move your arm now."

"Actually," he gasped, trying not to writhe, "no I can't." He felt her reach across him, tuck her hand under his chest, and grab his wrist. He could barely feel her touch against his skin.

"On three." She pulled immediately before he could tense.

"That wasn't very nice," he grunted when he could speak again.

She ignored his feeble attempt to tug his arm out of her hands and continued rubbing life back into the chilled flesh. "There's nothing wrong with it. It's just numb because you've been lying on it in the cold."

"Oh? Are you a Healer then?"

He sounded so indignant that she smiled and actually answered the question. "No, I was a mining engineer. I designed this mine."

"Oh." He'd wondered what kind of idiot would put a mine in a place like this. Now he knew.

Ari heard most of the thought and gritted her teeth. "Keep flexing the muscles." Untying the end of the rope from around her own waist, she retied it just under the Herald's arms. It felt strange to touch a young man's body again after so long. Strange and uncomfortable. She twisted and began to free his legs.

Jors listened to her breathing and thought of being alone in darkness forever.

:*I'm here, Chosen.*:

:*I know. But I wasn't thinking of me. I was thinking about Ari . . . Ari . . .*: "Were you at the Collegium?"

"I was."

"You redesigned the hoists from the kitchen so they'd stop jamming. And you fixed that pump in Bardic that kept flooding the place. And you made the practise dummy that . . ."

"That was a long time ago."

"Not so long," Jors protested trying to ignore the sudden pain as she lifted a weight off his hips. "You left the Blues the year I was Chosen."

"Did I?"

"They were all talking about you. They said there wasn't anything you couldn't build. What happened?"

Her hands paused. "I came home. Be quiet. I have to listen." It wasn't exactly a lie.

Working as fast as she could, Ari learned the shape of the stone imprisoning the Herald, its strengths, its weaknesses. It was all so very familiar. The tunnel she'd built behind her ended here. She finished it in her head, and nodded, once, as the final piece slid into place.

"Herald Jors, when I give you the word have your Companion pull gently, but firmly on the rope until I tell you to stop. I can't move the rest of this off of you so I'm going to have to move you out from under it."

Jors nodded, realized how stupid that was, and said, "I understand."

Ari pushed her thumbs under the edge of a rock and took a deep breath. "Now."

The rock shifted but so did the Herald.

"Stop." She changed her grip. "Now." A stone fell. She blocked it with her shoulder. "Stop."

Inch by inch, teeth clenched against the pain of returning circulation, Jors moved up the slope, clinging desperately to the rope.

"Stop."

"I'm out."

"I know. Now, listen carefully because this is important. On my way in, I tried to lay the rope so it wouldn't snag but your Companion will have to drag you clear without stopping–one long smooth motion, no matter what."

"No matter what?" Jors repeated, twisting to peer over his shoulder, the instinctive desire to see her face winning out over the reality. The loose slope he was lying on shifted.

"Hold still!" Ari snapped. "Do you want to bury yourself again?"

Jors froze. "What's going to happen, Ari?"

Behind him, in the darkness, he heard her sigh. "Do you know what a keystone is, Herald?"

"It's the stone that takes the weight of the other stones and holds up the arch."

"Essentially. The rock that fell on your legs fell in such a way as to make it the keystone for this cavern we're in."

"But you didn't move the rock."

"No, but I did move your legs and they were part of it."

"Then what's supporting the keystone?" He knew before she answered.

"I am."

"No."

"No what, Herald?"

"No. I won't let you sacrifice your life for mine."

"Yet Heralds are often called upon to give their lives for others."

"That's different."

"Why?" Her voice cracked out of the darkness like a whip. "You're allowed to be noble, but the rest of us aren't? You're so good and pure and perfect and Chosen and the rest of us don't even have lives worth throwing away? Don't you see how stupid that is? Your life is worth infinitely more than mine!" She stopped and caught her breath on the edge of a sob. "There should never have been a mine here. Do you know why I dug it? To prove I was as good as all those others who were Chosen when I wasn't. I was smarter. I wanted it as much. Why not me? And do you know what my pride did, Herald? It killed seventeen people when the mine collapsed. And then my cowardice killed my brother and an uncle and woman barely out of girlhood because I was afraid to die. My life wasn't worth all those lives. Let my death be worth your life at least."

He braced himself against her pain. "I can't let you die for me."

"And yet if our positions were reversed, you'd expect me to let you die for me." She ground the words out through the shards of broken bones, of broken dreams. "Herald's die for what they believe in all the time. Why can't I?"

"You've got it wrong, Ari," he told her quietly. "Heralds die, I won't deny that. And we all know we may have to sacrifice ourselves someday for the greater good. But we don't die for what we believe in. We live for it."

Ari couldn't stop shaking but it wasn't from the cold or even from the throbbing pain in her stumps.

"Who else do you want that mine to kill?"

"This, all this, is my responsibility. I won't let it kill anyone else."

Because he couldn't reach her with his hands, Jors put his heart in his voice and wrapped it around her. "Neither will I. What will happen if you grab my legs and Gervis pulls us both free?"

He heard her swallow. "The tunnel will collapse."

"All at once?"

"No . . ."

"It'll begin here and follow us?"

"Yes. But not even a Companion could pull us out that quickly."

:Gervis . . .: Jors sketched the situation. *:Do you think you can beat the collapse?:*

:Yes, but do you think you can survive the trip? You'll be dragged on your stomach through a rock tunnel.:

:Well, I'm not going to survive much longer down here, that's for certain—I'm numb from my neck to my knees. I'm in leathers. I should be okay.:

:What about your head?:

:Good point.: "Ari, you're wearing a heavy sheepskin coat, can you work part of it up over your head."

"Yes, but . . ."

"Do it. And watch for falling rock, I'm going to do the same."

"What about your pack?"

He'd forgotten all about it. Letting the loop of rope under his armpits hold his weight, he managed to secure it like a kind of crude helmet.

"Grab hold of my ankles, Ari."

"I . . ."

"Ari, I can't force you to live. I can only ask you not to die."

He felt a tentative touch, and then a firmer hold.

:Go, Gervis!:

They stayed at the settlement for nearly a week. Although the

Healer assured him that the hours spent trapped in the cold and the damp had done no permanent damage, Jors wore a stitched cut along his jaw as a remembrance of the passage out of the Demon's Den.

Ari was learning to live again. She still carried the weight of the lives lost to her pride but she'd found the strength to bear the load.

"Don't expect sweetness and light though," she cautioned the Herald as he and Gervis prepared to leave. "I was irritating and opinionated before the accident." Her mouth crocked slightly and she added, with just a hint of the old bitterness, "I expect that's why I was never Chosen."

Jors grinned as Gervis pushed his head into her shoulder. "He says you were chosen for something else."

"He said that?" Ari lifted her hand and lightly stroked the Companion's face. She smiled, the expression feeling strange and new. "Then I guess I'd better get on with it."

As they were riding out of the settlement to take up their interrupted Circuit again, Jors turned back to wave and saw Ari sketching something wondrous in the air, prodded by the piping questions of young Robin.

:*I guess she won't be alone in the dark anymore.*:

Gervis tossed his head. :*She never had to be.*:

:*Sometimes it's hard for people to realize that.*: They rode in silence for a moment, then Jors sighed, watching his breath plume in the frosty air. :*I'm glad they found the body of that cat—I'd hate to have to go back into the Den to look for it.*: Their route would take them no where near the Demon's Den. :*That was as close to the Havens as I want to come for a while.*: And then he realized.

:*Gervis, you knew Ari wanted to die down there!*:

:*Yes.*:

:*Then why did you let her go into that mine?*:

:*Because I believed she could free you.*:

:*But . . .*:

:*And,*: the Companion continued, :*I believed you could free her.*:

Brock

This is the second Valdemar story I wrote and it seemed to only make sense to use the same Herald and Companion as I had in the first. This is one of the few things I've ever written that makes me cry every time I read it.

"ID'S JUST A CODE."

Trying not to smile at the same protest he'd heard for the last two days, Jors set the empty mug on a small table. "Healer Lorrin says it's more, Isabel. She says you're spending the next two days in bed."

The older Herald tried to snort, but her nose had filled past the point it was possible, and she had to settle for an avalanche of coughing instead. "She cud heal me," she muttered when she could finally breathe again.

"She seems to think that a couple of days in bed and a couple of hundred cups of tea will heal you just fine."

"Gibbing children their Greens . . ."

That was half a protest at best and, as Jors watched, Isabel's eyes closed, the lines exhaustion had etched around them beginning to ease. Leaning forward, he blew out the lamp, then quietly slipped from the room.

"Oh, she's sick," the Healer assured him, exasperation edging her voice. "What could have possessed her to ride courier at her age, at this time of the year? Yes, the package and information she brought from the Healer's Collegium will save lives this winter, but *surely* there had to have been younger Heralds around to deliver it?"

Jars opened his mouth to answer.

Lorrin gave him no chance. "If she hadn't run into your riding sector, she might not have made it this far. She needs rest and I'm keeping her in bed until I think she's had enough of it."

Jars didn't argue. He wouldn't have minded an actual conversation—Lorrin was young and pretty—but unfortunately, she seemed too determined to run this new House of Healing the way she felt a House of Healing *should* be run to waste time in dalliance with the healthy.

"Have you good as new. You see. Good as new. Soft and clean."

Jars stopped just inside the stable door and stared in astonishment at the young man grooming his Companion. The stubby fingers that held the brush, the bulky body, the round face, angled eyes, and full mouth told the Herald that this unexpected groom was one of those the country people called Moonlings. He wore patched homespun; the pants too large, the shirt too small, both washed out to a grimy gray. His boots had seen at least one other pair of feet.

He'd already groomed the chirras and Isabel's Companion, Calida--the sleeping mare all but glowed in the dim stable light.

:*Gervis?*:

:*His name is Brock.*: The stallion's mental voice sounded sleepy and sated. :*Can we take him with us?*:

:*No. And how do you know what his name is?*:

:*He talks to us and he knows exactly-oh, yes where to rub.*:

Companions were not in the habit of allowing themselves to be groomed by other than Heralds' hands. Jors found it hard to believe that they'd not only allowed Brock's ministrations but were actually reveling in them. He stepped forward and, at the sound of his footfall, Brock turned.

His face broke into a broad smile radiating welcome. Arms spread, he rushed at the Herald and wrapped him in a tight hug. Staring up at Jors, their faces barely inches apart, he joyfully repeated "Brother Herald!" over and over while a large gray dog leaped around them barking.

:*Gervis?*:

:*The dog's name is Rock. He's harmless.*:

:*Glad to hear that.*:

"Brock . . . I can't breathe . . ."

"Sorry! Sorry." Releasing him so quickly Jars stumbled and had to grab the edge of a hay rack, Brock shuffled back, still smiling. "Sorry. I brushed." One short-fingered hand gestured back at the Companions. "Good as new. Soft and clean."

"You did a very good job." Jors stepped around the dog, now lying panting on the floor and ran his fingers down Gervis' side. There wasn't a bit of straw, a speck of dust, a hair out of place on either Companion.

:Better than very good,: Gervis sighed.

Jors smiled and repeated the compliment. *:Did you say thank you, you fuzzy hedonist?:*

In answer, the Companion stretched out his neck and gently nuzzled Brock's cheek, receiving a loud, smacking kiss in return.

"Okay. We go now." Brock bent and picked a ragged, gray sweater out of the straw and wrestled it over his head. "We go *now*," he repeated, placing both hands in the small of Jors' back and pushing him toward the stable door. "Or we come late and Mister Mayor is mad and yells."

"Late for... ?"

:The petitions.: Gervis' mental voice sounded more than a little amused and Jors remembered he'd intended to merely look in on the Companions on his way to the town hall.

Heading out into the square, he realized Brock was trotting to keep up, and he shortened his stride. "Does the mayor yell a lot?"

"Yes. A lot."

"Do you know why?"

Brock sighed deeply, one hand dropping to fondle the ears of the dog walking beside him. 'Mister Mayor wears the town," he said very seriously after a moment. "The town swings heavy heavy."

Okay; that made no sense. Maybe we should try something less complex. "Is Rock your dog?"

"He's my friend. They were hurting him. I . . . Wait!"

Uncertain of just who had been told to wait, Jors watched Brock and the dog run across to the town well where a pair of women argued over who'd draw their water first. Ignored in the midst of the argument, Brock began to draw water for them. He had no trouble with the winch, but while pouring from bucket to bucket, he splashed the older woman's skirt. Suddenly united, they turned on him. By the time Jors arrived, Brock had filled another bucket in spite of the shouting—although his shoulders were hunched forward and he didn't look happy.

The older woman saw him first, shoved the other, and the shouting stopped.

"Ladies."

"Herald," they said in ragged unison.

"Let me give you a hand with that, Brock. You bring the water up, and I'll pour."

"Pouring is hard," Brock warned.

"Herald, you don't have to," one of the women protested. "We never asked this . . ." When Jors turned a bland stare in her direction, she reconsidered her next word. ". . . boy to help."

"I know." His tone cut off any further protests and neither woman said anything until all the buckets had been filled, then they thanked him far more than the work he'd done required. He'd turned to go when at the edge of his vision he saw one woman lean forward and pinch Brock on the arm, hissing, "Now that's a *real* Herald."

"HERALD JORS!"

Across the square, the mayor stood on the steps of the town hall, chain of office glinting in the pale autumn sunlight, both hands urging him to hurry. *Well, he'll just have to wait!* Lips pressed into a thin line, Jors turned back toward the well, had his elbow firmly grabbed, and found himself facing the mayor again.

"Mister Mayor is yelling," Brock explained, moving Jors across the square.

"Let him. I saw what happened back there. I saw that woman pinch you."

"Yes." He turned a satisfied smile toward Jars, never lessening their forward motion. "I made them stop fighting. Heralds do that."

"Yes, they do." They'd almost reached the hall and Jors had a strong suspicion that digging his heels in would have had no effect on their forward motion. "You're stronger than you look."

"Have to be."

I'll bet, Jors thought as he caught sight of the mayor's expression.

"Brock! Get your filthy hands off that Herald!"

"Hands are clean."

"I don't care! He doesn't need you hanging around him!"

"I don't mind." Jors swept through the door, Brock caught up in his wake, both moving too quickly for the mayor to do anything but fall in behind.

"Heralds work together," Brock announced proudly. He clapped his hands as heads began to turn. "Be in a good line now. Heralds are here."

"Heralds?" a male voice jeered from the crowd. "I see only one Herald, Moonling."

"Heralds!" Brock repeated, throwing his arms around Jors' waist in another hug. "Me and him."

Oh, Havens.

:Trouble, Heart-brother?:

:I just realized something that should have been obvious-Brock believes he's a Herald.:

:So? You'd rather he believed he was a pickpocket?:

:That's not the point.:

But he couldn't let the townspeople chase Brock from the hall as they clearly wanted to do and Brock wouldn't leave because it was time for the Heralds to hear petitions, so Jors ended up sitting him at the table and hoping for the best.

He realized his mistake early on. Brock had a loudly expressed opinion on everything, up to and including calling one of the petitioners a big, fat liar-which turned out to be true; on all points. Unfortunately, short of having him physically carried out of the hall, Jors could think of no way to get him to leave. *:Have him check on Isabel.:*

:How . . .?"

:You're worried. You're projecting. And I'm only across the square. If he wants to be with a Herald, send him to check on Isabel. She's sick and she needs company.:

:That's a terrific idea.:

Gervis' mental voice sounded distinctly smug. *:I know.:*

It worked. Jors only wished the Companion had thought of it sooner. A Herald's office protected him or her from the repercussions of a judgment-no matter how disgruntled the losing petitioner might be, few would risk the grave penalties attached to attacking a Herald. Brock didn't have that protection. *Good thing he's safely tucked away with Isabel.*

"No, Brock's not here." Healer Lonin continued rolling strips of soft linen. "He left at sunset for the tavern."

"The tavern?"

"He's there every evening. He fills their wood box and they feed him–him and Rock."

"He works there?"

Lorrin nodded. "There, and the blacksmith's whenever there's a nervy horse in to be shoed–animals trust him. I tried to have him deliver teas to patients, but if he's carrying something, there's always troublemakers who try to take it from him."

"I'm surprised." Jars rubbed his elbow at the memory. "He's quite strong."

"Is he?" She set the finished roll with the others and picked up a new strip of cloth. "He's bullied all the time, but I've never seen him defend himself. Did you know that poorer mothers have him watch their infants if they have to leave them? I'll tell you something, Herald. When I came here I was amazed to discover this town has almost none of those horrible accidents that happen when a baby just starting to creep is left alone and burns to death or drowns–that's because of Brock."

"Where does he sleep?" This far north the nights were already cold.

"In various stables when the weather's good. By someone's hearth when it isn't."

"Has he no family?"

"His parents were old when he was born. Old and poor. They died about three years ago and left him nothing."

"Why doesn't someone take him in?"

"He doesn't want to be taken," the healer snapped. "He's not a stray cat, and for all he can be childlike, he's not a child. He's a grown man, probably not much younger than you and he has the same right as you do to choose his life."

"But . . ."

She sighed and her tone softened, "There are those who try to make sure he doesn't suffer for those choices but that's all anyone has a right to do. Besides . . ." One corner of her mouth quirked up. ". . . he tells me that Heralds never stay in one place so no one thinks they like some people more than others."

Simpler language but pretty much the official reason, Jors allowed. "How long has he believed himself to be a Herald?"

"As long as I've been here. I'm surprised you haven't heard about him from other Heralds. You can't be the first he's latched on to."

"He wasn't in the reports I read and I . . ." About to say he doubted Brock would come up in casual conversation between Heralds, he frowned at a distinct feeling of unease. "I should go now."

"There's no need to go to the Waystation tonight, I've plenty of room." Her smile edged toward invitation. "I doubt anyone will accuse you of favoritism if you stay here."

"No. Thank you. I need to . . ." The feeling was growing stronger. ". . . um, go."

He doubted she'd be smiling that way at him again, but personal problems were unimportant next to his growing certainty that something was wrong. Taking the steps two at a time, he hit the ground floor running and headed for the stables. *:Gervis?:*

:We can feel it, too. Calida says it's close.:

It wasn't in the stables or the corral but when Jars opened the small door, a pair of huddled figures tumbled inside.

Brock lifted a tear-drenched face up from matted gray fur and wailed, "Heralds don't cry."

"Says who?" Jars demanded, dropping to one knee.

"People. When I cry."

"People are wrong. I'm a Herald and I cry." He stretched out a hand, keeping half his attention on the big dog who watched him warily. Herald's Whites meant nothing to Rock, and he didn't lower his hackles until Gervis whickered a warning of his own. "What happened? Did someone hurt you?"

"Heralds don't tattle!"

His various tormentors had probably been telling him that for years. "If someone does something bad, we do."

"No."

"Yes. If we can't make it right on our own, we tell someone who can. Bad things should never be hidden. It makes them worse."

Brock drew in a long shuddering breath and slowly held out his arm. Below the ragged cuff of his sweater was a dark bruise where a large hand had gripped his wrist.

"Is that all?"

"Rock came. The man ran away."

"Who was it?"

"A bad man."

No argument there. "Do you know his name?"

"A bad man," Brock repeated, wiping his nose against the dog's shoulder.

:You catch him and I'll kick him.: The Companion's mental voice was a near growl. *:Calida says she'll help.:*

"It's a bad bruise, but it is just a bruise. Healer Lonin wrapped it in an herb pack and she says he'll be fine. He won't stay, says he's not sick enough, but I can't just let him wander off into the night."

"Coors you cand."

"And I can't take him to the Waystation and I can't stay with him because that would be seen as losing impartiality. So, do you mind if he spends the night with Calida?"

Isabel managed a truncated snort. "Fine wid me, bud you'd bezd ask her."

Leading Gervis and the chirras out of the stable, Jors turned for one last look at Brock curled up against Calida's side. The elderly mare had been pleased to have the company and had positioned herself in such a way that Brock could pillow his head against her flank. Rock had snuggled up on the young man's other side and although his face was still blotchy, Jors had never seen anyone look so completely at peace.

: Why do you two care about him so much?: he asked as he mounted.
:He believes he is a Herald.:
:Yes, but . . .:
:And he acts accordingly.:

The next day during petitions, the mayor tripped over Rock sprawled by the table. Jerking his chain of office down into place, he snarled, "That dog is vicious and ought to be destroyed."

Jors pushed Brock back into his chair. "Who says this dog is vicious?"

The mayor's lip curled. "I heard he attacked a man last night."

"I heard that, too, Herald," called out one of the waiting petitioners. .

"Brock, show everyone your arm." The bruises were dark and ugly against the pale skin. "The man Rock attacked did that and would have done more had the dog not come to his master's defense. This dog is no more vicious than I am."

"We've only your word on that, Herald. You can't truth-spell a dog."

"No but I *can* truth-spell the man who made the accusation if he's willing to come forward."

No one was surprised when he didn't.

Mid afternoon, as Jors was returning to the hall after a privy break, the town clerk fell into step beside him and apologized for the mayor's earlier behavior. "It's just he feels responsible for the whole town, and it weighs on him and makes him short-tempered. Believe me, Herald, he's a whole different man when he can take that chain off."

"Mister Mayor wears the town. The town swings heavy heavy."

Brock's explanation suddenly made perfect sense.

It had been arranged that Brock would spend another night with Calida.

"Companions need Heralds. Lady Herald is sick. *I* am not sick. I am here." He threw his arms around Jors. "I see you tomorrow, Brother Herald."

"No, not tomorrow, Brock. Tomorrow, I'm going to see the tanners." Tanning was a smelly business, tanners set up their pits downwind of towns, far enough away they could work without complaint but not so far they couldn't get skins or find buyers for their hides. These particular tanners had chosen distance over convenience and had settled nearly a full day's travel away. The townspeople he'd spoken to about them had made it quite clear that the animosity was mutual. No one went near the place unless they had to. "I'll stay overnight, then go back to the Waystation the next day. The day after that, I'll be back in town. That's why I brought my chirras in today, so he won't be left alone at the station."

"No."

"It's okay. Gervis travels very fast, I won't be gone long."

"No!" Brock released him, stepping back just far enough to meet Jors' eyes. 'Don't go!" Pulling the hair back off his face with one hand, he grabbed the Herald's wrist with the other. "See?" An old scar ran diagonally from the edge of a thick eyebrow up into his hairline.

"The tanners did that?"

"I bumped mean lady's cart. Don't go." His eyes welled over. "Mean lady is there."

Jors pulled free of Brock's grip and squeezed his shoulder. "I'll be fine. Really. The mean lady won't do anything to me." The sort of people who'd strike a frightened Moonling were unlikely to be the sort who'd strike a healthy young man in Herald's Whites. "But I have to go and check on them. They haven't been into town for a long time and it's almost winter."

"Not alone."

"Don't worry, I'll have Gervis." He gave the trembling shoulder another squeeze then swung himself up into the saddle. "You stay with Calida, and I'll see you in two days."

He supposed he'd been half expecting it. When Jors came out of the Waystation early the next morning there sat Brock—which was the half he supposed he'd been expecting—on Calida—which was a total surprise. It wasn't often a Companion would choose to bear anyone but her Chosen and those exceptions were almost always Heralds.

"Good morning, Brother Herald!"

Actual Heralds. "Brock, what are you doing here?"

The young man's crestfallen expression insisted on better manners. Jors rubbed a hand over his face and sighed. "Good morning, Brock."

The smile returned. "It's early!"

"Yes, it is. What are you doing here so early?"

"I go with you. To tanners."

"No, you don't,"

"Yes, I go with you."

"No."

"Yes."

Jors hated to do it, but . . . "What about the mean lady?" The smile faltered as Brock sucked in his lower lip. "You don't want to see the mean lady."

"Don't want you to see mean lady alone." He took a deep breath and squared his shoulders. "I go with you."

"That's very brave of you." And he meant that. Courage was only courage in the face of fear. "But even though I know you mean well, you can't just *take* a Companion."

Brock's eyes widened indignantly. "Didn't take!"

:*Calida says if she hadn't wanted him to ride her, he wouldn't be here.*: Gervis scratched his cheek on a post and added thoughtfully. :*He's very bad at it.*:

:*At what?*:

:*Riding.*:

:*No doubt. What does Isabel say about this?*:

:*Herald Isabel trusts her Companion.*:

:*That's not very helpful.*:

:*It should be.*:

One more try. "Brock, by taking her Companion, you've left Herald Isabel alone."

"No." He leaned carefully forward in the saddle and stroked Calida's neck. "Left Rock."

Jors reached for Calida's bridle, but the Companion tossed her head, moving it away from his hand. "Calida, you *have* to take him back."

The mare gave him a flat, uncompromising stare.

:She says, "make me.": Gervis translated helpfully.

:Yeah. I got that. What do you think I should do?:

:Help him down.:

:You think this is funny, don't you?: Jors demanded doing as the Companion suggested.

:I think this is inevitable, Chosen. You might as well make the best of it.:

Even with Jors' help, Brock stumbled as he hit the ground, fell, rolled, and bounced up, declaring, "I'm okay!"

:Now, get ready.: Gervis shoved at Jors' bare shoulder. *:We'll be moving slowly and Calida says it's going to rain.:*

:And won't that *make this a perfect day?:*

:No. She says it's going to rain hard and I don't like to get wet. I want to be there before it rains.:

That began to look more and more unlikely as the morning passed and the clouds grew darker. Brock managed to stay in the saddle at a fast walk and Calida refused to go faster. Once or twice, Jors was positive he was going to fall off, but at the last instant he'd shift weight and somehow stay mounted.

:His balance is bad. But Calida's helping.:

:Why is Calida doing this?:

One ear flicked back. *:So he won't fall off.:*

:No, I mean why is Calida allowing any of this? Why is she allowing Brock to ride her? Why is she allowing–insisting–he come along today?:

:She has her reasons.:

Jors sighed. He knew that tone. *:And you're not going to tell me what those reasons are, are you?:*

:He's very happy.:

:I can see that.:

Happy was an understatement. For all he held the pommel in a death grip, Brock looked ecstatic. *This is really not helping his delusion that he's a Herald,* Jors realized. Something would have to be done about that and since the two of them were spending what was likely to be a full day traveling together, now would be the time to do it. Maybe *that* was why Calida had brought him.

There'd be no point in bluntly saying, *"Brock, you're not a Herald."* The townspeople said that all the time, shaded in every possible emotion from amusement to rage, and it had no effect.

"Brock, do you know what makes a person a Herald?"

"Heralds help people. Heralds can cry. Heralds tell when bad things happen." He beamed proudly. "I remember the new things."

"Yes, all those things make a Herald, but . . ."

"I'm a good Herald."

". . . but there's other things."

Brock twisted in the saddle to look at him and Calida adjusted her gait to prevent a fall. "Heralds wear shiny white."

"Yes . . ."

He looked down at his gray sweater, then looked back at Jors smiling broadly. "Clothes are on the outside."

:*And a Herald is on the inside.*:

:*I get it.*:

A sapphire eye rolled back at him, distinctly amused. :*Just trying to help.*:

"Brock, all those things are part of being a Herald, but the most important part is being Chosen by a Companion. You don't have to be a Herald to be a really good person but you *do* have to be Chosen. Do you understand?"

Brock nodded. "Companions have Heralds."

"You don't have a Companion."

"Yes!" He bounced indignantly, lost a stirrup, and nearly went off. "Have Calida," he continued when he was secure in the saddle again.

"But she's Herald Isabel's Companion. Herald Isabel is letting you ride her."

"No. Calida is letting."

:*He's got you there.*:

Jors sighed. "Riding a Companion isn't the point, Brock. You're not Calida's Herald."

"Not her Herald," Brock agreed, his smile lighting up his whole face. "A Herald."

Between the less than successful conversation and the glowering sky, Jars had picked up a pounding headache. They rode without speaking for a while, Brock humming tunelessly to himself. Finally, more to put an end to the humming than for any real desire to know, Jors turned in the saddle and said, "So, you were going to tell me how you saved Rock."

"Kids were hurting him." Brock's placid expression turned fierce at the memory. "I made them stop." Although he wouldn't defend himself, he seemed quite capable of defending the helpless. "He was hungry. I counted his bones. One, two, three, four . . ."

"Where did he come from?" Jars interrupted, unsure of how high the other man could count and not really wanting to find out.

"Don't know. Now, he is my friend." The broad brow furrowed as he searched for words. "Some mean people aren't mean now because he is my friend."

That was hardly surprising. Rock was a big dog. Probably a hunting dog of some kind who'd gotten separated from his pack and managed to finally find his way back to people. "Why did you call him Rock?"

"So when kids are mean, it doesn't matter."

"I don't understand."

Brock stared down between Calida's ears and chanted, "Brock, Brock, dumb as a rock." Then he grinned and turned just far enough in the saddle to meet Jars' gaze. "Rock isn't dumb. I fooled them."

He looked so proud, Jors found himself grinning in return. "Yes, you did. That was very smart."

"I am a smart Herald."

It was a good thing he didn't need affirmation because Jors had no idea of what to say. :*And now,:* he sighed quietly as large drops of cold water began splashing against his leathers, :*it's raining.:*

:*I know. I'm getting wet.:*

:*So am I.:*

:*I'm bigger. There's more of me, so I'm more wet.:*

In a very short time all four of them were so drenched there was little point in comparisons. Fortunately, as they crested a rise in the trail, the tanners' holding came into sight on the other side of a small valley. Neither Companion needed urging toward the river running through the valley center although they both stopped well back from the bank. The water was brown and running fast, the log bridge nearly awash.

:*What do you think? Is it safe?:*

Gervis stepped cautiously out onto the edge of the logs. :*If we move quickly.:*

But Calida hesitated.

:*What is it?:*

:*Calida says the river's already undermining the bridge supports. That the bridge is going to wash away.:*

:*Tell her that if it does, better we're all on the side with shelter. I'm half drowned and half frozen and Brock's got to be colder still. She's got to get him out of this weather.:*

Eyes wide, the mare stepped up beside Gervis who took her arrival as his cue to leap forward. One stride, two, three. As Jors

watched anxiously from the other shore. Calida slowly followed, placing each hoof with care.

Wood screamed a protest as the bridge supports caved.

The huge logs dipped and skewed out from the bank, dragged by
the river.

Calida half-reared as her front hooves scrambled for purchase in
the mud.

Brock bounced over the cantle and disappeared.

"No!" Jors threw himself to the ground. Stumbling to the
Companion's side, he grabbed the mare's saddle and heaved. Step by
step, as she managed to work her way forward, he worked his way
back until, to his amazement, he saw a very muddy Brock holding on
with both hands to Calida's tail, his feet in the river. A heartbeat later,
with solid ground, beneath all four of them, he dropped to his knees
and gathered Brock up into his arms.

"Are you all right?"

He looked more surprised then frightened and returned the hug
with wet enthusiasm. "I fell."

"I know. The bridge broke."

Brock twisted around to look, and clutched at Jors' arm. "I'm
sorry!"

"It's okay. It wasn't your fault." His heart slamming painfully
against his ribs, Jars grabbed a stirrup and hauled himself onto his
feet. "Come on, we're almost there."

The tanners' holding looked deserted as they stumbled up to the
buildings. Jors called out a greeting, but the wind and rain whipped
the words out of his mouth.

Brock grabbed his arm. "Smoke," he said, pointing to the thin gay
line rising reluctantly from a chimney. "I'm cold."

"Me, too."

All thoughts turned to a warm fire as they made their way over to
the building, the Companions crowding in close under the wide
eaves.

:We'll be right back as soon as we find someone.:

:Hurry, Chosen.: Gervis sounded completely miserable. Covered in
mud almost to his withers, his mane hanging in a tangled, sodden
mass, he looked very little like the gleaming creature who'd left the
Waystation that morning. Calida, if anything, looked worse.

Jors considered leaving Brock with the Companions, but the
other man's breathing sounded unnaturally hoarse so he beckoned

him forward as he tried the door. The sooner he got him inside the better.

The door opened easily. It hadn't even been latched.

"Hello?"

Stepping inside wasn't so much a step into warmth as a step into a space less cold. It looked like they'd found the family's main living quarters although the room was so dim, it was difficult to tell for sure. The only light came from a small fire smoldering on the fieldstone hearth and a tallow lamp on the floor close beside a cradle.

"No." Brock charged across the room, trailing a small river in his wake. "No fire beside baby!"

Remembering what Lorrin had told him about Brock and babies, Jors held his position by the door. The younger of two, what he knew about babies could be inscribed on the head of a pin with room left over for the lyrics to *Kerowyn's Ride*.

Squatting, Brock picked up the lamp. "No fire beside baby," he repeated, began to rise, and paused. "Baby?" Leaning forward, he peered into the cradle.

"Is it all right?" The lamp and the fire together threw barely enough light for Jors to see Brock. He couldn't see the baby at all.

Setting the lamp down again, Brock stretched both hands into the cradle. When he stood and turned he was holding a limp infant across both palms, his broad features twisted in sorrow. "Baby is dead."

:Jors!:

Jors spun around as the door slammed open and five people surged into the room. They froze for an instant, then the man in front howled out a wordless challenge and charged.

Bending, Jors captured his attacker's momentum then he straightened, throwing the other man to the floor hard enough to knock him breathless. The immediate threat removed, he faced the remaining two men and two women. "I am Herald Jors. Who is in charge here?"

"I am," the older woman snarled.

The hate in her eyes nearly drove Jors back a step.

He didn't need Brock's whispered "mean lady" to know who she was. It took an effort, but he kept his voice calm and understanding as he said, "The child was dead when we arrived."

"Dory came to say the babe was sick, not *dead*," she spat as the younger woman ran silently forward and snatched the body from Brock's hands. "The Moonling killed him."

"He did not . . ."

"You're here and he's there," she sneered. "You can't see what he did."

Spreading his hands, he added a mild warning to his tone. "And you weren't even in the building. I understand this is a shock . . ."

"You understand nothing, Herald." She placed a hand on the backs of the two remaining men and shoved. "Have the guts to support your brother!"

They sprang forward, looking like nothing so much as a pair of whipped dogs.

"Jors?"

He ducked an awkward blow. "Outside, Brock. Now!" If anything happened to him, the Companions would get Brock to safety.

"There's two of you and one of him, you idiots! Don't let him protect the half-wit!"

:Chosen?:

:It's all right.:

Fortunately, neither man was much of a fighter. Jors could have ended it quickly, but as they'd just suffered a sudden terrible loss and weren't thinking clearly, he didn't want to do any serious damage. After a moment, he realized that had it not been for the old woman goading them on, neither would have been fighting. *Maybe I should have Gervis deal with . . .*

He'd forgotten the first brother. The piece of firewood caught him on the side of the head. As he started to fall, he felt unfriendly hands grab his body.

"No!"

Then the hands were ripped away, and he hit the floor. Two bodies hit the floor after him, closely followed by the third.

"Never hit a Herald!"

"Get up, you cowards! That's a Moonling—not a real man!"

"But, Ma . . ."

He killed *my* grandson!"

Hers. Jors thought muzzily. *Not grief Anger. Anger at the loss of a possession.*

"You never loved him!"

Apparently, the child's mother agreed.

"You always complained about him! You said if he didn't stop crying you were going to strangle him! If anyone killed him . . ."

"Don't you raise your voice to me, you cow. If you were a better . . ."

"ENOUGH!"

The doors slammed open again. Hooves clattering against the floor boards, the Companions moved to flank Brock. From Jors' position on the floor, it looked as if there were significantly more than a mere eight muddy white legs.

"Don't lie there with your idiot mouths open! They're just horses!"

"They're not *just* horses, you stupid old woman!"

:Gervis?:

:I'm here, Heart-brother.:

Jors felt better about his chance of recovery. Gervis was angry but not frantic.

"A baby is dead. Is time for crying, not fighting. A Herald is hurt. You hurt a Herald."

:Is that Brock standing up to the mean lady?:

:It is.:

:Good for him.:

"You will cry, and you will make the Herald better!"

"I will *not.*"

No mistaking that hate-filled voice.

"Then *I* will."

Nor the voice of the child's mother.

For the first time, Brock sounded confused. "You will cry?"

"No. I will help the Herald."

:Out of spite . . .:

:You need help, Heart-brother. Your head is bleeding. Spiteful help is still help.:

Jors got one arm under him and tried to rise. *:If you say . . .:*

:Chosen!:

His Companion's cry went with him into darkness.

Jors woke to the familiar and comforting smell of a stable. For a moment he thought he'd dozed off on foal-watch, then he moved and the pain in his head brought everything back. *:Gervis!:*

:I'm here.: A soft nose nuzzled his cheek. *:Just open your eyes.:*

Even moving his eyelids hurt, but he forced them up. Fortunately, the stable was dark, the brightest things in it, the two Companions. He could just barely make out Brock tucked up against Calida's side, wrapped in a blanket and nearly buried in straw. *:How long?:*

:From almost dark to just after moonrise. Long enough I was starting to worry.:

He stretched up a hand and stroked the side of Gervis' face. *:Sorry.:*

:The young female made tea for your head. There's a closed pot buried in the straw by your side.:

The tea was still warm and tasted awful, but Gervis made him drink the whole thing. *:I take it we're in the stable because you and Calida wouldn't leave me?:*

:The old woman said the young woman could do as she pleased but not in her house. I do not want you to be in her house.: The obvious distaste in the young stallion's mental voice was hardly surprising. Even on short acquaintance the old woman was as nasty a piece of work as Jors ever wanted to get close to. *:Brock told two of the young males to carry you here.:*

:He just told them what to do and they did it?:

:They are used to being told what to do.:

:Good point,: Jors acknowledged.

:And,: Gervis continued, *:I think they were frightened when they realized they had struck down a Herald.:*

:They knew *I was a Herald!:*

:Knowing and realizing are often different. Had the blow struck by the child's father been any lower, they would have killed you and that frightened them, too. They were thankful Brock took charge. He saw you were tended to, he was assured you would live without damage, he groomed us both, and then he cried himself to sleep.:

:Poor guy. Good thing he was there. If he hadn't been, I wouldn't have put it past the mean lady *to have finished the job and buried both our bodies.:*

:The Circle would know.:

:We'd still be dead. Is this why Calida insisted on bringing him?:

:She has told her Chosen we need no assistance and convinced her not to ride to the rescue. The Herald Isabel agreed but only because she felt the towns-people would lay the blame on Brock.:

:That's ridiculous.:

Gervis sighed, blowing sweet, hay-scented breath over Jors' face. *:There is already much talk against him taking a Companion.:*

All of which he needed to know but didn't answer his question. About to ask it again, he stopped short. *:Calida can reach Isabel from here? I couldn't reach you from here!:*

:Nor I you.:

He sounded so put out by it, Jors couldn't prevent a smile. *:Never mind, Heart-brother. Calida and her Chosen have been together for many* *years; when we've been together for that long, I'll hear you if I'm in Sorrows and you're in Sensholding.:*

:I'd rather we were never that far apart.:

Jors wrapped one hand in Gervis' silken mane. *:Me either.:*

:Sleep now, Chosen. It will be morning soon enough.:

When Jors opened his eyes again, weak autumn sunlight filtered into the stable. An attempt to rise brought Gervis in through the open door. He pulled himself to his feet with a handful of mane and throwing an arm over his Companion's back, managed to get to where he could relieve himself.

:The old woman made them bury the child this morning.:

:They're only a day's ride from town; they can't wait for a priest?:

:The bridge is gone. The priest cannot come.: He pawed the ground with a front hoof and added. *:I don't think the old woman would send for a priest even if he could come.:*

:Do you know where they are?:

:Yes.:

Jors took a deep breath and, holding it, managed to swing himself up on Gervis' bare back. *:Let's go, then.:*

The tanners had a graveyard in a small clearing cupped by the surrounding oak forest. When Jors arrived, the three men had just finished filling in the tiny hole. As Jors stopped, half hidden by a large sumac, Brock wiped the tears from his face on Calida's mane and stepped up to the grave.

"There is no priest. I will say good-bye to the baby."

"I'm not listening to a half-wit say anything," the old woman snarled. She turned on one heel and started down the hill. "I only came to see the job was done right. Enric, Kern, Simen; back to work, there's hides to be sammied."

Two of the three moved to her side, the third looked toward the young woman and hesitated. "He was my son, Ma."

"He was my son, Ma." She threw it mockingly over her shoulder. "Look around you, Simen. I've buried a son, two daughters, and a husband besides, and it don't make hides tan themselves. Stay and listen to the half-wit if you want."

"Dory?"

She lifted stony eyes to Simen's face. "Better do as your ma says," she sneered. "'Cause you always do as your ma says."

Scarred hands curled into fists, but they stayed at his side. "Fine. I'll go."

"I don't care."

"Fine." But when he turned, Brock was in his way. Jors tensed to urge Gervis forward, but at the last instant, for no clear reason, he changed his mind.

"Stay and say good-bye." A heavy shove rocked him in place but didn't move him. "Stay." And then gently. "Say good-bye to baby."

Simen stared down into Brock's face, then wordlessly turned back to the grave.

Brock returned to his place and rubbed his nose on his sleeve. "Sometimes," he said, "babies die. Mamas and papas love them, and hug them, and kiss them, and feed them, and they die. Nobody did anything bad. Everyone is sorry. The baby wasn't bad. Babies are good. Good-bye, baby."

"His name," Simen said, so quietly Jors almost missed it, "was Tamas."

Brock nodded solemnly. "Good-bye, Tamas. Everyone is sorry." He lifted his head and stared at Tamas' parents standing hunch-shoul-dered, carefully apart. "Now, you cry."

Dory shook her head. "Crying is for the weak."

"You have tears." Brock tapped his own chest. "In here. Tears not cried go bad. Bad tears make you hurt."

"You heard Aysa. She buried a son and two daughters. She never cried."

"She is the mean lady," Brock said sadly. "You can't be the mean lady." He opened his arms and, before Dory could move, wrapped her in one of his all-encompassing hugs.

Jors knew from experience that when Brock hugged, he held nothing back.

It was a new experience for Dory.

She blinked twice, drew in a long shuddering breath, then clutched at his tattered sweater and began to sob. After a moment, Brock reached out one hand, grabbed Simen and pulled him into the embrace.

"Cry now," he commanded.

"I . . ." Simen shook his head and tried to pull away. Brock pulled him closer, pushing Dory into his arms and wrapping himself around them both. Simen stiffened then made a sound, very like his son might have made, and gave himself over to grief. All three of them sank to their knees.

:These people need help.:

Gervis shifted his head. :*It seems they're getting it.*:

With the funeral over, Jors pulled himself into something resembling official shape and sought out Aysa.

"Your son attacked a Herald."

"*His* son just died. He was mad with grief."

"You goaded his brothers . . ."

"To stand by him," she sneered triumphantly. "I never told no one to hit you. And now I'm givin' you and that half-wit food and shelter. You can't ask for more, Herald."

Given that he and Brock were trapped on her side of the river, he supposed he'd better not. "About the bridge . . .

Without the bridge, there was no way back. The river wasn't particularly wide, but the water ran deep and fast.

"You come out here to stick your nose in on us, then you're stuck out here till we head in to town and we ain't headin' nowheres until them hides is done. We wasted time enough with Dory having that baby. You want to leave before that, then you and the halfwit can rebuild the bridge yourself."

"That's fair. I can't expect you to drop everything and assist me." His next words wiped the triumphant sneer from her face. "I'll have them send a crew out from town."

"You can't get word to town."

He smiled, hoping he looked a lot more confident of the conversation's outcome than he felt. "There's a Herald there and I already have. By this time tomorrow, there'll be a dozen people in the valley."

"Liar."

"Heralds can't lie, Ma."

"Shut up!" Aysa half turned and Kern winced away as though he expected to be hit. Lip curled, she turned back to Jors. "I don't want a dozen people in the valley! And it don't take a dozen people anyway. And the water won't be down enough tomorrow."

"Then I'll have them come when the water goes down."

"You won't have no one come. My boys'll rebuild."

"Then the townspeople can help."

"My boys don't need help. They ain't got brains for much, but they can do that. You let them know in town I'm hostin' you *and* the half-wit till then."

It was a grudgingly offered truce, but he'd take it. Jors wasn't surprised that Aysa'd refused help. The last thing she'd want would be her sons exposed to more people, to people who'd make them realize they were entitled to be treated with kindness. Over the next few days, while they waited for the water to recede, she proved that by keeping him by her side, keeping him from interacting with anyone else at the holding.

Brock, she considered no threat. Which was a mistake.

Because Brock treated everyone with kindness.

"You call that supple? I could do better chewin' it! How could you be doin' this all your life and still be no damned good? You're pathetic." Enric and Kern leaped back as she threw the piece of finished leather down at their feet. "Pathetic," she repeated and stomped away.

"Mean lady calls me names, too," Brock sighed, coming out from behind the fleshing beam and picking up the hide.

Enric ripped it out of his hands. "We ain't half-wits."

"Mean lady calls me half-wit. Not you."

"You *are* a half-wit!"

"Are you pathetic?"

Kern jerked forward, face flushed. "You callin us pathetic?"

"No. It hurts when people call names." Brock looked from one to the other. "Doesn't it hurt?"

"If your half-wit falls in a liming pit," Aysa snarled as Jors caught up, "my boys'll stand there and laugh."

"You taught them that."

"I'm all they got."

"They're terrified of you."

"Good."

"Dory isn't."

"You think one of my boys is stupid enough to pick up a weakling?" Aysa nodded toward the garden where Dory heaped cabbage into a basket. "But she does what I say like the rest. If she doesn't like it, she can leave any time."

While they watched, Dory lifted the basket, gave a little cry and let it fall.

Aysa snorted. "'Course that baby left her stupidly weak."

Jors took step toward the garden but stopped as Simen came out of the chicken house and hurried across to his wife.

"Simen! You get back to work, you lazy pig."

His mother's voice froze him in his tracks. Then he shook himself, and began retrieving the spilled cabbages.

"Simen!"

He ignored her.

"This is your fault, Herald. Turning a woman's family against her." Muttering under her breath, she strode toward them.

Dory looked up, saw her coming and stood, hands on hips.

"You think you can face me down, girl? Simen, get up!"

He stood.

"Now get back to work."

He took a step forward and put his hands on Dory's shoulders. "When I'm finished here, Ma."

Aysa's mouth worked for a moment, but no sound emerged. Finally, she spun on one heel and stomped away.

The corner of Simen's mouth curled. "You'd best help here, Herald. I wouldn't follow her right now."

The river was low enough the next day.

The bridge took only a day longer to rebuild and for the most part involved fitting the original pieces back into place.

Jors stared the completed bridge in amazement. "That's incredible."

"Nothin' incredible about it, Herald," Enric snorted. "Damned thing goes out every other season. Easier to build it so it breaks apart clean."

His bare torso red with cold, Kern shrugged into a sheepskin coat. "Supports slip out so they don't shatter, logs end up in the same place, we float 'em back and rebuild. Any idiot can do it."

"Trust me, I've crossed a hundred rivers–or maybe a couple of rivers a hundred times–but I've never seen anything like this."

"Ma says it's not . . ." Simen paused, frowned, and looked up at the Herald. "It's really good?"

"It's really good."

The brothers exchanged confused looks and Jors had the horrible suspicion this was the first time they'd ever been praised for anything.

The next day while Jors was checking Calida's girth strap for the trip back to town, Dory came out of the house with a bundle. "It's for Brock," she said, folding back a corner. "I want you to give it to him for me."

At first Jors thought it was white leather. Made sense; they were tanners after all. Then he realized the leather had been cut and sewn into a fair approximation of Herald's whites. Dory had clearly taken the pattern from his and sized it to fit Brock.

"I saw he didn't have none of his own."

Oh, help. "Dory, you know he's not . . ."

"Brother Herald! We go now? What you got?" His hands and Dory's together closed the bundle.

"It's a surprise," Dory said, her cheeks crimson. "For later."

"Not for now?"

"No."

"Okay." He took Calida's reins and stood waiting patiently while Jors tied the bundle behind Gervis' saddle.

:You seem upset, Chosen.:

:I can't tell her Brock's not an actual Herald while he's standing there. He'll say he is, I'll say he isn't, and I'm not sure that in this place at this time, I'd win the argument.:

:You shouldn't argue.:

:Oh, that's helpful.:

:Thank you.:

The whole family went with them to the bridge. Jors didn't know why the rest came, but he was certain Aysa just wanted to make sure they were off her land. He wanted to say something, something that would convince them they didn't have to live inside the darkness of an old woman's anger, but before he could think of the right words, Brock hugged Dory. And Simen. And Enric. And Kern.

Then he scrambled up into the saddle and, from the safety of Calida's back, took a deep breath, looked Aysa in the eye, and spoke directly to her for the first time. "Why don't you love your babies?"

Her lip curled. "I buried my babies, half-wit."

He nodded toward the three young men standing to her right. "Not them."

She turned, looked at her sons, looked back at Brock and muttered, "Half-wit." But there was little force behind it.

Jors had no idea he was going to do what he did until he did it.

"Jors, you hugged mean lady."

"Yeah. I know." Although he still couldn't believe it. "Everyone else got hugged, I just . . ."

She'd pushed him away with such force that he'd slammed back into Gervis' shoulder.

"You are the bravest Herald. Ever, ever."

"Thank you."

Then she'd snarled something incomprehensible, turned, and stomped away.

He'd probably accomplished nothing at all by it. The bundle Dory had given him pushed against the small of his back.

The weather remained clear and cool and just as the sun was setting, they stopped outside the village.

"Gate will close when sun is set," Brock warned.

"I know. Brock, I think you should go back to Haven with Isabel."

"Lots of Heralds in Haven?"

"Yes."

Brock sighed and shook his head. "No. I have to stay here. I am the only Herald."

"Brock, you're not . . ." He couldn't say it. . Brock waited patiently for a moment then smiled.

"Is it later?"

"Yes . . ."

"What's Dory's surprise?"

"Um . . . it's um . . ."

Both Companions turned their heads to look at him. Their expression said, *this is up to you.*

:He believes he is a Herald.:

:Yes, but . . .:

:And he acts accordingly.:

"I couldn't do it, Isabel. They're just clothes and I know that but if I gave Brock those whites, then there'd be fake Heralds showing up all over the place."

"A bad precedent to be sure," the older Herald agreed.

"There has to be a line and that line has to be the Companions. Sometimes it seems like we're barely keeping order in chaos now. I couldn't . . . No matter how much . . ." Jors ran both hands back through his air, he couldn't believe how much the decision, the right decision had felt like betrayal. "It wouldn't make any difference to Brock. He knows who and what he is, but for the others in the village, those who made fun and called him names . . ."

"Come here, I want to show you something." Isabel took his arm and pulled him to the window. "What do you see?"

Jors squinted down into the stable yard. "Brock's grooming Gervis again."

"While you four were gone, I talked to a lot of people. Seems that whenever a Herald comes into this village, the Companion manages to spend time with Brock. Even if it's only a moment or two." They watched as Calida crossed the yard and tried to shoulder Gervis away. Brock laughed and told her to wait her turn. "You were right not to give him the Whites," Isabel continued, "but you were also right when you said it makes no difference. He couldn't be Chosen because, as Heralds, we have to face dangers he'd never understand, but the Companions know him. All Brock needs from us is our love and support. Now, since Healer Lortin has finally allowed me out of bed, what do you say you and I go down there and give our brother a hand with the fourfoots?"

Jors grinned as Brock gamely tried to brush both tails at once.

Heralds wear shiny white.

Brock wore his Whites on the inside.

All The Ages Of Man

I thought I'd try something a bit different for the third Valdemar story. Although I was still using the same Herald and Companion, I wanted to see if I could stay true to the source material and write something funny. Just between us, this damned near killed me to write as it kept sliding down the slippery slope toward earnest and had to be hauled back up again by the back of its pants. Sometimes, Heralds just seem to need a good whack upside the head . . . which is eventually what I went with.

"I'M TOO YOUNG FOR THIS."

Although Jors had spoken the words aloud, thrown them as it were out onto the wind without expecting an answer, he received one anyway.

:*So you keep saying.*:

"Doesn't make it any less true."

:*You are experienced in riding circuit,*: his Companion reminded him. :*All you must do is teach what you know.*:

Jors snorted and shifted in the saddle. "So *you* keep saying."

Gervis snorted in turn. :*Then perhaps you should listen.*"

"I'm not a teacher."

:*You are a Herald. More importantly, you are needed.*:

And that was why they were heading north east, out to the edge of their sector to meet with Herald Jennet and her greenie. To accept said greenie from the older Herald and finish out the last eleven months of her year and a half of Internship. The Courier who'd brought the news of Jennet's mother's sickness had also brought the news that the Herald able to replace her was already in the Sector but way over on the other side of a whole lot of nothing. It was decided

283

he'd start his circuit from there and Jennet would backtrack the much shorter distance to meet up with Jors.

The girl's name was Alyise, her companion's name was Donnel and that was pretty much all Jors knew. He couldn't remember ever seeing anyone of that name amidst the Grays during the rare times he'd been at the Collegium over the last few years and he only remembered her Companion as a long-legged colt.

The thing was, he liked being on the road and he much preferred the open spaces of the Borders to any city so he went back on Circuit as fast as he could be reassigned. That didn't give him much time to learn about the latest Chosen and when he did meet up with other Heralds, he was much more interested in finding out what his year-mates had been doing.

"Jennet has got to be ten years older than I am. At least. And she's a woman."

Strands of the Companions mane slid across Jors' fingers like white silk as Gervis tossed his head. : *What does her being a woman have to do with this?*:

"Women are better at teaching girls. They understand girls. Me . . ." He rubbed a dribble of sweat off the back of his neck. ". . . I don't get girls at all."

: *You seemed to understand Herald Erica. I remember her continuously agreeing with you.*:

"Continuously agreeing? What are you talking about?"

: *Raya and I could hear her quite clearly outside the waystation. She kept yelling yes. Yes! Yes! Yes!*:

"Oh, ha ha. Very funny." Jors could feel Gervis' amusement—the young stallion did indeed think it was very funny. "As I recall, Erica and I weren't the only two keeping company that night."

: *We were quiet.*:

"Well, I'm sorry we kept you from your beauty sleep and you needn't worry about it happening again for, oh, about eleven months."

: *You do not know that the new Herald will find you distasteful. Raya told me that her Herald found you pleasant.*:

Jors sighed. Pleasant. Well, he supposed it was preferable to the alternative. "Thank you. But that's not the point. I'll be Alyise's teacher, her mentor; I can't take advantage of my position of power."

: *You will be Heralds together.*:

"Yes, but . . ." He felt a subtle shift of smooth muscles below him echoed by a definite shift of attention and fell silent.

:Inar says we will meet in time for us to return to the Waystation outside of Applebay before full dark.:

If that was true, and Jors had no reason to doubt Jennet's Companion, they were a lot closer to the crossroad than he'd thought. He glanced over his shoulder to check on Bucky and found the pack-mule tucked up close where Gervis' tail could keep the late summer insects off his face. And that was another possible problem. Mules were mules regardless of who they worked for and mules that worked for Heralds could be just as obstinate and hard to get along with as any other. They'd be adding a new mule to the mix.

It was a good thing Companions always got along.

And speaking of . . .

"Why didn't Donnel contact you? Can't he reach this far?"

:Inar is senior to Donnel as you will be senior to his Chosen.:

"You'll be senior to Donnel as well then."

: Yes.: Sleek white sides rose and fell as Gervis sighed.

Jors grinned. "Wishing Alyise's Companion was a mare?"

His grin broadened as it became quite clear that Gervis had no intention of answering.

"She's a good kid," Jennet said, glancing over at where the youngest of the three Heralds was carefully packing away the remains of the meal they'd shared. "Eager, enthusiastic . . ."

"Exhausting?" Jors suggested as her voice trailed off.

"A little," the older Herald admitted with a smile. "But you're a lot younger than I am, you should be able to keep up."

"That's just it. I'm too young to be doing this. I'm no teacher."

"You have doubts."

He only just managed not to roll his eyes. "Well, yes."

"Does your Companion doubt you?"

"Gervis?" Jors turned in time to see Gervis rising to his feet after what had clearly been a vigorous roll, his gleaming white coat flecked with bits of grass. "Gervis has never doubted me."

"Then, if you can't believe in yourself, believe in your Companion. And now that I've gifted you with my aged wisdom . . ." Grinning, she bent and lifted her saddle. ". . . we'd best get back on the road."

Lifting his own saddle, Jors fell into step beside her. "I'm sorry to hear about your mother."

"Yes, well, she wasn't young when I was born and she's never been what you could call strong so I can't say that I'm surprised. I'm just glad that the Borders are so quiet right now and that there was someone close enough . . ." She smiled so gratefully at him that Jors felt himself flush. "*Two* someone's close enough."

Inar, given his head, had disappeared southward almost too fast for the eye to follow. One moment he, and his Herald, were a white blur against the gold of summer-dried gasses and the next, they were gone.

Gone. Leaving Jors alone with Alyise.

Alone with an attractive eighteen year old girl.

No. Alone with another Herald.

One he just happened to be responsible for.

Oh Havens.

:*She is a Herald. That makes her responsible for herself.*:

:*I was broadcasting?*:

Gervis snorted. :*Donnel probably heard you.*:

Jors doubted that since Donnel—with a fair bit of that long-legged colt in him still—was dancing sideways away from a bobbing yellow wildflower. Alyise was laughing, probably at something Donnel had said. Their mule, right out at the end of its lead rope, turned his head just far enough for Jors to see that he looked resigned about the whole thing.

Which reminded Jors of something he'd meant to ask Jennet and forgotten. No matter, Alyise would know what had happened to their second mule.

"Spike?" She giggled. "Oh Jennet left him back at the Waystation Supply post saying you'd have enough on your plate without having to deal with Spike too. He's not a pleasant fellow although honestly, I think most of it's an act and he's really much nicer than he pretends. You know?"

Jors had no time to answer. He suspected she hadn't intended him to as she rattled on without pausing.

"She left a lot of her gear there except for the bits she gave to me. I seem to go through soap really, really quickly, I can't think why, I mean, we're all in whites but if there's something to smudge on, I'll smudge. I may be the only Herald ever who really appreciated her grays. So Jennet gave me her extra soap and a tunic that was getting too tight for her—across the shoulders of course not in front because I'm well, a little better endowed there—but no worry about her being caught short because she didn't leave behind or give me anything she'll need because she's heading home. But you knew that didn't you because you were there when she left."

The punctuating smile was dazzling.

The Waystation outside Appleby was much like every other Waystation; there was a corral for the mules, a snug lean-to for the Companions, a good sized, well stocked storeroom, and a single room for the Heralds. The biggest difference was that the fireplace had been filled in with a small box-stove, flat-topped for cooking and considerably more efficient at heating the space.

"Not to mention there'll be a lot less warm air sucked up the chimney," Jors observed examining the stove-pipes. This was new since this the last time he'd been by.

"I think it's less romantic though."

"What?"

Alyise smiled as he turned. "I think a stove is less romantic than an open fire. Don't you think there's just something so sensual about the dancing flames and the flicking golden light?"

"Light." Jors cleared his throat and tried again. "We'd better light the lanterns."

She pushed russet curls back off her face with one hand, grey eyes gleaming in the dusk. "Or instead of lighting the lanterns, we could just leave the doors of the stove open and sit together close to the fire."

"Fire."

"Pardon?"

"You light the fire." His palms were sweaty. "In the stove," he expanded as she stared at him, head cocked. "So we can cook. I have to go check on Gervis."

:*I'm fine.*:

:*Good.*: He got outside to find his Companion standing by the door and gazing at him with some concern. :*She's . . . I mean, I'm supposed to be teaching her.*:

:*Donnel says his Chosen is glad you are a young man. She has been with Jennet for seven months.*:

:*Hey, I've been on my own for eight and that's . . .*: He paused as Gervis snorted. :*Yeah. Sorry. Way too much information. The point is, it wouldn't be right.*:

:*If that's how you feel.*:

:It is.:
:Good luck.:
:Oh, that's very helpful.:
:Thank you.:

Never let anyone tell you that Companions can't be as sarcastic as cats, Jors muttered to himself as he turned and went back inside. The curve of Alyise's back stopped him cold. Her pants hung low on the flare of her hips, low enough to expose the dimples on the small of her back just under her waist.

She smiled at him over her shoulder as she pulled a sleeveless tunic out of her pack. "I just had to get into something that wasn't all sweaty. I don't know what it is about spending the day in the saddle that makes me so damp since Donnel's doing most of the work but from my breast bands right on out everything is just soaked through. I guess the good news is that, at this time of the year, I can rinse them out tonight and they'll be dry by morning unless it rains, of course, but I don't think it's going to. There's really no point in having the village laundry deal with them." Her brow wrinkled as she pushed her head through the tunic's wide neck. "Does this village even have a laundry?"

"Laundry?" He tried not to stare at the pale swell of her breasts as she pulled the tunic down and turned to light one of the lamps with shaking hands. He was not ready for this kind of responsibility.

"Men."

Was she allowed to laugh at him? There was too much about this mentoring that he didn't know.

"I don't suppose you even noticed," she continued, slipping out of her pants. "Ah, that's better. Shall you cook or shall I?"

"Me!" Cooking would be a welcome distraction. "You can tell me about your time with Jennet. So I know what you've covered . . . done."

"Okay; how much of . . ."

"Everything!"

Everything took them through dinner and into bed. Separate beds. Alyise seemed fine with that Jors noticed thankfully since he wasn't certain his resolve would stand up against a determined assault. Long after her breathing had evened out into the long rhythms of sleep, he lay staring up at the rough wood of the ceiling and wondered just how authoritarian he was supposed to be. All Heralds were equals, that was a given. Except when they weren't, and that was tacitly understood. *I'm just not ready for this yet.*

:*Sleep now, Heart-brother.*: Gervis's mental touch was gentle. :*Many tasks seem less daunting in the morning.*:

Jors woke just after sunrise to discover that Alyise had already gone out to feed and water the mules.

"I can never stay in bed after I wake up," she explained with a sunny smile. "My mother used to say it's because I was afraid I'd miss something but I think it's because I didn't want to get bounced on by my younger sisters and I'll tell you, that habit stood me in good stead when I was a Gray because you know how hard it is to get going some mornings and the first up has the first shot at the hot water and there were mostly girls in my year; six of us and one boy. What about yours?"

"My?" When did she breathe?

"Your year; how many boys and girls in your year?"

"Oh. Three boys, two girls."

"How . . . nice."

He heard Donnel snort, realized she was staring at him, and a moment later realized why. He'd gotten a little panicked when he'd seen her bed was empty and raced outside wearing only the light cotton, drawstring pants he'd slept in. With the early morning sun behind him, he might as well be naked. *Oh yeah. This is going to help me maintain some kind of authority.*

:*Authority does not come from your clothing.*:

And that would have been more reassuring had his Companion not sounded like he found the entire situation entirely too funny. :Maybe not, but it sure doesn't come from . . .: It occurred to him that while he was standing talking to Gervis, Alyise was still staring. Appreciatively. "I'll just go and get dressed. We'll be heading into Appleby right after we eat."

And thank any Gods who may be listening for that, he thought as he made as dignified as retreat as possible into the Waystation.

Appleby wasn't so much a village as it was a market and clearing center for the surrounding orchards that gave it its name. Jors told the younger Herald all he knew about both the area and the inhabitants as they rode in from the Waystation but since his available information ran out some distance before they arrived, Alyise took over the conversation.

Her mother made a terrific apple dumpling but wouldn't give out the recipe not matter how much Alyise or her sisters begged.

Donnel was very fond of apples, especially the small, sweet pink ones that grew further north.

She loved apples sliced and dried and hoped she'd be able to buy some of last years if they had a moment before they left town.

Her grandfather used to carve apples and dry them whole and they turned into the most cunning old men and women dolls' heads.

Just when Jors was about to suggest she stop talking, she finished her story about how an apple peel taken off in one unbroken spiral would give the initial of true love when tossed over a shoulder and fell silent, straightening in the saddle and transforming from girl to Herald.

:*Neat trick.*:

:*Why does she need to be anything but what she is when she is with you?*: Gervis asked reasonably.

:*She doesn't.*:

:*And why do you . . .*:

:*Because I'm her teacher!*:

:*Herald Jennet was also her teacher. Do you think Herald Jennet behaved differently than herself?*:

:*Herald Jennet has had more time to be herself!*: Jors pointed out.

Gervis tossed his head, setting his bridle bells ringing as they passed the first of the buildings. :*You are not Herald Jennet,*: he said as the first wave of laughing children broke around them.

:*That's what I keep saying!*:

The Companion carefully sidestepped an overly adventurous and remarkably grubby little boy. :*Maybe you should try listening.*:

And that was all he was willing to say.

Go not to your Companion for advice, Jors sighed. *For they will tell you to figure it out for yourself.*

Judgments in Appleby were, not surprisingly, mostly about apples. More surprisingly, Jors found Alyise to be an attentive listener—both to the petitioners and to him. Although she deferred to Jors as the senior Herald, she expressed her opinions clearly and concisely when asked for them and in turn asked intelligent questions when she needed more information. Having been more than a little afraid of what the day would bring, Jors was impressed and grateful that he could set aside personal doubts and concentrate on the job at hand.

Late that afternoon, when they'd finished with official business and had moved on to the more social aspects of being a Herald—

trading the gossip that kept the far flung corners of the kingdom telling the same stories–Jors glanced over at Alyise within a circle of teenage girls and wondered if it counted as a conversation when everyone seemed to be talking at once.

"Herald Jors."

He turned to see the eldest of the village councilors holding out a cup of cider.

"Don't worry, it's one of this year's first pressings. Windfall from the early apples. It has absolute no trade value so you needn't fear you're being bribed."

A tentative sip curled his tongue. "Tart," he gasped.

"A little young," the councilor admitted, grinning. "And if you don't mind my saying, you seem a little young yourself to be teaching the ray of sunshine there."

"I've been doing this for a while, Councilor." On the outside, Jors remained calm and confident. Inside, a little voice was saying, *Oh that's just great. It's obvious to everyone.* "And Alyise is a trained Herald. I'm only here to help guide her through her first Circuit.

"Oh, I'm not criticizing, lad. And given that one's energy, it's probably best you're no greybeard. I imagine she'd be the death of an older man."

The councilor obviously believed he was sleeping with Alyise. That was a belief he'd have to nip in the bud. "Heralds aren't in the habit of taking advantage of their Interns."

"Advantage?" The elderly councilor glanced over at Alyise and began to laugh so hard he passed a mouthful of cider out his nose. "Oh lad," he gasped when he had breath enough to speak again. "You *are* young."

There wasn't a lot Jors could say to that.

: *You seem fine in the villages,*: Gervis pointed out as they headed toward the Border.

: *It's different in the villages.*: Jors told him. : *We have well defined roles and I know what I'm supposed to do.*:

: *You've always known what to do in a Waystation before. You've always know what to do with another Herald before.*:

He glanced over at Alyise who'd turned to check on the mules. : *I've never been responsible for another Herald before.*:

His Companion sighed and raised his head so Jors could get at an elusive itch under the edge of his mane. : *You're beginning to worry me.*:

There wasn't a lot Jors could say to that either.

Six days later Alyise handed him a mug of tea and said, "Is it because you like boys? It's just that I've been as obvious as I know how without coming right out and saying we should bed down together," she explained a few moments later, after they cleaned up the mess. "I mean, I was with Jennet for seven whole months and you're cute and well, it's been a while, you know."

He knew.

"Your ears are very red," she added.

Jors attempted to explain about being responsible and not taking advantage of her while he was in at least a nominal position of power. Alyise didn't seem to quite understand his point.

"You're a little young to take such a grandfatherly attitude, don't you think?"

"That's it exactly."

She wrinkled her nose, confused. "What's it?"

She was adorable when she wrinkled her nose and some of the tea had splashed on her tunic drawing his eye right to . . .

"Maybe you should talk to Donnel about it," he choked out. "I need to check the um . . . mules."

"I just checked them."

"I meant the . . . um, stores!"

"Gervis explained to Donnel who explained to me and I think I understand the problem." Alyise smiled at Jors reassuringly when he came back inside. "I was kind of dumped on you unexpectedly wasn't I? I mean, there you were, out riding your circuit, just the two of you hearing petitions and riding to the rescue and being guys together and all of a sudden Jennet finds out her mother is sick and you've got me. I know Heralds are supposed to be adaptable and all but this is a situation that could take some getting used to for you so I expect it's all a matter of timing."

"Good. So we're um . . ." He tried, not entirely successfully, to pull her actual meaning from the cheerful flow of words.

Her smile broadened. "We're good."

"Okay." Still, something felt not quite right. :Gervis?:

He could almost see his Companion roll sapphire eyes. :*I dealt with it, Chosen.*"

:*But . . .*:

:*Let it go.*:

Not so much advice as an unarguable instruction.

"So . . ." Jors brought his attention back to the younger Herald. ". . . there were some tax problems in the area we're heading for next. We should go over them in case they come up again."

"Jennet and I ran into a few problems just like this back last month. Well, not just like this because that's one thing I've learned since I've been out is that no two problems are exactly the same no matter how much they seem to be and . . ."

He let her words wash over him as he pulled the papers from his pack. So they were good. That was . . .

. . . good.

Why did he feel like he was waiting for the other shoe to drop?

Last year's tax problems didn't reoccur but new problems arose and Jors did his best to guide Alyise through them. She was better with people than he was and as summer passed into fall, he allowed her to hear those petitions that dealt with social problems and tried to learn from her natural charm as she learned from his experience.

Given her unflagging energy and exuberance, he felt as though he was running full out to stay ahead of her and he never felt younger or more unsuited for his position as her teacher as when he saw her in the midst of a crowd of admiring young men.

Not that she ever forgot she was a Herald on duty, it was just . . .

:*Just what, Chosen?*:

:*You're laughing at me again, aren't you?*:

No answer in words, just a strong feeling of amusement. Which was, of course, all the answer Jors needed.

Frost had touched the grass by the time they reached the tiny village of Halfrest grown up not quite a generation before around a campsite that marked the halfway point on a shortcut between two larger towns. A shortcut only because the actual trade road followed the kind of ground sensible people built roads on rather than taking the direct route more suitable to goats.

Jors had a feeling that without the mule tied to her saddle, Alyise and Donnel would have been bounding like those goats from rock to rock, Alyise chattering cheerfully the entire time as they skirted the edges of crumbling cliffs.

The Waystation was brand new, the wood still pale and raw

looking. No corral had been built for the mules but a rope strung between two trees would take the lead lines giving them plenty of room to graze. While there was no well, the pond looked crystal clear and cold.

"If you have a Waystation," Jors said as they carried their packs inside, "you're more than just a group of people trying to carve out an uncertain life. You're a real village."

"And that's important to them, to be seen as a real village?"

"This was wilderness when the elders of this village came here with their parents. They're proud of what they've accomplished."

He reminded her of that again as they rode into Halfrest which was, in point of fact, nothing much more than a group of people trying to carve out an uncertain life. Livestock still shared many of the same buildings as their owners and function ruled over form. Only the Meeting Hall bore any decoration—graceful, joyful carvings tucked up under the gabled eaves gave some promise of what could be when they finally got a bit ahead.

"Because a real village has a Meeting Hall?" Alyise asked quietly as they dismounted.

He nodded and turned to greet the approaching men and women.

They had not had an easy year of it. There had been sickness and raiders and heavy rains then sickness again.

"We had no Harvest Festival this year," a weary woman told them, pushing graying hair off her face with a thin hand. "With so many sick there were few to bring the harvest in so when the fields were finally clear the time was past. We had little heart for it besides. But there are two pigs fattening, pledged for the festival last spring. One came from my good black sow and I feel I should be able to slaughter him for my own use."

"He was pledged to the village," an equally weary looking man interrupted.

"He was pledged to the festival!"

As there had been no festival it would seem sensible to give the pig back to the woman who had pledged it, perhaps requiring her to give some of the meat to those in need. But this was Alyise's judgment and Jors sat quietly behind her allowing her to make up her own mind with no interference from him. He glanced around the Hall, from the work-roughed and exhausted villagers to the sullen knot of teenagers clumped together by the door. No one looked hungry or ill used, just tired. They'd been working non-stop for weeks. It was no wonder they'd skipped their festival, all they probably wanted was a chance to rest.

"I have heard all sides of the argument," Alyise said at last. "And this is my judgement." She paused, just for a moment, and Jors had the strangest feeling the other shoe was finally dropping. "The pig was pledged to the Harvest Festival. Have the festival."

"But the harvest has been in long since and . . ."

"The harvest is in," Alyise interrupted, her smile lighting all the dark corners of the room. "I think that's worth celebrating." Before anyone could protest, she locked eyes with the woman who owned the pig. "Don't you?"

"Well, yes but . . ."

"The sickness is past. The raiders have been defeated. And that's worth celebrating too." The man who had protested the reclaiming of the pig seemed stunned by her smile. "Don't you think so?"

"I guess . . ."

"And the rains have stopped." She spread her arms and turned to the teenagers by the door. "The sun is shining. Why not celebrate that?"

Shoulders straightened. Tentative smiles answered her question.

No one stood against Alyise's enthusiasm for long. Soon, to Jors surprise, no one wanted to. The pigs were slaughtered and dressed and put it pits to roast. Tables were set up in the hall. Food and drink began to appear. Musicians brought out their instruments.

"I'd have thought they were too tired to party," Jors murmured as half a dozen girls ran giggling by with armloads of the last bright leaves of fall.

"My mother has a saying; if you don't celebrate your victories, all you remember are your defeats. The food they're eating now won't be enough to make a real difference if the winter is especially hard but the memories they make, good memories of laughter and fellowship, that could be enough to see them through." Alyise gestured toward the carvings. "They know joy. I just helped them remember they knew. You know?"

He did actually.

:*Careful Chosen.*: Gervis adjusted his gait as Jors listed slightly to the left.

"You lied to me." Alyise's whites were a beacon in the darkness. Which was good because he didn't think he could find her otherwise.

Except that she was on Donnel and that made it pretty obvious where she was now he considered it.

"What did I lie about?"

"You said that was apple . . . apple jush. Juice."

She giggled. "It was once."

"Jack. That wash apples jack." He wasn't drunk. Heralds did not get drunk on duty even at impromptu Harvest Festivals where the apple juice wasn't. Which he wouldn't have had any of had Alyise not handed him a huge mug just before they left to toast the celebration and the celebrants.

Now the night was spinning gently around him and he suspected that getting the Companions settled for the night was going to be interesting.

Fortunately, it seemed that Alyise was less affected.

"Hey." He set his saddle down with exaggerated care. "You had some of that too!"

"Some," she agreed, the dimples appearing. "Come on inside."

Her hand was warm on his arm. Then it was warm under his tunic. And her mouth tasted warm and sweet. And . . . Wait a minute. He pulled back although his hands, seemingly with a mind of their own, continued working on her laces.

"I don't think . . ."

Her eyes gleamed. "What?"

He couldn't remember. :*Gervis?*:

:*She got you drunk and now she's taking advantage of you.*:

:*What?*:

:*It was Donnel's suggestion but it seemed sound.*:

The bunk hit the back of his legs and he was suddenly lying down holding a soft, willing, body.

:*Help.*:

His Companion's mental voice held layers of laughter. :*Say that like you mean it, Heart-brother.*:

Actually, for a while, he wasn't able to say anything much at all.

Jors stood staring down at the pond watching the early morning sun tease tendrils of fog off the icy looking water, trying to work the kinks out of muscles he hadn't used for far too long. Alyise was as enthusiastic in bed as she was about everything else and he'd been hard pressed to keep up.

He guessed he had been a bit of an ass about that whole position of power thing. Still . . .

:*What is it, Chosen?*: Gervis velvet nose prodded him in the back.

:*I'm still her mentor for another seven months. What if this changes things between us?*:

:*You think she will no longer trust your judgement because you have shared her bed?*:

Put that way it sounded a bit insulting. :*Well, no.*:

:*Then what is the problem?*:

There didn't seem to be one. Jors leaned against his Companion's comforting bulk and thought about it.

He wasn't Jennet.

Alyise was a Herald. That made her responsible for herself.

Donnel said his Chosen was glad he was a young man.

They had well defined roles in the villages.

There was no reason for them not to continue sharing a bed as long as they both remained willing. No reason at all for it to detract from his ability to teach what he knew or learn what she offered.

Jors grinned. He had other nights like last night to look forward to and days of cheerful conversations combined with an enthusiastic welcome to whatever the road ahead might bring, and a high energy approach to life that definitely got results since a village-wide party turned out to solve a petition about a disputed pig.

His grin faded as a muscle twinged in his back.

"Havens," he sighed, as he realized what the next few months would bring, "I'm too old for this."

Gervis weight was suddenly no longer a comforting presence at his back but rather a short, sharp shove.

The water in the pond was as cold as it looked.

Being is Believing:
Action, Character, and Belief
in the Work of Tanya Huff

THE CENTRAL THEME RUNNING THROUGH the work of Tanya Huff involves the relationships between our actions, our character, and our beliefs. One of the traditional questions in ethics is whether the fundamental moral problem is what we should do or what we should be; modern ethicists tend to focus on our actions, while classical ethicists focus on our character.[1] Huff's response seems to be that they are two sides of the same coin: our characters shape our actions and our actions make us into particular kinds of people. Similarly, just as being and doing are related, belief also plays an important role. The beliefs that we have about ourselves and others shape what people are able to be and what they are able to do.

Let us start by considering the relationship between what we are and what we do. Sometimes this relationship is explicit; for instance, Tony explains to Brianna: "We're wizards. It's what we do."[2] Similarly, Huff's description of Mrs. Ruth evokes the connection between the two: "She'd known her time was ending for months now. It was, after all, what she did. What she was. She knew things."[3] However, frequently the relationship is more subtle. The crow in "Finding Marcus" talks about how it is in dogs' natures to search for their masters; similarly, it is in crows' natures to get bored easily and seek stories to entertain themselves. Each of them is playing the part that they were made to—what they are determines (at least to some extent) what they do. This may make it seem as if our actions are greatly constrained by who we are, which reeks of predestination or determinism. However, that only follows if our nature is unchanging; being sapient, part of our nature *is* the ability to change.

In "I Knew a Guy Once" Huff explicitly emphasizes the notion that our choices shape who we are. Able Harris does not tell the bar

having the right buildings will do this–it will make them into a town.[10] And, at least for them, it does. This raises an interesting question as to whether this belief-shaped reality is relative to the beholder; Jors and Alyise, after all, did not particularly see Halfrest as a "real town" simply because it had those buildings. There may be some limitations as to how much we can shape reality simply with our beliefs; my believing the world is flat will not, in most universes, actually make it flat. Our beliefs can, however, greatly affect our experience of reality.

One of the most interesting presentations Huff gives of the relation of belief to being with respect to people is in "Tuesday Evenings, Six Thirty to Seven." The Brownies come to Missus Owl because they are tired of being Brownies; they wish to become something else. She agrees to help, but this generates problems; since the sort of Brownies she deals with are not normally short, foul-mouthed men of magic, she has to conceal them from the rest of the community. When the Guider from the main office comes to meet the Brownies, she and the minister's wife have very different experiences. As Big Tam puts it, "The dark one, for all she was here to check you out, truly wanted to see Brownies so that's what she saw and heard–wee girls. The other, well, she'd convinced herself that there were no such thing as Brownies hadn't she? So that's all she saw."[11] Quite directly, the beliefs that the two women hold shape their experience of reality. The Guider sees what she wants to see–a happy troop of little girls collecting badges and learning things. However, since the minister's wife does not believe the Brownies exist, she is not able to see them; her belief in their non-existence translates into their actual non-existence, at least so far as she is concerned.

The way in which other people's beliefs affect us are not necessarily this extreme; beliefs can shape what we are in much more subtle ways. Frequently we gather encouragement and confidence from other people–as children, we gain strength from our teachers and parents, and as adults we gain it from our peers and our colleagues. If I am uncertain that I am capable of something, being told that someone believes in me is sometimes all I need–if someone believes I have strength, I actually have the strength. Huff touches upon this idea at the end of "The Demon's Den," when Ari discovers that Gervis believes she was chosen for something other than being a Herald. Since Gervis believes Ari has a purpose, she starts to see herself that way as well; he gives her the confidence to stop seeing herself as a worthless person who should have died and start seeing what she can still accomplish. His belief in what she can do shapes her belief in herself—and that, in turn, shapes what she is.

In addition to being shaped by other people's beliefs, therefore, we are also shaped by our own. The little girl in "Choice of Ending" will always know she is loved, according to Mrs. Ruth, and this will shape the kind of life she has; she may be a rebellious teenager, but she will come through it okay because of this knowledge. The beliefs we have can sustain our character even through difficult times and even when other people doubt those beliefs. Brock, for instance, believes he is a Herald. He is not swayed by the arguments of other people that he has no Companion, he is not wearing Whites, and so forth. As he points out, "Clothes are on the outside."[12] What we are is not simply a matter of what other people believe or of external trappings like our clothes. What we are is a matter of our character—how we act and what we believe.

Brock himself is a culmination of both of the themes running through Huff. As Gervis puts it, "He believes he is a Herald . . . And he acts accordingly."[13] What Brock believes himself to be shapes what he is—he is the kind of person that Heralds are, a person who is kind and honest and helpful. And because he is that kind of person, he does kind and truthful and generous acts. His belief shapes his character which shapes his actions. Huff leaves us, therefore, with an extremely optimistic outlook. If we can change the person we are by believing hard enough, if we can become the person we want by doing the actions we think they would do, there is hope for us all: goodness is within our grasp. Perhaps our hearts are not naturally as big as Brock's. But if we believe in ourselves long enough, we may be able to change that.

Erica L. Neely
University of Illinois at Urbana-Champaign
Urbana, Illinois

1 John Stuart Mill exemplifies the modern approach to ethics, Aristotle the classical approach.

2 "After School Specials," p. 58

3 "Choice of Ending," p. 22

4 "I Knew a Guy Once," p. 17

5 "All the Ages of Man," p. 296(?)

6 "I Knew a Guy Once," pp. 11-12
7 "Not That Kind of a War," p. 152
8 "Not That Kind of a War," p. 157
9 "After School Specials," p. 59-60
10 "All the Ages of Man," p. 295(?)
11 "Tuesday Evenings, Six Thirty to Seven," p. 119
12 "Brock," p. 269(?)
13 "Brock," p. 282(?)

TANYA HUFF: BIBLIOGRAPHY
(as of June 2007)

NOVELS by Date of Publication (23)

Child of the Grove, DAW Books, Inc., May 1988
The Last Wizard, DAW Books, Inc., March 1989
Gate of Darkness, Circle of Light, DAW Books, Inc., November 1989
The Fire's Stone, DAW Books, Inc, October 1990
Blood Price, DAW Books, Inc., May 1991
Blood Trail, DAW Books, Inc., February 1992
Blood Lines, DAW Books, Inc., January 1993
Blood Pact, DAW Books, Inc., November 1993
Sing the Four Quarters, DAW Books, Inc., December 1994
Fifth Quarter, DAW Books, Inc., April 1995
Scholar of Decay, TSR Ltd., December 1995
No Quarter, DAW Books, Inc., April 1996
Blood Debt, DAW Books, Inc., May 1997
Summon the Keeper, DAW Books, Inc., May 1998
The Quartered Sea, DAW Books, Inc., May 1999
Wizard of the Grove, (Omnibus *Child of the Grove* and *The Last Wizard*) DAW
    Books, Inc., January 1999
Valor's Choice, DAW Books, Inc., April 2000
The second summoning, DAW Books, Inc., March 2001
Of Darkness, Light And Fire, (Omnibus *Gate of Darkness* and *The Fire's Stone*)
    DAW Books, Inc., December 2001
The Better Part of Valor, DAW Books, Inc., March 2002
Long Hot Summoning, DAW Books, Inc., May 2003
Smoke and Shadows, DAW Books, Inc., April 2004
Smoke and Mirrors, DAW Books, Inc., June 2005
Smoke and Ashes, DAW Books, Inc., June 2006
The Blood Books, Volume One–Price & Trail, (Omnibus *Blood Price* and *Blood
    Trail*) DAW Books, Inc., July 2006

The Blood Books, Volume Two–Lines & Pact, (Omnibus *Blood Lines* and *Blood Pact*) DAW Books, Inc., August 2006

The Blood Books, Volume Three–Debt & Bank (stories), (Omnibus *Blood Debt* and *Blood Bank*) DAW Books, Inc., September 2006

A Confederation of Valor, (Omnibus *Valor's Choice* and *The Better Part of Valor*) DAW Books, Inc., December 2006

Smoke and Ashes, **pb**, DAW Books, Inc., June 2007

Heart of Valor, **hc**, DAW Books, Inc., June 2007

SHORT STORIES by Date of Publication (63)

"What Little Girls are Made Of," *Magic in Ithkar 3*, ed Andre Norton & Robert Adams, TOR, October 1986 (collected *What Ho, Magic!* 1999)

"Third Time Lucky," *Amazing Stories*, November 1986 (reprinted *On Spec* Fall 1995, collected *Stealing Magic* 1999 & 2005 and *Magical Beginnings* 2003)

"And Who is Joah," *Amazing Stories*, November 1987 (reprinted *On Spec* Winter 1995, collected *Stealing Magic* 1999 & 2005)

"The Chase is On," *Amazing Stories*, July 1989 (collected *What Ho, Magic!* 1999)

"The Last Lesson," *Amazing Stories* September 1989, (reprinted *On Spec* Summer 1996, collected *Stealing Magic* 1999 & 2005)

"Be it Ever so Humble," *Marion Zimmer Bradley's Fantasy Magazine*, Winter 1991 (reprinted *Best of Marion Zimmer Bradley's Fantasy Magazine*, Warner October 1994, collected *Stealing Magic* 1999 & 2005)

"Nothing up Her Sleeve," *Amazing Stories*, 1991 (collected *Stealing Magic* 1999 & 2005)

"Underground, *Northern Frights*, Mosaic Press, 1992 (collected *What Ho, Magic!* 1999)

"I'll Be Home for Christmas," *The Christmas Bestiary*, DAW Books Inc., 1992 (collected *What Ho, Magic!* 1999)

"Shing Li-ung," *Dragon Fantastic*, DAW Books Inc., 1992 (collected *What Ho, Magic!* 1999)

"First Love, Last Love," *Marion Zimmer Bradley's Fantasy Magazine*, Fall 1993 (collected *What Ho, Magic!* 1999)

"Word of Honour," *Tales of the Knights Templar*, Warner 1995 (collected *What Ho, Magic!* 1999)

"The Harder They Fall," *Marion Zimmer Bradley's Fantasy Magazine*, Summer 1995 (collected *What Ho, Magic!* 1999)

"A Debt Unpaid," *Northern Frights 3*, Mosaic Press, 1995 (collected *What Ho, Magic!* 1999)

"This Town Ain't Big Enough," *Vampire Detective*, DAW Books Inc., 1995 (collected *What Ho, Magic!* 1999 and *Blood Bank* 2006)

"Swan's Braid," *Swords Of The Rainbow*, Alyson Publications, April 1996 (collected *Stealing Magic* 1999 & 2005 and collected *Relative Magic* 2003)

"What Manner of Man," *Time Of The Vampires*, DAW Books Inc., 1996 (collected *What Ho, Magic!* 1999 and *Blood Bank* 2006)

"In Mysterious Ways," *Bending The Landscape*, White Wolf Publications, March 1997 (collected *Stealing Magic* 1999 & 2005 and collected *Relative Magic* 2003)

"February Thaw," *Olympus*, DAW Books Inc., 1997 (collected *What Ho, Magic!* 1999)

"Symbols are a Percussion Instrument," *Tarot Fantastic*, DAW Books Inc., 1997 (collected *What Ho, Magic!* 1999)

"A Midsummer Night's Dream Team," *Elf Fantastic*, DAW Books Inc., 1997 (collected *What Ho, Magic!* 1999)

"Mirror, Mirror on the Lam," *Wizard Fantastic*, DAW Books Inc., November 1997 (collected *Stealing Magic* 1999 & 2005)

"The Cards Also Say," *The Fortune Teller*, DAW Books Inc., 1997 (collected *What Ho, Magic!* 1999 and Blood Bank 2006)

"The Demon's Den," *Sword Of Ice*, DAW Books Inc. 1997 (collected *Finding Magic* 2007)

"The Vengeful Spirit of Lake Nepeakea," *What Ho, Magic!*, 1999 (collected *What Ho, Magic!* 1999 and *Blood Bank* 2006)

"The Lions of al'Kalamir," *Stealing Magic*, Tesseracts Books 1999 (collected *Stealing Magic* 2005, collected *Relative Magic* 2003)

"Now Entering the Ring," *On Spec*, Winter 1999 (collected in *Relative Magic* 2003)

"Burning Bright," *Earth, Air, Fire, Water*, DAW Books Inc, November 1999 (collected in *Relative Magic* 2003)

"Death Rites," ASSASIN *Fantastic*, DAW Books Inc, 2001 (collected in *Relative Magic* 2003)

"Someone to Share the Night," *Single White Vampire Seeks Same*, DAW Books Inc, January 2001 (collected in *Relative Magic* 2003)

"Oh Glorious Sight," *Oceans Of Magic*, DAW Books Inc, February 2001 (reprinted in *Year's Best Fantasy and Horror 2001*, collected in *Relative Magic* 2003)

"All Things Being Relative," *Villains Victorious*, April 2001 (collected in *Relative Magic* 2003)

"Sugar and Spice and Everything Nice," *The Mutant Files*, DAW Books Inc, August 2001 (collected in *Relative Magic* 2003)

"To Each His Own Kind," *Dracula in London*, Ace Publishing, November 2001 (collected in *Relative Magic* 2003)

"Nights of the Round Table," *Knights Fantastic*, DAW Books Inc., April 2002 (collected in *Relative Magic* 2003)

"Playing the Game," *Be Very Afraid*, Tundra Books, 2002

"Nanite, Star Bright," *Once Upon a Galaxy*, DAW Books Inc, September 2002 (collected in *Relative Magic* 2003)

"When the Student is Ready," *Apprentice Fantastic*, DAW Books Inc, November 2002 (collected in *Relative Magic* 2003)

"Another Fine Nest," *The Bakka Anthology*, Bakka Publishing, December 2002, (collected in *Relative Magic* 2003 and *Blood Bank* 2006)

"We Two May Meet," *DAW 30ᵗʰ Anniversary Anthology*, 2002 (collected in *Stealing Magic* 2005 and *Finding Magic* 2007)

"Succession," *Pharaoh Fantastic*, DAW Books Inc. December 2002 (collected in *Relative Magic* 2003)

"Sometimes, Just Because," *Relative Magic*, September 2003 (collected in *Stealing Magic* 2005)

"I Knew a Guy Once," *Space, Inc*, DAW Books Inc., 2003 (collected in *Finding Magic* 2007)

"Brock," *Sun in Glory*, DAW Books Inc., 2003 (collected *Finding Magic* 2007)

"Scleratus," *The Repentant*, DAW Books Inc., 2002 (collected in Blood Bank 2006)

"He Said, Sidhe Said," *Faerie Tales*, DAW Books Inc., 2004 (collected in *Finding Magic* 2007)

"Finding Marcus," *Sirius the Dog Star*, DAW Books Inc., 2004 (collected in *Finding Magic* 2007)

"Jack," *Little Red in the Big City*, DAW Books Inc., 2004 (collected in *Finding Magic* 2007)

"Slow Poison," *In The Shadow of Evil*, DAW Books Inc., 2005 (collected in *Finding Magic* 2007)

"A Choice of Endings," *Maiden, Matron, Crone*, DAW Books Inc., 2005 (collected in *Finding Magic* 2007)

"All the Ages of Man," *Crossroads & Other Tales of Valdemar*, DAW Books Inc., 2005 (collected *Finding Magic* 2007)

Tuesday Evenings, Six Thirty To Seven, Eeriecon chapbook, 2006 (collected in *Finding Magic* 2007)

"Blood in the Water," *Army of the Fantastic*, DAW Books Inc., May 2007 (collected in *Finding Magic* 2007)

"After School Specials," *Children of Magic*, DAW Books Inc., June 2006 (collected in *Finding Magic* 2007)

"Not That Kind of War," *Women at War*, DAW Books Inc., 2006 (collected in *Finding Magic* 2007)

"Under Summons," *MythSprings*, Fitzhenry and Whiteside, 2006 (collected in *Finding Magic* 2007)

"Critical Analysis," *Slipstreams*, DAW Books Inc., 2006 (collected in *Blood Bank* 2006)

"So This is Christmas," *Blood Bank*, 2006

"A Woman's Work," *If I Were an Evil Overlord*, DAW Books Inc., March 2007 (collected in *Finding Magic* 2007)

"The Things Everyone Knows," *Under Cover of Darkness*, DAW Books Inc., Feb 2007 (collected in *Finding Magic* 2007)

"Blood Wrapped," *Many Blood Returns*, hc, ACE, September 2007

"Exactly," *Places to Go, People to Kill*, DAW Books Inc, 2007

"Music Hath Charms," *Hotter Than Hell*, Harper Collins, 2007

SHORT STORY COLLECTIONS (4)

What Ho, Magic!, Meisha Merlin Publishing Inc, March 1999
Stealing Magic, Tesseracts Books, 1999 (simultaneous hc & trade)
Relative Magic, Meisha Merlin Publishing Inc, September 2003
(rp)*Stealing Magic*, Edge Science Fiction and Fantasy, 2005
Finding Magic, ISFiC Press, 2007

NON FICTION (3)

"'Thanks for the Reenactment, Sir.'," *Finding Serenity*, BenBella Books Inc. 2005

"What Is She Wearing," *Totally Charmed*, BenBella Books Inc. 2005

"It's All in the Numbers," *Star Wars on Trial*, BenBella Books Inc. 2006

FINDING MAGIC

November 2007

Finding Magic by Tanya Huff was published by ISFiC Press, 707 Sapling Lane, Deerfield, Illinois 60015. One thousand copies have been printed by Thomson-Shore, Inc. The typeset is Berthold Baskerville, Adobe Garamond Titling, Adobe Garamond and Zapf Dingbats printed on 60# Nature's Natural. The binding cloth is Arrestox B Black. Design and typesetting by Garcia Publishing Services, Woodstock, Illinois.